SomeTimes a Light Surprises

**Center Point
Large Print**

**This Large Print Book carries the
Seal of Approval of N.A.V.H.**

SOMETIMES A LIGHT SURPRISES

Jamie Langston Turner

CENTER POINT PUBLISHING
THORNDIKE, MAINE

This Center Point Large Print edition
is published in the year 2009 by arrangement with
Bethany House Publishers,
a division of Baker Publishing Group.

Scripture quotations are from
the King James Version of the Bible.

The text of this Large Print edition is unabridged.
In other aspects, this book may vary
from the original edition.
Printed in the United States of America.
Set in 16-point Times New Roman type.

ISBN: 978-1-60285-529-8

Library of Congress Cataloging-in-Publication Data

Turner, Jamie L.
  Sometimes a light surprises / Jamie Langston Turner.
    p. cm.
  ISBN 978-1-60285-529-8 (library binding : alk. paper)
  1. Widowers--Fiction. 2. Large type books. I. Title.

PS3570.U717S67 2009b
813'.54--dc22

2009011479

for

KALYN REBEKAH SMITH TURNER

I first saw you in early fall standing outside our church with your family. You were starting college, and your parents teased about how many pairs of shoes you had brought along. I saw you months later at a winter concert, wearing a formal gown and carrying flowers our son had given you. I saw you that spring, when the four of us went out for dinner before school was out. "I want you to love her," our son told us. I was cautious, wary, uncertain. A mother is slow to give her heart to a girl. Months went by, you returned to school, I saw you again. And again. Many times throughout that year and the next and the next. And quietly, surely, it came to pass, though I can't say when it happened. All I know is this. When I saw you in white on your wedding day, your shining eyes fixed on our son, I knew I had grown to love you as a daughter.

Contents

ONE

Not on Sundays

Sitting at his desk, Ben stared at the photo, an old one with faded colors. It had been in his wallet for at least twenty-five years, stuck behind an expired library card and his voter registration, but transferred every time he changed wallets. He rarely looked at it and wouldn't be looking at it now if he hadn't been searching through his wallet for something.

In the picture Ben was standing in front of a fireplace, holding the twins, one in each arm, as if they weighed no more than five-pound bags of sugar. They must have been around six years old, which would have put him in his early thirties. Chloe was standing next to him, holding Grant, and Shelly was in front of her, smiling stiffly at the camera as if worried that the automatic timer wouldn't go off. The twins were wearing princess dresses and silver ballerina slippers, with sparkly crowns on their heads. Each one had an arm around his neck. Hard to believe, since they had no use for him now.

"What I Lost"—that could be the title of the photo. Or "What I Gave Up"—that might be closer. A wife and four children. One dead, the others as good as dead.

Just then Caroline stuck her head in the office

door. "Good, you're here. I was hoping you hadn't forgotten about the interview. She'll be here any minute." She shut the door just short of a slam.

Why Caroline thought his mere presence meant he hadn't forgotten, Ben couldn't say. As a matter of fact, he didn't know a thing about the interview even though he was sure Caroline must have written it neatly on his appointment calendar, something he usually failed to look at each morning.

He put his wallet back in his pocket and closed the book on his desk. It was a book he often consulted, a thick volume of word and phrase origins titled *Say It Ain't So, Joe: A History of Common Expressions.* He had been looking for *high on the hog,* but he hadn't found it among the entries.

Ben stood up and replaced the book on the shelf where he kept it. Probably not many people knew that the title of the book came from the notorious baseball scandal involving Shoeless Joe Jackson, an outfielder for the Chicago White Sox in 1919. Supposedly some kid had tugged on Jackson's sleeve when he came out of the courtroom after admitting his guilt in selling out to gamblers: "Say it ain't so, Joe," the kid had said. Probably not many people knew that Shoeless Joe Jackson had grown up right here in Greenville, South Carolina, either. Time had been kind to his reputation. There was a life-sized statue of Shoeless Joe downtown in the West End not far from the Liberty Bridge.

Turning back to his desk, Ben shuffled through some papers and found the application. He took it over to the window, held it at arm's length, and squinted down at the name. Kelly Kovatch. Female. Age twenty. He shook his head in disbelief. Kovatch? Surely not. But yes, that's what it said. Not exactly what you would call a common name around these parts.

Could it be that this girl was the daughter of Kay Kovatch? The age would be right. The name, too. Kay Kovatch would have been the type of mother to give all her kids names that began with the same letter as her own. He looked at the address on the application. He didn't recognize the street name, but that didn't mean anything. It was a Derby address, which would fit.

Ben couldn't remember exactly how many children had trailed along behind Kay Kovatch the last time he had seen her, coming out of the Derby Public Library one summer evening, but it was an immoderate number by today's standards, that much he knew. It could have been as few as five, but he thought it was probably more. And she was obviously in the last few weeks of another pregnancy. That would have been over ten years ago now. He had sat in his car and watched her corral them all into a red minivan, talking and laughing the whole time.

It had been only months after that last sighting of Kay Kovatch that Ben had finally packed up and moved from Derby, South Carolina, over to Greenville, something he should have done long before. He hadn't been back to Derby since, though he had continued to subscribe to the Derby *Daily News* for reasons he couldn't explain—until a year ago, when he had canceled his subscription after being blindsided by a headline one morning: *LOCAL MURDER STILL COLD 20 YEARS LATER.*

He wished he had looked at the application before now. He could have told Caroline to call the girl and tell her not to bother coming in, the position was already filled. Caroline would have tightened her mouth at the lie, since it wasn't her own, but she would have done it. If there was one thing Caroline understood the value of, it was a well-timed lie. Ben glanced at the clock on his wall. Maybe he could still get out of it if he acted immediately. He could tell Caroline he had just remembered something urgent and would be back in an hour. He could tell her to cancel everything for the rest of the afternoon and . . .

But he heard her voice now on the other side of his office door. "Yes, he's expecting you. Have a seat and I'll let him know you're here. You can leave your coat and umbrella out here if you want to." He heard the click of Caroline's heels as she approached the door again. She was two years older than Ben but seemed to have twice the energy. Brisk, busy Caroline, an overripe Barbie doll with her dyed strawberry blond hair, all her matching clothes, complete with shoes in every color—today it was purple. Ben couldn't imagine how much room a woman like her would take up at home. She was divorced, though, so she didn't have to compete with anybody for closet space.

He sighed. He'd have to see the girl now. But he would make it fast. He would act very apologetic that she had made the trip over here for no reason, especially in the bad weather. He would tell her that the job had just been given to someone else only minutes before—too late for him to contact her. He would wish her well, stand to see her out, shake her hand if she offered hers, and act solicitous about her safety on the way home during this unseasonable cold snap. He would urge her to be careful in case the roads were slippery. Then he would close the door and throw her application into the trash can.

Caroline tapped on his door and opened it. "Next applicant is here," she said.

"Say it ain't so, Joe," Ben said without looking at her.

Caroline frowned at Ben. He was always saying that. He was standing over by the window as if in deep thought. Sometimes he aggravated the fire out of her, the way he always talked in circles and muttered things to himself, but other times she almost felt sorry for him, as she did now. He looked beaten down. He was holding a piece of paper in his hand, staring down at it. No doubt he had misplaced his glasses again. Catching sight of them on the bookcase, she came forward swiftly, whisked them off the shelf, and handed them to him. "Here, you might need these." They were an old pair of reading glasses with oversized black frames. Clark Kent glasses.

Ben nodded. "Helpful Caroline, always Johnny-on-the-spot," he said. He put his glasses on and gave her a distracted smile.

Caroline returned to the door. "Are you ready for her?" she said. He looked a little rumpled with his shirtsleeves rolled up and his necktie loosened, but that was nothing new. He was actually a fairly nice-looking man and would be even nicer-looking if you could disregard his quirks, which were many.

Caroline often watched other women when they talked to Ben. He was the kind of man a lot of women liked, quiet and smart yet with a needy look in his eyes. Many of them acted as if they would like to take him home and meet those needs. "Big old lonely guy like you," their eyes said, "shouldn't be living by yourself. You need some female companionship." She was sure at least two of the employees here at work, both too young, had their caps set for him. In Caroline's opinion, he needed someone closer to his own age. Not herself, though. Not on your life. She knew too much about men in general and this one in particular. He would drive her out of her mind.

"Yes, yes, let's go ahead and get this show on the road," he said, waving the piece of paper at her.

Caroline opened the door and stood beside it. "You can come on in," she said to the girl. She swung the door open wider and added, "Don't be nervous. Mr. Buck's harmless. Most of the time." Kelly Kovatch, Caroline's appointment book said. A tall girl with a long neck. Lots of things about her were long, in fact. Long matronly looking brown skirt, long-sleeved apricot blouse in a shiny fabric, long feet in brown loafers. Caroline liked to compare people to animals. This girl was a giraffe. Her blouse, buttoned all the way up to the top button, looked a couple of sizes too big around the neck but too short at the wrist.

And very long eyelashes, Caroline noted as the girl passed her at the door. But then there was her hair—a short little shiny bob, much too neat to look stylish by today's standards. She wore a small tan cap of some loosely woven fabric, which gave her head an acorn-like effect. No jewelry, but she carried a tan shoulder purse, strapped diagonally across her chest. She had a pretty face and conscientious eyes. "I'm right out here if you need anything, Mr. Buck," Caroline said, and then to the girl, "We'd sure love it if you were the right person. When Trish up and moved to California on us, we sure didn't expect to have so much trouble finding somebody to take her place." Then she closed the door.

So much for telling the girl the position was already filled, Ben thought. He waved a hand toward the two wing armchairs in front of his desk. "Have a seat," he said. He hadn't yet looked at her directly but was aware of her height. He was guessing she was an attractive girl if she looked anything like her mother. Physically attractive, that is, which in her mother's case hadn't begun to make up for all the other ways in which she was anything but attractive.

He sat down at his desk and pretended to be studying the application. He turned it over and saw the section marked Educational Background. Of course—he might have known. The girl had been homeschooled from grades five through twelve. That was exactly the kind of thing Kay Kovatch would have thrown herself into. She would have become convinced that the public schools were dens of wickedness. And private schools would have been out of the question for a woman who stayed home and kept having babies, a woman whose husband drove a UPS truck for a living.

If Ben's own wife had lived, Kay would no doubt have tried to rope her into the homeschooling thing, too, for she had been the kind of woman who had considered it her mission in life to teach other women how they should run their families. She had been outspoken about the fact that a woman belonged at home with her children instead of holding a job in the workplace.

And she had been very persuasive. Chloe had known Kay only a few weeks when she had told Ben one night in bed that she was praying about whether to quit her part-time job at the animal shelter. Praying about it—that's exactly what she had said. Chloe, his intelligent, strong-willed wife, who had never said a prayer in her life until she had met Kay Kovatch at an evening exercise class at the YMCA.

"Well, let's see, Kelly Kovatch," he said now, deliberately mispronouncing the last syllable.

"It's Kovatch, Mr. Buck. It rhymes with watch. My father said it was a common name in Hungary, where his ancestors came from—as common as Smith is here."

Ben nodded. "And my name's Buckley," he said. "Caroline likes to take shortcuts."

He lifted his eyes now and looked at her. She sat very tall with her back away from the chair, her chin lifted slightly, her dark eyes boring a hole through him. The phrase *spitting image* came to his mind. He quickly glanced away. He had read in his *Say It Ain't So, Joe* book that the phrase *spitting image* had originated in the South, perhaps as an altered form of "spirit and image." He wondered what Kelly would say if he said right now, "You are the very spirit and image of your mother." Except that her mother had been more filled out. This girl was all skin and bones. And flat-chested as a boy, a fact accentuated by the purse tightly strapped across her torso. A very pretty face, though. With longer hair she could pass for Natalie Wood in *West Side Story*.

He remembered the very first time he had set eyes on Kay Kovatch over twenty-one years ago. She was at his house visiting Chloe one day after lunch when he had run home to get something. She and several of her children. He glanced down at the date of birth noted on the application. Not this girl, though; she wouldn't have been born yet—not quite yet, though it struck him now that her mother must have been pregnant with her that first time he saw her. Kay and Chloe had been sitting at the kitchen table with an open Bible between them.

No doubt he had noticed Kay's good looks at the time. But after what she had done to his wife, he had never again thought of her as pretty. When she tried to speak with him two months later at the graveside, he had turned and walked away. And afterward when she had called and offered to help with the children, he cut her off and told her they were taken care of. The last time she called, he had said nothing, only hung up on her.

"So now that we've got our names straight," he said to the girl, "let's get started. This shouldn't take too long." He looked back down at the application. He had done dozens of these interviews in the past couple of weeks, but suddenly he forgot how he usually started. All he could think of was how he had come home another day shortly after that first one to find Chloe down on her knees by their bed, a Bible spread out in front of her.

"Mr. Buckley, may I say something first?" Kelly leaned forward. She was sitting directly in line with the floor lamp by the door so that its soft glow appeared to emanate from her head.

Ben nodded and made an inviting motion with his hand.

"I didn't write this on the form," the girl said, "but I need to tell you up front that I'm willing to work as much as you need me, except not on Sundays."

Of course. He might have known this, too. Kay Kovatch's kids wouldn't violate Sundays by going to a job out in the big bad world. Their God was a jealous God, visiting the iniquity of the fathers upon the children unto the third and fourth generation, and all that. Actually, this part was good. It would make it even easier to tell her she wasn't right for the job. He already knew exactly what he would say: "Well, Ms. Kovatch, then I'm afraid we can't use you. You see, it wouldn't be fair to the other employees. We need to have everyone available anytime the store is open and the need arises." In fact, he opened his mouth to say the words, but she spoke again.

"I'll work extra hours any other day of the week. And I'll work hard. I have a good eye for design." She looked at him steadily. No cajoling or begging. She was simply stating a fact.

If he had felt like being rude, he could have pointed out that her good eye for design was nowhere evident in her appearance. And it wasn't that he didn't have the capacity for rudeness. He had told the last applicant as soon as she walked into his office that since clean air was important to him, they might as well not waste their time with a job interview. The woman had reeked of cigarette smoke. After she had stalked out, Caroline had come to his door, her arms folded disapprovingly.

"What did you say to her?" she had said.

"The truth." There was absolutely no reason to apologize. "You could help me screen some of these people, you know," he had told Caroline. "I assume your nose is in good working order."

Ben looked back down at Kelly Kovatch's application, frowning and shaking his head. He would make it seem that he regretted deeply having to turn her down. Just as he opened his mouth again to speak, however, his eye caught something on the application that almost made him laugh. At the bottom of the back page, under Previous Job Experience, she had printed very neatly "baby-sitting, cooking, cleaning, washing, ironing, giving flute lessons, pet care, yard work, tending vegetable garden, painting, car care, selling bread, teaching Sunday school, organizing parties, sewing, drawing, piano, calligraphy, home decorating, carpentry, cutting hair, writing plays." And under Previous Employers she had written "Parents (Mr. and Mrs. Charles Kovatch), Pastor (Rev. Ian Shamblin), Neighbors (Whitleys, Hodges, Dillards, Gerbers)," with addresses and phones numbers for each one.

What a child she was to think she could venture out into the marketplace with such credentials. No college education and no real work experience. Ben wondered if she had ridden her bicycle over here. Maybe it had those little pink plastic streamers on the handlebars.

He opened his mouth to speak, closed it, then opened it again. "Ms. Kovatch," he said, "you are . . ." The phrase *manifestly unqualified* was the one that came to mind, but for some reason he couldn't get it out.

"I can do the job," the girl said. "In fact, I brought pictures to show you."

"Pictures?" Ben asked.

"Yes, I have a pictorial portfolio of my work." And the girl unzipped her purse and pulled out a small photo book.

A pictorial portfolio. Kay Kovatch had probably coached her to call it that. They had probably acted out the whole job interview at the kitchen table while younger brothers and sisters read history lessons and did math problems. Or maybe the entire family had gathered to watch the mock interview, clapping proudly at the end. Kay Kovatch would be in her fifties now, so surely she was done having babies. Still, there could very well be close to ten children, with this girl most likely somewhere in the middle.

He leaned forward and took the photo book, scolding himself for not having already ended this interview. There was no chance he was going to hire this girl, so why drag it out? He would hate having someone around who constantly reminded him of the woman who had brought about such a change in Chloe during those last couple of months of her life and, in doing that, had made his own life so miserable.

What made a girl like this one actually think she could succeed in today's business world anyway? He wondered what she would do the first time she heard Lester and Morris in the break room. And he wondered what Lester and Morris would do when they saw the likes of Kelly Kovatch working on the showroom floor, when they had to take directions from her about what to install or where to move things. He could imagine their eyes as they looked her up and down, took in her sharp bones and angles, her clothes hanging off her broomstick frame, every button securely fastened.

Ben opened her photo book and flipped through a few pages. Maybe as soon as next week this would strike him funny, but it certainly didn't right now. The pictures had been printed on regular paper, so the images were fuzzy. It looked like she had tried to cover all the bases, though; he'd give her that. She had evidently had a hand in decorating every kind of room you could think of. Below each picture was a caption rendered neatly in a variety of calligraphy scripts. One picture showed the inside of a playhouse, with the caption "Karla and Kitty's New Playhouse."

"I helped my dad design and build that for my sisters two summers ago," Kelly said. "I made the braided rag rug out of all our old clothes."

Ben nodded. Kay Kovatch's kids would know how to recycle old things.

Another picture showed a nursery with a half-dozen cribs and three baby swings. "Charity Bible Church Nursery," the caption read. The walls were painted green, with a wallpaper border depicting a cartoonish Noah leading pairs of animals to the ark. The curtains were green with white trim, and the carpet was dark green. Toys were stowed neatly in white bins against one wall, and large colorful pictures hung above them. There were close-ups of these: Mary and Joseph with baby Jesus, Jesus blessing the children, Jesus teaching on a hillside, Jesus walking on the water.

"I drew the pictures," Kelly said. "They were chalk drawings I did for Vacation Bible School two years ago, and we had them framed."

Ben looked closer. No doubt the grainy quality of the photo made the drawings look better than they actually were.

"One of my brothers helped me paint the walls and put up the border," she said, "and I made all the curtains and the cushions for the rocking chairs."

Ben turned a page and saw the caption "Mrs. Hodges' Fifth-Grade Classroom." The photo showed a bulletin board with a big pink flamingo standing on one foot and the title "Ornithologically Speaking" in cutout letters across the top and winding down the side. Pictures of different kinds of birds were mounted and displayed all around the flamingo, with typed paragraphs beneath each one.

"That's our neighbor's classroom," Kelly said. "She teaches fifth grade at Derby Elementary School. She gave me two boxes of old *National Geographic* magazines and asked me to come up with some bulletin boards. That was one of the last ones I did for her."

Ben looked at the girl. She was staring at him. He heard sleet pelting against the windowpane behind him. He swiveled his chair to the side and looked toward the wall. His office was stark—beige walls, only the barest furnishings. He could guess what the girl must have thought when she walked in—that whoever got this job would do well to start here. This is how he liked it, though. He didn't want an office with stuff all over the walls and tabletops. He couldn't stand clutter, although he knew people would find that hard to believe, given the perpetual state of his desktop.

Ben turned back to the photo book on his desk. The next page showed a picture of a long table covered with dozens of science projects. The caption read, "Piedmont Home Education Association Science Fair."

"They asked me to organize the display for that last spring," Kelly said. "There were about a dozen more tables as big as that one. I did all the posters and labels and award certificates and then arranged all the projects by age groups. That big one of the model oil rig was the winner for the high school division."

Ben wished he had thought to ask Caroline how many more applicants were scheduled for interviews. He knew this girl was the last one today, but what if she were the last one, period? He doubted that she could handle the job of floor designer long-term, but maybe she could tide them over until they could find somebody professional. And he could always use another floorwalker; the newest one had already given notice that she had found another job. If nothing else, at least they would have another pair of hands to do all the packing and dismantling when it came time for the move later this year. Ben hadn't told anyone except Caroline about the move yet, but he knew they were all talking. They had to suspect something was up when they were practically the only business still open in the whole mall.

He had known when they first leased this space, a former department store, that it would be only temporary, three or four years at the most. When they had moved in, the owner had told him there were plans to close the mall, maybe to tear it down unless someone came forward with an offer to buy it. There had been talk of a German firm wanting it for office space or the city using it for a new vocational school. But nothing had come of any of it, and a deal was now in the works to sell the whole tract of land for a subdevelopment, which meant everything would be leveled.

Still, there was the question of whether he could tolerate the sight of Kay Kovatch's daughter every day. Ben picked up the girl's application again and turned it over. "So has the work around the neighborhood and church dried up?" he said. "Is that why you're interviewing for a job?"

"Well, not really. We just felt like it was a good time. I'll be twenty-one in a couple of months. And it sounded like an interesting job."

Ben closed the photo book. "This is a big enterprise we've got here at the Upstate Home and Garden Bazaar, Ms. Kovatch. Just over a hundred different vendors and growing all the time. It's not quite the same as sewing curtains or putting together a science fair."

"Right," she said. "I wouldn't expect it to be." Her eyes never left his face. "I can do anything you give me to do, Mr. Buckley."

He leaned back in his chair and looked up at the ceiling. For some reason he remembered one of the last things Chloe had ever said to him. It was only days before she died. "You're not nearly as gruff on the inside as you try to make people think you are." She had been leaning over him from behind, tickling his ear with a strand of her hair. He hadn't even answered her but had gotten up and walked away.

He straightened his chair and looked back at Kelly. He took his glasses off and pushed the photo book across his desk toward her. "And if someone decided to let you try," he said at length, "could you start on Monday?"

When she left his office a few minutes later, Ben swung his chair around to face the window. "Say it ain't so, Joe," he said aloud. "Please, say it ain't so."

TWO

Silly Word Games

"Don't some days just seem to go on forever?" Caroline said a few minutes after the girl left. She stood in the doorway of Ben's office, hands on her hips.

Ben was sitting at his desk with the phone book open to the yellow pages. He didn't look up.

Caroline took one of her shoes off and peered inside it, adjusted something, then slipped it back on. "I mean, they say time speeds up as you get older," she said, "and it's mostly true, but then there are these days that just crawl. Especially when it's bad weather and *especially* when it's Friday. It feels like it should have been five o'clock hours ago."

"You used to be better at hinting," Ben said. He turned a few pages in the phone book but still didn't look up.

"That's not true," Caroline said. "I'm still at the peak of my powers in every area, hinting included." She came forward and stood in front of his desk, staring down at him. She tapped an index finger along the edge. At times, especially when he was so intent on tracking down something, he made her think of a large spaniel with his long ear-lobes and mane of wavy dark hair. Or a blood-hound. She wouldn't be surprised to see him start sniffing the phone book.

Finally he raised his eyes. "What? Are you worried about a little sleet?"

"I wouldn't exactly call it worried," she said, "but I did just get my car back from the body shop, you know. I'm not real excited about sliding into a ditch." He looked back at the phone book and ran his finger down a column, moving his lips as he did. He was such a strange man sometimes. If he needed a phone number, why didn't he just ask her to find it the way he usually did?

"Mr. Buckley," she said. This is what she called him when she wanted his attention. In so many ways it was like having to deal with a big over-grown child.

"Ms. Mason," he said. This was what he called her when she was in what he described as her "schoolteacher mode." His finger came to a stop and he held it there, bending closer to the page.

"The weather says the sleet could go on all night," she said. "This is like a bad April Fool's trick."

"April Fool's Day was three days ago, Ms. Mason."

He glanced up at her, holding his finger in place. "Did I ever tell you how the tradition of playing pranks got started? It happened when the Julian calendar was replaced by the Gregorian and the—"

"I don't care about that, Mr. Buckley. I just thought you might be interested in knowing that the weather says it could keep sleeting all night."

"I don't pay you to listen to the radio, Ms. Mason," he replied. "Next thing I know, you'll be turning up the music and dancing." He took a pencil out of the cup on his desk and underlined something in the phone book, then opened a drawer and peered into it. "I won't have you rolling back the rugs and tripping the light fantastic on company time, Ms. Mason." He looked up at her again. "That means to dance, you know. The phrase was made popular in a forties tune titled 'The Sidewalks of New York,' but John Milton actually used it in a poem a long time before that."

Caroline sighed. "Fascinating, I'm sure. And

very funny, too. Since when did we have a radio in the office, Mr. Buckley? You know very well I can read the weather on the Internet."

"Oh yes, the Internet, Ms. Mason. I keep forgetting how technologically savvy you are." On a pad of yellow Post-it Notes he wrote something down in his minuscule handwriting, then opened his shirt pocket, stuck the note neatly inside, and patted it down. He stood up and went to the window. "Why, look, Ms. Mason, there must be fifty or sixty cars down there in the parking lot. I wonder what all those people are doing out on a treacherous day like this."

Caroline turned to leave. He was so irritating when he got sarcastic. But she stopped at the door and looked back at him. He was still standing at the window, so she couldn't see his face, yet the sight of his broad shoulders slumped forward did something to her anger. Even as she wondered how his wife had ever put up with him, she felt the kind of pity you feel for somebody helpless and deformed.

"Well, what are you still hanging around for, Ms. Mason?" he said, his back still to her. "Why don't you go ahead and leave? Or are you hoping I'll offer to escort you to your car?"

Caroline sighed again. "If a person could only have a normal conversation with you."

He turned from the window and slapped the phone book shut. "Well, I'm waiting," he said.

"Waiting for what?" she said.

"You didn't finish."

"Finish what?" She tried to think if he had asked her to find a piece of correspondence earlier or schedule an appointment with somebody. She prided herself on keeping up with details. She might be a couple of years older than Mr. Buck, but she liked to think she was a shining example of how a woman of sixty could still be mentally sharp. And physically, too. People routinely told her she didn't look a day over fifty.

"Your dependent clause, Ms. Mason." Ben shook his head sadly. "You said if a person could only have a normal conversation with me. I was waiting for the rest of the sentence."

"Oh really, Mr. Buck, you and your silly word games! Ever since you read that old grammar book." She nodded toward the bookcase, where he kept his 1950 edition of *The Harcourt Grammar Handbook*.

He cocked his head and studied her a moment. "Yet another unmoored dependent clause, Ms. Mason." He came forward suddenly, making shooing motions with his hands. "Well, go on. Leave, Caroline, leave. Off with you. Begone. You're wasting time. You come in here hinting around to leave, and when I give in, you keep hanging around sputtering your trivial palaver."

She glared at him a moment, her eyes narrowed. "Byron's on floor duty tonight," she said. "He's

31

coming in at five." She walked out of Ben's office to her own desk and quickly started clearing it, not that it needed much tidying. She wasn't one to strew things about. She liked to clean up her messes as she went along. She glanced at the clock. She wasn't all that worried about the weather, had actually stretched the truth a little, but she hated the rush hour traffic on Fridays. If she could get home before five, she would miss the worst of it. Maybe she'd swing into Little Caesars and get one of those five-dollar Hot-n-Ready pizzas on her way. She could put a salad together at home. Maybe Donald would stop by if she called him. If he knew there was food involved, there was a fifty-fifty chance he'd come. Without the food, it was more like one to ninety-nine.

"Too bad that girl didn't work out," Caroline called through Ben's open door. "I told you the salary was too low. Real designers don't work for peanuts." She swept some paper clips into her palm and deposited them into their proper slot inside her top drawer, then shut down her computer. "Of course, from the looks of her, I don't think she was anything close to a real designer. She looked more like she belonged in the 4-H club."

"Why are you shouting?" Ben was standing two feet from her desk, holding his stapler, which was splayed open. "Do you even know what the four *H*s in 4-H stand for, Caroline?"

"Here, give that to me." She took the stapler

from him and whipped open a side drawer. Briskly she replenished the staples, then closed it up and handed it back to him. She opened the bottom drawer, took out her purse, and walked over to the coat-tree by the door. She tossed her purse on the couch. "Heart, hands, something, and something," she said, putting on her coat. "Two of my brothers were in 4-H back in Indiana."

"Head and health," Ben said. "And by the way, what makes you think she didn't work out?"

"Oh, just a wild guess," she said, wrapping her black chenille scarf around her neck, then looping the two ends together under her chin. She picked up her purse. "Maybe because she was *crying* when she left your office?"

"She was?"

"Bye, Mr. Buck, have a good weekend, and I'll see—"

"But I hired her. She's starting Monday."

Caroline stopped, her hand on the doorknob. "Mr. Buck, you're getting worse and worse about acting serious when you're joking and acting jokey when you're serious. It gets tiresome. Try to get some rest this weekend."

"Oh, and one more thing," Ben said.

"What?"

"Did I ever tell you that you have something in common with Amadeus Mozart? He was a Mason, too." He paused a split second as if waiting to make sure her eyes registered puzzlement. "Only the Freemason kind," he added. "They've been around since the Middle Ages, you know."

"Nobody but you could possibly care about that, Mr. Buckley." She wheeled and left, her heels click-clicking against the shiny linoleum in the hallway. She didn't feel one bit guilty skipping out before five—a solid week of working for that man earned a woman early release on Friday.

She hoped the sleet hadn't made the pavement slippery. She would have to watch her step walking to the car. She remembered what Donald had said the time she turned her ankle stepping off a curb last year: "Mother, that kind of thing is to be expected when you insist on wearing shoes designed for women half your age." He had shown no sympathy whatsoever, hadn't even asked if she needed an ice pack or something from the drug-store.

Twenty-five minutes later Caroline kicked off her shoes at the back door and set the pizza on the table. The newspaper hadn't been securely wrapped, so she spread it out on the breakfast bar to dry and went to turn up the thermostat. Donald hadn't answered his cell phone when she called, so she had left a message. He wouldn't call back, she knew that, but if he decided to take her up on her offer, he would probably be here within ten or fif- teen minutes, since Prime Systems, where he worked, wasn't far from her house. She turned the oven on low and set the pizza box inside.

Minutes later, changed into a bright pink fleece warm-up suit, she was back in the kitchen chopping up carrots when she heard a car door slam. Why was it, she wondered, that even when your grown son was a big spoiled baby in a lot of ways, your heart still gave a little leap whenever you thought he might be dropping by? She went quickly to the back door and unlocked it. Donald hated it when he had to wait for anything. He had his own key to her house but didn't want to go to the trouble of finding it among all the others on his key ring.

"Hello there," Caroline said cheerily when he entered. "So you got my message? Are you hungry? Have the roads gotten any worse in the last hour?" This was her usual way of conversing with Donald—a series of questions piling up, most of which he ignored.

Sometimes he did manage a response, usually to the last one, as he did now. "My mother the alarmist," he said, "all worried about the relative condition of the roads now as compared to an hour ago, which would be hard to ascertain since I have no way of knowing what they were like at—" he glanced at his watch—"at four-fifteen." He walked across the floor, his rubber soles making little squeaking noises. It wouldn't occur to him to take off his wet shoes by the door, although it had always been a requirement when he was a little boy. Caroline saw that he was wearing the same old ratty sport coat with a limp yellow polo shirt underneath. The sport coat was a wool camel plaid, one he had picked up secondhand somewhere. It was badly pilled, and one of the wooden buttons was broken in half.

He stopped at the breakfast bar and turned to the sports page of the newspaper. Sighing, Caroline went back to her carrots. Donald could be so nice-looking if only he cared about putting his best foot forward. It was no wonder he was still single. All he cared about was computers and sports. But she excused him regularly and fondly, though with fake exasperation, to whoever would listen. It was one of her favorite topics of conversation: "Young People Today." Donald was thirty-eight.

"Weren't you cold without your winter coat?" she asked. "Did you get your brakes fixed yet? I guess they must have been wrong about that groundhog back in February. This is *not* what I would call an early spring! Whoever heard of sleet in South Carolina on the fourth day of April? Things still busy at work?"

"Uh-huh," Donald grunted. Caroline had no idea what kind of work he did except that it involved computers and software. He had a high IQ and could be very witty when he felt like it. Once she had stopped by Prime Systems to show him a letter from his father, actually one of those giant picture postcards, from Hawaii this time, and she had found him leaning over the low modular wall dividing his cubicle from the next one.

He was in the middle of telling a story to a co-worker, a bald man who was shaking with laughter: ". . . and then she gives me this look like I just poked her in the watusi with a cattle prod and says, 'That *wasn't* what I had in mind, you cretin,' and she starts getting all her stuff together to leave, but then I—" The bald man had seen Caroline by then and had alerted Donald by means of jiggling his eyebrows and bobbing his head in her direction. Donald had broken off, turned around, and immediately become a different person. "What are you doing here?" he had asked in a challenging tone.

Caroline wished she had heard the whole story. She wondered what he had said to make someone call him a cretin. She wasn't even sure what a cretin was, but it didn't sound very complimentary. Donald was such a stranger to her in so many ways. She would like to follow him around for a day and spy on him. She was intensely curious about his relations with women, but he always avoided her questions along those lines. He often told her that she asked too many questions. He said he could understand why his father had finally packed up and left town.

She went to the refrigerator and got out a jar of olives. She would add some of those to the salad since Donald was here. He used to eat entire jars of olives, popping them into his mouth like candy. She got out the celery, too. "Did your landlord ever give you that refund?" she asked. Donald had been feuding with his landlord about his last month's rent, when he had been forced to go to a motel for several days after his furnace quit working. "I think that man is half-crazy if you ask me. Did you ask him about fixing the doorbell?"

"Uh-huh," Donald said.

"Uh-huh what?" Caroline asked. "The refund or the doorbell?"

Donald was sitting on one of the stools now, his hands resting on either side of the newspaper, his head bent. "Sweet. I knew they'd trade him, the loser," he said.

Though she felt like throwing the cutting board at his head, Caroline knew better than to get upset at him. The last time she had blown her cool, he hadn't spoken to her for three weeks. The truth was, he could get along without her company a lot better than she could get along without his. She'd finally had to go to his apartment with takeout from the China Palace as a peace offering. That's when she found out that his doorbell wasn't working—or at least that's what he said when he finally came to the door, which he opened only after she pounded on it and called out, "I have Chinese!"

Later, as she was leaving, she had pressed the doorbell to test it. It rang clearly with a delicate chiming sound. "It's got a short," Donald had said. "Sometimes it works; sometimes it doesn't."

She speared several olives and added them to the salad, then broke off a stalk of celery and rinsed it. "Refund or doorbell?" she asked again now, careful to keep her voice neutral, pleasant.

He looked up. "Huh? Oh, neither."

"But you said 'uh-huh.'"

"You said he's crazy. I was just agreeing." He went back to the paper.

Caroline chopped off the leafy top of the celery with a vengeance, then started mincing it to add to the lettuce. She thought of Gilda Bloodworth, one of the floorwalkers at work, whose son Ryan was a clerk at the sporting goods store, the only other place still in business at the mall. Sometimes Ryan stopped by to see Gilda during his afternoon break, and several times Caroline had seen them standing face-to-face, deep in conversation. Once she had seen him give his mother a quick hug before running back to work. "I'll tell you the rest later!" he had called back to Gilda. Of course, Ryan Bloodworth was younger than Donald, probably only in his midtwenties, but how did it happen that some women had sons like that when she had one who wouldn't notice if she fell off the face of the earth, one who seemed to make a game out of pushing her to the end of her patience?

She had often wondered about Mr. Buck's son. She knew he had four children, a son and three daughters, though he never talked about them unless she asked him direct questions, and even then he gave her precious little information. They were all married and lived in different states. She wondered if his son called him regularly, asked his advice, sent him gifts. She wondered if the boy had as many odd habits as his father. In the four years she had worked at the Upstate Home and Garden Bazaar, Caroline had never once seen a picture of Mr. Buck's children or his grandchildren. She had asked him one time why he didn't put some pictures and other homey touches around his office, and he had said solemnly, "Because this isn't my home, Caroline." She had never even heard him say the girls' names, but she did know somehow that his son's name was Grant. Grant Buckley. It had a nice ring to it.

She could smell the cardboard box in the oven, so she turned the temperature down lower. She thought of poor Mr. Buck and the time he had started a fire in his kitchen from a pizza box in the oven. He wasn't much of a cook; he had admitted that numbers of times. "A burnt offering but no sweet-smelling savor," he had told her the next day at work after the fire. He said some of the most peculiar things, which is what came of spending so much time at the public library, where he camped out every night after work and on weekends. He had told her he had a regular spot at one end of the sofa.

She had seen it for herself one Sunday afternoon, when she had stopped by the library out of curiosity. Sure enough, there he was, sitting at the end of the long, curved sectional sofa under the skylight, wearing his big ugly glasses and poring over a book in his lap, with a stack of five or six more on the floor at his feet. Three other men were seated on the sofa. Maybe they were regulars, too. Maybe the four of them went out for coffee after a night of reading. More likely, since they were men, they didn't even know each other's names.

She got out several cans of pop and several bottles of salad dressing and set them on the counter. "I've got Coke, 7-Up, and diet ginger ale," she said. She got out two glasses. "What do you want? You want to sit at the bar or at the table?"

Donald gave a scornful laugh and swatted at the newspaper. "What is that coach thinking?" he said. "He does the same stupid thing four times in one season. Total insanity."

Caroline had no idea what he was talking about. Growing up, she had seen only one use for sports: to justify the existence of cheerleaders.

She put two placemats on the table, along with plates, napkins, forks, and the bowl of salad. She really wasn't much of a cook, either, and she didn't apologize for it. When you'd had to spend most of your adult life working full time to support a child and a lazy husband, you couldn't be bothered with kitchen work.

She filled the glasses with ice, then took them to the table. "Okay, we're ready," she said briskly, clapping her hands. "You want to bring the dressings over? Or you can just pick up whichever one you want. And whatever you want to drink. Come on and sit down, and I'll get the pizza."

Donald looked up from the newspaper. "I'm already sitting down." He turned his head and looked back at the table as if it were on the other side of the Sahara Desert instead of only four feet away.

"Well, I've got everything over here," Caroline said. "Come on, it's ready."

Donald sighed but heaved himself off the stool and made his way to the table. "Oh yes, let's do make everything as complicated as possible," he said.

It took great willpower for Caroline not to say what she was thinking: "You're shuffling—pick your feet up! You look like a deadbeat! Hold your shoulders back! Get a haircut, shave that stubble, and for heaven's sake, get some decent clothes!" A warthog—that was Donald's animal counterpart.

She picked up a can of Coke in one hand and a bottle of honey mustard dressing in the other. She deposited them firmly on the table, then stalked to the stove to get the pizza.

Behind her Donald said, "This all you got to drink? I wanted Dr Pepper."

THREE

A Third and Fateful Time

Ben left his office and ambled through both floors of the Upstate Home and Garden Bazaar, speaking to several of the floorwalkers who had just come on duty for the evening. "Making his presence known" was what he called it, and it was something he tried to do at least twice a day, often more. He had delegated so many responsibilities here at work that he had very little real work to do. He knew he could be gone for weeks without being missed, but he had no intention of going away for even one week. He liked to keep an eye on things.

He walked by to check on the progress of the Clearance Mart on the second floor, a section recently set apart for sale items. The idea was for the vendors themselves to decide which merchandise they were ready to move out, then do their own markdowns and tag the things to be transferred. The large sign at the entrance of the Clearance Mart read *NEW ITEMS ADDED DAILY!* Lester and Morris were down at the far end, replacing several squares of carpet that had been damaged from a leak in the ceiling.

Ben stopped to study a pair of large black ceramic monkeys on the floor by the clearance sign. Easy to see why those hadn't sold. Next to them was a tall lamp with a shade that looked like a misshapen pink Easter bonnet. Two customers were sifting through a box of leftover Christmas ornaments on a table. The Clearance Mart was something else the new girl could help with. It was in serious need of some organizing and sprucing up. Right now it had all the pizzazz of a Goodwill store.

Downstairs, Ben found Byron, the evening supervisor, returning stuffed animals to a toy chest in Funtime Furnishings, a showroom of merchandise geared to children. "Look at this mess," Byron said. "Somebody must've let their kids play in here while they shopped." He was holding a stuffed gorilla in one hand and a furry white rabbit in the other.

Ben picked up a pink poodle and tossed it into the toy chest. "Looks like we need to put up another one of those 'Look, Don't Touch' signs," he said, "only make it bigger this time." He smoothed out a small rug shaped like a slice of watermelon and rearranged some books on top of the old-fashioned school desk.

"Well, today it's the Cayman Islands," Byron said. He was getting married in two months, and every day he gave them all an update on his fiancée's latest honeymoon choice. He heaved a sigh of exasperation. "I never should've told her she could pick the place. It's driving me crazy. You got any advice?"

Ben smiled and shrugged. "What can I say? When I was your age, weddings and honeymoons were a lot simpler."

"Where'd you go on yours?" Byron asked.

Ben picked up a wastebasket shaped like a little tree stump and studied it. It had fake bark and several knotholes, with a little squirrel face peeking out of one. "Atlanta," he said. "Two whole days." He put the wastebasket back down.

Byron whistled. "Whoa, big spender." He bent down to pick up a floppy green frog and a large gray kangaroo, then stuck a foot under the miniature kitchen table to retrieve a wooden truck. "So did you—?"

"Who usually walks this zone?" Ben interrupted. "Is it Melody? She needs to keep on top of things better than this. We can't be letting children trash our showrooms."

"I already talked to her," Byron said. "She said it wasn't this way when she left at five, so it must've happened sometime in the last hour. Gilda was tied up with a woman at the jewelry case in Pearls and Diamonds, so she didn't see anything, either. Hey, look at this. I guess it's supposed to be a toadstool." He was holding a child-sized tan umbrella over his head. Evidently he didn't know it was bad luck to open an umbrella inside. Ben nodded but didn't say anything. Byron could talk as much as a woman once he got started.

Ben straightened a pair of Winnie the Pooh

bookends. "Well, I need to be on my way," he said.

As he walked away, Byron called out, "Oh, say, thanks for the suggestion about our honeymoon! I'll ask Deb how two days in Atlanta sounds to her."

Ben could have reminded him it wasn't a suggestion; it was only the answer to a question. But he didn't. He walked to the escalator and started down. Though he didn't want to think about honeymoons, his own or anybody else's, he couldn't help it now. He had run across the word numbers of times in his *Say It Ain't So, Joe* book. Supposedly it came from a special drink for newlyweds in ancient times. Sweetened with honey, it was thought to bring good luck if they drank it every day for the first thirty days after they were married. Personally, Ben put more stock in the *American Heritage Dictionary* explanation, which said that the word had its origins in the simple notion that the first weeks after marriage—or the first "moon"—were the sweetest.

"I'm the luckiest girl in the history of all time," Chloe had whispered on the first of the two nights they had spent at a hotel in Atlanta. They were lying in the dark on the ninth floor with the drapes wide open. It had stormed off and on all night, a flamboyant show of lightning and loud claps of thunder, but well past midnight it stopped, and a silver moon emerged from behind the clouds in the black sky.

The luckiest girl in the history of all time never dreamed that her good luck would run out less than fourteen years later.

It was well after six by the time Ben finally finished his rounds and walked out back to the employees' parking lot. The sleet had already stopped. The wind, which had been blowing hard all day, seemed to have sucked the moisture away with it. The air was crisp and nippy, more like October than early April. He looked up at the sky. The wind must have blown most of the clouds away, too, for he could see glints of evening stars.

So Caroline had snookered him about the weather. Or maybe the vagaries of spring had wrought a magical change in only a couple of hours. No, it was more likely that Caroline had snookered him again. He didn't mind, though. After a week of Caroline, he was always ready for her to go home on Friday afternoon. As a secretary—or administrative assistant, as they called themselves now—she was very efficient, but sometimes efficiency in a woman could wear a man out. Ben needed her, he knew that, but he also needed regular breaks from her. He liked Saturdays and Sundays, when she wasn't there bustling around.

He walked past Lester's maroon 1969 GTO. The car was polished to a high sheen, the front end sitting higher than the rear as if poised for takeoff. It had whitewall tires and a black leather interior, including a steering wheel cover. A black lace garter hung from the rearview mirror. Les treated his car better than a lot of men treated their wives and children.

He didn't see Mo's truck anywhere; maybe it was broken down again. Ben wished it would break down permanently. It was an old ice cream truck with faded pictures and words on the side. Someone in his neighborhood—at least that's what Mo claimed—had taken black paint and crossed through the *R* in *DELICIOUS TREATS*.

Ben got into his white Lincoln Town Car and sat there for a full minute before starting the engine and backing out slowly. An old person's car—that's what his Town Car was. Les had told him so repeatedly. But Ben didn't care. His mother had given it to him when she quit driving three years ago. Ben had been glad to get rid of his other car, an ailing BMW with over 300,000 miles on it and a dented front bumper he had never bothered to have repaired.

His philosophy about cars was practical. If it got you from one place to another, who cared what it looked like? But this one looked fine, really fine, for what it was. His mother had kept it in pristine condition, taking it in for regular oil changes and tire rotations, checking on every little squeak, driving it through the car wash every other week. She had taken better care of it than many women did their husbands.

And it truly had been a town car for her—only the proverbial trips to the grocery store and beauty shop, and occasionally to her bridge club. She had also taken her very last trip in it. Late one night less than two years ago she had called Ben to drive her to the emergency room at the hospital, where she died suddenly and quietly the next morning on the way back from X rays—one of the few things she had ever done without a lot of deliberation and fanfare.

Ben drove slowly past Les's car. More than once he had pointed out to Les the irony of it all—that his GTO was a lot older than Ben's old person's car. "So at least you're not totally hopeless," he would tell Les. "At least you know the worth of old things."

Age was a running joke between them. He called Lester and Morris youngsters, kids, upstarts, and whippersnappers, and they called him Old Man. Ben liked to tell them that he was alive when the polio vaccine was discovered and when Jackie Robinson played in the major leagues, that he heard the actual speech when JFK said, "Ask not what your country can do for you, but ask what you can do for your country," that he would have been at Woodstock if his cousin's car hadn't thrown a rod on the way there, and that he saw Nixon resign from office on television.

"You whippersnappers probably don't even know," he told them recently, "that *whipper-*

snapper is an altered form of the older word *snip-persnapper*." Les said no, he wasn't interested in old words, so he didn't know that and didn't care, either. "You two are pathetic," Ben would some-times say when he was in a bantering mood. "I feel sorry for you, really. No wisdom, no experience, no traditional values."

Les would shoot back with something like "Yeah, that really stinks. We ain't got nothing going for us but youth and vitality and good looks."

The grunts—that's what everybody at the Bazaar called Les and Mo, though the official job title was Facilities and Resources Management Team. Together, the two of them could figure out how to fix anything, could lift and haul like machines, could build shelves, partitions, fake windows, and mantels, whatever the vendors requested for their displays. A few days ago they had constructed a pagoda-like façade, fitted with hundreds of little hooks so the Asian Treasures vendor could hang his pearl and jade necklaces and rice paper lanterns.

They made a funny-looking pair. Short and mus-cular, Les had long, lank hair and an incongruously round, mischievous face like Spanky on *The Little Rascals*, while Mo looked more like Buckwheat—a very tall six-foot-four Buckwheat with dread-locks. Les talked freely, usually said more than he should, but Mo kept his thoughts to himself.

Except for a few memorable occasions such as the incident with a new vendor a month or so ago.

"All I was doing," the vendor had complained to Ben, her voice quivering, "was telling them how I wanted the racks set up!" To which Les had responded, "Yeah, set 'em up, then take 'em down, then set 'em up again and take 'em down again, then set 'em up a different way—must've changed her mind ten times." It was a custom drapery business, so the setup had involved tall wooden racks with long poles and many rolls of fabric. Les had finally told her exactly what she could do with her rolls of fabric, and even Mo had lost his cool and let loose with a few expletives.

Ben knew all about the irritations of dealing with indecisive women. He had grown up with a mother who agonized over what kind of bread to serve with a meal and would put on five different outfits every morning before finally deciding what to wear. Nevertheless, he had been firm with Les and Mo, had summoned them to his office as if he were a school principal, had asked the woman to stay for the meeting so he could make sure nothing got lost in the translation.

"You can't say things like that to vendors or customers or anybody else around here," he told them after she repeated her accusations. "I'm ashamed that two of my employees would stoop to such behavior. Besides being flagrantly rude and unprofessional, it's bad for business. You owe her an apology." They had both grumbled insincere apologies. "And if I ever hear you use bad language on the job again, I'll have to let you go," Ben added sternly, even though he knew he would have a hard time following through with such a threat because everybody at the Bazaar depended on them so much.

So where to go now for a bite to eat? Ben stopped at the mall exit, considering which way to turn. Downtown could fill up a lot of time, but it was too cold to be walking around outside. He'd heard some of the people at work talking about a place called Naturally Good that had just opened up near the new shopping park on Woodruff Road. It sounded like a combination of a health food store, a grocery store, a deli, a florist, and a restaurant. Maybe he'd check it out and then go over to the new Barnes and Noble to do some reading, since the library closed early on Friday nights.

He turned left and headed down toward the lights and crowds of Greenville's busiest new hot spot. Twenty-one years later and he still hated Friday nights.

Chloe had been a few weeks shy of her fourteenth birthday the first time he saw her, when she and her brother Dylan had ridden by bus from Alabama to visit their grandparents, who lived next door to Ben and his mother. The Buckleys had just moved into the house earlier that summer, in a subdivision called Montroyal in Derby, South

Carolina. Once a thriving textile community, Montroyal had originally housed all the mill employees, but by the late sixties it had become a popular place for young couples to buy their first homes, small brick affairs containing two bedrooms and a bath.

Closer to the old mill, which had eventually been razed, were a half dozen larger, nicer homes where the managers and their families used to live, on a street named Amaryllis. These homes had four bedrooms and two baths, a screened porch, a patio, and a one-car garage, and it was one of these that Ben's mother had bought the summer after she got a final settlement from the power company. By then Ben's father had already died of lung cancer after working around asbestos for over twenty-five years.

All the streets in Montroyal were named after flowers. Most of them were your average, well-known flowers like Rose, Lily, Tulip, and Violet. The developers of Montroyal must have thought long and hard to come up with a special flower for the name of the managers' street—and they must have been pleased when they hit upon Amaryllis, a pretty-sounding name though not the easiest flower to spell. The Buckleys had bought the home at 5 Amaryllis, next door to Chloe's grandparents, the Quantrilles, who had lived there ever since the homes were first built.

Ben had just turned eighteen that summer. He

was working at the Dairy Queen and heading off to the University of South Carolina in the fall without a clue of what he should major in. Somehow Ben and Dylan Quantrille had begun shooting baskets at the park on the corner of Amaryllis and Lilac whenever Ben wasn't working, with Chloe watching from the sidelines at first, sitting cross-legged on the grass.

She was a cute kid. Didn't say much but wasn't shy, either. She often laughed at something the boys said, but it was a straightforward laugh, more like a woman's than a little girl's. She sure looked like a little girl, though. Freckled face and braces on her teeth. She was starting to get some height on her but was skinny as a fence post. Her blond hair was straight and fine and slid over into her eyes when she didn't keep it pinned back.

Sometime during that two-week visit with their grandparents, another boy had shown up to shoot baskets, and somehow Chloe had ended up playing two-on-two with the boys instead of sitting on the grass. "I better warn you, she's pretty good," Dylan had told Ben before they started. Ben had taken that to mean she could dribble the ball without bouncing it off her foot. When she sank a shot from twenty feet out during warm-up, he thought it must be luck. When she moved farther out and did it two more times in a row, then went in for a layup, he swallowed hard and bent down to tighten the laces on his Converse high-tops.

Clearly, this was no ordinary little sister trying to keep up with her big brother. He had never seen anything like it. Not that she was better than Ben himself, but he knew if she challenged him to a game of horse, he would probably think of something very important he needed to tend to at home right away. The one thing he recalled about that first time was that they kept switching the teams around, and, coincidentally, whoever played with Chloe always won. He also remembered that her blond hair was dripping wet when they finally finished.

He didn't see her again until the summer after his junior year of college, when her whole family came to visit her grandparents for a few days. He had a steady girlfriend at USC by now. Home for just a month that summer, he had found a job with a lawn care business. He saw Chloe only once that time, after he got home dirty and sweaty from a twelve-hour day behind a lawn mower and weed eater.

She was sitting by herself on the front steps of her grandparents' house, drinking a tall glass of something orange and slushy-looking. She waved to him and called his name as he got out of his car. "Hi, Ben!" Very natural, very friendly, like a cousin or old classmate. He tried not to stare but waved back and said, "Hey there, how's it going?" She was still a kid compared to him, of course, but she was also living proof of the radical transformation that takes place in little girls between the time they're fourteen and seventeen.

He could close his eyes now and still see her on her grandparents' front steps that day, head tilted back, drinking. A prettier, younger Meryl Streep. A Grace Kelly kind of beauty with a little Maria Sharapova mixed in. But those were only rough comparisons. Chloe outshone them all.

Two years and a couple of broken relationships later, Ben saw her again, this time at Christmas. He had finished college by then, had started grad school in business management at the University of Georgia, and had decided that women weren't worth the risk they posed to a man's wallet and heart. He almost didn't come home that Christmas, but changed his mind at the last minute and arrived home late on Christmas Eve. On Christmas Day they saw each other "a third and fateful time," as they liked to tell it later.

Ben pulled into a parking place in the lot at Naturally Good. It was surprising how many people were wheeling grocery buggies to their cars a little before seven o'clock on a Friday night— buggies with all kinds of leafy things sticking out of the tops of brown paper bags. He could tell this was the kind of place Chloe would have loved. She had always been big on eating healthy foods, had bought organic things long before they became a fad. He thought of the drinks she used to whip up in the blender. She would throw all kinds of stuff together. He used to tell her she would make a great hippie.

She was midway through her sophomore year of college that third and fateful time he saw her. She was attending Western Alabama University on an academic scholarship. Evidently they didn't know how well she played basketball when they were offering scholarships. She had her eyes set on graduating early, then going for a master's degree and eventually a doctoral degree. At the ripe age of nineteen, she already had a list of ideas for a master's thesis and another for a doctoral dissertation.

But the wonder of it all was that she wasn't like a lot of smart girls Ben had known—either introverted and out of touch or arrogant and in your face. She was nice, genuinely nice, and she didn't seem to have the foggiest idea that she was anything great to look at. The two of them had talked for four straight hours at the Quantrilles' house that Christmas evening, and Ben hadn't taken his eyes off her the whole time.

"Somebody's got a spring in his step," his mother had said when he came home that night. "And a gleam in his eye and a funny little smile on his face."

"And somebody else has an overactive imagination," he had said back. But they both knew the truth. He had fallen hard.

Outside the automatic sliding glass doors of

Naturally Good, Ben passed a woman wearing a black spandex warm-up suit. She was talking on a cell phone, pacing in front of a large chalkboard advertising things Ben had never heard of: spinach gnocchi, panettone, sea beans, galanga root, Peppadews. Brow furrowed, the woman was gesturing dramatically with her free hand: "So I mean, like, what am I supposed to *do*? I feel like my life is in limbo now. How can he do something like that and then just leave? I mean, I am *so* not impressed with stupid stuff like that!"

The thought crossed Ben's mind that somebody ought to tell her how so not impressed people were with women her age who tried to talk like teenagers. The woman had to be fifty if she was a day. Did she really think she looked good in spandex? As the glass doors slid closed behind him, he heard her say, "Gross me out!"

How unfair, he thought, that a woman like that would probably live to be a hundred, while Chloe got only thirty-three years.

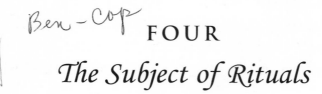

FOUR

The Subject of Rituals

Sunday morning found Ben sitting in his car like a cop on a stakeout. He felt a little foolish, actually, but now that he had gone to the trouble to get here, he meant to see it through. He wasn't sure exactly why, after the interview with Kelly Kovatch, he had been so intent on looking up the address and phone number for Charity Bible Church, then writing it down and carrying it around on a Post-it Note for two weeks. But here he was. He had felt devious calling the church office to ask about the times of the services. As if he would ever consider going to one.

From his curbside vantage across the street from the church, he surveyed the small building. So this was where Chloe had gone when she climbed out of their bed those seven Sunday mornings before she died. Two miles past the north edge of the Derby city limits, it certainly hadn't been the closest church to their house, but it was attractive enough as churches went—redbrick with a modest white steeple, two stained-glass windows flanking the big front door, and four wide curved concrete steps leading from the door down to the neatly landscaped lawn. Close to the street a few pale lavender irises, survivors of the cold snap, were just opening up around the base of the redbrick marker, which read *CHARITY BIBLE CHURCH* and underneath, *Ian Shamblin, Pastor.*

In the phone book the church was listed under "Independent," which fell alphabetically between "Holiness" and "Jehovah's Witnesses." Some of the churches in the Independent category had unusual names—The Church of the Open Door, Children of Harmony, Higher Ground Tabernacle,

Loaves and Fishes. Charity Bible Church sounded bland compared to many of them.

Though the months directly following Chloe's death were a blur, Ben knew that sometime later he had tried to get to the bottom of whatever it was that had pulled her away from him. He had read the books on her bedside table—a biography of some missionary, a couple of books called devotionals, and, of course, the Bible, or more specifically, the first five books of the Bible. He assumed that the red ribbon between Deuteronomy and Joshua marked how far she had read. That's where he had stopped reading, too.

But nothing made any sense. At some point he had given up trying to understand how a bright, independent thinker like Chloe could swallow all the malarkey of organized religion. He had gone back and forth from scorn to disbelief to amusement while reading the endless lists of rules, very strange rules, set forth in those first books of Chloe's Bible—things about wave offerings, scabs on the skin, donkeys and oxen being yoked together, lying carnally with a bondmaid. Maybe it had still been too close to her death to sort through everything; maybe now it was too far away.

He glanced at the church again, but it was closed up tight. No sign of life, only a packed parking lot. Even though his big reasons for sitting here might not be totally clear, he knew exactly what he wanted short-term. He wanted to see the Kovatch family. He wanted to see what the years had done to Kay Kovatch, wanted to see her husband and count all the younger Kovatches. Maybe he wanted to feel superior, to sneer just a little as they trailed out of church like some Norman Rockwell painting. Maybe he was hoping they wouldn't look all that happy.

He was also mildly curious about the rest of the people at this church. Maybe it took time, a lot of it, to understand something like how your wife could be suddenly and totally transformed from normal to severely religious, how she could give her heart away to someone else, someone she couldn't see or hear or touch. Maybe observing the people would somehow throw a glimmer of light into that dark corner.

Even though Ben knew it had been here for at least twenty-one years, the church looked new, except for the massive door, which was an authentic church-looking door, like something you would expect to see along a cobblestone street in Europe—a big arched double door of dark wood, pointed at the top, with little multi-paned windows centered in each half for decorative effect. Or maybe they were functional; maybe the preacher used them for checking the congregants before they entered. Maybe he stood behind the windows and asked questions before letting the people in one by one: "Have you been purified with the water of separation?" "Have you eaten only of beasts that divide the cloven hoof?" "Are you wearing vestures of fine linen?"

Ben turned the ignition back on and lowered the driver's window a few inches. Typical of April in South Carolina, the weather today was a good thirty degrees warmer than it had been two days ago. Tomorrow it could be down to freezing again, and by Friday there could be a heat wave.

He turned his attention back to the paved parking lot. Judging from the vehicles, the members of Charity Bible Church represented every economic stratum. Old pickup trucks were parked right next to luxury cars, and SUVs sat next to economy compact models. Vans, station wagons, even a paneled utility truck—the church members drove everything. It was hard to see how so many people could fit into such a small church. They must be jammed into the pews hip to hip.

A classic two-tone green '57 Chevy was parked off by itself on the grass, and two motorcycles were pulled up close to the front door. No red minivan like the one he remembered, but a big family like the Kovatches would probably wear out a vehicle every few years. Near the portico by the side door was a small white bus with *CHARITY BIBLE CHURCH* printed on the side in big block letters. Maybe the preacher let the Kovatches use that for their transportation to and from church.

Ben looked at his watch. Almost twelve. He hoped the reverend Ian Shamblin wasn't one of those preachers who didn't know when to stop. He probably wasn't the same one Chloe had listened to twenty-one years ago, but Ben couldn't be sure. He had always walked away whenever she started talking about church.

He picked up the library book he had brought along: *Presidential Shenanigans, Scandals, and Secrets*. He didn't normally check books out of the library, but he had gotten caught in the middle of something interesting in this one just as the closing lights started flashing one night.

He opened the book to a chapter titled "Mental Disorders in the Oval Office" and read the first two paragraphs. According to the author, at least nineteen presidents—over forty percent of the nation's leaders—had "very likely" suffered from some kind of psychiatric illness. Ben was instantly skeptical. He wondered just how Jacob B. Aspen, the author, had determined that. He scanned the list of the nineteen presidents and their very likely disorders—everything from severe overeating to bipolar tendencies to alcoholism. The most common was depression. There was one case of hypochondria, and Ulysses Grant supposedly had a phobia about blood, a funny thing for a war general to have.

He turned over a few pages and saw another chapter title: "Sexual Dalliances in the White House." But that wasn't anything he wanted to read about. It made him angry to think about presidents messing around that way when they were supposed to be devoting themselves to the business of running the country. One of the few things he agreed with the religious lunatic fringe about was the importance of marital fidelity.

Ben caught a movement out of the corner of his eye and looked up to see a woman in a peach-colored dress descend the steps of the church and head down the sidewalk toward the parking lot at a brisk clip. Maybe the preacher was winding things up inside. A minute later a man in a dark suit swung open both sides of the double door, then bent down to latch something at the bottom of each half. People started exiting, first only a trickle and then whole regiments of them. Children spilled out onto the lawn, squealing and racing toward the brick marker, and grownups stood around talking. Other people were coming out the side door, so Ben tried to keep an eye on those, too. He might not know Kay after so many years, but he felt sure he would recognize Kelly, even from a distance.

There appeared to be as much variety in the people's clothing as in the cars they drove, so much so, in fact, that Ben wondered if perhaps two or three churches were joining forces today. Maybe it was one of those homecoming services he used to read about in the Derby newspaper. Two people wearing jeans, a man and a woman, got on the motorcycles and sped off. Some men had on polo shirts, while others were wearing neckties and suits. Some women wore pants, others skirts. A couple of them had decked themselves out like Ben's mother used to when she was going to one of her garden parties—bright flouncy dresses with high heels and elaborate hats. One black woman wore a blue and yellow caftan with a matching turban.

One by one the cars in the parking lot disappeared. Most of them turned right and headed back toward Derby, but some turned left and passed right by Ben's car on their way toward Filbert. Several of the drivers slowed down and looked at Ben.

Two women in a brown Pontiac came creeping by. The looks on their faces told Ben exactly what they must be thinking: "Wonder who *that* is. Somebody ought to write down his license plate." The one in the passenger seat, an older woman with a flowered scarf tied around her head, said something to the driver, who slowed almost to a stop. They both stared hard at him as if they expected to see his picture on the news that night and knew they would need to come forward to testify.

Old biddies—that was the phrase that came to Ben's mind. The woman with the scarf said something else and the driver leaned forward and stared harder, then nodded. Ben could imagine what they were saying: "Men sitting in parked cars by themselves are never up to any good. The nerve of somebody like that lurking around a *church*!"

Exactly what you could expect from the religious far right, Ben thought—always assuming the worst of other people. But then he guessed he was doing the same thing—assuming the worst of the religious far right. As the brown Pontiac finally moved on, he saw a bumper sticker on the back: "When the trumpet sounds, this car will have no driver!"

Behind them, an old man driving a hearse-like black Cadillac tipped his hat and waved to Ben. Ben thought of his grandfather, who had worn a black derby hat like that every day of his life. Always playing practical jokes on people, that was his granddaddy. Mad as a March hare—or *a marsh hare*, which had been the original phrase, according to his *Say It Ain't So, Joe* book.

Ben thought suddenly of a true story he had recently read at the library about a man on death row who requested fried wild hare for his last meal. It had to be wild, the man specified—none of that chickeny-tasting tame rabbit. The man had also wanted collard greens, fried onions, and corn fritters to go with his wild hare. And loganberry cobbler for dessert. The whole story was told by the cook at the prison, who'd had to locate a wild hare, then skin it and cut it up and fry it. The inmate had eaten every bite and pronounced it acceptable, but the dish of cobbler he had thrown against the wall and declared a forgery. A forgery—that was the word he used, which, ironically, happened to be one of the many crimes, along with murder, of which he was guilty. "You think I can't tell a loganberry from a blackberry?" he had yelled. He had been so angry at the cook it had taken four men to restrain him as they led him to the electric chair.

Ben looked back at the church. How careless of him to let his mind wander. The crowd had now thinned to the point that the parking lot was almost empty. Only two children were still playing tag around the brick marker, where a couple of the irises were trampled. But as of yet no sign of the Kovatches. He had either lost them in the shuffle of people or else missed them as he was day-dreaming. Maybe they didn't even attend this church anymore. Or maybe they were out of town for the day.

And then he saw them. They were exiting from the side door. Kelly, her dark head bent, was walking along slowly with an older woman wearing a tan coat with the hood pulled up. Maybe a grandmother. Theirs would be the kind of family that would absorb the older generations into their household. Kelly was wearing a long black dress with a white collar. She looked like a Puritan. A tall man in shirtsleeves and a necktie followed closely. No hat and very little hair. Too young to be the grandfather, so probably Kelly's father. An assortment of others were walking behind him, all sizes and all with dark hair. Kelly appeared to be the oldest child, but it was hard to tell from this distance. No doubt some of the other children were grown and married by now.

Ben kept watching the door for signs of Kay. Maybe she was still rounding up the younger children. Or picking up grandchildren from the nursery. One of the teenagers, a gangly boy, ran ahead, slid open the side door of a gray Econoline van, and disappeared inside. It was a large van, the kind with a ladder up the back. Someone called out to the two children by the marker, who went zipping off toward the van. The older woman pushed the hood of her coat back and turned to watch them before allowing Kelly to assist her into the front passenger's seat.

And it was at that moment that Ben suddenly realized two things at the same time. First, that he had failed to count the number of children getting into the Econoline, and second, that the woman was not Kelly's grandmother. She was Kay Kovatch.

At last the van began to move to the exit of the parking lot, then turned right toward Derby. Only two cars were left in the parking lot now. Ben started his Lincoln Town Car, pulled a U-turn, and slowly headed back to Highway 11.

"You making it okay?" Charlie Kovatch said. "Maybe we shouldn't have tried so much yet. That's a long morning. We could have just gone to church and saved Sunday school for another time."

The usual commotion was going on in the back of the van. One of the children said, "Did not!" and there was laughter.

Kay leaned back against the headrest, her eyes closed. "I believe we already had this discussion," she said. "I knew it was going to be hard, but it was time to try." She reached over and patted Charlie's arm. "I'm okay. Just tired. Don't worry."

"What's for lunch?" Kyle asked from the back.

Kelly spoke up at once. "Tacos. And the more help I have in the kitchen, the sooner we eat."

"I gotta check the ducks soon as we get home," Kyle said. "But I heard Kitty say she wanted to help. Kirk, too." A noisy discussion ensued, during which someone suggested duck stew for an upcoming meal. "Over my dead body!" Kyle howled. Someone else said no, it would taste better over rice.

"It was good to get out," Kay said to Charlie, "but I think I'd better stay home tonight. I can probably do both services next week, but one is enough today."

Charlie nodded but kept his eyes straight ahead. He knew she would never admit what the rest of them already knew. Even Kyle, at ten, knew the truth. The treatments were over. The doctors said they couldn't do anything else. Charlie had told all the kids exactly what the oncologist had said: "It would take a miracle now to save her." But one look at Kay and anybody could tell that a miracle wasn't in the making for her.

For a little over a mile Ben followed the gray van. So he had succeeded. He had tracked down Kay, had seen the whole kit and caboodle of Kovatches. He didn't really know what he had expected to feel afterward, but it wasn't this mixture of sadness and guilt. He had accomplished nothing by spying on the Kovatches—nothing except to see them at the site of one of their weekly rituals.

It was the same ritual Chloe had adopted during the weeks right before she died. If she had to turn religious, he had told her right after she had become "converted," as she called it, he wished she would have chosen something High Church, something with grand art and pipe organs and solemn rites, not one of the little dinky churches the South was so famous for.

He thought at first that he might be able to shame her into an early defection. He told her if it were the Episcopal church downtown, or even the Lutheran or Presbyterian, he might be persuaded to go with her sometimes. Those people didn't wallow around in their religion the way so many lower-class Protestants did.

But Chloe had grown up in a Roman Catholic family. She had had enough of dry high-church rituals, she had told him. What she had now was *real*. Yeah, *real* dumb, he had said.

He remembered an argument over the subject of rituals another day, though it had started out in a light, teasing mode. Ben said there was something about the idea of rituals that was comforting and safe, even beautiful. They could add order to life or at least trick you into feeling like things were in order. The trouble with them, Chloe said, was that they could so easily become as hollow as a dry gourd. Shake them, she said, and all you heard were a few hard seeds rattling around inside. Form without substance. Chloe had always liked coming up with analogies.

But, on the positive side, Ben had pointed out, hollow gourds could be a good thing. You could drink out of them. Or build birdhouses out of them. Or make a pair of maracas and dance a rumba. Instead of laughing with him, as she once would have, Chloe had pressed her lips together and closed her eyes as if in prayer. After the first week or so, he had quit trying to make her laugh. He started getting mad and told her she had lost her sense of humor. Then he started ignoring her, or trying to, thinking that if he closed himself off from her, she would miss him so much she would do anything to get him back. But seven weeks passed, and then one afternoon she was found on the kitchen floor, dead.

In the years since, Ben had adopted rituals of his own, though none of them religious, of course. He had a Sunday ritual, one he had been forced to alter slightly today for his detective work. It was a ritual he usually enjoyed, as much as he could be said to enjoy anything. After breakfast he liked to take a long walk, or a run on the rare occasions he was feeling ambitious, which hadn't happened in many months. His cat, Ink, who sometimes behaved in very uncatlike ways, often followed him on these jaunts, but always far enough behind so as not to give the idea that she felt any affectionate attachment to him.

On Sundays when it was raining or especially cold, he went to the gym, and Ink stayed at home, stretched out inside the bay window. At the gym the treadmill had a certain symbolic attraction for him. You got on it and just kept moving, though not really going anywhere. You didn't have to work out any strategy or route, and your mind could fall into an almost trance-like state.

After his exercise he always came home and took a shower. Starting at noon, he spent three hours at the branch library nearest his house and then drove across town for a midafternoon meal at the Olive Garden, where he ordered the same spicy soup, salad, and garlic breadsticks every Sunday. After that he would drop in at the Bazaar for a half hour or so to check on things and make his presence known before going back to the library until it closed at six.

At home on Sunday evenings he always sat in his leather recliner and watched sports on television while he ate mixed nuts, popcorn, and pretzels and drank two cans of beer. Then to pacify the part of his conscience that questioned his eating habits, he always finished up with an apple—a tart, crisp Granny Smith.

He had rituals for other days of the week, too—certain times, for example, of checking his stocks and other investments online at home, certain financial programs on TV, certain places to eat. It might not be a very manly way to live life—such sameness from week to week—but it was something he had fallen into, and now it was all he knew.

Up ahead he saw the Kovatches' gray van turn off Highway 11 toward Derby. He could have followed them but had no desire to do so now. He cared nothing about seeing Kay Kovatch make her way into the house, where she would probably have to lie down while someone else fixed her something to eat. He was momentarily relieved to realize that he felt no trace of satisfaction over Kay's obvious illness—he assumed that's what made her look so old and weak.

At least he hadn't sunk so low as to rejoice over someone's misfortune. Surely that showed the capacity for compassion. Or maybe he was only fooling himself. That was another thing he knew hard-core Christians were right about: the deceitfulness of man's heart. For he had to admit that he felt no particular sadness over her illness, either.

· · ·

Two hours later Kelly appeared at her mother's bedside. "Daddy said you wanted to see me." Kelly didn't like the way her mother's bedroom smelled now. It used to be one of her favorite places in the whole house, with all the pretty greens and pinks she herself had helped put together, but now it was something close to anger that she felt whenever she came in here and saw the blinds closed, the trash can full of used tissues, and all the bottles and cups sitting around.

And the smell—a sickly sweet smell with a vinegary edge to it. Kelly didn't even know what the smell was from. It was something none of them ever talked about. Maybe it was a combination of the musty darkness and all the leftover medications and chemicals. Maybe all the sick spells in the bathroom had wafted out and absorbed into the bedroom walls. Maybe it was just the smell of worn-out life.

Kay patted the bed. "Here, sit down." She pushed the extra pillows and Kleenex box aside and eased herself over to the middle of the bed to make more room.

Kelly could tell from her mother's face how much effort the smallest things took now and how much pain resulted. If God had to take her mother's life, she didn't know why he had to let her suffer like this. She touched her mother's cheek with the tips of her fingers. "Did you sleep? Daddy said you didn't want anything to eat."

Kay sighed. "No sleep. No food. Funny to be so tired you can't sleep or eat." She took Kelly's hand in one of hers and kissed it. They sat in silence for a few moments. Kimmie was playing the piano downstairs in the living room, but it sounded plinky and far away.

Kay rubbed the back of Kelly's hand. "I wanted to talk to you about your job. I didn't even get to hear how the interview went, except Daddy said they hired you. He said you were so happy you cried." She closed her eyes and smiled. "They must have liked you."

"Or else they were hard up," Kelly said.

Kay gave her head a little shake. "No, don't say that. They saw something they liked." She opened her eyes again. "That's going to keep you busy. I hope it's not too much."

Kelly touched her mother's hair—coarser, curlier, shorter now but still mostly dark. Young-looking hair. "Don't worry. We've got it all figured out. We had a powwow about the housework. We can cover everything with a little redistributing." She leaned down closer to her mother. "Remember, we prayed about the job, Mom. I'm sure it's the right thing." As if prayer always worked, she thought.

Kay nodded, then took in a slow breath and released it just as slowly. "So what did the man say at the interview? Or was it a woman? Did they like the pictures? Tell me about it."

"It was a man," Kelly said. "He was nice to me. I guess he liked the pictures okay. I don't think he looked at them very closely. He doesn't seem very happy."

Kay's eyes searched Kelly's face. "Really? What's his name? I can pray for him." Before Kelly could answer, her mother was seized with a spasm of coughs. It was an awful gasping, sputtering sound like an old engine about to die.

Kelly quickly filled a small glass. "Here, can you drink some water?" She slid an arm behind her mother and tried to lift her to a sitting position.

The coughing finally subsided, and Kay took a sip of water, then pushed it away.

"Do you want me to read something to you?" Kelly asked.

"No, I think I'm ready to sleep now. Can you just pray before you go?" She took both of Kelly's hands in her own and closed her eyes.

Kelly couldn't have told anyone what she prayed—her heart wasn't really in it—but when she came to the end, Kay tugged on her hand and whispered, "No, not yet. You forgot to pray for that man—the one who's not very happy."

When Kelly finished this time, her mother was asleep. She sat and watched her shallow breathing, each exhalation too faint to blow out even the smallest birthday candle.

FIVE

Curses and Judgments

On a Sunday morning two weeks later, Caroline
Mason was searching through a cupboard in her den
for a newspaper article. It had appeared in the Derby
Daily News over a year ago, on the twentieth
anniversary of Chloe Buckley's death, and had outlined all the events surrounding the murder, the
investigation, and all the false leads that eventually
dried up and left the local and state authorities with
a cold case. Caroline knew she had saved the article,
but now she was having trouble finding it. She
wanted to read it again and check on something.

She pulled out a stack of old magazines stashed
on one of the shelves under the television. She had
always meant to go through them again and clip
out pictures for decorating ideas, so she took them
over to the sofa and set them on the floor so she
would see them later and be reminded to start on
them. There used to be a time when she never
forgot projects but dispatched them promptly, as
soon as they came to mind. She remembered
coming home after work, brimming with energy
and ready to dig into repainting a room or putting
up wallpaper or refinishing a piece of furniture.
And now she couldn't even get around to cutting
out pictures.

She opened the other cupboard door at the bottom of the entertainment center but saw only her videotapes and DVDs, no sign of the newspaper article. There used to be a time also when she kept her videos in alphabetical order, but now they were all mixed together. She took out *Sleeping With the Enemy* and set it on top of the TV. Maybe she would watch that while she worked on the magazines tonight.

Donald used to make fun of her movie preferences. "Other people's mothers like nice stories on the Hallmark Channel," he would say. "But mine? She likes murder, mayhem, psychosis, and terror." Caroline never had pointed out to him the element he was missing: the fact that the women in her favorite movies outwitted the men in some way. Killing them was just one of the many possibilities. She had her limits, though. *Silence of the Lambs*, for instance. She didn't like that one at all. It was too creepy. She had seen it once and still had nightmares about the underground pit in the killer's house.

She went to the spare bedroom, where her desk was. She stood in the doorway a moment, studying the pink and maroon décor she had worked so hard to pull together. She suddenly realized she was getting bored with it. It all looked so stiff and prim and confined, and the lampshade—covered with pale pink netting embroidered with little maroon flowers—suddenly struck her as particularly tiresome. Well, she couldn't do anything about it now, after having just spent so much on the living room.

That was the trouble with working at the Upstate Home and Garden Bazaar. She was forever seeing things she wanted for her house, things she didn't really need and often couldn't afford. And to make matters worse, it seemed that her tastes were constantly shifting. She remembered a time, for example, when she had turned up her nose at contemporary furnishings, but more recently she had begun seeing something clean and refreshing about all those sleek, straight lines and uncluttered surfaces. As if she could just throw all her old stuff out and start all over!

She had come to the spare room intending to go through the drawers of the desk, but her eye caught the pink wicker magazine basket beside the floor lamp. There among back issues of *Southern Living* she saw the edge of a newspaper sticking out. She pulled it out and was pleased to read the headline: *LOCAL MURDER STILL COLD 20 YEARS LATER*. She took it back to the den and sat down on the sofa to read it. She didn't know if Ben had seen the article when it appeared on the front page last year, but everyone else at work surely had. Even though it was in the Derby paper, not the Greenville *News*, several copies had shown up at the Bazaar and were passed around quietly among the employees. Caroline herself had taken her copy and shared it with Nora and Melody in the break room over lunch. She scanned through it now to find the part she was looking for.

Of the four Buckley children, it was the youngest who got home from school first that mild March Friday twenty years ago. It was a hard thing for a child to see—his mother lying dead on the kitchen floor with the electrical cord of the vacuum cleaner tied around her neck. The boy, seven, did what every well-trained child should do in an emergency. He called 9-1-1.

There, that was what she wanted to check on. She had been talking to Byron and Jillian in the break room two days ago about a story she had seen on *Cold Case Files*, one of her favorite television programs. The conversation had led naturally into a rehashing of the murder of Mr. Buck's wife, a subject of which Caroline never tired. She proceeded to tell the whole story, since Byron had never heard it all, but when she got to the part about the boy calling 9-1-1, he interrupted to ask if she knew that for a fact.

"I'm not sure they even had 9-1-1 in Derby twenty-one years ago," he had said. But here it was in print. Caroline looked at the byline. Surely this Celia Coleman person had checked her facts before writing the article. She'd no doubt had access to all the official reports, had probably even gotten to see police photos of the crime scene. Caroline felt a little thrill of horror go over her at the thought of the photos.

Police reported that the boy then ran next door and pounded on a neighbor's door. Leah Jorgensen said that when she saw him at her back door, she knew at once that something was dreadfully wrong. "He was always such a quiet little fellow," she said, "but that day he was screaming and crying at the same time, and pointing over to his house saying, 'My mommy, my mommy, my mommy!' over and over."

Caroline paused. She wondered what Donald would have done at that age if he had come home and found *her* strangled with an electrical cord. Sometimes it was hard to remember Donald as a child. She hadn't been very good about taking pictures when he was growing up, but she did have one of him with a new bicycle on a Christmas morning. He must have been nine or ten. He was standing beside the bicycle, his arms folded, looking out of sorts. She didn't remember now exactly what his complaints were, but the bicycle wasn't the one he wanted.

If she had been in some kind of serious accident, she couldn't imagine Donald running to a neighbor's house, crying, "My mommy, my mommy, my mommy!" He might have leaned down and shouted, "What do you think you're doing? Get up, Mother!" She could imagine him stepping over her body on the kitchen floor to fix himself a snack.

Before the ambulance and police arrived, the

boy's oldest sister, twelve, had come home with a friend who was planning to spend the night. The friend's mother had dropped the girls off and left already. After Leah Jorgensen went next door to see what was wrong, she took the boy and the two girls back to her house to wait for help to arrive.

Fifteen minutes later, after attempts by emergency workers to resuscitate their mother had failed, the boy's twin sisters, ten, also arrived home. They had ridden the bus with their brother but had stopped at a friend's house instead of going directly home.

Leah Jorgensen and other neighbors stayed with the children until their grandparents could be reached. The children's father, Benjamin Buckley, was out of town on business for the day and, due to a series of accidents and miscommunications, could not be contacted until four hours later.

Meanwhile police secured the site and searched the Buckleys' house and grounds for evidence of the killer. Police reported the back door was open with no sign of forced entry. They also reported a dirt stain and some debris that appeared to have been tracked onto the carpet in the den. No fingerprints were found other than those of family members. There was no evidence of sexual assault.

Caroline paused again, imagining the whole scenario as a movie, with the children arriving home one by one, totally unsuspecting, perhaps calling out to their mother as they came through the front door: "Mommy, I'm hungry! Can I have a cookie?" "Hey, Mom, guess what I made on the spelling test?" "Mom, can we have pizza tonight?" It would make for a riveting opening.

But Caroline didn't like movies that exploited children. She often wondered how parents could let their children act in adult movies, especially violent ones. Like that cute little Amish boy in the Harrison Ford movie *The Witness*. It was another of her favorite movies, but every time she watched it, she wanted to find out who the boy's real-life parents were and send them a scolding e-mail. People would do anything for money, even sell their own children's innocence.

Forget the movie, though. The real-life situation was riveting enough. She wondered how Ben's four children had held up afterward. And Ben himself—what in the world would it have been like for him when they finally tracked him down in Charleston and told him his wife had been murdered? She wondered exactly who had broken the news to him and where he was at the time.

Caroline sat on the sofa and read the rest of the article, which told of the neighbors' testimonies about what they saw, possible suspects and motives, and the results of the investigation, which could be boiled down to nothing, nothing, and nothing.

Ben Buckley, employed at the time by Schafer-Maxx-Pryor in Greenville, had left home early that morning for Charleston, where he was to conduct an audit of the Bright Gems Daycare Facilities. On his way, he stopped at the Columbia office of Schafer-Maxx-Pryor to leave some papers and arrived in Charleston before noon. He ate lunch before proceeding to the Bright Gems administrative office.

Due to an electrical storm the night before, however, the telephones at Bright Gems were not in service.

Back in the Greenville office of Schafer-Maxx-Pryor, the first emergency call was taken by a new receptionist, who reported that Mr. Buckley was not working that day but was in Boston for his parents' 50th wedding anniversary. It was, in fact, another employee, Ken Hucklebee, who was in Boston. The mistake caused further delays in notifying Ben Buckley of his wife's murder.

Caroline read the rest of the article, slowly and attentively. Surely there must have been some telltale clue the police had missed in their investigation. When she finished the article, she went back to the first paragraph and read it all again.

Stretched out almost full length in his recliner, Ben aimed the remote at the television. His bowl of popcorn was empty, as were the other bowls and the two beer cans. The Sunday night offerings on TV had been lackluster tonight. Even though it was NCAA time, he couldn't generate any enthusiasm. How had these two teams even made it to the playoffs? He couldn't remember a game with so many fouls, turnovers, and missed shots.

He stopped at an obscure channel called Offroad, which combined out-of-the-ordinary news and sports coverage. This was where he had watched billiard tournaments, eating contests, and women's boxing in the past. Tonight it was the World Domino Tournament.

He would have thought such a tournament was a joke if someone had told him about it, but the looks on the contestants' faces, sweaty with concentration under the bright lights, convinced him they were totally serious. The announcer's voice was just as serious: "Wainwright still holds the lead. You can tell he's trying to keep his head at this critical point in the game."

Ben sat up in his recliner and leaned forward. The domino players were full-grown men. The camera zoomed in on one of them—a man in a white turtleneck, with a little plume of curly blond hair sticking up in front. He had a thin face, deep-set eyes, and an enigmatic smile, as if he knew he had the game in the bag.

The camera shifted to the other contestant—a dignified, imposing man with a long beard, wearing a dark silky-looking shirt with a mandarin collar, the kind of man you thought of when you said the word *judge* or *king* or *priest*. In another era this man could be holding a scepter or shield or incense for an altar. Instead, he was frowning down at an angular network of black tiles with white dots on them. In a hushed tone the announcer said, "McClure has every reason to look worried, with the boneyard shrinking and twenty-five grand on the line. He knows he could be dead if things don't turn around in the next couple of plays."

Ben wondered what had ever become of the set of ivory dominoes he and his brother Walter had played with as kids. Not the real game of dominoes, of course, but their own game, played on the large tray that hooked onto Walt's wheelchair. That seemed like eons ago. His mother had probably thrown the dominoes out after Walt died, along with everything else that reminded her of him. She hadn't had an easy life of it, his mother. Losing a son, then a husband.

Ben rose abruptly and turned off the television. He didn't want to think of Walt or his mother or his father. And what did he care who won the World Domino Tournament?

He took his bowls and the empty cans into the kitchen. He had no interest in eating his ritualistic apple. What good would that do after all the junk he had eaten tonight? He nudged the cat off the rug under the sink and rinsed out the bowls, then put them in the dishwasher. Ink meowed indifferently and padded out of the kitchen into her bed in the laundry room.

Ben turned out the lights in the kitchen and den and went back to his bedroom. His knee was still hurting. He should have known the day would end badly by the way it had started, with a short, uncomfortable morning walk due to the stiff knee. In fact, nothing in his usual Sunday routine had given him any pleasure today. Nothing at the library had interested him much, except a picture book about edible insects, which was a big mistake to look at before lunch. The soup at Olive Garden, which he usually enjoyed, had been so full today of undercooked celery and macaroni noodles that every bite made him think of beetle carapaces and soft-bodied mealworms. Besides that, the tea was too weak and not sweet enough.

And when he had stopped in at the Bazaar after that, he had walked by the Field and Forest Accessories showroom only to spot a sorry piece of junk labeled Deer Antler Hat Rack with a price tag of $79.99. He had stopped to examine it before concluding that it wasn't worth even $7.99. At least the vendor could have had the decency to label it Imitation Deer Antler Hat Rack. Ben had nothing against using lower-priced materials to achieve an effect, but those antlers looked like nothing more than plastic sticks.

He undressed and stepped into the shower. He had already had one shower today, but maybe another one would relax him, make him feel less like a grumpy old man. He adjusted the shower head, then closed his eyes and let the water beat on his face. He tried to think of something good but instead kept going over the dissatisfactions of the day.

He adjusted the shower head again, this time to "mist." What a misnomer. It was more like "dribble." He thought about all the shoddiness he had to put up with on a daily basis. Not just cheap fake antlers but ninety percent of everything else. The real McCoy was becoming an endangered species. He reached up and yanked the lever to turn the shower off.

Ten minutes later he was sitting on the edge of his bed holding his alarm clock, another piece of plastic even though it was supposed to look like real cut glass. It was a wind-up clock since he had learned long ago not to trust electricity when it came to getting up in the morning. He started winding it, twisting the silver knob on the back harder than he needed to.

He turned the clock around and looked at the face. Almost midnight. He checked the time against the electric clock on his nightstand, then made sure the alarm was set for six-thirty. Less than seven hours before he had to get up and face another week of work. And then another one after that and another after that. He turned it back around and twisted the second knob to wind the alarm.

And the priest shall take the young pigeon and

wring off its head from its neck, but shall not divide it asunder.

It was surprising how many verses from Chloe's Bible had stuck with him over the years, coming back to his mind at random times, often lodging in his mind for days. And it always seemed to be the bad things he remembered. As he pulled back the covers and lay down, he thought of all the curses and judgments mixed in with those weird rules in the Bible: *And your strength shall be spent in vain: for your land shall not yield her increase. Ye shall be delivered into the hand of the enemy. Ye shall eat, and not be satisfied. Ye shall remember the former days.*

SIX

No Easy Answer

Early in the morning on the eighth day of May, Kelly Kovatch sat by the bedside, fanning her mother's face with a green silk fan that had been used only for decoration until now. A picture of geishas beside a blue lake was painted on one side, and a long black tassel was attached to a little silver ring at the end. Her mother's eyes were fixed on the picture on the fan, and Kelly wondered if the two of them were thinking the same thing, that such serenity was more than literally a world away.

"Does that feel better?" Kelly said.

Her mother nodded. She reached out and touched Kelly's hand. "It won't be long now, you know." Her voice was only a whisper.

In the past few weeks Kelly had seen the last traces of hope vanish from her mother's eyes. The hospice nurse came once a day now, a stout woman named Sheba. "That's right—Sheba," she'd said when she introduced herself the first day. "As in the queen of." Sheba was a good nurse. They all liked her. She took care of business but with a compassionate touch. And she was honest. She had told them it could be today or another six weeks. "You can never really tell," she said. "Your mother is a mighty strong woman in here." She thumped her broad fist over her heart. "If all it took was willpower, she could still be here all the way through summer, maybe even up to Christmas." She had looked away, then added sensibly, "But we all know it takes more than willpower."

"I've got to leave for work now," Kelly said to her mother. "Kerri's coming up to read to you in a little bit. She's cleaning up something in the kitchen."

Her mother's eyes darted to hers. "What? Did something spill?"

"Just sugar," Kelly said. She didn't need to tell her mother it was a full five-pound bag Kerri had just opened and was getting ready to pour into the canister as soon as she washed the sugar scoop. At least that was the plan until Kirk blew in. It was a family joke, though sometimes it wasn't all that funny, that Kirk couldn't seem to keep track of what his arms and legs did these days. Somehow in the simple process of getting his cereal bowl out of the cupboard, the bag of sugar had ended up on the floor.

Kelly stood up. She folded the fan and set it on the bedside table. "I'll be back by five-thirty," she said, taking her mother's hand. "I think Karla's on supper duty tonight. She's downstairs looking through your recipes. She's trying to figure out how she can use the leftover baked potatoes from last night. Kimmie's going to help her, though, so they'll do fine." She leaned over to kiss her mother's forehead. It was odd how she always managed to get used to the smell after being in the room awhile. "You need anything before I go?" she asked.

Kay smiled weakly. "Oh, I need a lot of things, honey, but nothing you can get for me." Kelly tried to pull her hand away, but her mother held on. "This dying by degrees is sure hard," she said. "Hard on everybody." She grimaced. "But any kind of dying is hard, I suppose."

Kelly couldn't think of anything to say. She couldn't see how her mother's slow dying could possibly be part of God's perfect will—something Pastor Shamblin was always preaching about.

She glanced at the clock. She gave her hand another little tug, but her mother squeezed harder.

"I had a friend once who died real suddenly," Kay said. "Somebody killed her. I never told you about her, did I? She died only a few months before you were born."

Kelly wondered if the morphine was making her mother imagine things. "No, you didn't tell me about that," she said.

"I've wondered if that wouldn't be a better way to die," Kay said. She let go of Kelly's hand suddenly and turned her head away. "It's hard seeing all of you every day and knowing . . . it might be the last time." She coughed softly, ending with a dry, airy sound like wind blowing through a hollow reed. "But I shouldn't talk like that," she said. "God knows exactly what he's doing. He gives and he takes away. Sometimes he does it fast, and sometimes slow."

Kelly sat down on the edge of the bed. She wondered if her mother could be struggling over the question of God's goodness the same way she was. "I could stay home from work today if you want me to," she said, laying the back of her hand against her mother's cheek.

But Kay turned to her and shook her head. "No, no, you go on. I'm tired now. I'm going to try to sleep. Maybe I'll dream again." Her eyes brightened. "I saw you in a wedding dress last night standing by your daddy."

Kelly laughed. "That was a dream all right." She kissed her again and walked to the door. "I'll see you when I get home tonight. I'll tell Kerri to wait a little while before she comes up."

"Are the blinds closed?" her mother asked. "It seems so bright in here."

"They're closed," Kelly said. "But I can pull the drapes."

"No, that's okay. Leave them. I don't want it pitch dark."

Kelly stood at the door a moment watching the covers rise ever so slightly with each breath her mother took. As she stepped out into the hall and shut the door behind her, she suddenly remembered something her mother used to tease about when Kitty and Kyle were babies, when she was flying around the house cooking meals for eleven children, folding laundry into different stacks, and supervising school lessons at the dining room and kitchen tables. "One of these days," she would say, "I'm going to lie in bed till noon. You just wait and see. I might even stay in bed all day if I feel like it!"

Kay heard her daughter's footsteps recede down the hallway and down the stairs. She needed to talk to Charlie again tonight and make sure he wouldn't forget to keep praying about a husband for Kelly. Poor Charlie, he had a lot on his mind right now. She needed to remind him where the list of questions was. They had made it up together when Neil was courting Krista six years ago, and the four of them had sat on the back porch one summer night as Neil answered each one. Maybe they needed to revise the list for the next boy. It was going to take someone special for Kelly, someone not put off by a smart girl and someone who could see past her serious side.

She also needed to talk to Charlie again about the children's schooling, but every time she tried to start a discussion, they kept getting stuck. There wasn't an easy answer to anything these days. And time was getting away from them. Nothing at home was running on schedule anymore, and there was no easy answer to that, either.

Oh, and she needed to tell Kelly to make sure Kitty and Kyle both had new flip-flops to take to camp in July. A few weeks ago the children had helped her downstairs so she could watch them transplant monkey grass along the front sidewalk. That's when she had noticed that Kyle was wearing one green flip-flop and one of Kitty's smaller pink ones. Only weeks ago—Kay couldn't imagine being able to make it downstairs now.

She was so tired. And her memory was so unreliable now. She opened her eyes and fumbled on the bedside table for the little notebook and pen she kept there. "Courtship ?s," she scrawled slowly, then "fl-flops." There, that would help her—if she could read her own handwriting, that is. She lay back against the pillows, then reached over to the table again for the sock she kept there.

It was one of Charlie's black ones that had a hole in the toe. She laid it over her eyes to block out the light.

The door opened again. "Mother, you want me to wait?" It was Kerri. She came partway into the bedroom. "Kelly said you might not be ready yet for me to read, but I wanted to check before I started anything else."

Kay lifted a hand. "No, not now, honey. Come back later." She heard the door close. If she had the energy, she could have offered a little joke of some kind: "Imagine being too tired to even listen to a story!" There were other things she wanted to say. Things like "Did you get the sugar all cleaned up?" and "Don't forget to mail Keith's birthday present tomorrow, okay?" and "Make sure Daddy's work pants get pressed." She also wanted to know if Kenny had sent the pictures of the new baby yet. She felt a desperate need to see this latest grand-child, the one named after her.

But she had used up all her words for now. She heard Kerri's footsteps on the stairs and felt relieved. There, she was all alone now.

Just before she drifted off, she thought again of Chloe Buckley. She would get to see her old friend soon. Theirs had been a short friendship but had grown surprisingly fast—until that awful day. The only thing that worried her now was that Chloe might ask about her husband, Ben. The last thing she had said to Kay on the phone the night before she died was "Please keep praying for Ben." It would make perfect sense for her first question in heaven to be "Tell me, were our prayers for Ben ever answered?"

But Kay wouldn't have an answer. She had meant to keep up with him, had even tried a couple of times, but she hadn't persisted. Then he and his children had moved out of their house and in with his mother so she could help with the children, and the last Kay had heard, the kids had all left home and Ben had left Derby, too, and moved over to Greenville. She had always meant to contact him again but never did.

From downstairs she heard laughter. That was good.

"Hey, you changed your mind yet about that offer?" Lester Lattimore called to Kelly as she came in through the back door of the Bazaar. He was standing in the doorway of the storage supply room wrapping a long orange electrical cord around his elbow. She reddened but replied firmly, "No, I haven't." She heard him laugh as she quickened her steps.

"Want to go to Hooters with me and Mo some night?"—that was the standing offer, first put forth a week after she had started work back in early April. Lester had described for her several times since then how much fun they could have, had told her it was only mild fun, however, compared to what they could have later, after she got loosened up. He had suggested she bring some different clothes to change into, had said she'd look good in some of the things the waitresses wore. Kelly had seen the billboards for Hooters. She knew what the waitresses wore, and she knew it was a place where people drank and carried on and listened to loud music.

She also knew Lester was making fun of her. She had a feeling it would only get worse if he saw he was annoying her, so she tried never to let on. The less she said around him, she figured, the better. He was the type who loved to twist people's words and turn something innocent into some kind of innuendo. It wasn't that he was smarter than other people, but he had the advantage, if you could call it that, of having a lot of worldly experience. She often didn't have any idea what he was talking about.

He had laughed uncontrollably, for instance, the day he asked her about the dented front bumper on the Ford Taurus she drove to work. All she had said was "That happened when my sister was learning to drive. She stopped too fast and somebody ran into her from behind and knocked her up against a mailbox."

Lester had almost fallen on the floor from laughing so hard. "Her sister got knocked up against a mailbox!" he kept saying to Mo, who finally said, "Yeah, yeah, heard you the first time."

Mo rarely spoke to her, but when she had to talk to the two of them for some work-related reason, he was always the one she addressed. His eyes didn't give away much, but she thought there might be a chance that Mo had a heart. Lester, he just had a mouth.

Caroline was the one who took the call some two hours later. Ben happened to be standing in the doorway of his office at the time, asking her to find him some new, sharpened number-two pencils. Not the cheap mechanical ones she preferred, but "real pencils made out of real wood," he said, "with real erasers on the end." He was holding a stubby one in his hand, sniffing it near the pointed end and saying, "I want a pencil that smells like a tree, not one of these plastic ones"—and he held up a red Bic in his other hand—"that go click click click. Why try to improve on tradition and simple efficiency? Let's get back down to brass tacks around here, Caroline!"

She was glad the phone rang at that moment as it relieved her from having to say, "Yes, Mr. Buck, I'll attend to it right away." Some weeks it seemed that he wasn't happy about anything, that he just poked around in every nook and cranny until he found something to gripe about. Two days ago he had complained about her new cologne, which she had ordered from QVC and for which she had paid dearly, and yesterday he had told her that the music track over the intercom system was getting on his nerves and needed to be changed. He was always coming up with something new for her to take care of while he just sat and puttered in his office or walked around the showroom floor.

Even as she reached for the phone, he was still talking: "And speaking of brass tacks, don't they make those anymore? I was noticing the cheap plastic things on the bulletin board in the break room the other day. What's the deal with those? Did somebody find them at a closeout sale or something?"

Caroline felt like telling him to go sit on one of those cheap plastic tacks, but instead she raised an index finger and said to him, "Hold on a minute," then kept her voice calm as she spoke into the phone: "Upstate Home and Garden Bazaar. This is Caroline Mason, administrative assistant. How may I help you?"

She listened to the person on the other end of the phone now, then spoke clearly and, she hoped, sympathetically. "Yes, I will go find her myself. Yes, I understand. I'll tell her to come right home. I'm very sorry. Yes, thank you." She hung up the phone and rose from her desk. "I have to go find Kelly Kovatch now," she said, hoping to convey to Mr. Buck that his demands about pencils and tacks were of no account in the face of real problems. She started toward the door leading out into the store.

"Wait. Why do you have to find Kelly?" Ben said.

"It's a family emergency," she said.

"I'll get her," he said. "I was going out to walk the floor a little anyway. What's the message?"

She bit her tongue. She wished she hadn't said anything. She wanted to do this herself for two reasons. One, to get away from her desk for a few minutes so she wouldn't go crazy listening to one more word out of Mr. Buck's mouth, and two, not that she relished the idea of bearing bad news, but it did give one a momentary sense of importance. She could go with Kelly to get her things, even walk her out to her car. Maybe she could find out more about her mother's final illness, something she had never heard her mention.

Though she had been working here for a month now, the girl was still a total mystery. Caroline wondered how somebody like her would respond to the news she had just heard over the telephone. Losing your mother anytime was hard. But right here before Mother's Day—well, that would be especially hard.

"Is it her mother?" Ben asked. "Has her mother died?"

Caroline opened her mouth and closed it. Now, how in the world had he guessed that? "Yes," she said with a little sigh. "I didn't even know her mother was sick. Did you?"

But Ben just shrugged. "I'll find her and tell her to go home," he said. He put the two pencils down on her desk. "And here, I'll just leave these to remind you of our little conversation. I'm sure they sell nice wooden ones at any respectable office supply. Oh, and be sure to get yellow number twos." He put his hands in his pockets and left, whistling something under his breath. He took a few steps, then turned back. "Oh, and just in case you were wondering about the expression *getting down to brass tacks*, Caroline, it came from the days when they had general stores. They would nail brass tacks into the counter and—"

Caroline interrupted. "It doesn't matter, Mr. Buck. I don't care where it came from."

"Well, I'm disappointed to hear that," he said. "You should always care about learning." He resumed his whistling and walked out.

Caroline sat back down. At least her first goal was accomplished. With Mr. Buck out of the office for a few minutes, maybe she could regain a little of her sanity. If she was lucky, maybe he would get sidetracked out on the floor and give her a nice long break. She still wondered how he knew about Kelly's mother. Maybe the girl had confided in him during the interview. Maybe that's why she had been crying when she left his office that day.

Caroline tried to imagine how somebody like Mr. Buck would break such bad news to somebody like Kelly Kovatch. The world was sure full of odd people, and a high concentration of them seemed to work right here at the Upstate Home and Garden

Bazaar. Caroline held her hands out in front of her and studied her nails. She was getting tired of the French manicure and was ready to go back to her favorite shade: Poppies Flambeau.

As she turned back to her computer, she thought again of Kelly. Plain, somber, diligent, unmanicured Kelly. All the other employees seemed to be as puzzled by the girl as Caroline herself was. It wasn't that she was unfriendly exactly, but a little standoffish—and just *so* different. She didn't know a thing about movies or TV, for instance. A few of the employees made fun of her behind her back. Nothing mean, just a little mild mocking.

In the break room one day Caroline had been telling the others about a book she was reading in which a woman was murdered at her own wedding. In an effort to draw Kelly into the conversation, Caroline had asked her if she liked to read. She had nodded politely between bites of a sandwich. "Yes, I'm reading a very interesting biography of John Paton right now," she'd said.

Nobody had spoken for a moment. Then LaTeesha Rutherford, one of the floorwalkers, had said what the rest of them were thinking: "Who's that, Double-K? You talking about *George* Patton, that general dude?" LaTeesha liked to make up nicknames for people. Besides Double-K for Kelly, she always referred to Lester and Mo as Mo'-or-Less. And Roy Fox, the assistant business manager, was Viceroy.

"No, John Paton," Kelly said. "He was a missionary to the New Hebrides."

"The new *what*?" LaTeesha said.

"Hebrides."

"Sounds like a disease." They had all laughed as LaTeesha lapsed into a deep doctor-like voice: "Sorry to tell you this, honey, but you got you one awful case of the Hebrides."

Kelly smiled but shook her head. "No, it's a group of islands in the South Pacific. It's off the coast of Australia."

LaTeesha had feigned interest. "Sure enough? That's a kick. A book about a missionary on an island. Can I read it after you?"

Kelly nodded eagerly. "Well, it's not my book, but I'm sure you could borrow it. It belongs to a friend at my church." She paused, then added, "The natives in the New Hebrides were cannibals."

Someone by the drink machine snorted then covered it up with a cough.

"Oh, I love books like that, Double-K," LaTeesha had said. "I just eat 'em up."

Even Kelly had laughed at that.

Ben found Kelly in an unoccupied showroom upstairs next to the carpets. An artist had made arrangements to rent the space and would be moving in soon. Kelly was writing something on a clipboard. She had a tape measure draped around her neck. Ben wondered if anyone had ever told her that besides Natalie Wood, she also favored Audrey Hepburn a little, especially with her short haircut. He wondered if she even knew who Audrey Hepburn and Natalie Wood were.

"Hello, Ms. Kovatch," he said. "Getting things set up for the new vendor?"

"Yes, sir, I'm working on it," she said. She tucked the ballpoint pen behind her ear and clasped the clipboard to her chest. "He asked for some pretty specific things."

"Oh? Such as?"

"Well, he wants a wide molding all the way around the top of the partition. He's going to hand paint it with blue pomegranates."

"Blue pomegranates?"

She nodded. "That's going to be the name of his showroom. The Blue Pomegranate."

Ben cocked his head. He already knew this, of course. "I wonder if he simply plucked that name out of the air or if he happens to know the origin."

"Oh, he knows the origin," she said. "He told me all about it."

Ben smiled. "But you probably already knew, didn't you?"

She gave him a funny look. "Well, yes sir, I did." She paused. "Do you—"

"Oh yes, I know about the blue pomegranates on the hem of the high priest's robe," he said. "And about the breastplate and the ephod and the table of showbread and the Urim and Thummim and—" He stopped abruptly.

Kelly didn't know what to make of this surprising speech. But he spared her the trouble of saying anything by adding, "I'm sorry, Ms. Kovatch. I didn't mean to waste your time. Forgive me. I came to tell you that you're needed at home right away."

She put a hand to her mouth. For a moment they stared at each other. Then he eased the clipboard from her hands. "Here, I'll put this on your desk in the workroom. And this, too." He took the tape measure from around her neck. She handed him the pen from behind her ear.

She started away, then turned back. "But should I . . . ? How will this . . . ?" She waved a hand around the empty showroom.

"Don't worry about this," Ben said. "It can wait. You go get your things and go on home."

"I made some notes for Lester and Mo," she said, pointing to the clipboard.

"Okay, I'll tell them."

As she walked quickly away, Ben couldn't help wondering if her eyes would be so clear, her hand so steady if she had been caught unawares as he had been twenty-one years ago. What a luxury to have time to prepare for letting go of someone instead of having her yanked from you in a blinding instant.

And from the victim's point of view, it was a

luxury, too, to be allowed to die a little at a time in your own bed instead of being attacked and murdered. Compared to Chloe, Kay Kovatch had drawn an easy card in the game of death.

SEVEN

A Slow, Sad Dream

"Hey. They told me I could find the grand panjandrum in here somewhere."

Caroline looked up with a start. A tall, thin man in jeans and a white T-shirt stood at the door of her office. He motioned back through the door into the hallway. "You know, Mutt and Jeffster out there? They directed me here."

He was carrying a hammer in one hand. His T-shirt showed a picture of a little cartoon man in a chef's hat running up a hill carrying a banner, beneath which was printed *HAVE YOU SEEN THE MUFFIN MAN?* Furthermore, the front of the shirt was smeared with all kinds of colors, as if the man had used it to wipe his hands while finger-painting.

Caroline was stunned. Whatever he was talking about, she couldn't take it in. All of a sudden her mind was flooded with stories she had read in the newspaper of mentally unstable people showing up in stores and restaurants and going on shooting rampages. One man had attacked a woman in a grocery store just last year with a screwdriver, of all things. She tried not to look at the hammer the man was holding. She didn't want to set him off.

The man raised his voice a little and took several steps toward her desk. "Uh, excuse me, ma'am. May I please talk to the high muckamuck? The royal rajah?" He paused, then added hopefully, "The head honcho?" He had very blue eyes behind his rimless glasses. Caroline had recently seen a TV report about a serial killer in Georgia with disarmingly blue eyes and a gentlemanly manner. Suddenly she couldn't remember if they had caught him or if he was still on the loose.

The man lowered his eyebrows and spoke softly. "She has ears, for I see them—but does she hear? Perhaps she is like the lady Alexander Pope wrote about, the one with a single fault." He held the hammer aloft and raised his voice. " 'When all the world conspires to praise her, the woman's deaf, and does not hear.' " Suddenly his eyes brightened and he pointed the hammer at her. "Hey, wait just a minute, maybe *you're* the main maharani around here! Pardon my execrable sexism, ma'am. No insult intended. I'm actually a very progressive-minded individual normally. I have profound respect for the many talents of women."

Caroline stood up behind her desk and pressed the intercom into Ben's office. She tried to remain calm, but her voice was tight: "Mr. Buckley, could you come out here, please?" No answer. She side-stepped toward Ben's office door, which was closed. "Mr. Buckley," she called, "there's someone here to see you." She knocked and swung the door open, keeping the blue-eyed man within sight. She cast a glance into Ben's office, but it appeared empty. Of all times for him to go missing, just when she needed him. She thought sure he was in here. Had he let himself out by the window? "Mr. Buck!" she called shrilly.

She heard a guttural half groan, and from behind the desk Ben pulled himself up. On his knees, he blinked at her across the room, then slowly rose to his feet. "What is it, Caroline?" he said. "You sound hysterical."

Her mouth fell open. "Did you lose something on the floor, Mr. Buckley?"

Ben fixed her with a stern look. "Yes, I lost consciousness, Ms. Mason." He yawned.

Caroline stepped into his office and spoke with quiet intensity. "You mean . . . you were *sleeping*? On the *floor*?" She looked pointedly at the sofa against the wall.

Ben raised his eyes to the ceiling. "Never let it be said that you are not quick on the draw, Caroline. Or that you cannot get a bead on a faraway target. Or that you cannot smell a rat or read between the lines or get one's drift."

She stepped closer to his desk. "Mr. Buck," she whispered fiercely, "there is a crazy man out by my desk. I need your help. Maybe the two of you can relate to each other. He talks nonsense, too."

She was calmer now. The sight and sound of Mr. Buck had reminded her suddenly that speaking in riddles might not necessarily be a warning sign that someone was about to get violent.

"Well, show him in, by all means," Ben said, yawning again and stretching. "Maybe we can do mumbo jumbo together. That comes from an African dialect, you know, and . . ."

Caroline spun around. "I'll go tell him to come in," she said.

But the man had followed her and was already standing at the threshold of Ben's office. Smiling pleasantly, he stepped inside. "Thank you, ma'am," he said to Caroline with a slight bow. He advanced toward Ben, his hand extended. "So it's Buckley, is it? Macon Mahoney here. New vendor of linocut prints. I think we might have talked by phone a while back."

"Ah yes, the Blue Pomegranate, I presume," Ben said.

" 'Which, if cut deep down the middle, shows a heart within blood-tinctured,' " Macon Mahoney said.

Caroline eased out of the room but left the door open. Just as she had suspected, these two were on the same wavelength, somewhere in a distant corner of outer space.

Ben motioned to the two chairs in front of his desk. He wasn't sure what the man meant by "blood-tinctured." Maybe he was quoting something. He made a mental note to check it in his *Oxford Dictionary of Quotations*. Or maybe the fellow really was just a little off-balance, as Caroline suspected.

"No, no, I'm not staying," Macon Mahoney said, flourishing the hammer. "I just popped in on a little reconnaissance mission of my showroom, hoping to get some prints hung. A few minutes ago I had a scintillating interchange with your two . . . uh . . . construction engineers, is that what you call them? They said they 'don't have no orders about no carpet on no walls,' to quote them. I told them I talked with somebody named Kelly about it a few days ago—an intelligent no-frills type—and, to quote the short guy, I was told that '*she* don't tell *us* what to do.' "

"Oh yes, that," Ben said, sitting down to leaf through some papers on his desk. He pulled a piece of yellow legal paper out and squinted at it. "Yes, it looks like our designer made a note of all that before she had a chance to talk with them. She had to leave suddenly yesterday for a family emergency, so I told her I'd advance the ball down the field for her." Ben felt in his shirt pocket, then started patting the papers on his desktop.

"Maybe you should invest in several pairs," Macon Mahoney said. "I know a place that sells them for a dollar." Forming a circle with a thumb and forefinger, he put it to one eye and smiled at

Ben. "My wife keeps them all over the house. She has them on the kitchen counter, the desk, the washing machine, you name it. There's even a pair in the medicine cabinet."

Ben nodded. "Good idea. I'll keep that in mind. Ah, here they are." He pulled his glasses out from under an empty Steak 'n Shake sack. He held up the sack before tossing it into the wastebasket. "Evidence of my epicurean tastes," he said.

"Hey, no need to apologize. You've got an incurable burger gourmand standing right here in front of you." Macon pointed to himself. "So . . . is the carpet a go? Will you tell the friendly duo out there? And can we talk about the color? For the purest and most thoughtful minds are those which love color the most, you know."

Ben stood back up. Caroline was right. This guy did talk nonsense. "Let's go see them right now," he said. "I know we've got several rolls of leftover carpet stored somewhere in the basement. I'm sure they can figure it out. Those two can do anything, believe it or not—they're smarter than they look. Smart but a little strange."

"All is strange, yet nothing new," Macon said, leading the way out of Ben's office.

Ben felt like taking issue. All was strange indeed, but this was an entirely new kind of strangeness. As they passed through Caroline's office, he said, "I forgot to ask . . . exactly why is it that the Blue Pomegranate needs carpeted walls?"

"Well, just between us burger epicures," Macon replied, "carpet is more cordial and accommodating to displays of art. A blank white wall is like somebody slapping a burger on a bun without any condiments. Nothing to complement or enhance the flavor." He winked at Caroline and gave her a thumbs-up sign as they passed her desk. "Although a really fine burger, like good art, can stand on its own merits."

Caroline watched the two men disappear through the doorway. There went two peas in a pod. Maybe *they* knew what they were talking about, but not one word of what she had just heard made the least bit of sense to her.

Erin Buckley Custer was trying to choose a birthday card for her father. Or rather, she was trying to decide whether she was going to choose one, for it was the last thing in the world she wanted to do. She had never sent her father a birthday card. No card, no present, not even a phone call. But she didn't feel one bit guilty about it since he never sent her anything on her birthday, either. Not once since she had left home for college thirteen years ago. She doubted that he even knew when her birthday was.

She pulled out a card with a fishing rod and a mounted deer head on the front under the words *On your special day, Dad*. Inside it said, *May you enjoy all your favorite things!* She put it back. Her dad didn't fish or hunt. For a card like that to make sense, it would need a picture of a television, a wad of money, and a stack of books on the front. He used to golf, swim, and jog years ago, when she was a little girl, but that stopped after her mother died.

She pulled out another card with a cartoon picture of a bearded, scrunch-faced man pushing hard with one hand against a big golden gate and with the other against a big blue globe. *To a dad who would move heaven and earth for me* was the message inside. She put that one back, also. She wasn't going to be a hypocrite and send him something cute, funny, and totally untrue. Her father might have paid for things she needed growing up, but that was as far as it went. He had never gone to any trouble for her, had never given her anything that couldn't be bought with money.

A cheerful woman wearing a flowing yellow print dress and dozens of silver bangle bracelets appeared at Erin's elbow, also looking through the cards for fathers. She plucked out a card and said, half to herself but also in a tone that included Erin, "Oh, isn't that adorable?" The picture on the front was a little bear pitching a red ball to a fat father bear holding a bat. *You make a hit with me, Daddy*, the words said.

Erin nodded and murmured politely. She took a step away. She hated it when other women, total strangers, tried to strike up conversations with her while shopping.

"Of course, this one is for a child, so it won't work for me," the woman said, "but I do wish they made more cards with Daddy on the front instead of Dad or Father. I still call my daddy *Daddy*, don't you? I think most Southern women do. Have you run across any grown-up cards that say *Daddy* on the front?"

Erin shook her head. "No, I don't remember any."

The woman pulled out another card. "Oh, I just love these cards with pictures of dogs on them. Look at this fellow. Doesn't he look like a sad sack?" A loose-jowled, floppy-eared dog was sitting in the middle of scattered confetti wearing a little red polka-dotted birthday hat and staring droopy-eyed into the camera. Extra folds of grayish-brown skin hung slack all over his body. "Looks like he's wearing his daddy's suit, doesn't it?" the woman said, laughing.

Again Erin nodded but didn't smile this time. What made women do this in stores—act like they were your best friend? She took another step away from the woman. Down near the bottom of the rack she saw a card that looked promising. *Happy birthday, Dad*, it said on the front. Just plain and noncommittal, with a picture of a sailboat on a lake. Nothing fancy or funny. That might work. She opened it. *Though I don't tell you as often as I should, / You're everything that's strong and wise and good.* The poem went on for many more lines, but she read no further. There was no way she could sign her name to a card like this. Strong and wise and good? Not on your life. Not in all the ways that mattered most to a daughter.

"Okay, that settles it!" the woman said, her bracelets jingling as she waved the dog card happily. "This is the one. Look at what it says inside!" She stepped over and held it up to Erin. *Hey, Daddy! Party till your clothes get wrinkled!* it said. The woman laughed a lusty, booming laugh. "Isn't that perfect? And it says *Daddy*, too!"

Erin mustered an obligatory chuckle.

"He's going to absolutely love this!" the woman said. "I wonder what kind of dog that is. It's sure not one you see very often." She turned and walked off toward the front of the store.

If Erin had been a friendlier sort of person, she might have called after the woman and told her it was a Shar-Pei. She might have told her she had first seen one at a local dog show her mother took her to a few weeks before she died. It had won Best in Show, in fact, even though the American Kennel Club didn't officially recognize the breed until several years later. Erin had been delighted that the Shar-Pei had won even though her mother thought the Pomeranian should have. She could have gone on to tell the woman that she had inherited her mother's love of dogs, of animals in general, that she worked at an animal shelter just as her mother had. But she didn't say any of this, of course. She

115

had learned long ago that people didn't really care about other people.

After looking halfheartedly through several more cards, Erin finally told herself she would look at only three more. If none of them was right, then it was over, that was the end. She wasn't wasting any more time in this place. Remarkably, the very next one she picked up was suitable. The front showed a footpath disappearing into a wooded area, with mountains and a winding river beyond. *For your birthday, Father*, it said at the top, and then inside, *May your journey through the coming year be a pleasant one*. She turned the card over and saw that it was only $1.99. That was a lot better price than most of the others. She quickly walked to the cashier to pay for it. She was more than ready to be done with this little chore.

The woman in the yellow dress was chattering to the sales clerk as she rummaged around in her billfold for the exact change, so Erin stopped a little distance away to look at some monogrammed key chains that didn't interest her in the least.

It was Shelly, Erin's older sister, who had sent her an e-mail the day before, reminding her of their father's birthday coming up. "I know he'd like to hear from you," it said. "This is number fifty-eight." This was followed by some boastful bits of news about her three children, and then at the end, "We're all grown-ups now, Erin. We need to put the past behind us and reach out to Dad. God has spoken to me, and I feel very strongly about this. We need to make a real family out of ourselves before it's too late. Grant is sending Dad a gift card to Olive Garden, and Lydia is ordering him a book from Amazon. Won't you make it a hundred percent and at least send him a card?"

Shelly hadn't said what she herself was giving him; she was probably hoping Erin would ask. Shelly liked for people to know how generous she was. Doing alms in secret wasn't her mode of operation. Whatever she had sent their father, it was probably expensive. She always went overboard with everything. She had sent Erin a blue cashmere sweater for her last birthday. Erin had sent her an e-card for hers, two days late.

From the door of her parents' bedroom, Kelly watched her father. Charlie Kovatch slid the closet door open and stood there looking from one end to the other. Kelly knew the funeral home had called again about clothes. It should have been already taken care of, but there had been so much else to do.

Charlie pulled out a pink dress and held it up, then the pansy dress Kay used to wear on Sundays—a black background with purple and yellow pansies printed on it. He put both dresses on the bed.

"Daddy?" Kelly said. "Can I do anything to help?" She stepped inside the bedroom.

Charlie was back at the closet now. He looked at Kelly and held up a dark green knit suit. It had a gold pin shaped like a cluster of leaves fastened near the neck of the jacket. "I'm looking for some clothes to take to the funeral home," he said. "They called again this morning. They need them right away." He added the suit to the dresses on the bed.

Kelly looked at the things he had laid out. She knew her mother wouldn't want to be buried in the dark green. It was a suit Kelly's grandmother had sent several years ago, something she had originally bought for herself but had never really liked. Grandmother Vandenberg had always considered the whole family a charity case, had sometimes said things to her mother like "Well, if it doesn't fit you, maybe one of the girls can wear it." At Christmas she gave them boxes of canned goods and toiletries in giant sizes.

"I think the pink is best," Kelly said to her father. "Mother always looked pretty in that, even though she didn't wear it much."

"She didn't?" Charlie said.

Kelly held it up. It had a little crocheted collar and pearl buttons down the front. Her mother hadn't liked the way the dress gapped around the buttons when she sat down. It wouldn't gap lying down, though.

"I can take it to the funeral home if you want," Kelly said.

"No, I'll run it down there," Charlie said. He

took the pink dress from Kelly and laid it across the chair beside the bed. He returned the other things to her closet and slid the door shut.

"Is there . . . anything else you want help with?" Kelly asked. She knew they had asked for under-wear.

Charlie shook his head. "No, that's all. Thank you for helping with the dress." Hands by his side, he looked toward the window. It was open, and light and fresh air were streaming in. Kelly could tell he was waiting for her to leave so he could get the other things by himself.

"Well, call if you need me," she said, and she pulled the door closed, leaving a crack. She heard him open a drawer and close it, then open another. She waited a few seconds, then looked back in. He turned from the dresser to the bureau and stood looking at the five drawers. He opened the middle one and closed it again, then the bottom one. Kelly knew that was where her mother kept small gifts she found on sale. She even had names taped to them.

He closed the bottom drawer and opened the second one. That was it. He began going through it, looking for the right things. They weren't very nice-looking pieces of lingerie, Kelly knew that, most of them limp and well-worn with stretched-out elastic and torn lace. Her mother had found it hard to spend money on herself.

Charlie picked out the best of the lot and closed

the drawer. He set the things on the bed, then opened the bottom drawer again. He emptied one of the plastic bags of gifts Kay had bought for other people and put her funeral underwear inside it.

EIGHT

Rich in Symbolism

During one of his rounds at work the next week, Ben stopped at the Blue Pomegranate to check on the progress of things. Les and Mo had by now covered the back and two side walls of the small showroom with a smoky blue carpet, the same carpet in fact that was already on the floor.

Around the top of the three walls Macon had installed a wide pale blue molding with a hand-painted pattern of twining ivy, blue pomegranates, and golden bells. He had also installed, with Les and Mo's help, indirect lighting on suspended tracks as well as dark wood baseboard.

As Macon explained it, all of these finishing touches were especially important in a showroom without furniture—that is, without furniture in the normal places, against the walls. There were two upholstered chairs positioned at the showroom entrance, but facing the back wall. They were skirted, with low backs and round seats—like chairs at a woman's dressing table—and covered in a soft gray brocade with a muted leaf design.

Macon had gotten Les to secure the two chairs to the floor so that patrons wouldn't be shifting them around. And unlike some of the other showrooms with signs on the furniture that read "You May Test But Don't Rest," the Blue Pomegranate had an elegantly hand-lettered sign on a little stand against the backs of the two chairs that read "You Are Welcome to Sit in Reverent Contemplation and View the Art." Another sign, a larger framed one displayed on an easel to one side, identified the name of the showroom: *THE BLUE POMEGRANATE*. In smaller letters beneath the name was written "Original Linocuts by Local Artist Macon Mahoney."

The Trio Gallery, which exhibited Macon's art under contract, was allowing him this new venue at the Upstate Home and Garden Bazaar with the proviso that he display only prints instead of single originals like watercolors, acrylics, batiks, and the like. Macon's prints, however, were nothing like the prints in some of the other showrooms, all of which had a manufactured look in spite of the ornate frames and double or triple matting—prints of things like hunting scenes, impressionistic landscapes, and Picasso-like abstracts. Macon's linocuts were colorful, intricate pictures made by carving reverse images into large blocks of linoleum and then printing them off on a press, one at a time. They might be called prints, but they were real art.

Macon's intention was to display his framed prints on the three carpeted walls top to bottom, and now that the other showroom details were finished, he planned to bring in several pictures each day. So far he had hung only six, all of them on the back wall. As he had explained to Ben, he was busy framing his pieces at home, taking his time and using a wide variety of styles and colors since he wanted each one to be different—"something for Grandma and the grunge both," he said, though Ben doubted that anybody from the grunge element would be buying this caliber of art.

Approaching the Blue Pomegranate, Ben saw two women just seating themselves in the gray chairs, obviously not for the purpose of reverent contemplation, however, for they were engaged in a lively conversation. Since Ben liked to overhear customers talking about the merchandise in the various showrooms, he pretended to be studying some hand-carved figurines in the Everything Wood showroom across the aisle. More than once he had used overheard comments in the monthly newsletters he wrote for Caroline to type and distribute to the vendors.

"Look at that pretty molding up there," one of them said. She had a headful of messily styled jet-black hair that looked like it had been tossed about in a high wind. "Somebody sure went to a lot of trouble."

"The Blue Pomegranate—funny name, isn't it?"

the other one said. "The only pomegranates I've ever seen are a sort of orangey red. Have you ever eaten one?" She made an indelicate gagging noise. "I tried one once. It was a little thing, so sour it turned my mouth inside out. I think they're mainly for decoration, not eating."

Ben thought she might be confusing pomegranates with persimmons. He could have stepped forward to set her straight, for he had read a whole encyclopedia entry on pomegranates not long ago. He could tell her that a pomegranate could sometimes grow as big as a grapefruit and that it was prized as food in many parts of the world, whether eaten raw or cooked in dressings, desserts, soups, and jams.

He could have also told her that it was a fruit rich in symbolism. For the Jews it symbolized righteousness and for the Greeks, fertility and good luck. It could be eaten prayerfully in one country, therefore, but broken apart in raucous celebration in another. As for the color, she was partly right. They were red, though not the orange red of a persimmon. You would certainly never see a blue pomegranate growing anywhere.

The women were talking about the six linocuts now, each choosing the one she liked best. The wild-haired woman preferred the scene of an open-air produce market titled *Where Country Folks Shop*, but the other one liked *Theresa's Garden Bower* best. "That would look gorgeous over my buffet in the dining room," she said. "I wonder how much it is." She got up from the chair and moved closer to read the price on the small tag mounted next to the picture. She shook her head. "That's amazing."

The other woman got up and joined her, and the two of them studied all the price tags. "But you know," the black-haired one said, "I can understand why someone would do it. I might even get motivated to start cooking again if I had one of these hanging in my dining room."

"If you had any money left to buy food," the other one said, laughing.

They stood another few moments, then moved on down the aisle to the Klassy Kitchen showroom. Ben walked over to the Blue Pomegranate and looked at the price tags for himself. He couldn't help wondering if Macon Mahoney was overreaching the clientele of the Bazaar. Only serious art lovers would pay these kinds of prices for something to hang on a wall.

But then he reminded himself of the prices in the Pomp and Pizzazz showroom downstairs, which featured high-end furniture and accessories. It was one of the most popular showrooms in the store, the one that regularly turned in the biggest average monthly profit. Just last week someone had bought the L-shaped yellow leather sofa for over four thousand dollars, and then the same woman had come back the very next day and paid another three thousand for the matching chair and over-sized ottoman. So it was conceivable that someone would pay a couple of thousand for a real piece of art even though it might not be as practical as something you could sit on.

Ben didn't consider himself a true art connois-seur, but he did like Macon Mahoney's work. His favorite of the six prints, *Strike Up the Strings*, depicted an orchestra in an opera house with a fat little bearded conductor wearing a lime green bow tie and a royal blue tuxedo with tails. All of the players were wearing bright, boldly patterned clothes reminiscent of the seventies.

Ben looked up at the border of blue pomegran-ates and thought about the conversation he'd had with Macon Mahoney only a couple of days ago right here in this very spot. Macon had been on top of a stepladder, nailing one end of the molding in place while Mo stood on the floor, arms raised, supporting the other end. When Macon noticed Ben, he greeted him but kept working, speaking around a couple of nails in his mouth. "Hey, I was just telling my friend Mo here about the signifi-cance of the blue pomegranates. Do you know anything about them?"

"Oh, not much," Ben said. "Only that they were sewn onto the hem of the priest's garment, along with purple and red ones, alternating with golden bells—pomegranate, golden bell, pomegranate, golden bell, and so forth all the way around." He didn't know why he said so much and immediately wished he hadn't.

Macon had twisted himself around on the ladder and looked down at Ben. He took the nails out of his mouth. "Whoa. What are you—a rabbi or something?"

"No, just a heathen Gentile with a pretty good memory," Ben said. He never told people he had a photographic memory, or used to. It wasn't anything to brag about, especially when it wasn't working so well anymore. "Well, at least sometimes," he added, "but mostly only for trivial things."

"But 'mighty contests rise from trivial things,' you know," Macon replied. Mo was staring at Macon's feet on the ladder, his eyes unreadable.

Ben edged away. "Well, I'd better be on my way now."

"I bet you like to read," Macon said. "So do I. There's no end to what you can learn by reading." He turned back to hammer in another nail but kept on talking, louder now. "Like this—it's something I ran across yesterday. 'Come, dear old friend, Lady Resignation, and sing me your familiar old song.' It was in a letter Albert Einstein wrote somebody."

Ben couldn't think of a response to this. He was sorry he had come by here and even sorrier he had stopped to watch.

"But anyway, back to blue pomegranates,"

Macon said. "It's a good name for my showroom, you know. It makes a perfect symbol for the Christian artist."

This was getting worse. Ben didn't want to talk about Christian artists or anything else with this man. He looked at his watch as if remembering an appointment. "Well, I've got to run," he said.

Ignoring the hint, Macon pounded in another nail. "It's God's stamp of approval on art, on the whole concept of creativity, really!" he shouted. He dismounted the ladder and stepped back to study the molding, talking the whole time. "Not only did he command a *picture* of something to be embroidered on a holy robe, but he also made it nonliteral. He's doing a lot more there than just describing a priest's robe, you know? He's saying, 'Hey! Use your imagination! It's okay to play with reality! Change up the colors! Have fun!'" He paused a moment to fish another nail out of his pocket. "So now if anybody asks about the name, you'll know what to tell them." He nodded to Mo. "You, too." He mounted the ladder again.

"Right," Ben said. "Well, I'll be seeing you."

"Say, wait just a minute, speaking of heathen Gentiles," Macon said from the top of the ladder, "what else does a man like you know about the Bible?"

Numbers of things sprang to Ben's mind. He could have talked about not eating the eagle, the vulture, or the screech owl, or not boiling a kid in its mother's milk or eating leavened bread in the month of Abib, or the rule about setting apart all the firstling males of the flocks.

But he didn't say any of those things. He merely shook his head. "Not much really." He gave a little wave as he turned to leave. "I've got to go check the A.C. now. I think the whole system is shot."

"Well, speaking of Albert Einstein," Macon called out cheerily, "one might think of his famous theory and be tempted to think all of life is relative. But it isn't, you know. There are absolutes. Very definite absolutes."

Ben could have easily countered. "Speaking of relatives," he could have said, "did you know that one of Einstein's sons ended up in a loony bin near Zurich, Switzerland?" But he didn't. He just kept walking toward the escalator.

Standing in the Blue Pomegranate showroom now, days later, Ben felt ashamed to think of how much he had wanted to match wits with Macon Mahoney. Such juvenile behavior. He knew one thing for sure: He needed to avoid Macon whenever possible. He might be an interesting, funny, nice enough guy, but he made Ben uneasy. Artists in general were weird enough, but add religion to the mix—well, speaking of loony bins.

When Kelly came out to get in her car at a quarter past five the next afternoon, Lester Lattimore was sitting in his maroon GTO, which was backed into the parking space. Her heart fell. He hadn't been at work since she had come back after her mother's funeral, and it had been a relief not to have to worry about what he might say or do next.

He was parked two spaces away from Mo's ice cream truck on one side and several spaces from her Ford Taurus on the other side. He had his windows down so that his music, which sounded more like a hurricane ripping through a metal tool warehouse, pulsed across the parking lot. He appeared to be looking down at something he was holding in his hand, so Kelly could only hope he wouldn't lift his head. Unfortunately, she had to pass in front of his car to get to hers, but if she was careful, maybe she could make it. Maybe he was taking a little nap—that would be nice. She sent up a quick prayer that he wouldn't see her.

For an instant she considered going back inside to wait a few minutes. Maybe he would leave soon. But she couldn't do that. She was already a little late leaving work, and it took a good twenty minutes to get home. Then supper and dishes had to be squeezed in before prayer meeting at seven. She had told Kerri she would help her get supper together. At least they still had plenty left from the food people had brought in for the funeral.

She started toward her car, walking close to the building so as to stay as far away from Les as possible. As long as he didn't look up, she was safe. If she got close enough to her car, she could make a dash and maybe get inside before he had time to say anything. Then she could lock the doors and be on her way.

But he did look up. She cringed when she heard his voice: "Hey, hey, Kelly babe, you ain't trying to dodge me, are you?" He turned the music off, then got out of his car and started ambling toward her Taurus. He had on ragged jeans and a black T-shirt with the sleeves rolled up. He walked with his arms away from his body, slightly bent, the way muscular men did to show off their biceps. Kelly wondered if his tough act might be an attempt to make up for being short.

"I been off work a couple of days," he said, "so I been missing you. Thought I'd come by and get my paycheck." He held it up. "Hey, I got an idea— let's you and me go someplace and spend it." He tossed his head back and made little glugging sounds, pretending to guzzle something. He grinned at her. "Come on, you'd have fun! How come you keep on turning me down, good-looking guy like me? I ain't nobody to hold off. I could show you . . ." He dropped his voice and wiggled his eyebrows. "Well, ain't no limit to the things I could show you."

Kelly knew she could probably get Les into trouble if she complained to Mr. Buckley, but she also knew Les would laugh it off and lie about anything she said. She would rather not tattle on him. She kept hoping he would get tired of teasing her and leave her alone. In fact, she prayed about it every night. She had even prayed that he would find another job somewhere else and leave the Bazaar altogether. But evidently God wasn't interested in her prayers right now.

Les had reached her car and was standing by the driver's door. She slowed down, then stopped. Even though it was still daylight, there was no one else back here where the employees parked. She glanced back toward the store exit and clutched her keys tighter. She didn't think Les would really do anything, but he still made her nervous. She felt pretty sure he would back down in a hurry if she ever tested him by accepting one of his offers. She would never do that, though—pretty sure wasn't sure enough. She knew better than to play with chances. Besides that, the thought of saying she would go anywhere with Lester Lattimore, even as a joke, gave her a sick feeling.

He took hold of her door handle and tried to open it, but it was locked. He cursed, then made a face. "Sorry. You didn't hear that, okay? I was just gonna open the door for you like I always do for ladies." He leaned against her car and grinned at her again, a mean grin as if he liked seeing her scared. When he smiled, his eyes turned into little slits and almost disappeared in his round face, which was pitted with old acne scars. He had gotten his hair cut in front and had it spiked up, probably something he thought looked good. Kelly tried to remember everything her mother had ever told her about what to do if you were accosted by a man. Look him straight in the eye—that was the only thing that came to her right now. That, and where to kick him if he got too close.

They stared at each other for several long seconds. Then his smile faded, and he pushed his lower lip out. "You been missing me this week?"

"No," she said, lifting her chin. "I've been off a couple of days, too."

"Aw, too bad I didn't know that. You should've called. We could've done stuff together. I was thinking about this place down past—" Suddenly his eyes flicked to the side, and he stood up straight. He took a step away from her car. "But, hey, you look like you're in a hurry now, so . . ."

Kelly glanced behind her and saw Mo coming toward them. She didn't have much use for him, either, but right now she was very glad to see him.

Les walked back toward his car and waved at Mo. "Hey, what's up? You been holding things down this week? I'll be back in tomorrow." He yanked his head toward Kelly. "Me and her was just catching up. She was saying how much she missed me."

Kelly stepped to her car quickly and unlocked the door. She didn't hear Mo say a word, but he sauntered over toward Les. The two of them watched her as she backed out and pulled away. She glanced over at Mo's ice cream truck as she drove past it. She wished he would paint over the words and pictures on it, especially the words. She remembered the day two weeks ago when Les had stared right at her chest and under his breath had said, "Deeee-licious!" Then he had laughed, of course.

NINE

A Candle Burning

Another Friday, another suppertime, which was just another sandwich, this one at Panera Bread out by the new Barnes and Noble. Ben didn't usually pay this much for a sandwich, but at least it was a very good sandwich, though maybe not as good as it might have been on a different day of the week.

Today was his birthday, his fifty-eighth, and though he had thought about it a few times during the day, he had felt no sense of joy. But neither did he feel more gloom than usual for a Friday. Caroline had brought two boxes of Dunkin' Donuts to the break room at work, and he had eaten one Boston cream and one blueberry, which was more celebrating than he usually did on his birthday.

He sat at a window table by himself, finishing his tea, reading a newspaper someone had left behind. The headline said, *ISRAELIS MOBILIZE ON BORDER FOR ALL-OUT ATTACK*. Well, what else was new? Israel was always scurrying around its borders, getting ready to attack or be attacked. You had to admire them, though. Snatch three of their soldiers, and you would pay for it. They weren't going to sit down to discuss it. Instead, they were going to unleash their bombs on you and keep at it unrelentingly until you gave back what belonged to them.

An American living in Lebanon was quoted in the paper: "It happened so fast. We all know what Israel is capable of, but nobody was ready for this kind of bushwhacking." A picture of the man showed him with his arm in a sling and a bandage on his forehead. What was he doing living in the Middle East, anyway? Ben wondered. He had trouble feeling sorry for him even though he knew what it felt like to be bushwhacked. That's what Fridays felt like to him, always leaping out from the edge of the week to remind him that bad things could happen without warning.

He turned the page of the newspaper and found himself looking at an article titled "Taming Your Time," accompanied by a jumbled picture of calendars, clocks, watches, computers, PDAs, and cell phones. He scanned it and saw that it was one of those self-help articles about how to use your time wisely. Probably written by some thirty-year-old who had no idea how many tricks time could play on a person.

At the bottom of the same page was another

article titled "Religious Ritual Turns Deadly" about a sect of snake handlers in West Virginia. Just one more of the many strong arguments against modern religion, if extreme wackos like that could be part of anything called *modern*. He took another drink of his tea and glanced up to see two people, a man and a woman, looking for a place to sit. The woman looked away quickly with a tightening of her lips, but the man stared pointedly at the newspaper in Ben's hands.

Okay, he could take a hint. He was ready to go anyway. He folded the newspaper and stood up, gathered his empty plate and cup, and disposed of it all in the trash bin.

He exited the restaurant and, looking across the parking area, decided to walk to Barnes and Noble. It would be getting dark soon, but he was in the mood for some light exercise. His knee, which had been sore for over a month now, was feeling better, but there was a painful twinge in his lower back that had served as an excuse not to exercise for the past several Sundays. Next to Panera was an ice cream place called Cold Stone Creamery. Maybe he would do that later—finish his birthday with an ice cream cone. No need to feel guilty eating ice cream when it was your birthday, even if you had already eaten two doughnuts you didn't need. At least he was offering the sacrifice of exercise now to atone for the sin of ice cream to come.

A carload of teenagers cruised up beside him.

They were packed into an older model Chevy Impala. The driver hung her head out the window. "Hey, you parked somewhere close?" she yelled to Ben. She had purple streaks in her hair and a large fleur-de-lis tattoo on her upper arm.

He nodded and pointed to his Lincoln Town Car. "I am, but I'm not leaving," he said. "I'm walking somewhere."

She said a swear word, then gunned the accelerator and almost hit a car backing out of another parking space. There were shrieks of laughter from inside the car as she shot back in reverse to give the other car room. Ben wished she hadn't found a space so easily. More and more he found it hard to tolerate the teenagers of today.

Inside Barnes and Noble, he wandered around for a while, browsing here and there. Eventually he came to a shelf labeled "Judaica" and stopped. He had never seen this shelf before since it was in the corner of the store devoted to religion. He scanned the titles and collected several books. Jewish culture was a subject that fascinated him, especially the rituals. The chair he preferred was already taken, so he carried the books to a table and sat down at one end. A teenager sat at the other end, engrossed in what looked like math homework, a strange thing for a boy his age to be doing on a Friday night. But probably no stranger than the way Ben himself was spending his Friday evening.

Though the Jews carried them to extremes, Ben

knew rituals were useful. He thought of his own rituals, sad though they were, as walls around his sanity. One by one over the years he had laid them on top of one another the way the Israelites piled up all those stones for a memorial. Except their rituals were always for remembering, whereas his were for forgetting.

He opened one of the books, titled *Judaism: Its Beauty and Truth*, and started reading a chapter dealing with the custom of *tzum*, or fasting. Ben saw this as heavy-duty religious activity, to give up food and drink for prayer and meditation, but according to the author, "the divine returns for such a gift of devotion to Jehovah are many." Ben didn't consider himself a glutton by any means, but he couldn't imagine going without food on a regular basis.

The author of the book, a man by the name of Obed Friedman, also pointed out that a time of genuine fasting meant giving up more than simply food. "When one gives himself totally to communion with God," he wrote, "he also fasts from sinful thoughts, from unkind words, from selfish deeds." If entered into completely and sincerely, "fasting preempts all forms of unholiness known to man and results in a spiritual cleansing unattainable by any other means."

Ben turned over several pages to a chapter titled "*Kashrut*,"which concerned Jewish dietary laws, and read awhile. Then he skipped to another chapter and read about the *mezuzah* to be hung on the doorpost.

He looked up from the book. The boy at the other end of the table was punching numbers on a calculator with the eraser of his pencil—an old-fashioned yellow wooden pencil, Ben noted. A girl in denim shorts was sitting on the floor nearby, hunkered over a large book in her lap and twirling a strand of hair around her finger. A man standing nearby was flipping through a large atlas. At the end of the aisle a steady stream of people walked past. Probably no Jews among them, though—at least not devout Jews. They would all be at home right now preparing for the Sabbath tomorrow.

He turned to another chapter titled "*Avelut*," the Jewish rituals of mourning. Not what he wanted to read about on a Friday night. Yet he did. He read the first page and then continued through six more. He read about *aninut*, the time of the death and burial. He read about sitting *shiva* for seven days, about the ceremonial meals marking the stages of grief: the *se'udat havra'ah*, which was the first meal after the funeral; the *shloshim*, after thirty days; and the *yahrtzeit* at the end of a year.

He stopped again. Chloe had told Ben about some of the Roman Catholic traditions she remembered from childhood, but in his opinion the Catholics couldn't hold a candle to Jews when it came to rituals. He suddenly recalled reading somewhere that candles figured prominently in a lot of Jewish rituals. He flipped back to the table of contents and saw, in fact, that there was a whole chapter on the lighting of candles. He turned to it and skimmed through several pages.

There were special candles for everything. Two candles to burn throughout the entire Sabbath, then *havdalah*, lit at the close of the Sabbath, to signify the separation between Holy *Shabbat* and the new week of work in the ungodly world. He read about the *menorah* and *Chanukah*. There was even a special candle lit before lovemaking.

He abruptly stopped reading and closed the book. Chloe had loved candles. She had always kept one on their bedside table. In college she had made her own, and early in their courtship she had melted dozens of them, all different colors, into a canning jar and given it to him for his birthday. After they were married, she had always liked a candle burning while she bathed.

Ben set the book aside. Jewish rituals had suddenly lost their interest. He never should have read any of this. *Se'udat havra'ah*—the words came back to his mind, and all at once he remembered the first meal he had eaten after Chloe's funeral. There had been food at home, a whole dining room table covered with Southern bereavement casseroles. His mother had expected him to come home that afternoon to eat with her and the children and with Chloe's parents and all the rest of the relatives.

Instead, he had gotten into his car alone and had driven up old Highway 29 for two hours. Then he had turned around and driven back to Derby. At dusk he found himself at the Dairy Queen where he used to work as a teenager. He ordered a burger to go, and after getting his food, he had driven to a park where he and Chloe had once eaten when they were dating. He couldn't explain why he was doing it; it certainly wasn't because of hunger. It had felt like a weak thing to do, yet something he couldn't stop.

The park was beside a man-made lake in a sub-division outside Greenville called Minnow Brook. It was chilly that March day of the funeral, so no one else was there. Ben had carried the white paper bag to a picnic table and unwrapped his hamburger and his French fries. He took a few bites, but the food had cooled off considerably by then. It grew darker and colder as he watched the lights come on in the houses across the lake and listened to the slapping of cables against the flagpole by the gazebo.

He knew his mother was probably worried sick, had very likely already called the police to file a report, so finally he got up and threw the rest of his food into the trash can. He got into his car and sat there for a long time before making his way back home. His mother would be getting the children to bed by now. What kind of father would do this— leave his own children on the day of their mother's funeral? That was the question that came to him as he drove home, along with an answer: a miserable father, that's who.

Well, that was the trouble with reading. You might start off in what seemed like a harmless direction, but so often you stumbled into an ambush. You'd be reading about Jewish rituals one minute, then wallowing in self-pity the next. He hated it. He knew other men recovered from the death of their wives; he had observed hundreds who had gotten on with life. But none of those men had been married to Chloe. Their wives were like Catholic rituals compared to Jewish ones. None of them could hold a candle to Chloe.

The boy at the other end of the table was jerking his head back and forth between his paper and the calculator, looking perplexed. He made an exasperated sound, then turned back a page in his math book and read something. Furiously he erased something on his paper and wrote something else very carefully, studied it a moment, then wrote something else, nodding and chewing on the inside of his mouth. He appeared to have found a solution. Well, good for him.

Ben looked at the stack of books sitting in front of him. He thought of all the effort that had gone into writing all those words down. Any one of these volumes could have been the work of a lifetime for somebody. Normally he was careful to reshelve the books he read, but tonight was different. He got up from the table and left the books sitting there, stacked neatly.

Crossing the parking lot, he stopped suddenly as a car lurched backward out of a parking place. Of all the moments he could have ended up in this exact spot, it had to be right now, at the same split second the teenagers in the Impala were leaving. Someone inside the car cried, "Watch out, Becky! You almost nailed that old guy!" To which Becky replied, "Tell *him* to watch out!" Followed, of course, by derisive teenage laughter.

From where he stood, Ben could see there was a line in the ice cream place, a long one. But he didn't feel like ice cream now anyway. He would go home on his birthday and listen to Lady Resignation sing her old song.

As usual, the kitchen was a busy place on Friday night. Kelly was unloading the dishwasher while Karla, Kirk, and Kimmie were playing a game of Scrabble at the table. Kerri was stirring up lemonade in a pitcher, and Kyle was standing in front of the open refrigerator, staring into it. Kitty was putting together a jigsaw puzzle in the den just off the kitchen.

Friday nights had always been one of Kelly's favorite times of the week before her mother died. Her father had always gone along for the ride, as he liked to say, but her mother had always been the planner. Occasionally they would go for a literal ride, but usually it was a stay-at-home night. Sometimes they would check out a good family movie from the library and watch it together.

"So where's the rest of the roast beef?" Kyle asked. "I wanted a sandwich."

At the table Kirk laughed and pointed his thumb at himself. "*This* little piggy had roast beef," he said, then pointed to Kyle. "And *that* little piggy had none."

Karla let out a squeal. "Look! I can spell *jewel* on a triple word."

"No fair!" Kirk said. "Were you watching her, Kimmie? Did she cheat?"

Charlie appeared at the doorway.

"Hey, Daddy," Kerri said. "Want some lemonade? We've got cookies in the oven."

He shook his head. "No, I'm going on to bed. Tomorrow's my Saturday to work. I've got to be up early."

Kelly took a handful of silverware out of the dishwasher basket and started putting it away. "I'm working tomorrow, too," she said. "But only in the afternoon. There's that picnic at church in the evening if we want to go. It's only hot dogs, but they'll have other things, too."

"We've *got* to go," Kirk said, looking up from the Scrabble board. "I signed us up for volleyball, Dad. We're on a team with Stan and his dad."

"Don't forget me," Kyle said. "I'm playing, too."

He had gotten a jar of peanut butter out of the cupboard.

Suddenly all the children were looking hopefully at Charlie. Kelly calmly continued to place the silverware one piece at a time in the drawer. No one said a word, but Kelly knew what everybody was thinking. She knew they all wanted to go to the picnic except her father, but she also knew none of them would go without him. It had been two weeks since her mother died. Last weekend her father hadn't known what to do with himself, so he had finally gone into his workshop and started straightening shelves. One by one they had gone to the door and asked if he wanted them to help, but every time he said no, thanks, it was a one-man job.

It was early for a picnic, not even officially summer yet, but even if it were later, Kelly knew that a church picnic was the last thing her father would want to do on a Saturday. He didn't like crowds of people, never had, unless they were all family. But the younger children were still looking at him, waiting for an answer.

"Well," he said at last, "I guess we can go. I won't get off till after three, though."

"It doesn't start till four," Kimmie said quickly. "Everybody's supposed to bring a dessert, so I'll make a sheet cake tomorrow."

"They're having sack races and water balloons for the kids!" Kitty called from the den.

"Hop to it, squirt," Kirk said, and everyone groaned.

Charlie said good-night and left the kitchen. As Kelly finished putting the silverware away, she thought of how hard everything must be for him now. He had depended on her mother for so much. She thought of him going upstairs to the bed where he slept alone now. She remembered all the nights she used to hear her parents praying together in their room before bed. She wondered if her father still prayed before he went to sleep or if he was struggling as much as she was with prayers that seemed to go unanswered.

"One day at a time"—that was something her mother always used to say. But it had always sounded a lot easier then than it did now.

TEN

What Might Have Been

It was almost eleven o'clock the next morning when Erin, who always slept late on the Saturdays she didn't work, fumbled to answer the phone on her nightstand. It was her sister Shelly, who lived in Raleigh, North Carolina. Erin had actually been expecting the call on Friday and knew it must have taken great self-control for Shelly to wait a whole day. She swung her feet out of bed and walked over to open the blinds. Her husband's truck wasn't in the driveway, so Reuben was either working or else he was at Home Depot, one of his favorite places to spend money on weekends.

Shelly small-talked for a while until Erin finally interrupted her. "Okay, okay, I know why you called, so you can quit beating around the bush." She sighed and added, "Yes, yes, I did it."

Shelly laughed an embarrassed sort of laugh and said, "You did what?"

"Come on, Shelly, cut it out. We're grown-ups now, isn't that what you said? You don't have to play games with me. Yes, I sent him a stupid birthday card." She closed the blinds again. All that sunshine hurt her eyes. She sat back down on the edge of the bed.

Shelly laughed again, clearly relieved. "Well, that's good. I know he appreciated it."

"Oh, you do?" said Erin. "And how do you know that? Did he tell you? I'm guessing he didn't feel one ounce of appreciation. Did you even talk to him?"

"Well, no, not yet," Shelly said. "But I'm going to call him tomorrow to find out if my gift arrived on time." She paused briefly, then, "It was this bicycle that folds up. We ordered it from L. L. Bean. It was Mark's idea. We thought Dad might like to take up cycling since he's not running as much as he used to."

So that meant it was a pricey gift, just as Erin had suspected. "And he hasn't called yet to thank you?" she said. "My, I'm so surprised. We'd better get off the phone quick. He's probably trying to get through to you right now."

Shelly clucked her tongue several times. "I don't do things for Dad because I expect to be thanked," she said. "That's not how *families* work, Sis. You have to——"

But Erin cut her off. She hated it when Shelly called her Sis. "Yeah, well, it's a good thing to keep all your expectations low when it has anything to do with him," she said. She couldn't bring herself to refer to him as Dad. And she would certainly never call him Daddy. Those days had ended long ago.

"Erin, I've said this before and I'll say it again. I wish you could stop *just once* and try to put yourself in Dad's place. It was rough for all of us, sure, but especially for him. Think of what he must have gone through afterward. Yes, so he neglected us for a while, but at least he made sure we had Grandma." She gave a little impatient huff. "Haven't you ever heard of *mercy* and *compassion*?"

Erin didn't have the energy to reply to such a question, nor to listen to the rest of Shelly's little speech, which she had heard numerous times before. She held the receiver away from her ear. Why didn't telephones have mute buttons? She wondered if Shelly ever realized how goody-goody she sounded, how proud of herself for being the bright and shining example of Christian piety to her younger siblings. She would like to ask Shelly someday if she thought their father had ever stopped *just once* to try to put himself in his children's place.

Of the four children, Shelly was the only one who had gone with their mother to her new church during those final weeks before she died. And now that they were all grown, she seemed to think it was up to her to be the religious one in the family, to continue what their mother had started. It would never cross her mind that one of her sisters might have also tried to read parts of the Bible, might have even visited several churches before giving up on the possibility of healing and recovery, of understanding why this God her mother had talked about so much had turned his back on her and all the rest of them one afternoon twenty-one years ago.

Erin put the receiver back to her ear. ". . . to put the past behind us," Shelly was saying, "and look ahead. We've just *got* to pull together and do this. I feel a real conviction about it." She stopped talking for a moment, then cleared her throat and said, "Well, that brings me to the real reason I called, Erin. I have something I want you to consider. I've already talked to Grant and Lydia." Which was obviously her way of saying, "I've saved you, the most stubborn, for last." Her tone was motherly and instructive.

Erin imagined a slow, heavy vapor rising up around her. This had the sound of a greater emotional outlay than sending a birthday card. She said nothing.

Shelly hastened on. "Just listen first, okay? You don't have to commit to anything today, but I want you to think about it. *And* talk it over with Reuben." She spoke as if she knew she could count on Reuben as an ally. Then she took a deep breath and spilled it all at once. No long introductory explanation as usual. In fact, she spoke so rapidly and economically that it almost sounded as if she were reading from a prepared script.

It was a family trip she was planning. *Family*, she said again firmly, as in all four siblings, their spouses and children—and their father. She had already looked into renting a house for the third week of July in Flat Rock, North Carolina. It was a place called Hearthside Cottage at a mountain resort near a lake. The word *cottage* was misleading, she said, for it would sleep twenty. With sixteen of them there would be plenty of room. They could split the cost four ways.

She had written their dad about it in her birthday card, so she would follow up on it when she called him tomorrow. She had already put a deposit on the house and had to confirm within two weeks. Of course, they could still go even if their father didn't, but he was pretty much the main reason for the whole trip. She came to the end of her speech and, uncharacteristically, she stopped. Shelly was known for going on and on, repeating herself and adding meaningless filler.

The summer ahead suddenly lost its attraction for Erin. A week in the same house with her brother and two sisters and all their kids was bad enough, but with her father included in the picture, the idea was about as appealing as a freeway accident. Reuben would be okay with it, would most likely put a positive spin on it the way he always did with everything. Reuben actually liked being around her family more than she did.

She heaved a sigh and rubbed her hand across her face. Surely she could think of an excuse for the third week of July. Unfortunately nothing came to mind right away except the truth—that this was absolutely the last thing in the world she wanted to do at any time during the year.

Just days before, ironically, she and Reuben had been talking about taking some time off this summer, but for some reason they couldn't come up with any place they really wanted to go. "Let's wait and see," Reuben had finally said. "Who knows, maybe somebody will invite us somewhere, or maybe we'll think of something we really *need* to do with our vacation days." Oh, great, she had told him, that was her idea of a summer vacation—something they felt obligated to do.

"Like I said, I don't want an answer now," Shelly

said. "I'll call you again in a few days. But think about it, Erin—and *please try* to have an *open* mind."

Her meaning was clear: "Please shock me and be reasonable for once."

"Well, I have to go now," she added briskly. "We're taking the kids to a carnival! Ta-ta for now." Then she hung up.

As she put the receiver down, Erin heard the far-off sounds of sirens. It sounded like a whole caval-cade of fire trucks, ambulances, and police cars. It was a sound she had always hated. She thought of Shelly, so pleased over her happy life, her opti-mistic plans to knit the family together, her little speeches about forgiveness and mercy. Erin hoped a big storm would come up and flood the dumb carnival.

Part of Ben's Saturday ritual was working in the yard. Even in the winter he tried to find something to do outdoors on Saturdays—blowing leftover leaves, cleaning out gutters, raking up pine needles and sweet gum balls. If nothing else, he cleaned the outside of the windows again or washed down the siding. He frequently restraightened the shelves in the storage shed and was often on the roof checking the shingles for nails that may have worked their way out.

Now that it was almost summer, however, he wouldn't have to think up things to do outside.

There would be plenty of bona fide yard work. Today, in fact, he had already mowed the grass and was now using the weed eater along the driveway.

The woman next door came out to water the two big pots of ivy on either side of her front steps. Her husband followed her out and picked up a child's bicycle lying on the sidewalk. He didn't look at all happy as he wheeled it around to the garage. Ben put his head down and pretended not to see them. They had just moved in a few weeks earlier, and he didn't even know their names yet.

He had already noticed how lean and fit the man was, though, how he liked to wear athletic shorts and sleeveless cropped T-shirts to show off the fact that he didn't have an extra ounce of fat anywhere. Ben glanced down at his own T-shirt stretched over his middle. He had a long way to go before he got rid of the extra pounds that had appeared over the past few years. This was something Chloe would have watched out for. She would have helped him guard his health. They would have continued to exercise as they grew older together, and she would have been very careful about the food they ate.

Next door one of the children, a little girl, suddenly flew out of the house, down the front steps past her mother and into the front yard. She did a cartwheel, then a handstand, then walked on her hands before flipping herself upright and starting all over again. Her mother stood on the bottom step watching her, wearing an undisguised expression that said, "Isn't she something? Look what we made! Aren't we good? Aren't we lucky?" She glanced over at Ben and caught him looking. He felt compelled to wave but then quickly bent his head again and got back to his weed eating.

He remembered overhearing a man on an airplane one time, saying to another man across the aisle, "It was my kids who helped me survive. They kept me hooked up to life. I knew I had to be strong for them." Ben had never said that, to his shame had never even thought it, and he knew his children would testify that it was their grandmother, not their father, who had been strong for them.

His mother had always loved a challenge. After Chloe's death, she moved in to rescue them, taking over the running of their house—a gift of service that released Ben from all responsibility. It shouldn't have, of course, but it was as if he floated away from home in an emotional sense and never returned. He floated away more literally, too. He changed jobs and started traveling more, staying gone for weeks at a time. Looking back on all those years following Chloe's death, he was appalled at how few and how sketchy his memories of his children were.

At some point early on, his mother had told him they needed to get out of the house where "it happened" because it was too hard on the children.

When he made no objection, she organized the whole move back into her own house, the one on Amaryllis Street. So one day Ben had come home from a long trip and had taken up residence in the same bedroom he'd had as a teenager. It didn't matter to him. One room was as good as another.

What I Used to Have. This had been the theme of Ben's life for the past twenty-one years. Whenever it started playing through his mind, he heard the sound of a high wind, as if rushing through a door left open. And rising above it were all the heated words he had said to Chloe during the last few weeks of her life. Things like "You aren't the woman I married" and "You're ruining what we had together" and "We don't have anything in common anymore." He had acted more like a child than a grown man.

And close on the heels of these words were always the words of the two police detectives who had questioned him at length: "And is there anyone who saw you or talked to you during those four hours, Mr. Buckley? Anyone who can verify that you were indeed in Charleston during the time of your wife's murder?" And, later, "What can you tell us about the life insurance policy you took out on your wife two months ago?" And "Do you know any reason why the back door of your house would have been unlocked?"

Whenever these thoughts crept into his mind, he could always count on losing track of time. Last night, for example, he didn't know how long he had sat in his car while the parking lot at the shopping mall emptied and employees mopped the floors inside Panera and the ice cream place.

He had driven home in a sort of daze, which was compounded, when he pulled into his driveway, by the sight of a big box sitting on his front porch and then further by the discovery of its contents. A bicycle, of all things, in a box that small—he could hardly believe it. A printed message enclosed with the packing slip identified the sender: "Happy Birthday, Dad! From Shelly and Mark." He had taken the bicycle out of the box and unfolded it. He had never seen such a thing, a full-sized bicycle that folded up.

He glanced back up toward the open garage now, weed eater in hand, and saw the bicycle hanging on the two large hooks he had mounted late last night after taking the bicycle out for a trial run under the streetlights. If any of his neighbors had seen him, they had probably thought he was crazy.

As he moved from the driveway to trim around the base of the mailbox, he suddenly realized he had forgotten to get the mail the night before. Evidently the discovery of the bicycle had derailed his normal routine. Opening the mailbox now, he saw that it was quite full. For a moment he wondered if he had failed to check it for two or three days.

There was a book-sized package wedged in sideways as well as a fistful of regular mail. He laid the weed eater down on the ground. There were four envelopes, each bearing the return address of one of his children. This had to be Shelly's doing. He knew the other three wouldn't think of sending him a card unless they had been prompted. Or bribed. He wondered how Shelly had done it.

Part of him shrank from opening the cards. What kind of greeting card could sum up his brand of fathering? *Thanks, Dad, for financing my college education.* That was one that might work. He thought of others: *To a dad who made a fortune in the stock market.* Or *To a father who didn't ask a lot of nosy questions or impose a bunch of strict rules on us growing up.*

He took the mail inside and set it on the kitchen table. He would wait and open it all later. He wasn't up to it now. But then he changed his mind and decided to go ahead and open the book before finishing the trimming outdoors. The return address told him it was from his daughter Lydia, one of the twins. He was curious about what kind of book Lydia would send him. Of the three girls Lydia was the one who looked most like her mother. She was also the one who had turned out to be most like Chloe in temperament, not as cheerfully self-satisfied as Shelly and not as gloomy as Erin. She and Erin were twins, but fraternal. They were as different as night and day.

He opened the top of the bubble-wrap mailer and

turned it upside down. The book slid out onto the table face up. *Through the Year With Books and Writers.* That was the title. He picked it up. It wasn't a large book, but it had a nice heft. The cover design was a swirl of reds and browns with a dark wine-colored binding. It had its own red ribbon page marker—the same color as the marker in Chloe's Bible. He turned the book over. The back cover informed him that this was a "treasure trove of literary facts about writers" and that it was "marvelously and generously illustrated."

He turned back to the front and opened it. The endpapers were decorated with the same swirled design as on the cover. On the page facing the copyright was a quotation by Oscar Wilde: . . . *each day is like a year, / A year whose days are long.* Ben knew about days like that.

Happy Birthday, Dad. Love, Lydia—these words were written in a flowing script on this same page. It came to him as he stared at Lydia's message that maybe his children knew something about long days, too. He also realized that he never would have recognized his own daughter's handwriting if she hadn't signed her name.

He flipped through the book and saw that it was divided into days of the year, each entry identifying all the different events that had happened to writers on that day. He turned to his birthday, May 23. On May 23 in 1839 Henry Wadsworth Longfellow publicly critiqued Jane Austen's writing as "a capital picture of real life" but went on to say, "She explains and fills out too much." And on May 23, 1906, Henrik Ibsen had died at the age of 78.

He scanned other pages. He could imagine himself in years to come working these facts into his conversations with people at work: "Be sure to wear your coat, Caroline, or you could die of consumption as Emily Bronte did" or "No need to apologize for reading your pulp fiction in the break room, Nora. As Mickey Spillane once said, 'There are more salted peanuts consumed than caviar.'"

The book was indeed generously illustrated. He stopped to look at some of the pictures: a caricature of James Joyce, Eugene O'Neill in a kayak, Benjamin Franklin's epitaph.

He heard a meow and looked down to see Ink staring up at him. "No, it's not time to eat," Ben said. "And no, I'm not going to give in." The cat stared at him another moment, twitching her whiskers, then turned and padded out of the kitchen. Ben remembered something Chloe had told him once after they were engaged, that she was impressed by the fact that Ben was one of the few men she had ever known who appreciated cats. Her theory was that men were intimidated by cats because they were so much like capable women, who also intimidated them. Men simply didn't understand cats, she used to say, just as they didn't understand women.

He suddenly recalled something he had read years ago about circus lingo, that the circus term for the man who stood at the very bottom of the acrobats' inverted human pyramid was the *understander*. In so many ways, that's what a father and husband was, or should be—the understander for his family. And when the understander collapsed, so did the whole pyramid. Understanding—it often came to men too late, if at all.

Ben sighed and closed the book. It was a solid-feeling little volume, one he was sure he would return to often, like his *Say It Ain't So, Joe* book. It was a good birthday gift Lydia had chosen. He really ought to thank her—and Shelly, too. He glanced at the cards on the table, then headed back outside. He wasn't up to opening those yet.

ELEVEN

A Sort of Tithe

On the following Thursday morning, Caroline put the next week's work schedule on Ben's desk. She had no idea if he ever looked at it, but this was always the required order of things. Nora, the day-time personnel supervisor, made up the schedule, then sent it to Caroline to look over and post in the break room. Before she could post it, however, Ben had to see it and put his initials at the bottom.

Three years ago she had tried skipping this step

and had received a verbal reprimand she hadn't forgotten, one that started out, "Let me remind you, Ms. Mason, that I am in charge here. I am both the owner and chief executive of the Upstate Home and Garden Bazaar. You are a valued employee but an employee nonetheless. Though I have relinquished much of the responsibility around here, I am still the overseer of . . ." and blah, blah, blah. She had only thought she was saving him some trouble, but evidently the act of writing *BB* at the bottom of the page was important to him, like so many of the other little details he liked to control.

To Caroline's delight, today was one of the rare days Ben was out of the office. He was looking at three vacant properties this morning as potential future sites of the Bazaar when the time came for them to move. One was a furniture store that had gone bankrupt, another was an old movie theater, and the third was the former home of a company that sold gas logs, propane heaters, and such. Caroline was hoping Ben would get involved this morning in long conversations with the real estate people and then run into traffic jams getting from one place to another. She was glad that one of the sites was all the way out by the airport. If she was lucky, he might not be back until well after lunch.

Caroline moved a few papers on his desk and placed the schedule in a little clear spot right in the center of the ink blotter so he would be sure to see it. Mr. Buck was bad about setting things on top of other things. "Getting lost in the shuffle" wasn't just an expression around here. She would have stood the schedule upright between the rows of keys on his old manual typewriter if something else wasn't already there.

She stepped around his desk to look at it. It was another one of his lists of sentences, this one typed on a piece of thick blue cardstock. She had seen more of these lists than she could count, and each one simply convinced her further that Mr. Buck's mind was full of kinks. And also, that he had a lot of spare time on his hands. At the top of this list, she read, *Some Pomegranate, which, if cut deep down the middle, / Shows a heart within blood-tinctured, of a veined humanity.* The sentences were things he had read, she supposed, followed by abbreviations that meant nothing to her, this one "EB Brwn p. 98." The next sentence was *All animals are equal, but some animals are more equal than others*, and the next was *A poet doomed at last to wake a lexicographer.*

Caroline shook her head. She would never in a million years understand the way some people squandered the hours in their day. Two books were sitting on the extension of his desk beside the old typewriter. One was a dictionary with a yellow sticky note on the front cover on which he had written three words she had never heard of: *troglodyte, unctuous,* and *mansard.* The other book was one she wished she could throw out the window. The title was *Say It Ain't So, Joe*, and it was one of his favorite books, the source of all his half-baked theories about the origins of words and phrases.

She flipped it open and clucked her tongue at all the underlining and check marks. Her eyes lighted on an entry: *a lick and a promise.* At least that one was familiar. According to the book, the phrase started in England centuries ago and referred to a cat's licking its face quickly, with the intention of doing a more thorough job later. Well, that was the most ridiculous thing she had ever read. How could anyone trace a common saying to what a *cat* was *thinking*?

The next entry was *lickety split*, which had taken other forms throughout the years: *lickety-scoot, lickety-tuck, lickety-Christmas*. She flipped back to another page and saw *get the lead out of your loafers*.

Caroline slapped the book shut, irritated all over again by the thought that while she was busy keeping the Upstate Home and Garden Bazaar running smoothly, Mr. Buck was ensconced in his office, piddling around with books and typing out lists of totally irrelevant information on a *manual typewriter*.

The typewriter was another source of great aggravation. She scowled at it—a brown Remington with dark green key caps and an oversized carriage. Mr. Buck could afford the best computer on the market, or even a dozen if he wanted them, but he stubbornly hung on to this relic, saying he had one computer at home and that was enough, although she firmly believed he was holding out just because he saw how much it rankled her.

It was Caroline's conviction that he needed his own computer at work so that he could do things for himself that he asked her to do. But when she had mentioned this advantage to him one day, he had studied her solemnly for a long moment, then said, "Didn't I just approve a generous pay raise for you recently, Ms. Mason?" And it was true. He paid her very well. Evidently his point was that as long as he was paying her a good salary, he could ask her to gather twigs all day if that's what struck his fancy.

"Is Mr. Buckley here?"

Caroline jerked her head up to see Kelly Kovatch standing at the door, her hand poised as if to knock. The girl was wearing a dark blue jumper today and a light blue blouse with a Peter Pan collar. On her feet were little soft, round-toed Mary Jane shoes. No jewelry, of course, except for her plain Timex watch with its stretchy silver band.

Caroline stepped away from Ben's typewriter. "No, he's out right now," she said. "I was just putting something on his desk." It irked her that she felt she had to explain what she was doing in Ben's office by herself. As his senior assistant, she had every right in the world to be in here. She knew a lot more about running the everyday business of the Bazaar than anyone else, owner and chief executive included. "Why?" she asked Kelly. "Did you need to see him about something?"

"Yes, ma'am."

Caroline walked toward the door. "You know, Kelly, a simple yes or no is a perfectly acceptable answer around here. In fact, it makes a lot of people in the professional world feel uncomfortable when someone says *ma'am* and *sir* all the time." She swept past her and headed for her own desk, then sat down and swiveled her chair around to face the girl. "It's like rubbing your youth in their face. You might as well tell people they're old enough to be your grandparents."

Kelly's eyes registered surprise, but she kept her composure. Lifting her chin, she said politely, "All right, Caroline. Thank you for telling me. I never meant to offend anybody."

Caroline noted with approval Kelly's use of her first name, the result of another conversation they'd had recently in which she had told her that Mr. Buckley was the only one she needed to be so formal with. "Well, I'm not *offended*," she said, softening a little, "but it's something you ought to know." She looked up at the girl and offered a smile. "Mr. Buck should be back by one, maybe sooner. Could I help you with whatever it is?" She motioned to her computer. "I'm working on this week's employee memo, but there's no huge rush."

Kelly had a way of holding her hands at waist level, close to her body, fingers tightly interlaced. She stood that way now a few feet from Caroline's desk, then took a quick breath as if to say something but stopped. She shook her head and frowned. "Oh, that's okay. I guess I'll just wait and talk to him later. Thanks, Caroline." She started to walk away.

Caroline raised her voice. "I've been meaning to ask you how your family is doing, Kelly." Several times she had tried to imagine what kind of man Kelly's father might be and how he was taking the death of his wife. She pictured a man a little taller than average, with the beginnings of a middle-aged potbelly, graying hair going thin, and the patient eyes of a sheep. He was probably a man of few words. For some reason she was guessing that Kelly's mother had been the more assertive one, the organizer, the talker, the go-getter—the Thoroughbred racehorse type.

Kelly turned back to face her. "Oh, we're doing okay," she said. "It's been pretty hard for my dad, but we're all trying to . . . well, hold things together. Thanks for asking." She searched Caroline's face for a moment, then added, "We know my mother is happier where she is now, so that helps a lot."

After she left, Caroline kept hearing the words:

"We know my mother is happier where she is now." How confident she sounded at the advanced age of what . . . twenty? Caroline wanted to dislike the girl, almost succeeded on certain days, but then there were other times like right now when she came very close to wishing she could look into Kelly's heart and see her from the inside out, understand what was behind those dark, serene eyes, and feel what it must be like to have that calm assurance that whatever happened was meant to be. It was a feeling verging on respect.

Well, enough of all that. She had work to do. She needed to get the lead out of her loafers and finish up this employee memo lickety-scoot, lickety-tuck, and lickety-Christmas. She smiled at her own wit as she slipped off her olive green heels and put a hand to the olive green scarf at her neck to make sure the knot was still over to the side where it belonged.

She touched her keyboard. The screen saver of blue planets and galaxies faded to reveal the weekly memo she was composing, to be included with the Friday paychecks. This was another little job Ben had thought up within the past few months to add to everything else she did. He used to have her post reminders on the bulletin board in the break room, but he became convinced that people weren't reading them, so he had instituted the idea of individual memos inside the pay envelopes.

She had tried to tell him that this was no way to

guarantee that people would read them, but he had simply said, "Nevertheless, that's what we're going to do," and that was the end of that. Though she had dropped the subject, she couldn't help feeling a certain "I told you so" smugness, mixed with a desire to kick somebody in the pants, when just last week she had seen Lester Lattimore tear open his pay envelope, look at the check, then pull out the memo, spit his chewing gum into it, and wad it up.

Throughout the week now, Ben frequently called her on the intercom or handed her notes on little scraps of paper about certain matters he wanted to call to the attention of all the employees, and every Thursday morning she had to collect these and type them up into a memo, then print it out so Ben could make corrections or additions. If he had his own computer, of course, it would be so much simpler, but he evidently enjoyed circling things with his red pen and having her walk back and forth between his office and hers until that crowning moment when he carefully printed "Approved by BB" at the top.

She read over what she had already typed, then consulted her handwritten notes, sighed, and started typing the next item: "Please check the refrigerator in the break room for items you may have forgotten. Leftovers in Styrofoam containers are especially problematic when they start to smell. We had to dispose of several such containers recently." Caroline gave a little irritated snort at his use of the pronoun *we*. As if *he* had been involved in any way in opening all those containers and seeing all the different disgusting colors of mold that could grow on food!

It was three hours later when Ben walked into the basement entrance of the Bazaar, carrying a slim leather binder in which he had written all his notes from the morning's real estate talks. Seth and J.J. were on the dock unloading a dining room suite, and the vendor of Begian Classic Interiors was nervously looking on. The chairs were massive things, the size of thrones, with carved backs and arms and seats covered with a tapestry-like fabric, the kind of chairs that belonged in the banquet hall of a medieval castle. Each one was encased in plastic sheeting, which made them a little unwieldy to grasp by the arms. Ben stopped and watched for a minute as Seth carried another one off the truck, his neck muscles straining with the effort. It was hard to imagine normal-sized people sitting in chairs like these and scooting themselves up to the table. And if these were the chairs, Ben couldn't help wondering what the table looked like.

The vendor, whose name was Nazar Begian, had sold furniture and home accessories at the Bazaar ever since it first opened. He waved to Ben now and gestured excitedly toward the truck. "I have buyers for this goods already!" he said. Nazar, a shrewd businessman of Armenian descent, had lived in several different countries in his lifetime, the last one being Cambodia. Passably competent in five or six different languages, he still struggled with English. He had been in the United States fewer than six years.

Today Nazar was wearing black-and-white checked pants and a multicolored striped shirt, which showed that a person could have a good eye in a field like home furnishings yet miss the mark in another like fashion. Yet fashion was so culturally bound, Ben reminded himself, that maybe it was unfair to judge someone like Nazar, who had probably been used to wearing clothes that looked like pajamas in Cambodia.

"My buyers want these mahogany!" Nazar said. "They like old ways."

"Your buyers must be a family of giants," Ben said.

"No, they live close," Nazar said. "They will come today."

Ben nodded. From Nazar's replies it was often hard to tell exactly which words he misunderstood, and, oddly, he often used big words correctly. Recently, for example, he had told Ben that his daughter had worn a "cunning ensemble" to a costume party and another time that his son had "acquired a franchise" in New York.

Nazar also tried to use English idioms, often

with humorous effect, such as the time he had objected to having to pay for the cleaning of a bearskin rug in his showroom that some customer had spilled on. He had bowed his head and swung it from side to side, groaning with deep emotion. "Oh, Mr. Buckley, my friend, you put me on a hard place and a rock!" he had said. Once he had bemoaned to Ben that his sales during the past month were "under the par," and another time he described the popularity of gas fireplaces as "a flash in the pants." In Ben's opinion, however, you had to hand it to a person like Nazar, who bravely entered new cultures and tackled new languages. He couldn't imagine doing that himself.

"You are feeling good health?" Nazar asked now, stepping closer and frowning at Ben with concern.

"Yes," Ben said. "Yes, I am."

Nazar shook his head. "Your eyes have fatigue. You are pale like birch. You have a doctor, no?"

Trying to look nonchalant, Ben rubbed one hand along the side of his face. Pale like birch? He felt fine. But maybe it took someone like Nazar, without the American habit of soft-peddling the truth, to tell him he didn't look so fine. He wondered if others had noticed the same thing and had just been too tactful to mention it. Or too indifferent.

"Oh, I'm okay," Ben said. "I haven't slept very well for a couple of nights, that's all."

"You need different scenery," Nazar said seriously. "You spend all your existence here in this place." He pointed with both hands and lifted his eyes to take in the two floors of the Bazaar above them. "You need to leave this premise for vacation."

There was the sound of a heavy thump, and both men quickly looked back toward the truck. When he saw that it was only the sound of J.J. jumping from the dock back onto the truck, Nazar clasped his hands and laughed. "For all the stars!" he said. "I feared to see great smithereens!" He returned to the dock, pointed into the back of the truck, and called out, "Seth! J.J.! The table must take great care! It is all of one piece. You need assistance for this! Where are Morris and Lester for help?"

Seth came to the open end of the truck and spoke into his headset. "Hey, can you guys give us a hand on the dock?" There must have been a reply, for Seth laughed and said, "Yeah, J.J. can't hold up his end. Yeah, like right now. We got another truck due any minute."

"Well, so long," Ben said. He turned toward the elevator, then decided to take the stairs instead. He glanced back at Nazar, who was watching him, and gave a cheerful wave. He started up the stairs two at a time, hoping to demonstrate that he was full of energy and good health.

"You must go for vacation!" Nazar called. "I advise for your health!"

Breathing hard, Ben stopped at the landing outside the first floor and decided to take the escalator up to the second, telling himself this would be a good time for walking through both floors and making his presence known before returning to his office. He felt his heart pounding and scolded himself for trying to go up the stairs so fast. He opened the door and came out into the first-floor lobby next to the restrooms, where he sat down on a wrought iron bench beside a stone fountain, under the pretense of tying his shoe. He set his leather binder down beside him and leaned over.

As he fiddled with his shoelaces, Nazar's words kept running through his mind: "You need different scenery. You must go for vacation!" How funny that he should mention such a thing less than a week after Shelly's note about a big family vacation to the mountains in July, something he had immediately decided against.

Ben tried to remember his last vacation. He couldn't recall taking one since a trip to Savannah ten years ago, when he had looked into financing an upscale retirement complex—and that was actually only a business trip with a couple of short, unsatisfactory free days tacked on to the end.

His idea for the retirement complex had been to oversee the construction of the place from the ground up, something he thought he might enjoy more than spending the rest of his life doing audits and filing corporate tax forms at the accounting firm where he worked at the time. After building it, he could hire competent people to run the place for him. After that he might build another one in another city and keep expanding until he had four or five. His plan was to house his mother in one of them, of course, so she would quit talking about wanting to move into something smaller without all the worries of upkeep, which he knew was her way of suggesting that she move in with him again or that he move back in with her.

He had taken five vacation days from his job that time. For some reason he felt an urgent need to walk on a beach and hear the cry of seagulls. His mother had worried that he was losing his mind. "You never even liked the beach when you were growing up!" she had said. Which wasn't exactly true. What he hadn't liked was her fretting over every little thing at the beach. Sharks, jellyfish, sharp pieces of broken glass, sunstroke, under-tows—she was sure he would be transported home in a coffin if she wasn't constantly vigilant.

She had tried hard to deter him from going to Savannah: "Why don't you go to the mountains if you have to go somewhere?" She had hinted strongly that he ask her to go with him, but he ignored the hint. He knew it wouldn't be any vacation with her along.

For a number of reasons, the plans for the retirement complex had run into snags, so he had rejected the idea quickly and spent the last two days of the week walking on the beach, which had proved to be a disappointment, with all those fishy, salty smells and the things washed up on shore—crushed shells, trash, long slimy strings of weeds.

He sat up again and picked up his leather binder. So one vacation ten years ago—maybe Nazar had a point. Maybe Nazar Begian had been sent, like one of those Old Testament prophets, to tell Ben he needed to set aside a week or two for a vacation every ten years. One summer out of ten. He could look at it as a sort of tithe—something he owed his body for seeing him through another decade.

He thought again about Shelly's note on his birthday card. Flat Rock, North Carolina—it didn't sound like much of a vacation spot in his opinion, even if he had been inclined to face his children after all these years. She would be calling him back soon to get his answer, she had written in the card, but if he kept refusing to answer the phone, maybe she would give up eventually.

He heard footsteps and looked up to see Jillian Denton, one of the new floorwalkers, coming toward him.

She put on one of her frighteningly broad smiles. "Well, hi there, Mr. Buck!" she said. "You sure look comfy and relaxed. What are you doing sitting here all by your lonesome?" She laughed and shook her hair, a springy mass of auburn tangles, then plucked at it with one hand. Jillian was in her late twenties, unmarried but "seriously prowling," as Caroline put it.

"Oh, I was just thinking," Ben said.

Jillian leaned down and put her hands on her knees as if talking to a child. The neck of her yellow sweater gaped open. "And what might we be thinking about?" she said.

Ben got up from the bench and turned to look at the water running over the smooth brown stones of the fountain. "I'm sure we must be thinking about the same thing, Ms. Denton—getting back to work." And he gave her a quick, businesslike nod as he left.

TWELVE

What Kind of Father

A couple of weeks later, on a Tuesday morning in June, Kelly was working on a new display window when one of the girls at the customer service desk called her to the phone. On the other end was Iris, the owner of the Tasteful Trimmings showroom, all in a snit about a cloisonné vase.

"One of my best customers said she came in to buy it yesterday," Iris told Kelly, "but it wasn't there! I've checked all my records, and I've only gotten paid for two of those! So what's happened to the other one? And how many other things of mine have disappeared? What's going on around there? You people just let somebody pick up a vase that size and walk out the door without paying?"

Kelly told her she would check on it right away. She hung up and pulled the inventory list for Tasteful Trimmings. Iris was right. The store's records confirmed that only two of the large cloisonné vases had been sold. Surely no one would have the nerve to shoplift something that big.

Though she hated having to stop what she was doing, she printed off the list and headed upstairs to the showroom. She stopped in the aisle outside Tasteful Trimmings and let her eyes sweep every table and shelf, every inch of floor space. The vase was nowhere to be seen. She walked over to a small round table, pulled up the tablecloth, and looked underneath. No cloisonné vase, but there was a small teak tea chest hiding there. She set her clipboard down and pulled the chest out. Maybe it had gotten shoved under the table when someone vacuumed the floor last—whenever that was. She ran a finger over the faux mantel where a large clock and a pair of porcelain pheasants were displayed. Somebody surely needed to do some basic housekeeping here in Tasteful Trimmings. Maybe she would have time to do a quick dusting for Iris later today even though the vendors were supposed to do all that for themselves.

She stood in the middle of the showroom and made a slow circle, giving it another once-over. It was quite full of merchandise, mostly accessories like lamps, ceramic accents, bookends, framed prints, decorative pillows. It would be easy to miss something. But clearly the vase was not here.

There had been a testy exchange over the phone recently, when Iris had called to tell Byron where she wanted him to display two bronze lions whenever they arrived. When Byron told her she would have to get a friend or family member to help her out, he had listened patiently while she ranted at some length, and then he had replied calmly, "Well, I'm sorry you've been sick, Iris, but I can't do your job and mine both. The vendors have to take care of their own stuff. You know that. We make that very clear up front. It's stated in your contract—the one you signed and we have on file."

After he hung up, he observed to Kelly that whatever Iris's illness was, it hadn't affected her vocal cords or her lung capacity. He also told Kelly that from now on when Iris called to talk with a manager, he was passing the honors off to her, which was exactly what happened. Ever since, Iris had been asking to speak with Kelly each time.

The vase wasn't behind the red damask deacon's chair or the antique steamer trunk. It wasn't anywhere around or inside the cherry buffet, and it wasn't under the other round table next to the stack of Victorian hatboxes. Kelly sighed and looked down at the inventory list. Though she couldn't really spare the time, maybe she should run through all the items to see if anything else was missing. That way she could at least report truthfully that all the other merchandise was present and accounted for. She did sympathize with Iris, lying in bed worrying about her showroom.

She heard a *kik-kik-kik* sound, the kind you would make out the side of your mouth if you were calling a horse. She looked up to see Lester standing by a tall arrangement of pampas grass, one hip cocked, a thumb hooked into the pocket of his jeans. "Well, here she is, finally. I been looking all over for you, Never-on-Sunday." This was Lester's newest name for her since he had noticed that she was never scheduled to work on Sunday.

He looked her up and down. He was wearing a T-shirt with the faded words *BABE PATROL* on the front. The sides of his hair were slicked back today. If his behavior weren't so disgusting, Kelly might be tempted to feel sorry for him. It had to be calculated, all of it—the posture, the clothes, the hair, the attitude.

"Well, okay, you're not gonna talk, I guess," he said. "You're just gonna stand there staring at me. 'Course, I can understand that easy, you being you and me being *me* and all. You probably thinking—"

"Do you have a question?" Kelly said. She wondered why he hadn't just contacted her over her headset instead of walking around looking for her. But at least they weren't alone; there were plenty of people milling around.

He tossed his head back and laughed. "Do I have a question, she asks. Oh yeah, I got a question. I got lots of them." But before he could say more, a woman came up behind him, holding a little boy by the hand.

"Excuse me," the woman said loudly, "I'm looking for all those silk flower arrangements. Does anybody know where they are? I was sure they were up here on this floor, but I can't find them anywhere. This place is like a maze!"

"Here, I'll show you," Kelly said, picking up her clipboard. She walked past Lester without looking at him. "Floral Dreams—that's probably the show-room you're talking about," she told the woman. "It's on around the circle here on the other side of the escalator. It's sort of tucked back in a corner, so it's easy to miss."

Behind her, Les called out, "Hey, wait, you didn't tell me where them two lions go! J.J. just called up from the dock to say they're here, and Byron said ask you where to put them before we haul them up."

Kelly stopped and turned around in the aisle. "Oh, sorry, I didn't hear you ask," she said evenly. "Why don't you just set them on the floor by the mantel for now, one on each side, turned slightly toward each other. I'll be back in a minute, so we can see how they look after you get them up here. We might need to experiment with where to put them."

"Yeah, let's do that," Les said. "Let's *experiment*."

Kelly turned back around and continued on her way. It was creepy the way Les could take the simplest thing and twist it into something suggestive.

"Here we are," she said to the woman as they neared the Floral Dreams showroom. And then her eyes lighted on something that made her stop in her tracks. It was a large cloisonné vase sitting on the floor under an ebony sofa table on which were displayed two yellow ginger jars filled with red silk zinnias. She walked over and picked up the vase. Sure enough, on the bottom was a sticker with *TT* for Tasteful Trimmings printed on it.

How odd. She could have spent a good hour or two looking for this in a store the size of the Bazaar, but instead she had walked right to it. She knew what her mother would have said: "Well, praise the Lord. He brought that woman along to ask about the silk flowers just so he could lead you right to the missing vase!" Well, maybe so, but she also heard the voice of doubt: "So if God can fix a little problem like that, why does he leave so many bigger ones unfixed?" She could only imagine the look of disappointment in her mother's eyes if she had ever known one of her children had such a thought.

Kelly tucked her clipboard under her arm and carried the vase with her. There was no way to tell how something from Tasteful Trimmings had ended up in Floral Dreams, but it was hardly the first time this kind of thing had happened.

Customers often changed their minds about purchases and just set them down anywhere. Or sometimes they tried to hide things they were interested in so they could come back later and buy them. Well, anyway, she had found the vase without even trying very hard, so that was something to be thankful for. She might still do a quick run-through of the inventory list just to set Iris's mind at ease when she called her back.

Heading back to Tasteful Trimmings, she saw Mr. Buckley strolling toward her, his hands behind his back, looking pensively at the floor. Maybe she should stop and talk with him right now about Lester. A few weeks ago she had almost done it, had in fact gone to his office only to find him gone for the morning. But later she had reconsidered, rebuking herself for being such a chicken. She was always telling Kitty and Kyle at home not to be tattletales but to hold each other accountable and work their differences out. She needed to follow her own advice, not go complaining to the boss.

"Hello, Kelly." Mr. Buckley stopped and smiled politely. "Nice vase." He pronounced the word as if it rhymed with *was*. "How are things going?"

Kelly nodded back. "Things are going fine, Mr. Buckley, thank you." She noticed that the tips of his shirt collar were curled under, and she wondered briefly if he did his own laundry. If so, he obviously didn't do ironing. She thought of her father's nicely pressed shirts. But that was something her mother and, later, Kelly and her sisters had always done for him. She doubted that her father even knew how to operate the washing machine, and she had never seen him iron anything.

"Well, that's good," Mr. Buckley said. "So you're still finding enough to keep you busy around here?" He wasn't looking at her now but seemed to be studying a large white baker's rack in Klassy Kitchens, its shelves loaded with various fake foods: a layered cake, a big plastic round of cheese with a wedge cut out of it, several baskets of fruit.

"Oh yes, there's always plenty to do."

"Good, good, wouldn't want you getting bored." He was still not looking at her.

"And we'll have even more to do as soon as the big moving sale starts," she said.

He nodded but said nothing.

"Not to mention the actual move," Kelly added. "It will be plenty busy then." Sometimes with Mr. Buck a person had to keep talking since he didn't always hold up his end of the conversation.

He glanced at her, then looked away again. Maybe she should go ahead and talk to him about Les. She could describe the problem in a general, hypothetical way, as if it were happening to someone else, and ask what he would recommend. It really was the perfect opportunity. No customers in the Klassy Kitchens showroom. Just the two of them standing here in the aisle. Maybe God had planned this encounter. But something held her back.

She shifted the vase in her arms. "Well, I just found what I was looking for, so I guess I'd better get it back where it belongs."

"Yes, yes, I guess so." But he didn't move. He was looking at the vase in her arms now, squinting slightly. She wondered if he had daughters of his own and if he looked them in the eye when they sought his advice, *if* they sought his advice. What kind of father would Mr. Buck be?

Suddenly he was looking directly at her. "And how is your father doing these days?" he asked.

The question took her by surprise. "Oh, he's doing pretty well, thank you," she said, "but it's hard for him. He depended on my mother a lot." She probably should have stopped there, but when he didn't respond she added, "He says he tries to ask himself every day what my mother would want him to do and that helps him keep going." Still he said nothing, though he was staring at her more intently now, frowning slightly. "We're all trying to help him as much as we can," she continued. "And he's trying hard to help us, too. We're all just trying . . . to hold each other up." Finally she stopped.

It was an odd look that came into Mr. Buckley's eyes then. He looked confused and almost . . . hurt.

That was the best way to describe it. She wished she hadn't said so much. She hated to think she was responsible for that look.

He looked away, nodding slowly. "Well, then, onward and upward, Kelly," he said. "And by the way, that's a nice-looking window display you're putting together at the west entrance. I like what you've done so far." He met her eyes again for a brief moment. "Very copacetic, as they used to say in show biz."

"Thank you, Mr. Buckley." She had no idea what the word *copacetic* meant. It was funny that someone like Mr. Buck, who seemed to be so fascinated with words, wasn't very easy to talk to. She watched him walk away. He was such a different sort of man, a brooding type. Not that she was an expert on types of men, by any means. She knew he didn't go to church anywhere, but he seemed to know a lot about the Bible. At least she had heard him make a number of Old Testament references, sometimes very obscure things.

Well, she couldn't stand here all day thinking about the curiosities of Mr. Buck. Time to go face Lester and the lions.

At home that night Caroline finished her exercise routine with fifty sit-ups. The part of the movie she liked best was coming up, so she paused the VCR and went to check the locks on the front and back doors. Then she poured herself another half cup of decaf. She added a small scoop of vanilla ice cream and went back into the den. She settled herself on the sofa and started the movie again. This was where the hired killer let himself into the house with the hidden key, and the woman in the bathtub got out and came into the kitchen in her white velour robe.

Five minutes later the woman's white robe was splattered red, and there was a trail of blood from the kitchen back to the bedroom, where she was sprawled out on the floor sobbing into the telephone. A voice on the other end of the phone was saying, "Just hold on, ma'am. Someone is on their way to help you. Don't hang up until we get there. Just hold on, ma'am, we'll be right there." Then the camera shifted to show the woman's husband arriving home to find, to his great surprise, his wife alive and the man he'd hired lying dead in the kitchen with a meat thermometer sticking out of his neck.

Though Caroline had seen the movie at least a dozen times, this part still gave her the heebie-jeebies. The plot moved fast now and got complicated. The husband left his wife's side and raced to the kitchen, where he searched through the killer's pockets and pulled out a key just as the police arrived. Then there was a time lapse, and the chief of police was gently questioning the wife, who was now wrapped up in a blanket on the sofa, sitting next to her husband, who was pretending to be all lovey-dovey, totally concerned about her well-being.

Caroline studied the husband's face closely. She knew this man was an actor, of course, but she also knew that men in general were great at faking emotions they didn't feel. They knew what women wanted to see and hear, and they were ready to do whatever it took to get what *they* wanted. And any woman with a brain the size of a split pea knew what it was that men wanted. So why was it that women were so easily duped? This was the question Caroline often asked herself; in fact, she realized now that the question had momentarily distracted her from the movie.

So she stopped it and rewound it a little. She watched it very closely all the way to the end, when the husband lay bleeding on the floor of their posh apartment, shot dead by his wife after the police had left and he had tried to kill her. Everything was a mess, of course—furniture overturned, disheveled clothing, blood pooling by her husband's body—but the woman had come out the winner. Caroline ran the movie all the way through the credits and then turned the TV off and set about getting ready for bed.

This particular movie always frustrated her, because when she tried to review the plot after watching it, usually in bed as she was trying to get to sleep, she inevitably got mixed up. Did the exchange of money in the park happen before or after the wife discovered her house key didn't work? And when did she find out about her husband's financial trouble—was it before or after her husband showed her the police mug shot of her artist-lover? The important thing, though, was that the wife ultimately won. It was still a good movie, even if the exact order of events was a little bit of a jumble.

Or a *hodgepodge*—that was the word Mr. Buck had started lecturing her about at work today. They had just finished composing an employee memo about the upcoming mall demolition and the new site for the Bazaar, which was to be finalized within two weeks. She had cut him off, right as he was telling her that the word *hodgepodge* was originally *hotchpotch* and that it referred to a kind of porridge or stew in England. "Fascinating, I'm sure, but this is no time for word games, Mr. Buckley," she had told him. "With the sale starting tomorrow and then the move and all, you'll have a lot more important things to think about than all that!" The thought came to her that maybe she could arrange a way for his ridiculous *Say It Ain't So, Joe* book to disappear during the move.

It was provoking, though. Every time he told her about some silly word origin, she found herself thinking about that particular word or phrase all throughout the day, often even working it into a conversation without meaning to. Even now, as she ran her bath water, she remembered how Mr.

Buck had gone on to say, "Did you ever notice, Ms. Mason, how many common phrases are made up of rhyming words? Hodgepodge is only one of many."

And even though she had said sternly, "I *don't care*, Mr. Buckley," she had found herself thinking of other examples for the rest of the day, weaving them into her thoughts, even saying some of them out loud. Like hocus-pocus and razzle-dazzle and fuddy-duddy and hoity-toity. And as she'd left work, Melody had called out to her in the parking lot, "It's going to be a zoo around here tomorrow! See you bright and early in the morning!" To her surprise, Caroline had heard herself say, "Okeydokey!"

She adjusted the water temperature to make it warmer. She felt like a long, hot soak tonight. Maybe she would start that book tonight—the one about the ex-Marine who pushed his wife and two children off the side of a cliff in Utah, then tried to make it look like an accident. One itsy-bitsy problem, though: The eight-year-old girl survived the fall and had a very clear memory of what happened. Not only was the ex-Marine foiled by a woman; he was hung-chung by a little girl.

On second thought, maybe she should just soak in the tub with her eyes closed instead of starting the book. Maybe she had thought enough about murder for one evening.

THIRTEEN
The Same Language

Erin picked up the kitten and held him in front of her. "You're cute enough to take home," she said. The kitten had such a sweet, funny little black face with a ragged white tuft right between his eyes. He opened his tiny mouth exactly as if meowing but, as always, made absolutely no sound. Dirk, one of the other employees at the animal shelter, had come up with the perfect name for the little guy: Mewt.

Erin blew lightly in the kitten's face, and he went through his pantomime of meowing again. In her six years of working here, she couldn't remember a cat that didn't meow or a dog that didn't bark. Maybe Mewt just hadn't found his voice yet. Surely he would figure it out soon. She put him back in the cage with another kitten, a runty tabby Dirk had dubbed Caruso for the operatic gusto of his meows. Dirk's idea was that by putting them together, maybe Mewt and Caruso would somehow moderate each other's meowing habits and turn into two normal kittens. So far it hadn't worked.

"You are *not* cute enough to take home," Erin said to the tabby, but she ran a finger gently over his head, down his back, and up over his tail. He let out a long siren-like meow. She couldn't imagine having to live with a noise like that. If he meowed like that as a kitten, what would he sound like when full-grown?

She closed the cage and moved to the next one, which held two hyperactive gray kittens rolling around playfully like a big dust ball. They were emitting regular kittenish mews and timid snarly sounds.

Cleaning the cat cages wasn't Erin's favorite job, but it did give her an excuse to handle the kittens. She tried not to get attached to them, though, knowing that if they didn't get adopted within a certain time, they had to be "moved along," as Weldon put it. Weldon was the director of the animal shelter and the one who made the weekly deliveries to the landfill and occasionally the pet crematorium. Erin often referred to him as the boogeyman. He had asked Erin to do it once when he was strapped for time, but she had told him he was crazy. She wasn't doing his dirty work. Thankfully, Weldon liked her or she couldn't have gotten away with a flat refusal like that.

Caruso let out another long tenor wail. Erin reached back over and stuck her finger through the cage and wiggled it. "Hey you, pipe down," she said. "The boogeyman might come and get you early if you keep up that racket." Mewt swiped at her finger with a paw.

Just then she felt a swoosh of air as the door from

the hallway opened. She looked up to see Reuben holding a sack.

"Hey, Cat Woman, ready to eat?" he said. "I got good stuff. Meow meow."

Erin saw that the sack was from Subway. "You're early," she said. "But I'm just about done."

"Okay, I'll get the drinks. What you want?"

"Pepsi," she said. Then, "Hold on a minute. Come over here. Look at this."

Reuben walked over. Mewt chewed on Erin's finger, then swatted at it again. He opened his mouth wide but, as usual, made no sound.

"No," Reuben said firmly.

Erin looked up at him. Reuben's nose was wrinkled as if he smelled something bad.

"What do you mean, no?" she said.

"You know good and well what I mean," he said cheerfully. "We agreed on a dog. A watch dog. I never heard of a watch cat, did you?" He leaned over and kissed the top of her head. "Now hurry up. Food's getting cold."

"Sub sandwiches are supposed to be cold," she said. "Go on. I'll be there in a minute."

Reuben left and Erin finished up the last two cages. She stopped by Mewt's cage again on the way out. There wasn't any good reason they couldn't get a dog and a cat both. "I'm not giving up on you," she said to Mewt, who opened his mouth in what looked like a modest, hopeful meow.

She cleaned up and headed out to meet Reuben at their regular picnic table next to the old horse stable. The animal shelter would take in any kind of animal. Occasionally they had horses, though none right now. However, they did currently have a monkey, a pig, and a boa constrictor in what Dirk called their "exotic collection." Reuben had already spread napkins out as placemats, with the sandwiches and chips laid out, and he was sitting on top of the rail fence, staring up into the big oak tree, where a couple of squirrels were playing chase.

Cynthia, the one who handled all the paperwork for the adoptions at the animal shelter, often told Erin she was one lucky girl to have a husband like Reuben. She sometimes fussed at Erin. Just yesterday, in fact, after Erin had hung up from talking to Reuben on the phone, Cynthia had said, "You better watch it, girl. There's lots of women who'd treat that man of yours real, real nice. You might be gonna wake up one day and find out he's tired of you always carping at him. Listen to me, honey. I'm old enough to be your mama. I know a good man when I see one, and you got yourself one."

And Erin knew he wasn't a bad husband, really. In fact, he had a lot of advantages over other husbands she had observed. Approaching him now, she had to admit he was still as good-looking after ten years of marriage as he had been on their wedding day, maybe even more so. He had the kind of looks she used to associate with cowboys and rugged explorers like Lewis and Clark. He was fond, in fact, of western wear. Today he had on his oldest pair of cowboy boots, a pair of jeans, and a light blue chambray shirt with snaps instead of buttons. He had the sleeves rolled up.

His forearms had the hard, ropy look of men who spent their days wrestling with broncos or lumber. And in a sense he had spent a lot of time wrestling with lumber as the founder and owner of Custer's Last Fall, a tree trimming service. Since his accident two years ago, he spent most days on the ground, leaving the tree climbing and bucket work to Artie and Rod. He could have easily broken his back during the fall, but he'd gotten off light, with only two broken arms and a leg. Even though he didn't climb anymore, he still got plenty dirty helping with all the cutting, hauling, and chipping.

He dismounted the fence when he saw Erin coming, and together they sat down at the picnic table. "Long morning?" he said sympathetically, though she knew he had left home before she had even gotten up in order to be at his first job site by seven. They were taking out ten diseased oak trees that bordered a school playground.

Erin shrugged. "About like usual," she said. She lifted the bread of her sandwich and rearranged the meat and cheese, then pulled out half the pickles. Subway was bad to put on too many pickles all clumped together.

"Any new pups today?" he said. He took a huge bite of his roast beef sandwich, followed by a long swig of Mountain Dew.

"A couple." She pulled out some of the shredded lettuce, too, and laid it out on the napkin next to the pickles, then pressed the sandwich together. She hated sandwiches that were too thick to get your mouth around. "You forgot to have them cut it in half again," she said.

"Sorry," he said. "Here, I can do it with my pocketknife."

"You mean the one you dig around under your nails with?" she said. "No thanks." She took a small bite of her sandwich and gazed off toward the parking lot. The sounds of barking dogs punctuated the silence. One of them bayed like a hound treeing a raccoon, a constant, frenetic *Bar-roo! Bar-roo!* She knew exactly which one it was, too—a dingy white, nearly hairless midsized mutt that paced his concrete enclosure, stopping to throw himself against the metal bars of the door periodically. He was a new arrival, but not the kind of dog people were interested in taking home to play with their kids. No doubt he would be heading out in the boogeyman's truck one of these days soon.

They ate without talking for a while, during which Reuben finished off the rest of his sandwich and ripped into his bag of chips. Erin took another bite of her sandwich and chewed slowly.

A woman and little girl emerged from the front

door of the animal shelter. The little girl was cradling a cat in her arms, her head bent over as if whispering into its ear.

"I saw new holes in the yard this morning," Erin said. It wasn't totally true. She thought they were very likely old ones, but it was worth a try.

Reuben shot her a look. "Where?" For several weeks now he had been baiting the holes in their yard with poison. The plant nursery had told him what to use and exactly where to put it. They said it was probably voles. Not moles but voles.

"In the . . . front." She suddenly wished she had thought to take a spade out and dig a couple of new holes. It wouldn't have been hard with all the rain they had had lately.

He smiled and shook his head. "Nice try, but I counted them right before I left, and it was still eleven. All the bait was gone, too."

Erin sighed. "That poison is expensive. A cat would save money." She didn't worry about Reuben losing his temper with her. He was infinitely patient. "It would save a lot of trouble, too."

He stuffed the last handful of chips into his mouth and crunched down hard, then chewed fast as he studied her across the table. "Hey, what's the deal?" he said, the corners of his eyes crinkling good-naturedly. "We talked about a dog, remember? A dog that would let us know the next time somebody tries to break into the shop. So what's up with the cat business all of a sudden?"

She shrugged again and took another bite of her sandwich. She couldn't say why she suddenly wanted a cat so much. Well, not just any cat. She wanted Mewt.

"You were going to keep an eye out for a *puppy*, remember? And we were going to keep it here"— he waved a hand toward the animal shelter—"and then take it home after the trip to Flat Rock."

She heaved another sigh. "Oh, forget Flat Rock!" she said petulantly. "That's not any vacation."

Reuben dropped his empty chip bag into the Subway sack, then gathered up his sandwich paper and napkin and crushed them into a ball, which he lobbed toward the trash can nearby. "Well, we don't have to go," he said mildly, "but I think we should. We already said we would." He finished his Mountain Dew and stood up. "We can talk about the cat when we come back home." He walked over to deposit his can into the trash, then stood for a moment with his back to her. "I'm going to see that doctor this afternoon," he said offhandedly.

"I'm not asking you to do that!" Erin said.

"I know you're not. I never said you were." He turned around to face her, then looked at his watch. "Well, I need to get back to the school. We're hoping to finish it up today."

Ben studied the menu at Fuddruckers. He wanted a hamburger, but he knew he ought to order a chicken sandwich instead. It was still early, only minutes after five o'clock, so he had beat the supper crowd. He had left work before Caroline today, something he rarely did. He hadn't even told her he was leaving, had just walked out of his office, to the escalator, and out the downstairs exit.

"Can I help you, sir?" a girl behind the cash register said. Her name tag read "Scarlett." She had a stubby little black sprout of a ponytail on top of her head with shaggy strands of hair hanging down all around her thin face. Her lips were dark red, outlined with black, and she had on frosty green eye shadow. Both of her ears were studded with five or six silver beads around the sides and a small diamond on each lobe. Someday Ben was going to get up his nerve to ask one of these girls, "And just what are you going to do with all those holes when you grow up and have to start acting like an adult? What will it feel like to have the wind whistling through your ear lobes when you're an old woman?"

Lips slightly parted, the girl was staring at him with a look that said she had no use whatsoever for anybody over the age of thirty. He knew she would repeat her question, a little louder and slower, if he didn't answer right away. The look in her eye told him it was coming any minute now.

He looked back up at the menu board. High cholesterol and extra calcium somewhere around his heart—that's what the doctor had said a week ago when Ben had finally broken down and gone for a checkup. The doctor was a stout man who had spoken the words *exercise* and *diet* more than once during the visit, each time referring to Ben, though he was hardly a paragon of physical fitness himself. Ben had left his office with a prescription for a cholesterol medication and an appointment card for a stress test.

The chicken sandwich on the menu had a little red heart by it, signifying that it was a healthier choice. There was also an ostrich burger. He had read somewhere that ostrich was tasty, but he had no intention of finding out. He wasn't interested in eating the meat of any animal that fed on things like locusts, lizards, and sand. Something about the look of an ostrich made him think of tough, stringy meat. And it was one of the fowls labeled as an "abomination" in Chloe's Bible—there had to be a reason for that.

"Can I help you, sir," the girl behind the register said. Louder, of course, and more of a demand than a question this time.

Ben wondered if teachers today still pointed out the distinction between *can* and *may*. "You *may*, Scarlett," he said, "as soon as I've made up my mind."

She raised her eyebrows, then glanced away and blew a little puff of air out the side of her mouth as if to say, "Another old geezer."

"A hamburger," Ben said at last. "A half pounder, well done."

"Fries?"

"No." There, he was making a concession to the doctor. "Just the burger and a large drink."

She punched the order in, took his money, and slammed a plastic glass down on the counter with a resounding *whap*.

"First name?"

Ben had always wondered why they did orders this way at Fuddruckers. Evidently somebody thought it added a personal touch.

Just then someone behind the counter shouted into the microphone, "Barbara, your food is ready!"

In Ben's opinion, it created a stressful atmosphere to have somebody barking out people's names as you were trying to eat. It didn't add a personal touch at all.

The girl was staring at him, her mouth crimped in on one side. "I need your first name, sir," she said.

He glanced at her name tag again.

"Rhett," he said.

She gave him a brief skeptical look, then furiously typed in the name, after which she looked right past him to a woman who had just come in. "Can I help you, ma'am?" she called in a tone that made it clear she was done with the blathering old man who claimed his name was Rhett.

Ben took his cup and moved on to the drink dispenser, then sat at a small table against the wall under a poster of Elvis Presley. This Fuddruckers had a fifties décor.

"So why did you say you don't want to go to Myrtle Beach?" a woman at a nearby table asked the man sitting across from her. "I *know* you didn't like that motel last year, but for pity's sake, we don't have to—" The woman broke off and glanced at Ben, then lowered her voice and continued.

So other men had vacation issues, too. Ben thought again of the upcoming North Carolina trip Shelly was organizing as if it were the mother of all vacations. He thought of her follow-up phone call just days ago as she rattled off all the plans she had laid—a day-by-day schedule of events and activities. He was tired before she was half finished. "It's only three weeks away," she had said in her efficient voice, "and we're all counting on having you there." She had paused. "There will be sixteen of us altogether," and then, as if he would question the count, "Brittany's mother is coming with them. She's been down in the dumps lately." Ben knew Brittany was his son's wife, of course, but he had no idea who her mother was or why she would be down in the dumps. "So you *are* coming, aren't you?" Shelly asked at the end of her phone call.

Ben had sighed. He wasn't at all ready for this. He tried stalling. "Is Flat Rock anywhere near Pisgah? That was where that family went hiking and got mauled by a bear. One of the children died from a crushed rib cage, and the father lost his right eye."

The voice over the intercom interrupted his thoughts: "Phil, your order is ready!" Ben looked around. Things were starting to pick up here at Fuddruckers. By now a short line had begun to form in front of the cash register. Another cashier had joined Scarlett. Ben looked out the window into the parking lot. A half dozen little boys in blue soccer uniforms were spilling out of a van pulled up to the curb.

The woman at the next table had evidently changed topics. "And if I told her once, I told her a thousand times!" she said. She waved a fat French fry around as she talked. The man, chewing slowly, wore the defeated expression of someone who never expected to get in a word edgewise. "But she doesn't hear a word I say," the woman said, "or else she *pretends* she doesn't. I swear, it's like we don't even speak the same language!"

Ben suddenly remembered something that happened years ago at a party. After watching Chloe and Ben carry on an entire conversation using only gestures and facial expressions, a friend of theirs had said, "You two are morons. How do you do that?"

And Chloe had said, "We speak the same language."

"Yeah, well, too bad it doesn't have any words," the friend had said. "They come in handy every now and then for normal people."

Though Chloe was a great conversationalist, she wasn't an incurable talker the way a lot of women were. His mother, for instance. He remembered something his father used to say to his mother before he got so sick: "Just do me a favor right now and don't talk, okay?" After he got sick, he let her talk as much as she wanted.

A group of Hispanics—two men, two women, and three small children—pushed two nearby tables together and noisily settled themselves. Ben wondered if conversations in English sounded as fast to them as theirs did to him. He watched one of the men hail a bus boy. "Leetle chair?" he said, pointing to the smallest child.

Someone at a table across the room struck up "Happy Birthday," and others joined in as a little girl stood up on her chair and clapped her hands proudly.

Ben's thoughts returned to Shelly's phone call. "Flat Rock is down by Hendersonville, Dad. You know that," she had said. "We won't have time to be hiking up to Pisgah. Besides, that bear incident happened two summers ago."

"I know," Ben had said.

"So you'll come?"

"Say it ain't so, Joe," he had said.

"Please, Dad, say something that makes sense. I

need a definite answer. Can you just say yes or no? Preferably yes."

The phone call had ended soon after that. He had finally given in and said yes, and Shelly had said, "Well, good, that's settled, finally." It was a dangerous word, *yes*. Now the vacation in Flat Rock loomed before him like a bad weather forecast.

As he looked around Fuddruckers at all the people talking, he had a sudden guilty thought. You could know lots of words, yet be the world's worst communicator. He knew he often used words to hide behind or divert attention or avoid commitments. Or sometimes to impress people. Or to deliberately confuse. Or *obfuscate*—that was a good word. And he often did these things without even understanding why he wanted to. It had become a habit, a way of holding himself apart from other people. And it worked for that.

He thought about the paper work he'd had to fill out at the doctor's office recently. One section asked for a first contact, somebody you would notify first if a medical emergency arose. He had stared at the paper a long time before he finally wrote Shelly's name, even though he didn't know her phone number from memory or carry it in his billfold.

"Rhett, your order is ready!"

As he passed the table where the couple was sitting, the woman said, "And that doctor told her to take off fifty pounds or be prepared to die in a year, but *she* told *him* she'd rather eat and die happy than diet and live miserable." She laughed heartily and popped another French fry into her mouth.

Ben sucked in his stomach and walked briskly to the counter to get his hamburger.

FOURTEEN

A Brief Glimmer

Ben hated packing for a trip almost as much as the thought of the trip itself. He threw a large duffel bag onto the back seat of his Lincoln Town Car and dropped his golf shoes onto the floor. Playing golf this week ought to be a joke. He hadn't touched a golf club in ages. Typical of July, it was as hot and close and humid as a rain forest here in the Piedmont of South Carolina. Well, maybe it would be cooler in North Carolina.

He hung three extra shirts and a pair of khakis on the hook above the door. By now he had already attracted the attention of the dog across the street, a Chihuahua that kept watch at the storm door. The dog's name was Corky, and he scrabbled at the glass, barking furiously. Whenever the dog was outside with his owner, a frail-looking widow named Ava Cantrell, he strained at the leash and bared his teeth at anyone in sight. He seemed to have a particular aversion to Ben, maybe because he associated him with his cat, Ink, who had once gotten the better of Corky in a face-off.

At least Ava Cantrell didn't hold it against him even if Corky did. She had agreed to collect his mail and look in on Ink while Ben was gone.

He slammed the car door shut, then looked back at his house and sighed. Ink was stretched out inside the bay window, sunning herself. Lucky cat, Ben thought. He wished it were already the end of the week and he were arriving back home. He opened the driver's door and got behind the wheel. He sat there a moment and then turned the ignition. Time to get this dreaded show on the road.

Across the street Corky was still at it, springing up and hurling himself against the storm door. Ben backed out of the driveway and then stopped in the street to rev the engine, just to watch Corky pop another cork. Then he slowly pulled away and headed toward the 291 Bypass, which would take him to Highway 25.

Thankfully, it was only an hour's drive to Flat Rock, North Carolina, but he needed to gas up before he left Greenville, so he stopped at a station on the outskirts of town. It seemed that everybody else needed gas, too, for there was a car at almost every pump. Ben found an empty spot and pulled in. He inserted the nozzle, set the notch on the handle, and leaned against the side of the car as he waited. It smelled like rain, yet puffy white clouds were sailing lazily across the sky.

An old light blue Plymouth was sitting at the pump in front of him, and an elderly man slowly got out and went inside. He had a slight limp. Something about him seemed familiar, but not recently familiar. More like long-ago familiar. Usually good with names and faces, Ben couldn't pull this one up. The man was dressed in baggy walking shorts and a wrinkled Hawaiian-print shirt. He wore dark socks with slip-on canvas shoes and a tan fishing hat. He came back out and fumbled with the cap of his gas tank and finally got it off, then watched the numbers on the pump closely as the gas dispensed. A few gallons later it clicked off, and he replaced the nozzle, holding it with both hands. As he opened the door to get back into his car, Ben called out, "Don't forget your gas cap on top of the car."

The man frowned at him, then got into the car. Ben called out again, louder this time, but the man closed his door and started the engine, then bent his head to fasten his lap belt. Ben hurried over, grabbed the cap from the top of the car, and tapped on the window of the driver's side, which was partway down. The man looked up at him fearfully. One hand was shaking. Ben wondered if he should be driving a car.

"Your gas cap!" Ben shouted, holding it up.

The man's face cleared. "Oh yes, I see." The car rolled forward a few inches, and a look of alarm crossed his face. He stepped on the brake, and the car jerked to a stop. He opened the door as if to get out.

"Stay put," Ben said. "I'll do it for you. I had a car just like this one when I first started driving. I know where the gas tank is."

Nevertheless, the man swung the door open and started trying to undo his lap belt. It took only a few seconds for Ben to replace the gas cap. "There, that's got it," he said, coming back to the driver's door. "You're all set to go."

By now the man had one foot partway out of the car but still had his seat belt fastened. He looked up at Ben nervously and touched a hand to his hat. "Obliged," he said. Then he set about slowly shifting himself back into position.

It was at that very moment that Ben recognized him. He hadn't seen him in over twenty years, but he knew the face. And the last name—Hopkins. He was sure that was it. He had lived in the house directly behind Ben and Chloe's in Derby, their backyards adjoining. A reclusive man living with a grown son who was retarded. Ben remembered how upset the man had been about Chloe's murder, how he had broken down and cried when he came to the door late that night after it happened.

Ben's own gas pump had stopped by now, so he turned back to his car as the old man drove off. "Right here in our own neighborhood"—that's what Hopkins had said over and over that Friday night twenty-one years ago, sobbing as if it were his own wife who had been killed. And, "She was such a beautiful girl!" Ben had forgotten so much of that night, but the picture of Percy Hopkins weeping at the door, supporting himself with one hand braced on the doorjamb and stopping for breath with every other word—he had never forgotten that.

Hopkins was the only neighbor who had the slightest bit of information to offer about what happened that afternoon. He told the police he'd seen a tall man in a red hooded sweatshirt walking through the Buckleys' backyard around three o'clock. But the clue had led to nothing. For several years afterward, Ben had followed the investigation closely, had criticized those in charge of it, had made a nuisance of himself whenever he was in town, but gradually he felt the slow dying of hope. Old clues led nowhere, and there were no new ones.

One night on a business trip somewhere, he dreamed he killed a man in a red hooded sweatshirt with his bare hands—strangled him—and he woke up in the middle of the night with his heart pounding. For some reason, he found himself letting go after that, giving up, latching on to the dream as a sign that the killer was dead now.

A car honked and Ben looked up to see a Jeep sitting behind his car. A man leaned out and yelled, "Hey, you done?" Ben quickly replaced his gas cap, then got back into his car and started the engine. He pulled out of the service station slowly and turned toward Flat Rock.

Kelly sat down on a little stone bench in Shepherd's Valley Cemetery. This was the first time she had come here by herself. She had come once with her sisters just days after the funeral, to put an arrangement of silk orchids in the vase at the head of the grave, and once again with her father to see the headstone after it was in place. "A Woman of Virtue" was the simple inscription under her mother's name. That was an understatement.

This was the first Saturday Kelly hadn't had to work in weeks. She had a whole list of things to do at home, but she needed to do this first. She couldn't explain why, but it had been heavy on her mind for days now. The cemetery was quiet even though traffic moved steadily along Highway 11 in front of it. A white fence ran along one side, with a driveway leading up to a house. There were children's toys scattered around the front yard, but no one was in sight.

Kelly looked at the grave. It was hard to believe her mother's body was actually lying right there under the ground in a casket. It wasn't a very expensive casket, not as expensive as the one her grandmother had offered to pay for. But her father had politely refused, had told her grandmother he was paying for the one he knew Kay would want him to buy.

Kelly took a deep breath. Well, she needed to get this over with. Part of her knew it was a very silly thing to do, yet another part knew she wouldn't rest until she had done it. She glanced around at the little narrow road running through the cemetery. Her Taurus was the only car parked on it. She looked back at the grave.

"Well, okay, Mom, I can't stay long, but I need to talk," she said. "I need to confess some things and make a promise. I know you're not here, but I don't think God will mind if I pretend you are." A pair of small birds flew by, landed in a crape myrtle next to the road, and set up a warbling contest. Kelly listened a moment. "Do you hear that?" she said. "They must be singing for you." Her mother had always loved birds.

She stood and walked up next to the grave. Kneeling down, she rearranged the silk flowers a little. There, she could talk better now that she was closer. "I've been having some doubts about God since he took you away from us," she said. Saying the words aloud made her feel even worse, but she knew she had to do it.

She knew she didn't need to go into a lot of detail. God already knew all of this. "And I haven't let my light shine at work the way you prayed I would," she said. "I've been too afraid of speaking up and have kept to myself a lot. But God has spoken to me about that, and I'm going to try to do better from now on."

A van pulled into the long gravel driveway leading up to the house, and Kelly looked up. She saw children's heads bobbing around inside. She watched it all the way to the carport, where the doors slid open and three children tumbled out. Laughing and shrieking, they raced for the toys in the front yard. Their mother got out of the van and carried some bags of groceries into the house.

"And I read one of those Christian novels you gave me, and I hated it," Kelly said suddenly. She knew the other confessions were worse, but somehow this one sounded horrible. "I mean, I hated the fact that everything came out so happy at the end, because it didn't seem real. The girl acted too perfect even when things went wrong, and then the man came along at just the right time and loved her at first sight, and at the end they overcame all their problems and got married . . . *of course*, they got married. Everybody gets married. The whole world gets married. Somebody ought to write a novel that doesn't turn out so—"

She stopped as she suddenly remembered something else very bad. A couple of weeks ago Pastor Shamblin had preached about the rapture of the Church from the book of Thessalonians and said everything pointed to the fact that it was imminent. They were always singing songs about Christ's return at Charity Bible Church, and she knew Christians were supposed to hope it would happen very soon, maybe today. But right then, at that moment, Kelly knew in her heart she wasn't one of them. She had dreams for this life that she wanted to see fulfilled before that happened.

A truck honked its horn on the road outside the cemetery, a long deep blast, followed by a higher beep-beep of a car.

"Well, anyway, I want you to know I've asked God to forgive me for all these things," Kelly said. "For being selfish about what I want and timid at work and for wondering if certain things in the Bible are really true when they're written as plain as day. And I'm making a promise to God that I'm going to believe. No matter what. I believe he loves me. I believe he's done what's good and right and he always will. I believe he wants to bless me even if . . . it means a different kind of life than the one in that novel. I believe he knows what's best for me and for our whole family."

She plucked at a few blades of grass, then stood up. She looked around at all the other graves around her mother's and thought of all the lives and histories represented here. There were probably a lot of sad stories behind these graves. But maybe some happy ones, too. She looked back at the inscription on her mother's headstone and sighed. She couldn't imagine ever being the virtuous woman her mother was, but she meant to try.

It was a pretty drive up old Highway 25, past Travelers Rest, Jones Gap, and Bald Rock. Ben took it at a leisurely pace. He was certainly in no hurry to get to Flat Rock. He thought of all the things Shelly had planned for the week to come: a golf day, a hiking day, a drive to the Grove Park Inn for dinner, a tour of the Biltmore House in Asheville, a visit to Carl Sandburg's house, on and on it went. There was also a performance of *Cinderella* at the Flat Rock Playhouse. Shelly seemed to assume that all the adults would be delighted to sit through a staged fairy tale for two hours.

None of it held the slightest appeal, but even if it did, it was a bad time to be going away, with the big sale getting ready to start and the move itself slated for late August, only a month away. Not that anyone at work seemed to object to his being gone. In fact, he had a feeling Caroline was glad he would be out of the office. She had seemed especially cheerful the past few days.

More than once Ben had considered calling Shelly and canceling, but one thing held him back. It wasn't the thought of his children's disappointment, for that was something he could suppress quite easily, having done so for many years. What difference would one more failure in the fatherhood department make? Instead, it was Kelly Kovatch's words that kept coming back to him. That's what he couldn't forget: "He tries to ask himself every day what my mother would want him to do." That's what she had said about her father, and it blew Ben away.

He drove along Highway 25 slowly, taking the curves with the exaggerated caution of someone in no hurry to get where he was going. There were two cars behind him, but he wasn't going to let himself be pressured. He thought of Kelly's words again and felt a prick of shame that asking himself such a thing had never occurred to him in all the years since Chloe's death. A question suddenly presented itself to him: What would Chloe think of the man he had become? He knew the answer to that: not much.

He thought he heard a rumble of thunder, but the trees were so thick he couldn't see the sky. A fine mist began to coat the windshield even though shafts of sunlight fell across the road. Ben passed a pickup truck parked beside a little bridge. A man and boy were taking fishing poles and buckets out of the back. Ben thought of all the boys who had to grow up without a father's attention. Like himself, for instance. No fishing, no hunting, no playing catch in the backyard. His father had had an excuse, though, since he'd been sick for most of Ben's childhood.

Up until recently Ben had thought his own excuse for being a poor father was at least understandable. He'd been sick, too, in a different way. In a harder way. Not that he had publicly wallowed in his misery. That was one thing he could be proud of. He liked to think that most people who met him for the first time would never guess he had endured a tragedy. He wasn't a whiner or a martyr. He had always kept his troubles to himself.

He remembered a book he'd browsed through at the library about military discipline in the American armed forces. During World War II, platoon leaders used to give chronic complainers a card that read, "Your trials and tribulations have broken my heart. They are unique. I have never heard anything like them before. As proof of my deepest sympathy, I give you this card which entitles you to one hour of condolence from the nearest chaplain."

No complainer's card for me, Ben thought. He doubted that anyone at work, unless it might be Caroline, knew what he had been through. Somehow Caroline had a way of finding out everybody's most personal business. She had told him just yesterday, for instance, that Byron and Deb, his brand-new wife, had come home from their honeymoon to Acapulco on the outs with each other.

The road started climbing steeply, and the mist changed to sprinkles, though the sun was still shining. Ben turned on his windshield wipers.

Caroline very well could have gotten her hands on a copy of the Derby newspaper article last year that told about Chloe's murder. At least the article hadn't included all that happened afterward—the investigation of Ben himself as the prime suspect until a few people in Charleston had given him an indisputable alibi. One of them, a waitress at a sandwich and pizza place, had stated under oath in a courtroom hearing that she had served Ben lunch sometime between noon and twelve-thirty on the day of the murder, and the receipt Ben had absent-mindedly stuck in his shirt pocket for reimbursement verified it.

The waitress's middle-aged face came to his mind now—a woman as unlovely as a cracked sidewalk. Ragged gray hair, leathery skin, one eye that looked at you and the other that didn't. But who cared what she looked like? She had helped to save his good name.

She had identified him confidently. "I never forget a face," she said, " 'specially a spandy man like him." Those were the woman's exact words in the courtroom. When asked to explain *spandy*, she'd said, "You know, uptown and nice, like a gentleman." It was a word Ben had never heard before or since. It wasn't in his *Say It Ain't So, Joe* book or in any other dictionary he'd ever seen.

After the waitress finished her testimony, however, the possibility of Ben's hiring someone else to do the dirty work while he spent the day in Charleston had to be considered in some detail. The insurance policy on Chloe's life, taken out only months before and naming him as the sole beneficiary, was the thing that seemed to stick in everybody's craw—the policy Chloe had kept pestering him about after her boss at the Humane

Society had told the staff about a man at another animal shelter somewhere in the state who got kicked in the head by a horse and nearly died.

Chloe wouldn't drop the subject of insurance after that. She had finally made an appointment with an insurance man by herself and had a policy written up, with the premium taken out of her own checking account every month. And then, within two months she was dead. Thankfully, the insurance agent vouched for the fact that Chloe had been the one to contact him and set it all up.

Chloe's mother hadn't been on his side. He could still hear her words at the hearing, speaking of the weeks before the murder: "Chloe said Ben had clammed up and was acting very angry and unlike himself most of the time." Well, Mrs. Quantrille would probably clam up, too, if her husband turned religious on her all of a sudden.

At least Chloe's father had defended him. Somewhere Jim Quantrille's words were written in an official court record: "I don't believe Ben had any part in Chloe's death. I know him, and I know he loved her. He thought she hung the moon. No, I don't think he's capable of anything like that." And Chloe's brother, Dylan—he had agreed with his father.

He had lost touch with the Quantrilles after that, though they had continued to send Christmas and birthday gifts to the children. None of them had been much impressed with Ben as the years went by, however. They had made it known that they thought he was a poor excuse for a father. Both of the Quantrilles had died several years ago, and Dylan had moved overseas.

The road was steeper now. Ben looked off to the side and caught a glimpse of water far below him, just a brief glimmer beyond the trees. That must be the reservoir. He came to a small lookout point and pulled off the road. He got out of the car and stood looking down into the dense growth of trees. Past the fluttering of silver leaves he could see glints of the clear shining water. The silence was broken by the light patter of raindrops and the low rumble of thunder in the distance.

He looked up through the canopy of trees. How strange that he could still see patches of blue sunlit sky. A large bird wheeled and floated high overhead. He looked back toward the water, glittering like a sort of paradise beyond the wilderness. A scene from Chloe's Bible suddenly rose in his mind: An old man standing on a mountaintop looking out over the land of Canaan. After forty years of leading the people through the wilderness, all Moses got as a reward was a glimpse of the Promised Land. Not a very good payoff.

Ben stood there a long time, filled with dread for all the years ahead. And more immediately, for the days ahead. All of his children gathered in one place. And his grandchildren—how many were there now? Six, no, seven. All of those people he had failed so utterly. He couldn't believe he had agreed to do this. How could he possibly look any of them in the eye?

Though the prospect for the upcoming week was anything but joyful, it came to him that Chloe would surely be pleased to know he was on his way to a family vacation. She had always been big on family vacations when the children were small, especially camping trips. "I feel so alive out here!" That's what she always said when they were in the woods somewhere putting up tents. She had liked camping a lot more than he had. Being inconvenienced out in the middle of nowhere had never made him feel more alive, but he did it for her.

He turned back to the car and saw himself in the window glass. When had he gotten so slump-shouldered and slack, so spongy-looking? If that waitress in Charleston were to see him right now, *spandy* would be the last word to come to her mind.

FIFTEEN

One Long, Long Week

Erin was the first one to see their father's car pull up. She was standing by herself on the verandah of the house they were renting, holding a glass of iced tea, gazing out at the lake. The others were inside. She heard the crunch of tires on gravel and turned to see her grandmother's white Lincoln Town Car rounding the curve in the narrow road. She took a deep breath and looked away. Too bad her grandmother wasn't the one driving it.

When she glanced back, her father had stopped the car but hadn't gotten out. He was leaning forward over the steering wheel, head cocked, as if looking up at the sky. Maybe he was hoping it would fall on him. Erin knew that feeling. More likely he was wondering how the stock market was doing or naming the kinds of clouds he saw. She turned and went inside. She heard the others talking in the kitchen as she headed upstairs.

She and Reuben had the smallest bedroom at the top of the landing on the second floor. She walked inside and closed the door. She set her glass down on the nightstand and walked to the window above the verandah, overlooking the front yard. She could see through the ivory sheers to the circular driveway. Her father, still sitting in the car, was looking up at the house now. Erin stepped to the side so he couldn't see her.

The bedroom door opened. "Hey there." Reuben came in and closed the door. He walked up behind her and touched her shoulder. "I thought I heard you come upstairs. You okay, babe? What's up?"

She reached up and laid her hand briefly over his, then pushed it away gently. "I'm fine," she said, turning and walking into the bathroom. "I wish you'd quit saying 'What's up?' all the time."

She turned on the water at the sink. "And I don't want you hovering around me all week." She closed the door.

"Okay, I'll ignore you all week." Reuben was standing right next to the bathroom door, speaking into the crack. "I'll pretend we don't even know each other. I can hang out with the kids and call you Mrs. Custer. Except at night—could I sneak upstairs and sleep with you? Or would that qualify as hovering?"

Erin turned off the water and opened the door.

Reuben didn't miss a beat. "Or would you rather I sleep in the car, Mrs. Custer? I could take a couple of blankets and a pillow and—"

"Stop it," she said. "You're acting like a bozo—again." She walked to the bed and flopped down on her back, throwing an arm across her face. "It's so cotton-pickin' bright in this room. It's going to be impossible to get any sleep in here."

"Oh, maybe not," Reuben said. "The window faces west, so we won't get the full sun in the morning. And there's also a shade we can pull down. Did you see that?"

"Thanks. You've filled me with optimism."

She heard voices in the front yard.

Reuben moved to the window. "Ah-ha, the patriarch has arrived. Now Shelly can really get things cranked up."

Erin groaned softly. Her head was throbbing from all the talking and laughing downstairs, all the kids running in and out. Now her father was here. Two bad things stretched out before her: the week-long family frolic and the huge dark cloud of her father's presence. Either one by itself would be awful. She couldn't figure out how she had let herself get roped into this. She tried to breathe slowly but felt like there was a wad of wool stuck in her throat. She wondered what a panic attack felt like.

Reuben came over and sat on the edge of the bed. He bounced his weight on the mattress. "This is kinda rinky-dink, isn't it? Or maybe I should say cozy. We haven't slept in a double bed in ages."

"Like never, Reuben. You know that."

Reuben made a throaty, wolflike sound. "The better to snuggle with you, my dear."

"Oh, please." She rolled over on her side, away from him. She thought of their king-sized bed at home that took up half the bedroom. And the curtains were heavy, with a black-out lining. She would give anything to be curled up in her own bed right now with the curtains drawn, alone.

"Brittany's mother is a piece of work, isn't she?" Reuben said. "She could be a character in a book. Even her name—Vera Bridgewater. Sounds quirky and quaint and New Englandish, huh? And wet." He gave a goofy laugh. "And sturdy."

Erin didn't respond. Brittany's mother was the least of her worries right now. This whole family was a piece of work. What difference did one more nut case matter?

"The dark part of our brains is where the most useful learning takes place," Reuben said. "The part that lets us travel through time." He was talking in a funny voice, clipping his words.

Erin opened her eyes and looked up at the ceiling fan twirling lazily. "Okay, whatever that's supposed to mean." She sat up and reached over to the nightstand for her glass of tea.

Reuben was waving one hand back and forth as he talked, as if sweeping cobwebs out of the way. "It allows us to imagine consequences without having to endure them. That's why you don't need to try using cement as a facial treatment to know what a bad idea it is."

Erin took a long drink, then sighed. "I don't have the foggiest idea what you're talking about."

"Didn't you hear her? That's what Brittany's mom was saying downstairs while we were eating lunch. Joey asked her a question about her book." He leaned over and blew lightly into Erin's ear. "Why do you keep these things from me, babe? You never told me you had a sister-in-law whose mother was a counselor and a psychology professor. And a published author to boot."

Erin shrugged him away. "I hardly know my sister-in-law, much less her mother. I didn't even know she was coming. Besides, she's not a psychology professor anymore. She gave it up or got fired or something."

"She resigned two years ago. After her husband

died. Shelly explained it to all of us when *Vera Bridgewater* went outside to get something from the car." He spoke the name slowly, exaggerating each syllable. "Where *were* you? Weren't you sitting right next to me at the table? Maybe you were lost in the dark part of your brain." He gave a sudden bark of laughter. "I just thought of something. Brittany's name before she married Grant was Brittany Bridgewater. And now it's Brittany Bridgewater Buckley."

"Yep, that's the way it works," Erin said. She lifted her glass again and sucked in a piece of ice. "I sure hope Shelly doesn't have anything in mind."

"Like what?"

"It just seems odd to me that she's worked so hard to get us all here—and now Brittany's mother, who happens to write books about psychology, shows up. I hope Shelly didn't get her here to lead some big family counseling session."

"Nah, Vera Bridgewater wasn't Shelly's idea. She said Grant asked if they could bring her. She's been depressed. Guess you didn't hear that part, either."

"Well . . . still. I hope nobody's planning any round-table discussions." Erin chomped down on the piece of ice and chewed it quickly.

"Funny, though, she didn't seem depressed to me," Reuben said. "She was talking plenty. And the table's a rectangle, by the way."

Erin started on another piece of ice.

"But to be fair," Reuben said, "it's not like she was tooting her own horn or anything. She was just answering questions about her book. Pretty interesting stuff." He adopted his Yankee accent again: " 'The human mind is unparalleled for the disproportionate amount of time it spends in the past and future as opposed to the present moment.' " He laughed. "You have to wonder how they know that, though. I mean, who's to say a mouse doesn't spend most of his time dreaming of that last big wedge of cheese he ate or planning how to get the next one?"

Erin looked down at the remaining ice, little melting crescents in the bottom of her glass. She shook the glass so that they spun around in a tight circle. She wondered if Vera Bridgewater's book had any suggestions for how to go about skipping the present moment. She'd give anything to zip past these next six days to the future.

"Yeah, well," she said, sighing, "who really knows anything about anything?"

"You shouldn't do that," Reuben said.

"What?" Erin turned on him, glaring.

"Chew ice. It's bad for your teeth." Reuben stood up from the bed, fished his ChapStick out of his jeans pocket, and applied some to his lips. "I'm going back down. You coming?" He held out his hand. "Come on, I'll help you get past the first part. You know me—I can always think of something to say."

"Yeah, if only any of it made sense."

He adopted an offended expression. "Come on." He wiggled his fingers at her.

"In a minute," Erin said. "You go on." He started to say something, but she shook her head. "I said go." She turned her head away and closed her eyes. She heard him walk to the door and leave. She set her glass back down on the dresser and lay back on the bed again.

The voices weren't coming from the front of the house anymore, so they must have moved inside. She would wait till all the hellos and hugs were over. She knew she couldn't avoid her father all week, but she could put it off a little longer.

At half past seven, supper was just getting into full swing. It was later than he usually ate, but Ben had a feeling meals might not run on a strict schedule this week, that is, not timewise. Each of the four children had been assigned a night for kitchen duty, and they were eating out the other two nights. Shelly had announced the schedule shortly after he arrived, when they were all gathered in the living room. She was taking tonight. "Since the first night is always the hardest," she'd said.

She had made six large pizzas. Made them, not ordered them. Ben couldn't remember ever having homemade pizza before. She had set the table very properly in red, white, and blue, with large paper napkins folded into little hat-shaped affairs and set in the middle of each plate.

The table was big enough for all ten adults, and the six children were seated within sight, all of them cross-legged on the floor around the big square coffee table in the living room. Grant's two girls were wearing the little napkin hats on their heads. Lydia's baby was asleep in a bedroom somewhere.

Ben concentrated on eating his pizza slowly. There was tossed salad, too. He didn't want to get done too soon. In all of his dreadful scenarios of the week, for some reason he had never thought about having to sit with everybody at one table. He wished he were back home eating his normal Saturday night dinner at the K&W Cafeteria in Greenville, at a table by himself. If he went early enough, he could be in and out in twenty minutes.

This was a long table, and he was sitting at one end, with Shelly and Grant on either side of him. Shelly's husband was at the opposite end, flanked by Lydia and Erin. Shelly had mixed all the couples up, marking the places with hand-printed name cards. No doubt she had given a lot of thought to where to seat them all. She had probably drawn up a diagram first. Filling in along the sides were Erin's husband, Lydia's husband, Grant's wife, and Brittany's mother. Ben reviewed all the names, glancing around the table casually as he did so.

From where he was sitting, he could see his grandchildren in the living room, also, so he went through their names, too. Shelly's three had the yuppie names: Hunter, Quentin, and Mackenzie. Mackenzie was a girl. Grant's two were girls with old-fashioned names: Adelaide and Lavinia. And Lydia had a boy, Isaac, and the baby, Evanna.

He had everybody straight now. He ran through the names of his children's spouses once more for good measure: Mark, Reuben, Joey, Brittany. And then, of course, there was Vera Bridgewater. Vera from Vermont. He coughed suddenly and put his napkin to his mouth.

Shelly picked up his glass of Coke and handed it to him. "Here, something caught? You need a drink? The pizza's not too spicy for you, is it?"

He shook his head but took a drink nevertheless. "No, it's good, very good."

Shelly looked pleased. "Well, I try!" she said. But it was obvious that she felt she did a lot more than just try. She had made three different kinds of pizza, two of each kind, and was particularly pleased with the crust. She had already gone into some detail at the table about the five or six different crust recipes she had experimented with, finally concluding with "but this one is superior *by far!*" She went on to talk about the more expensive Boar's Head pepperoni she always used now because, as she put it, "I tried it once and was absolutely spoiled for life! It costs more, but like I always say, you get what you pay for!" She pointed out the dried cranberries and toasted almonds in the tossed salad as if no one could see them for themselves, then held up a tall wooden pepper grinder. "Anybody who wants it can have fresh-ground pepper on your salad."

From the other end of the table, Mark said, "Hey, Shel, did you tell them about the baking contest?" Mark was cut out of the same cloth as Shelly. They seemed to feed off each other, eager to share every speck of information about their successes. Ben wondered if their batteries ever ran down. He saw Erin and Reuben exchange looks across the table.

Shelly adopted a humble expression but launched into a detailed account of the baking contest, a citywide affair among all the Baptist churches in Raleigh, North Carolina, where they lived, a contest in which she had won second place—a fifty-dollar gift certificate. "I didn't care about the prize," she said breezily. "In fact, I think we gave it away, didn't we, Mark?" Mark confirmed this to be so, and as Shelly looked admiringly at the piece of pizza she was holding, she added, "The woman who won first place was related to one of the judges, we found out later."

Vera Bridgewater emitted what sounded like the beginning of a laugh—a single, breathy "Ha!" but broke it off abruptly and asked Grant to pass the pepper grinder.

"What was the first prize?" Brittany asked.

"Oh, I don't even remember," Shelly said. "It didn't matter one bit to me whether I *won* or not."

No one responded to this, but Shelly's daughter, Mackenzie, piped up from the living room: "It was a carrot cake, and they put her recipe in a magazine! That's what she made for dessert tonight."

Shelly shook her finger at Mackenzie but was smiling. "Oh, Kenzie, now you didn't need to go and tell *that*. I was going to surprise everybody." To everybody else she added, "Carrot cake is one of those that gets better the longer it sits, you know."

If he could say anything at all to his oldest daughter right now, Ben knew what it would be: "Shh, be quiet. Be very quiet." He wondered if before the week was over somebody might say it in stronger words.

Shelly got up and left the table, then came back out with one of the ham and mushroom pizzas, explaining as she circulated around the table that this was the kind Mark's boss really liked.

"He couldn't believe she'd made it from scratch," Mark said. "It was right after he came over for lunch that I got my promotion, so I told Shel it must've been her pizza that did it." Mark had already told them all about his new job with a software company, which involved a "*very* decent raise." He had winked at Shelly after he said it.

Lydia's little boy, Isaac, suddenly appeared at the table, holding a slice of soggy pizza crust from which he had scraped off all the toppings. He had tomato sauce all around his mouth and on his chin. "Mama, I want mustard," he said.

"Mustard?" Shelly said. "Did he say mustard? Whatever for?"

"Oh, he eats it on everything," Lydia said. She wiped at his mouth with her napkin. "Come on, sweetie, there's some in the fridge. We'll spread it on your crust then cut it in half." She headed toward the kitchen, Isaac following.

"Did you hear that?" Reuben said. "She's going to cut the mustard."

There was laughter.

Brittany leaned forward to look at Erin. "Does he do this a lot?"

Erin nodded. "Yeah, he suffers from the delusion that he's funny."

"Hey, you laughed at one of my jokes one time. You know you did," Reuben said, pointing across the table at Erin.

Ben studied Erin a moment. He knew he was safe in doing so. She wouldn't catch him looking at her because she hadn't so much as glanced in his direction since she came downstairs. She was thinner than he remembered, certainly thinner than either of her sisters. Her hair was light brown, pulled back in a low ponytail at her neck. Attractive in a wholesome, understated way but not as pretty as Lydia. You'd never know the two of them were twins.

"I wonder where that came from anyway," Reuben said.

"Where *what* came from?" Shelly said, sliding a piece of pizza onto his plate. "You mean this recipe?" She wore the smile of someone ready to share her secrets.

Reuben shook his head. "Cut the mustard—I wonder where that saying came from."

Mark offered the suggestion that it might have something to do with passing muster in the military sense. "Maybe the two words got mixed up somehow," he said.

"Do you know?" Reuben was looking directly at Ben. "Didn't I hear that you know a little bit about a lot of things—or is it a lot about a few things? Or maybe a lot about everything?"

"Well . . . no, not really." Ben put his fork down. "But I did read about that phrase. There are several different theories actually." Everyone was looking at him—everyone except Erin, whose eyes were fixed on her plate. "The word *mustard* was used by cowboys in the late 1800s," Ben said. "It meant the real thing, something especially good. And then it also showed up in—"

Suddenly the thin wail of a baby could be heard, and Ben stopped. Joey got up quickly and headed for the stairs. "I'll get her," he said.

"Is anybody ready for seconds on the pepperoni?" Shelly said. "There's plenty more!"

She headed back to the kitchen just as Lydia and

Isaac reappeared, Isaac happily carrying a small triangle of pizza spread with mustard while Lydia followed with the other half. "Did I hear Evanna?" she said.

"Joey's getting her," Brittany said. "You've got him well trained."

"Lavinia spilled Coke," Mackenzie called from the living room, and Vera Bridgewater jumped up and ran to the kitchen to get paper towels.

"Lavinia is not supposed to be drinking Coke," Brittany said. "Adelaide, what are you drinking? Do you have Coke, too?"

"Oh, I just gave them a taste," Vera called from the kitchen. "Let them live a little, Britt. They're on vacation." Brittany looked at Grant and sighed.

Well, so much for cutting the mustard, Ben thought. No one seemed the least bit interested in the rest of his explanation. But it didn't matter to him. He wasn't much interested in it himself. It didn't make a very good story; in fact, according to all that he had read, the bottom line was that no one really knew how the expression had gotten started. Like so much else in life, it boiled down to "Who knows?" That, and "Who cares?"

Ben picked up his fork again and speared several dried cranberries from his salad. He felt his ears filling up with the talk around him, and he drifted away. This was going to be one long, long week. But one good thing about it—with this many people, anything he would be called on to say would probably be interrupted. He could survive by coasting along.

The next time he looked up from his plate, Lydia was standing at the other end of the table, holding the baby, who looked stunned by the sight of so many people. Her eyes and mouth were three little round O's. Lydia was going around the table, naming everyone, as if Evanna were taking it all in. After every name Lydia lifted the baby's little hand and waved it.

She came to Ben. "And that's"—there was a slight break in her momentum—"that's your . . . granddaddy Buckley." She flapped Evanna's hand up and down, though the baby herself was now twisted around in Lydia's arms, looking over at the children's table, where Adelaide and Mackenzie were squabbling.

"Mustard is for sandwiches, not pizza," Mackenzie said sternly.

Apparently Adelaide didn't think much of the fact that her cousin was older and supposedly wiser. "Nuh-uh," she said, "mustard's for anything you want it to be for!"

Isaac, contentedly chewing his pizza, seemed oblivious to the quarrel.

"It's *not* for pizza," Mackenzie repeated.

"Oh, let's all be happy and get along," Shelly called out in a singsongy voice. She was back from the kitchen now with the pepperoni pizza.

Brittany lifted her eyes to the ceiling. Vera

Bridgewater, her lips pursed, gazed at Shelly impassively. Ben glanced around at the rest of the table. Joey was holding the bowl of salad in one hand, the salad tongs in the other, and Grant was lifting his plate for another piece of pizza. Mark was frowning worriedly over at the children's table, and Erin was staring straight ahead, pulling at one earlobe, her jaw set hard. Reuben was chewing pensively, his head down.

For some reason Ben was reminded of all those feasts described in that strange book of Leviticus in Chloe's Bible—all the altars and fires, the wave offerings and the lambs without blemish, all that bloodletting. Phrases swirled about inside his head: *Eat unleavened bread therewith, even the bread of affliction.* And *Thou wast a bondman in Egypt.* And *On the seventh day shall be a solemn assembly.*

It was a curious thing that he hadn't read Chloe's Bible for years now, but the only things he remembered were the gloomy parts.

SIXTEEN

Millions of Tiny Pieces

Caroline was looking through the miscellaneous piles on Ben's desk for a certain piece of paper. It was a handwritten estimate for the renovations to the restrooms at the furniture store they were moving into within a couple of months. Dustin, the new financial manager Ben had hired a few weeks ago, was asking for the original hard copy so he could "hold their feet to the fire," as he put it— "their" referring to the contracting firm, which was trying to jack up the cost now that the work was underway.

It embarrassed Caroline a little that Dustin was having to ask for the estimate. It was supposed to have been in the folder, which she should have checked before giving to him. She knew how bad Ben was to take something out of its place and then set it down somewhere else. Though the folder was an antiquated concept, Ben insisted on having all the moving costs in paper form. He didn't want to rely on the computer. "If the computer crashes, then what do we do?" he was fond of saying. If she could have a dime for every time she had heard him say that, she could buy a whole new wardrobe. "Here's the best computer right up here," he often said, tapping his head with an index finger.

Maybe now that Dustin had been hired, they could update things a little more around here. Maybe Ben would listen to a man, especially one like Dustin, who didn't seem to be out to impress anybody. He was a low-key sort of guy, not at all what you'd expect of a financial manager. Forties, married, nothing to look at but nice. He had told Ben the folder was an excellent idea, said it was always important to have original paperwork and printouts for backup records.

Of course, original paperwork was good only if you could keep track of it. Caroline heaved a sigh, stood up to stretch, and then sat down again in Ben's swivel chair. His desktop was covered with stacks of papers. She had gone through all but two stacks and still hadn't found what she was looking for, although she had found a whole host of things that needed to be thrown into the trash. Like all the typed quotations and lists of trivia. She leaned forward and picked up another one of them. *ARISTOTLE* was typed across the top of the paper. Caroline had only a vague idea of who Aristotle was. Some old guy in a toga who had lived eons ago on the other side of the world. The first quotation on the sheet was *The greatest crimes are caused by surfeit, not by want. Men do not become tyrants in order that they may not suffer cold.*

She read it again. All the *not*s were confusing, like those trick questions she used to hate on true-false tests in school. Besides that, she wasn't sure what *surfeit* meant. She read the quotation once more, but it didn't make any more sense than it had the first time. She put the paper down and glanced at her watch. Twenty minutes—that's how long she'd been wading through all this miscellany looking for the one thing on this whole desktop that somebody actually needed. Mr. Buck had no idea how maddening it was to work for somebody like him.

It was almost time to go home, but she didn't feel

the need to rush today. It was funny how calm and unstressed she'd felt the last couple of days without Mr. Buck around. She could get so much more done when he wasn't always looking over her shoulder or thinking up little extra jobs for her to do. Earlier this afternoon she had even had time to check a few Web sites for possible places to take her annual beach trip in August.

She was planning to ask Donald if he wanted to go with her for part of the time, even though she knew they would probably be ready to shoot each other before it was over. She imagined a headline in the newspaper: *MOTHER AND SON FOUND DEAD IN BEACH CONDO*. Still, it would be nice to have somebody to share a dinner table with every night instead of eating alone, even if it was your grown son, who irritated the stew out of you. One thing Caroline didn't cut corners on during vacation was the evening meal, and Donald knew this. If she offered to pay for a two-bedroom place and all the meals, she was pretty sure he would at least consider going along.

And who knew what might happen? They might have a nice waitress one night who was unmarried and in her thirties and looking for a man with a steady job . . . but Caroline didn't want to get her hopes up too much. That had happened too many times already. If Donald turned down the vacation invitation, well, she had gone solo plenty of times before and could certainly do it again.

She kicked off her pink slip-on heels, then gave herself a little spin in Mr. Buck's chair. When the chair came to a stop, it was facing the old manual typewriter on the desk extension. That was something else she'd like to throw in the trash. Maybe during the upcoming move she could get it out to the Dumpster behind the store, then tell Mr. Buck it had somehow disappeared. She would never have the nerve to do that, though, not if she valued her job, which she did. Mr. Buck overlooked a lot, but the littlest thing could set him off.

She still remembered the time one of the floor-walkers, a skinny boy with a crest of hair that made him look like a roadrunner, had tried to sneak a smoke in the bathroom. Mr. Buck had brought him back to his office and in a perfectly calm voice had said to him, "You can stay home and smoke all day long tomorrow. And the day after that and the day after that. In fact, you don't need to bother coming back to work here at the Bazaar ever again. We'll figure up your pay and mail your final check. Please clear your things out of the break room before you go." No warning, no second chances, no sympathy.

She couldn't help wondering how things were going for Ben in North Carolina right now. What she'd give to be a fly on the wall wherever he was, to study his children and grandchildren, to see what they were all doing. She wondered if Ben had taken some casual clothes along or if he was wearing his same old limp dress shirts and boring neckties. She wondered if he even knew how to relax. To her knowledge, this was the first time he'd gone on a vacation with his family since . . . well, for sure since she had started working here four years ago, but maybe even since his wife died. There was no way to know such a thing when Mr. Buck was so closemouthed about his personal life.

She'd finally badgered him into telling her that he'd be in Flat Rock, North Carolina, and he had given her one of his daughters' cell phone numbers, the one named Shelly, with stern instructions not to call unless it was "a true emergency." As if she'd call him just to chat. Of course, he didn't have a cell phone of his own. "I don't want to be controlled by electronic devices, Caroline." That's what he always said. He had a telephone at home and one on his desk at work, so why did he need one clipped to his belt? That was his way of looking at it.

She turned back to face the desk and reached for one of the remaining stacks of papers. She pulled it onto her lap and started going through it. More typed lists. One said, *DYING WORDS OF FAMOUS PEOPLE* at the top. Caroline read only the first five.

George Bernard Shaw, 94: "You're trying to keep me alive as an old curiosity, but I'm done, I'm finished, I'm going to die." (Good for him!) Died November 2, 1950.

Oscar Wilde, 46: "One of us had to go."
(Referring to himself and the ugly wallpaper in his
hotel room.) Died November 30, 1900.

Joel Chandler Harris, 59: "I am the extent of a
tenth of a gnat's eyebrow better." (Must not have
been, for he proceeded to die within minutes.) Died
July 3, 1908.

Johann Wolfgang von Goethe, 82: "More light!"
(Was he complaining that there wasn't enough or
perhaps exclaiming over a heavenly vision?) Died
March 22, 1832.

Washington Irving, 76: "When will this end?"
(Vague pronoun reference) Died November 28,
1859.

At the bottom of the page, he had carefully cred-
ited the source of his information: *Through the*
Year With Books and Writers, ed. Gregory P. Jacks,
Fort and Hudson Publishers, 1997 copyright, notes
in parentheses mine.

How like him. As if anybody cared who wrote
the part in parentheses. As if anybody cared about
the words of dying men for that matter. If he
wasn't so aggravating, Mr. Buck would be funny
with all his impracticalities and his little old-
mannish ways of doing things. She had often
wondered if he would be more normal if his wife
hadn't died so young. Maybe she would have kept
him from developing such strange habits.

Caroline quickly leafed through other papers:
pages torn from magazines, a computer printout of

stock information, the sports page from a news-paper, instruction manuals for a copier and a paper shredder, old employee applications. Across the top of one of these, submitted by someone named Lurlene Heffernan, he had printed neatly, "Not on your life! BB" That was one of Mr. Buck's wiser decisions, though. Caroline remembered that woman. She wore heavy perfume and brayed like a donkey when she laughed.

She came across a handwritten sheet, at the top of which Mr. Buck had printed *NAZAR'S MIS-QUOTES*. She assumed Nazar was Nazar Begian, one of the vendors, who had lived in all sorts of different countries before coming to South Carolina. Mr. Buck was always chuckling over things the man said. She could understand laughing over them, but writing them down on paper—well, she didn't see any point in that. She read the first few: *I will turn all stones to find a better price! He jumped into the frying pan and fire. She has a joint in her nose.* She wondered if anybody else in the world made lists of funny mis-takes foreigners made.

She came to the bottom of the stack without finding the estimate for the restroom renovations. Okay, one more stack to go. There were two books mixed in with this one. She slipped them out to set them aside. *How to Survive the Unexpected* was the title of one, by somebody named Clifford Farmer. A collage of photos cluttered the front jacket—trees ripped out of the ground, a car submerged in water, a raging fire, a grizzly bear reared up in attack mode, a closeup of an alligator's open jaws.

She flipped through it. Every page had its own title, along with an illustration of the catastrophe and numbered instructions for how to survive it. "How to Survive a Street Riot," "How to Escape from the Trunk of a Car," "How to Get out of Quicksand," "How to Detect a Rabid Animal," "How to Perform an Emergency Tracheotomy."

"Unbelievable," Caroline said right out loud. She stopped at a page with the heading "How to Survive a Shark Attack." She had no doubt that Mr. Buck had read the whole book and could repeat every step on every page. If she were to ask him how to fend off an attacking shark, she could just hear him: "Use your fist to make sharp jabs at the shark's eyes or gills. These are the most sensitive areas. Persist in fighting. A shark will not continue an attack if it doesn't think it has an advantage."

She slapped the book closed. Too bad the author hadn't included some things that the average person might really have to face, like how to survive working for a cuckoo boss or how to get your grown son to show you some respect.

She put the book down and picked up the other one: *Through the Year With Books and Writers.* She recognized it at once as the source of the deathbed quotations. She leafed through the pages.

Lots of pictures of writers, lots of names she'd never heard. She stared for several long moments at one identified as "the celebrated George Sand." A woman! She looked like an old poodle with that headful of curly black hair. Miguel de Cervantes had a little squirrel face, and Henrik Ibsen reminded her of a bobcat.

She closed the book and set it down on top of the other one, shaking her head. What must it be like to be so rich you could pay other people to do all your work while you spent your days poring over books like these? Now that he had hired Dustin to take over all the finances, Mr. Buck would have absolutely nothing to do. All his little typed lists would start spilling off his desk onto the floor. Slowly they would fill up his office. She would have to use a broom to clear a path whenever she came in here.

She began going through the last stack of papers. Just as she was starting to worry about how to tell Dustin the estimate was missing, she finally ran across it, between a ragged piece of sheet music and a magazine article about the Holocaust. She might have known it would be in the last stack she checked, near the bottom of the stack no less. Wasn't that the way it always worked?

She slipped her shoes back on and stood up. She was ready to get out of here now and get home. She would take the estimate by Dustin's office first. She set the rest of the papers down on the desktop with all the others. Just before she left, her eye caught the letter opener on Mr. Buck's desk, its blade tucked under the ink blotter. She thought of one of her favorite movies, in which a woman had stabbed her attacker in the eye with a letter opener and had then sprayed him with hairspray and lit a match. Caroline remembered the thrill of triumph she had felt watching the attacker, a large hairy apelike man, grovel on the floor, pleading for the woman to put out the match.

She pulled the letter opener out from under the blotter and studied the picture of Mount Rushmore on its ivory handle, then ran her thumb along the dull edge of the blade. She stood there a moment, then grasped the handle and raised it aloft, like a weapon, as if ready to attack.

"Uh, excuse me, ma'am, is it safe to come in?" The voice was pleasant, teasing.

Caroline looked up to see one of the vendors, that odd Macon Mahoney, in the doorway. She put the letter opener down quickly. He sauntered partway into the office.

"I was just getting something we need from Mr. Buckley's desk," she said tersely, holding up the paper. She walked past him quickly and flipped off the light switch at the door. "I have to take this to somebody right away. Do you have a quick question?"

"Yes, where was Moses when the lights went out?"

"I beg your pardon?"

"Nothing. It's a line from a play."

Caroline lifted her chin and fixed him with a look by which she hoped to convey that she was far too busy to stand around listening to his nonsense. "Do you have a *real* question?" she said with fake politeness.

He walked toward her. "I was looking for our mutual friend Ben," he said. Very good-natured, very easygoing. He gave her a broad smile, his blue eyes twinkling as he looked down at her. "But I guess he's not in, huh? I had an idea about the move. Thought I'd run it by him."

"He's out of town," Caroline said.

Macon tilted his head and studied her a moment, his hands stuffed inside the back pockets of his jeans. "Wild hair and bright countenance," he said slowly, nodding meaningfully. "That's another quote." With that, he turned and ambled off through the door and out into the hallway, whistling.

Caroline put a hand to her hair, then touched her face. What in the world was he talking about? She didn't know whether to be flattered or insulted. Men were usually so simpleminded, with such predictable, short-term goals. She could usually read them like the Sunday comics. Every now and then, though, one would stump her. She walked over to the small framed mirror above the fern stand. She turned her head from side to side and plucked at her hair with one hand. Her hairdresser had gotten a little aggressive with the color last time. Was that what Macon Mahoney had meant about "wild hair"? Or was it the style? She moved in closer to the mirror. "Bright countenance"? Well, she had to say she was holding her own for somebody her age.

The other team was winning by a big margin in the Schooldays Trivia game. It was Tuesday afternoon, and this was the activity Shelly had planned for Family Fun at Hearthside Cottage while the younger children had their naps. Erin guessed it hadn't occurred to her sister that some of the adults might be interested in a nap, too. Not that she was sleepy, but anything would be better than this.

If such a stupid board game mattered in the least, it would be embarrassing to be losing so badly. Shelly had divided them into two teams of four while she and Mark were serving as question-reader and scorekeeper. Erin was on a team with Grant, Joey, and Vera Bridgewater, who had asked them all to call her by her first name. Vera, who was responsible for more than half of their team's points, was obviously very smart.

Still, they were hopelessly behind since the other team had an unfair advantage, namely her father, who was clearly the master of all things trivial. She was amazed at what he knew: the longest highway across the United States, the composition of gypsum, the founder of the Camp Fire Girls, and

Abraham Lincoln's shoe size. He had even taken issue with one question about the British holiday called Boxing Day, saying that it could also refer to the day when the poor were given money from the alms boxes. Such vastly important things, all of them.

Erin felt her temperature rising a little with every correct answer he gave. That he could know all this minutiae yet know, or care, nothing about the people in this room, his own flesh and blood—well, she felt like breaking something made of glass into millions of tiny pieces.

She was sitting on one end of the sofa in the living room, and her father was across the room from her, seated on a chair by the brick hearth. She didn't really want to look at him, but for some reason she couldn't resist. Just quick looks, though, when she thought no one would notice.

He had put on weight since the last time she had seen him, at her grandmother's funeral a couple of years ago. Probably no more than ten or fifteen pounds, but enough to make him look bulkier. His face was fuller and his hair shaggier—no sign of a receding hairline or thinning, though. Not even much gray. She supposed some women his age would find him attractive. In his Bermuda shorts and loafers, he looked like somebody who lived at a beach resort and spent his days golfing and sailing. She wondered if he ever went out with any women.

She heard Reuben clear his throat. She looked at him and saw that he was staring at her hands, frowning. She glanced down to find them tightened into fists, pressed hard against her stomach. Slowly she unclenched them and lifted her eyes to the picture over the fireplace above her father's head. It was a big framed impressionistic art print of a woman and child walking through a field of wildflowers toward a lake. The woman was wearing a red bonnet, and she was well ahead of the child. Erin wondered why the mother wouldn't wait for the child or pick him up and carry him.

She took several long, deep breaths and then closed her eyes briefly. Next to her on the sofa, Grant and Joey were laughing about something, but Erin had no idea what. She opened her eyes again and looked across the room at Reuben. *I'm fine,* she said to him with a lift of her eyebrows, *so quit staring at me.*

Shelly fixed Grant and Joey with a stern look and put a finger to her lips. Erin looked at her father again. He had his hands on his knees, his fingers clasped loosely. He gazed down at the floor as Shelly read the next question to his team: " 'Who was the only U.S. President to hold a Ph.D. degree?' " It was technically Lydia's turn to answer, but they were playing team rules, which meant you could confer with the others before answering. Lydia shrugged and looked at her father, who leaned over sideways and whispered something to her. Lydia turned to Shelly and said, "Woodrow Wilson?"

Shelly looked none too pleased at the right answer. "This is getting way too lopsided," she said. "Why don't we say the teams can't talk? Everybody has to take turns answering by himself." She turned to Mark for approval, and he nodded but looked around at everybody uncertainly.

"No fair changing the rules in the middle of the game," Brittany said. "I always stink at games like this, so it's kind of fun being on the winning side for a change."

"Hey, we don't mind getting creamed," Grant said to Shelly. "Anyway, how do you know we're not just letting them get a big lead before we come from behind? Don't spoil our fun."

"Yeah, we're lulling them into a sense of false confidence," Joey said. "We're giving wrong answers on purpose!" He raised a finger and said, "A polecat is another name for the . . . panther!" This was the last wrong answer their team had given, the right one being skunk. He and Grant gave each other high fives and laughed like junior high boys. There was nothing like a little group competition to bring out the juvenile side of men.

"But there's no way you're ever going to catch up if they keep answering right," Shelly said to Joey. "You don't have a chance!"

"Really, it's no big deal," Joey said, laughing.

"Well, let's just go on, Shel," Mark said. "Just ask the next question. It's almost over anyway. They get to keep answering till they miss one."

Shelly pinched her lips together and took out the next card. She read the words fast and a little louder than necessary: " 'Based on average yearly rainfall, which state in the U.S. is the driest, with less than eight inches a year?' " She crossed her arms and looked at Ben, whose turn it was. The expression on her face was not a happy one.

"Arizona," Ben said.

He was right, of course, and the next question ended the game: " 'A calf is born with how many stomachs—one, two, three, or four?' " He answered that one correctly, too. It was four. Shelly set about packing up the game quickly.

While Reuben was clapping her father on the back and thanking him for leading their team to victory, Erin got up and left the room. In her opinion there was no reason at all to thank a man who knew all about rainfall and presidents and cows' stomachs but had never learned how to be a father.

SEVENTEEN

Preference for Shadows

Ben stood up from his chair at the edge of the swimming pool and stretched. Though it was getting dark, his grandchildren were still playing in the water. Joey and Grant were in the pool with them while Mark and Reuben were sitting in chairs beside Ben, talking about politics. Right now they were debating why a woman hadn't yet succeeded in winning the nomination to run for president.

"Not cutting out on us, are you, Ben?" Reuben said.

Ben picked up a squishy ball and threw it back to Quentin and Hunter, who were playing catch in the deep end. "Yeah, I think I'll take a little walk and then head back to the house. I'm going to turn in early." He felt like the day had lasted forever, and he wanted to get away by himself for a while. He would take a quick shower—get a share of the hot water for a change before it ran out—then read a little in his room before turning out his light. He hoped nobody offered to go back to the house with him. There seemed to be an unspoken conspiracy this week that he was never to be left alone.

"But you can't," Mark said, looking alarmed. "We're going to have ice cream back at the house." Shelly had already announced this at least a dozen times during the day, telling them all that she and Mark had brought their electric churn from home and she was going to mix up a special ice cream recipe with crushed Snickers candy bars.

Ice cream or solitude—it wasn't a contest. Not at the end of the fifth long day of the family vacation. One more whole day to get through, and then he could pack up and leave on Friday. "Sorry," Ben said. "I guess I just can't keep up with the rest of you. I'll tell Shelly I'm wiped out. Maybe she won't draw and quarter me. Maybe she'll even save me some ice cream."

"Well . . . but we were going to play a game, too," Mark said.

Mackenzie had materialized at the edge of the pool, all eyes and ears. "Where is he going?" She addressed the question to her father.

"Your old grandpop is pooped," Ben said. "I'm going to bed early. You eat an extra bowl of ice cream for me, will you, Mackenzie?"

She studied him disapprovingly. "Does Mother know?"

"I'm off to the firing squad right now," Ben said. "Wish me luck." And with that he started off in the direction of the house. He had no intention of telling Shelly anything if he could avoid it. All the protests and questions—he'd rather stay up and eat the ice cream than face all that. He was hoping he could sneak inside and up the stairs without attracting anybody's attention.

Behind him, Reuben called out a good-night and then switched the subject from women in politics. "Well, I sure wish somebody would quit talking about a flat income tax and *do* something about it."

Thankfully, no one followed Ben. He knew it wouldn't matter to anybody but Shelly if he missed the ice cream party. Even Shelly most likely wouldn't mind that much deep down, except that it would make one fewer audience member to witness yet another display of her kitchen skills. Lydia and Grant might not even notice his absence, but Erin would no doubt be elated. If Erin ever got elated about anything.

Ben made his way down the gravel road in the dusk, heading toward the porch light. All around him fireflies blinked on and off. It was a mild night, with a light breeze sifting through the pines. The sound of the crickets was incredible—a huge chorus of tweety chirps that blended into one loud sustained warble. It sounded like the East Coast Cricket Convention was in progress. And to think—only male crickets sang. If these were just the males, he couldn't imagine the size of the entire cricket population around Flat Rock.

As he grew closer to the house, he heard voices and could see that the women were sitting on the front porch. It wasn't a chummy communal sound, though; it almost sounded like they were arguing. Through the tall bushes bordering the porch, Ben could see the movement of the porch swing, and he heard Vera Bridgewater's voice clearly above the rest. She had a husky voice for a woman. He remembered suddenly a humorous metaphor he had read somewhere: *Her voice was so husky it could pull a dogsled.* He wondered if Vera had ever smoked.

". . . and everything I used to say to people in counseling sessions and everything I wrote about dealing with grief flew right out the window when I lost Reggie," she was saying now. "Well, when Reggie *died*—I hate all the euphemisms we use for death. Anyway, none of it meant a thing when he died. So back to what you were saying, you can *know* something in your head but still not be able to . . ."

Ben left the road so he could circle the house and go in through the back door. If all five of them were on the porch, he was safe. If they were divided between the kitchen and the porch, he was sunk. Cutting through the grass, he drew closer to the house. In spite of all the singing crickets, the women's voices were quite easy to distinguish.

"Well, all I'm saying is that there's something wrong at the very core of a man who can ignore his own children for years and years and years." That was Erin. So she did have a voice after all. Hard-edged and sullen. It was the longest sentence Ben had heard her say all week. He stopped walking and stood absolutely still. There was no doubt in his mind which man she was talking about.

"He *worshiped* the ground she walked on, Erin! He couldn't think of anything else after she died! Why is that so hard for you to understand?" This was Shelly. Combative and sure of herself. "And Grandma—she was part of the whole equation," she continued. "She moved in and took over Mom's place, so—"

"She didn't take over Mom's place," Erin said. "She never did that. I don't see how you can say that."

"You know what I mean. She did all the housework and cooking and—"

"Mom's place was a lot bigger than housework and cooking."

Lydia broke in. "Come on, Erin, you know what she's saying. If Grandma hadn't been there, he would've *had* to get more involved at home. In a lot of ways, looking back on it, Grandma treated him like another child—like he couldn't take care of himself."

Lydia's voice was so much like Chloe's that it hurt. That same rise and dip, the half-amused tone, the way you wanted to keep hearing more, like a favorite melody. And her face, too—it was hard for Ben to look at Lydia for very long at a time. Except for her shorter hair, she looked like Chloe's twin. Close to Chloe's age when she died, in fact. Just yesterday he had passed the bedroom where Lydia was nursing Evanna. Glancing in, he'd felt a tightening in his chest. She was humming to Evanna exactly the way Chloe had always done with each of their own babies.

"Remember how Grandma always used to make excuses for him?" Lydia added. "She would shoo us away and tell us not to bother him because he had a lot on his mind, and she'd always take the blame for stuff he forgot. 'He's a good provider'—remember that? That was one of her favorite things to say."

"Bingo." Vera Bridgewater. "You're at the heart of the matter, Lydia. Your grandmother in essence gave him permission to keep worshiping—wasn't your mother's name Chloe? She gave him permission to keep bowing down at Chloe's altar daily, offering himself as a sacrifice. That kind of behavior over so long a period of time has all the hallmarks of guilt. I wonder if your father felt guilty about something."

"Oh, Mother, quit it. You don't have to figure it all out." That was Brittany's voice.

Ben agreed with Brittany. He didn't want to hear another word from Vera Bridgewater or from any of the rest of them. Chloe's altar—he supposed she thought it was a clever metaphor. Offering himself as a sacrifice. That was ridiculous. And the part about guilt—what gave her the right to assign motives to people's behavior when she didn't even know them?

He didn't wait to hear more but quickly made his way around to the back door. Entering the kitchen, he heard the low whine of the electric ice cream churn and saw the bowls and spoons set out on the counter.

He passed through the kitchen and into the hallway. Quietly he took the stairs two at a time. The thought that troubled him was this: Out of all he had overheard on the porch, all the references to himself were either *he* or *him*. Not once had one of his daughters called him Dad or Daddy. Not even the stuffy-sounding Father. He was just a pronoun.

The next morning when Kelly walked past the Blue Pomegranate, she saw Macon Mahoney there, hanging a few new linocuts. She stopped and watched him a moment. His T-shirt today had a picture on the back of a penguin wearing bathing trunks and sunglasses. Underneath were the words *VISIT PINKY'S FUN PARK*. Macon was a nice man, also very comical, and she loved his work. Her dream was to save enough money someday to buy one of his pieces.

He glanced back and saw her. "Hey there, Kelly," he said. "Thought I'd fill a couple of these empty spaces in case somebody else wants to buy a dozen or so." Macon had discounted his prices by twenty percent during the sale, and though no one expected it to make much difference because his stuff cost so much to start with, some rich lawyer had shown up a few days earlier and bought six prints for his law firm.

Kelly walked into the showroom, her eyes fixed on one of the new pieces he had just hung. "That's what Mr. Buck needs for his new office after we move," she said. "That would be perfect." It was a larger piece, unlike anything else she had ever seen in the Blue Pomegranate. The others were all recognizable scenes—flower gardens, marching bands, barber shops, diners—but this one was more abstract than realistic.

"Hey, you're a woman of good taste," Macon said. The front of his T-shirt was smeared with paint, as usual. "That's one of my favorites, too, although a lot of people would twist up their faces and say, 'What is it?' And others—I won't mention my lovely wife's name—might say, 'Why did you make it so big?'"

Kelly moved closer and read the title on the card next to the linocut: *Sometimes a Light Surprises.* The foreground was dark greens and blues and purples—no distinct shapes, just overlapping blocks of deep color above which was something that could be interpreted as a skyline of trees and hills. Above this was a vast expanse of pastel shades—lavenders and pinks and pale oranges, swirls and streaks of color over a wash of gray. Though Kelly had never thought of such a thing, she suddenly wondered what the first sunrise must have been like in the Garden of Eden. What a surprise for Adam and Eve to wake up to that. The funny thing about the linocut was that the sun wasn't even on the scene yet, but somehow its presence was stronger because it was just out of sight.

"I could look at that every day for the rest of my life and never get tired of it," Kelly said. There was so much else she could say, but she didn't want to sound silly in front of a real artist like Macon Mahoney.

"Well, you'll probably be able to," Macon said, "since it will no doubt be hanging in the Blue Pomegranate that long. In fact, your grandchildren will probably be able to look at it for the duration of their lives, if the Bazaar stays in business that long. Theresa predicts it will forever languish in my inventory. Like the man in that poem—'a golden soul that groweth old alone.'"

Kelly didn't know that poem, but she shook her head. "I don't think so, but I do hope it stays around a little while. I'd hate for anyone to buy it and take it home before I have a chance to put a bug in Mr. Buck's ear—if I can get up my nerve to do that. If it ends up in his office, at least I could visit it regularly."

Macon laughed. "Aha. Quiet Kelly, she's a schemer deep down."

It was funny to Kelly that she could talk so easily to Macon. Maybe part of it was because she knew he was a believer, though certainly not like any of the other Christian men she knew—her father, Pastor Shamblin, her older brothers. But he was genuine; she knew that.

She stepped back and let her eyes sweep over the linocut once more. *Sometimes a Light Surprises*—that was a nice title for it. Bad things could happen fast, but she supposed good things could, too.

Carl Sandburg's home was set back from the road on a long, gentle slope of farmland. Thankfully, the tour was over—the house, the grounds, the goat farm, the folk singer. But even better than that, the week was almost over. Today was Thursday, and tomorrow Ben would get in his car and go home.

They were on a walking path, headed back toward the parking lot now. Ben trailed along behind the rest of the family, gazing out over the grassy pastureland—248 acres of it, the tour guide had said. He had learned a lot about Sandburg today, such as the fact that his formal education had stopped after eighth grade. He had taken some college courses but had never earned a college degree. He had held all kinds of jobs in his lifetime, from driving a milk wagon to washing dishes in hotels to harvesting in the fields of Kansas to political organizing. He was well into his thirties before he became a recognized American writer, having gradually "felt his way into poetry" by living, reading, experimenting. That was the way the tour guide said it.

The Sandburgs called their farm Connemara, which was an Irish word meaning "of the sea," though there was, of course, no sea near Flat Rock, North Carolina. Evidently the former owner, whose ancestors were from Ireland, had named it Connemara before the Sandburgs bought it in 1945 for $45,000. That included all the land, plus the three-story house with nine thousand square feet and all the outbuildings.

Ben had liked going through the house more than the goat farm. He liked Sandburg's office, a little hideaway in the southwest corner of the house that got very little sunlight until late morning. That's the way Sandburg liked it. Though Shelly had whispered to Mark, "How depressing, I would think he'd want a brighter place to work," Ben had no trouble at all understanding anybody's preference for shadows. In a pamphlet he had picked up at the beginning of the tour, he had read Sandburg's testimony about the need for a writer to "go away by himself and experience loneliness." It struck Ben that if that were the only requirement for becoming a writer, he himself could have written dozens of books.

Vera Bridgewater had taken notes during the tour. Evidently Sandburg's was one of the few American authors' homes she hadn't visited. Or worked in. She had been a cashier in the gift shop at Nathaniel Hawthorne's birthplace in Salem, Massachusetts, in college and had even served as a tour guide at the Mark Twain home in Hartford, Connecticut, years ago between teaching jobs. To hear her talk, you would think New England was the only place to experience real culture and history.

Far out beyond the Sandburg house, a tractor was moving across a field of tall grass. Ben stopped to watch it. He thought of the enormous job of taking care of 248 acres of farmland. A line of poetry came to him—one of the few Sandburg lines he remembered from school: *I am the grass; I cover all.*

Another Sandburg line came to him now, also. It was one the tour guide had quoted in the barn: *This old anvil laughs at many broken hammers.* The anvil was life, and the broken hammers were men, the guide had said. She was a tall, lean, dreamy sort of woman with a cloud of silver blond hair. As many times as she must have given this speech, she managed to give the impression that this was new and important information she had just learned and was divulging only to you. She went on to say that Carl Sandburg had faith in the common man. He also had faith in the healing power of time and the sustaining power of hope. And—this Ben found especially interesting—he had faith in ritual.

The tour guide made Sandburg sound like a much better writer than Ben thought he was. In his *Through the Year* book, he had read a famous deprecating remark some other writer had made about Sandburg's biography of Abraham Lincoln, something to the effect that the worst thing done to

Lincoln besides getting assassinated by John Wilkes Booth was to "fall into the hands of Carl Sandburg." But maybe he was better at writing poetry than biographies.

The tractor was turning now, heading back in the opposite direction, cutting another wide swath of grass. Ben intended to find a book of Carl Sandburg's poetry as soon as he got home and back into his library ritual. He wanted to find the poem about the old anvil and the broken hammers and read it all. He remembered the last thing the tour guide had said before they left the barn. He wasn't sure if she was quoting or just paraphrasing. Sandburg was a lover of life, she said, lifting her face to the rafters high overhead, "a lover of keepsakes, of dreams, of cradles, of fog, and sunset, and the northern lights."

No one had quite known how to respond to that. Ben suddenly felt like the theme music from the old *Twilight Zone* television program might start playing. Joey had raised his eyebrows at Reuben and coughed softly. They all filed out of the barn quietly and into the yard, where the mood was instantly broken by an old billy goat that butted his head against the side of a stall and let out a loud bleat.

"You coming, Dad?" Shelly called from the path up ahead, shielding her eyes with her bright yellow straw hat. It had a long floral scarf threaded through the brim so it could be tied under the chin, but Shelly had been carrying it over her arm like a purse all morning. Ben wasn't sure why she wasn't wearing it on her head, but maybe it had something to do with her hair. Shelly was very particular about her hair. They had all learned that the day little Adelaide had splashed her as she sat at the edge of the swimming pool.

"We're heading back to the house now," she said to Ben. "And then we're going to have a bite of early lunch before the children go for a swim and the kiddies go down for naps." Ben knew the lingo by now. The "children" were her own three while the "kiddies" were the younger ones, Grant's and Lydia's.

As he hurried to catch up with her, Ben realized that one of the things he was most looking forward to tomorrow was the relief from Shelly's close observation of his every move. That, and the affected way she often used language. Things like "Ruh-roh, no can do!" which she had said just a minute ago when she snatched up one of the kiddies who was petting a goat. Being around Shelly these past several days made it easy for Ben to understand how you could love someone yet not always like her very much.

"A penny for your thoughts," Shelly said to him as she fell into step with him.

Ben shook his head. "Nah, they aren't worth that much." He couldn't help wondering what Chloe would think of their oldest daughter if she were here. But he also wondered if Shelly might have turned out differently if Chloe hadn't died. Maybe her grandmother's fretful, opinionated ways had rubbed off on her during her teen years.

Shelly took his arm, as if she thought he needed assistance. "And then there's the matinee later this afternoon," she said, "and after that we're all driving into Hendersonville to eat. We want to get there early, in case it's crowded. But remember, nobody can get dessert! I've got that all planned back at the house."

"Oh good," Ben said. "Finally you've got some-thing planned."

She looked up at him quickly, a worried look in her eyes.

"I'm teasing, Shelly. You've done a great job organizing everything this week."

She waved a hand as if to indicate she hadn't done much at all but then laughed and said, "Mark says he doesn't need a day planner when he's got me."

He thought of what he'd overheard Erin say to Reuben last night: "I'm exhausted! I wish Shelly would just chill and let things happen instead of acting like every day's a big battle plan and she's the general."

Reuben had laughed. "Well, at least it makes it easy for the rest of us. We don't have to make any decisions. We just follow the general's orders."

"It's going to be strawberry shortcake," Shelly

said, returning to the subject of dessert. "I'm sending Mark to that produce market we passed yesterday for the strawberries, and then I'm making these little individual shortbread cakes, and . . ."

Shelly was easy to tune out. She was like one of those bedside clock radios with sound effects—waterfalls, surf, wind. You heard her, but only as background noise.

Hang in there just a little longer, Ben told himself. Eat a little lunch, sit through a play, then dinner, then the final dessert. And then tomorrow, at last, a sweet leaving.

"Hey, there you two are," Mark called out. "Just taking your good old time. You look like you're walking her down the wedding aisle, Dad."

Not a very nice analogy to make in the hearing of Ben's other two daughters, neither of whom he had walked down the aisle. Only Shelly had asked him to do that. No "Her mother and I" speech for him at the end of that walk with Shelly, though. Only "I do," which had seemed an unfitting thing for the father of the bride to be saying. He wasn't sure who had performed that role for the twins—they had gotten married in other states. He had found out about Erin's wedding after the fact, from Shelly, who had been told by Lydia weeks afterward. But he did know that he had given all three girls money for their weddings, and Grant, too. Very generous checks that none of them returned.

EIGHTEEN

Some Vision or Wonder

These appointments were so humiliating. Erin had already told Reuben that she couldn't do this anymore. She had told him that before, but she meant it this time. She wasn't going to keep subjecting herself to physical examinations and nosy questions by a doctor whose very title—fertility specialist—was too embarrassing to say out loud.

Erin didn't really trust him. She was becoming more and more convinced that these kinds of doctors liked to string their patients along, spreading the appointments out, trying first one thing and then another, acting disappointed with each failure but secretly glad to retain your dependence on them. The more things that didn't work, the more times you came back, and the more times you came back, the more money you paid them. Reuben didn't agree, said she was too cynical, but she knew what she knew.

She also thought such doctors developed a purely clinical view of sex, not to mention a basic disregard for people's privacy. She was sick and tired of the whole idea of "trying"—all the charts and assignments and tests. Like she was in school again and the doctor was the mean teacher nobody wanted. She had come to dread bedtime, had started staying up till she was sure Reuben had fallen asleep.

Sometimes Erin came to the appointments by herself, but Reuben was with her today. Dr. Webster said the timing was especially important for this one. She couldn't bring herself to repeat what he'd said at the last appointment but had simply told Reuben that she had an appointment at one o'clock on August 6 and she wanted him to come, too. She also asked him to meet her at home for lunch that day. And that was the most embarrassing part of all. Reuben had to know it was an assignment when she rushed him to sit down at the table and then stood up and put her arms around his neck from behind while he was taking the last bite of his ham sandwich.

"Hey, let's eat lunch at home every day," he'd said as he pulled her back to the bedroom. She couldn't even look him in the eye. The whole thing was so unnatural—bright sunlight streaming through the window, the sounds of the neighbor children playing next door, the thought of unwashed lunch dishes sitting on the kitchen table, knowing she had to go back to work later this afternoon. Not at all what she would call a spontaneous romantic interlude.

So here they sat in the waiting room of Dr. Jonas Webster, fertility specialist, with two other women, whose heads were buried in magazines. The outside door opened, and another couple entered and walked over to the receptionist's window. They were both wearing white shorts and sleeveless shirts, no doubt to show off their tans. It annoyed Erin that there were three other women here, presumably with appointments around the same time as hers. And Dr. Webster had only one partner. Why did doctors do this? She wished she had a dollar for every minute she had been stuck in some doctor's waiting room.

She watched the couple at the window. She couldn't help wondering if they were at the same point as Reuben and she in their "pathway to fertility," as Dr. Webster called it. The man gave their name to the receptionist, then hiked up his shorts and looked around at the available seats in the waiting room. The woman, who looked annoyed, left the man's side and took the nearest seat. He said something to her, but she shook her head and fixed her eyes on the floor.

"Hey, look at this." Reuben leaned over with the magazine he was reading. It was a picture of an elaborately frosted carrot cake garnished with little spirals of orange peel and the caption "Bugs Bunny Would Love This!" Reuben loved to look at food magazines. "I wonder if that's the recipe Shelly used for her carrot cake," he said in a cartoon voice, "minus the orange curlicues."

"Stop it. You don't sound anything like Bugs Bunny," Erin said. She pointed to the name and city printed under the recipe. "That's not it. Shelly made up her own recipe, remember. Or at least that's what she said."

"Oh, right, the recipe she entered in the contest," Reuben said. He laughed.

"Yeah, the contest she got second prize for," Erin said.

"The prize she didn't care anything about," Reuben said. He turned over several pages to a picture of a plump baked chicken on a platter, a tiny American flag toothpicked into its breast between the two golden brown drumsticks. The caption read, "Opt for a Heart-Wise July Fourth Picnic." Erin wondered if anybody had taken their suggestion. A whole baked chicken didn't seem like a very picnicky menu item.

An interior door by the receptionist's window opened, and a short blond woman emerged, holding a little girl by the hand and laughing a fake trilling sort of laugh. Speaking loudly as confident people often do, especially confident people who are rich, the woman stuck her head in at the sliding window and said, "You'll remind Jonas about that barbecue at six, won't you? It would be just like him to forget all about it between now and then!" The receptionist said she would, and the blond woman waved and said, "Catch you later!" then looked down at her daughter and said, "Come on, sweetie pie, now that we've fed Daddy his lunch, we've got to get you to your ballet lesson."

Yes, Erin thought, go get in your new BMW that

we're helping pay for and drive your kid to her ballet lesson before you head home to your million-dollar bungalow by the golf course at the country club. Rich people were so hard to take. She tried to imagine the doctor's wife putting in a day of real work at the animal shelter. She'd like to give her the job of changing all the paper in the puppy cages—the sick puppies.

Just before they walked out the door, the little girl asked her mother something, to which the doctor's wife replied at full volume, "Yes, we can get you the new swimsuit since your swimming coach bragged on how well you did last time! Why, I couldn't have *begun* to swim the length of the pool when I was your age."

Without lifting his eyes from his magazine, Reuben said, "She and Shelly would get along famously."

"Or else hate each other," Erin said.

A nurse stepped into the waiting room and called a name. One of the two women got up. She was overweight but had a cheerful, hopeful face. The man in the white shorts said, "I sure hope this doesn't take all afternoon. Some of us have to work." It was clear that he was speaking for the nurse's benefit, but she gave no sign of having heard him. Erin wondered what kind of work he did in his shorts and loafers without socks.

Reuben turned a page and said, "Hey, here's an article about that place outside Nashville Joey told me about. He said we ought to meet them there sometime."

Erin said nothing. She didn't even glance over at the pictures. Of her three siblings, Lydia was the only one she would drive any distance to see, but traveling anywhere was out of the question for now. She didn't want to take any more trips to see anybody for a long time. The trip to Flat Rock had done her in.

Physically, yes, but more than that, emotionally. Her siblings and their spouses and all the nieces and nephews, not to mention her father. It was too much. Even Brittany's mother, Vera Bridgewater, had been a source of irritation. Every day since returning from the trip, Erin kept hearing her voice.

It was from one of the many conversations on the porch. It was just the women that day; the men had gone to play golf, which Reuben pronounced "basically a joke" because none of them knew how to play very well. But it was a joke they all seemed to enjoy, judging from their endless banter about it afterward. Mark had even taken along a video camera, and they all insisted that the women view the tape. They kept rewinding and replaying the part where Joey reared back to drive the ball over a pond and down the long fairway, only to shank it into the water less than ten feet away. They were especially pleased that the recorder had picked up the sound of the plop very distinctly.

Reuben declared the golf game to be the best time of the whole week. "No offense," he'd told Erin, "but there was a lot less tension with just the men together."

But while Reuben was off having his best time of the whole week, Erin was stuck at the house with the women. On the porch that day, Shelly had decided she needed to preach a little sermon to the rest of them, which resulted in something very much like an argument between her and Vera Bridgewater about the subject of life after death.

In the beginning Lydia and Brittany joined in, too, but by the end it was just Shelly and Vera going at it. Erin kept out of it. But she heard the whole thing, and it was Vera's last little closing speech that she couldn't get out of her mind.

The problem with the idea of another life after this one, in Vera's opinion, was that it made this life seem somehow less important, and that led to troubling behavior. *Troubling* behavior? Shelly had demanded. Like *what*? Shelly was not a graceful arguer. Her neck got so stiff that it actually quivered and turned splotchy red. She got her words tangled up, also, and overdramatized everything.

"Well, like 9/11," Vera had said calmly. She never got her words tangled up. She was a small woman, much smaller than Brittany, and she sat on the glider with one leg tucked under her and the other swinging, like a child. She gestured languidly as she talked. "Why did those hijackers crash their planes into the towers?" she said. It was easy to imagine her in front of a college classroom, completely in charge.

"Because they were, were . . . full of . . . well, they were *satanic*!" Shelly had cried.

"They were seeking the prize of immortality," Vera said. "They expected to be lifted up as heroes in the afterlife and rewarded for all eternity with the things that most appeal to men's appetites." She stressed the word *men's*.

Shelly sputtered a response that made no sense— "Well, you can't use *that* to . . . well, to just throw everything out the window!"—and then fell silent.

After several long seconds had passed, Vera spoke quietly, as if talking to herself, but all of them heard every word: "But even something like 9/11, as horrible as it was, can serve a valuable purpose, can't it?" No one replied, but she went on. "At least it did for me. It reminded me of how very delicate and breakable this gift of life is that we hold in our hands. And how very brief. I remember apologizing in the following days to everybody I had wronged. I even went to a couple of people who had done *me* dirty and asked if we could forget the past and be friends. And you know what they said? Every one of them. They said sure, they would like that. And you know what else? One of those women was the first one to show up at my door to help me out after Reggie died. Nobody could ask for a better friend than she is today. All because we were shaken out of our narrow, selfish perspectives by a horrible tragedy. And all because we were both willing to let go of the past."

Willing to let go of the past—that was the phrase that kept haunting Erin. One of those catch phrases that sounded impossibly virtuous. In Erin's opinion, doing such a thing was way too easy on the offender.

It was obvious that Shelly was confused about how the argument had gotten off its theological track. She kept glaring at the rest of them, as if admonishing someone to jump in with a response. But still they all sat speechless.

"And so, it's just a choice I've made," Vera said. "I've decided to fasten my hopes and efforts on today, this life right now, and be thankful for the consciousness I've been given to live it fully." She stopped and heaved a half groan, half laugh. "Oh, I know—it all sounds so philosophically noble, doesn't it? That's my brain speaking, not my heart. To be honest, some days I want to take my chances and skip to the next part the way those hijackers did. This life right now doesn't thrill me very much."

Brittany had sighed and wearily reminded her mother of all the pleasures of life she still had—her children and grandchildren, tons of friends, reading, gardening, music, cooking, traveling, writing. From her tone, this was clearly a speech she had given many times before.

And Vera had nodded, then looked off to the side of the house, where a huge rhododendron was blooming. "And it's all nice. It really is," she said. "But you girls will find out someday that none of it can make up for losing your husband." Then she inhaled sharply and held up both hands. "Wait a minute, what am I saying? I hope to heaven none of you ever have to find that out."

Suddenly the door beside the receptionist's desk opened again, and the overweight woman came back out. She had her head down, but it looked like she was crying. Maybe she had filled out a chart wrong and Dr. Webster had dismissed her to go home and try again. Erin felt an ache of sympathy for her. But who knew why the woman was crying, if she even was. Maybe she was happy. Maybe Dr. Webster had told her she was going to have quadruplets.

Kelly was sitting on the edge of the sofa in Caroline's office, waiting for Mr. Buckley to get off the phone. It was her first summons to his office. She'd heard other employees talk about being called in, usually not for anything good, but so far all her encounters with Mr. Buck since her hiring interview had been friendly, casual ones out on the floor. He was always polite to her but usually seemed preoccupied and in a hurry to get on his way. Even though he had complimented a couple of her window displays, she wasn't sure he liked her as a person very much. But then he was a funny man. He didn't seem overly impressed with anybody.

She was trying to prepare herself for anything. Maybe he was going to release her. Or maybe he had found a designer with more experience and was going to ask Kelly to be a floorwalker. She had already made up her mind that she would do that if he asked. It wouldn't be as interesting a job, but she would get used to it. She was trying to convince herself not to think of it as a demotion. The floorwalkers' main responsibility was to circulate in their zones, answering questions and keeping an eye on the shoppers and the merchandise.

The hardest part, the part she was already dreading, was having to follow up on suspected shoplifting activity. That wouldn't be fun. Recently LaTeesha had reported a woman slipping jewelry inside her purse in the Pearls and Diamonds showroom, and there was a big, ugly scene outside the store before it was over. The woman had pretended to be insulted and had threatened to sue LaTeesha for every cent she was worth. LaTeesha told her that would be the lowest settlement a court ever awarded.

"It sure looks bare in here, doesn't it?" Caroline said. She was sitting at her desk across the room, looking at Kelly over the top of her computer screen.

Kelly nodded and smiled. "Yes, it does." She

looked around to where the pictures on the walls used to be and the two little tables and the magazines and the brass umbrella stand and the coatrack. All of the smaller things had already been moved to the new offices, even though the official moving date for the Bazaar was still three weeks away. They would move the big items later, closer to the grand opening at the new location on Labor Day.

Kelly was hoping to have the opportunity to suggest putting the tables and brass coatrack inside Mr. Buck's new office to make it look more executive. The three pictures, too—they were nice, understated abstracts in blues and purples. They would look nice on the wall behind his desk. And there was a blue plaid sofa in Mr. Begian's Classic Interiors showroom downstairs that could replace the plain gold one he had now, which could be put somewhere else. They could use a sofa in the break room, in fact. Then, of course, Macon Mahoney's large linocut. She had already mentioned it, but she wasn't sure Mr. Buck had been paying attention at the time.

Kelly realized, however, that she might not have any say about where things went. She might not even have a job after today. She looked at her watch. Five minutes past two. She didn't hear Mr. Buck talking anymore behind his office door, so maybe he was finished with his phone call. Seconds later, though, she heard his voice again.

She leaned back and tried to stop fidgeting with the fringed ends of her belt.

"I don't think it's anything bad, in case you're worried," Caroline said.

Kelly clasped her hands together tightly in her lap. "Thank you, Caroline," she said. "Sometimes I have a bad habit of expecting the worst."

"Well, knowing *him*," Caroline said, nodding in the direction of Mr. Buck's office door, "he might be just wanting to tell you about something interesting he read in one of his books." She rolled her eyes upward and shook her head. "He was standing in here before lunch today eating a bag of peanuts and going on and on about where the word *goober* came from! I finally said to him, 'Mr. Buck, that is fascinating, I'm sure, but I'm in a tizzy trying to get this report finished before I leave for the beach tomorrow—and no, I don't care where the word *tizzy* came from, either!' "

Kelly laughed. Caroline could be very amusing.

Maybe somebody had complained to Mr. Buck about her work, though Kelly didn't know what it could be or who would have done it. But there was a lot to remember here; maybe she hadn't followed some employee procedure correctly. Everybody knew Mr. Buck liked things to be done a certain way. Just a few days ago in the break room, Nora was telling everyone that Mr. Buck had sent her a memo that her desk was a shambles and needed to be straightened, which was funny, because everyone knew Mr. Buck's own desk was anything but tidy. His favorite method of organizing was to stack things up. But he was the boss. He got to make the rules and break them, too, if he wanted.

Caroline went back to her typing, and a minute later Mr. Buckley's office door swung open. Kelly stood up as he stepped out. He had a book in one hand, a finger hooked inside as a page marker. He lowered his head and studied her over the top of his reading glasses.

Kelly's heart gave a little lurch. He looked so serious. Was that book about how to succeed at your job, and was he planning to read to her out of it?

"Hello, Ms. Kovatch," he said. "Would you care to come in? Caroline, please hold any phone calls." Kelly's heart was pounding now. Usually he called her Kelly, not Ms. Kovatch. "And by the way," he said to Caroline as Kelly entered his office, "the call I just finished could have been taken by someone else."

"He asked for you by name," Caroline said.

"Nevertheless," he said, and shut the door.

Kelly took a seat in the metal folding chair in front of Mr. Buck's desk. The wing chairs and bookcase had already been loaded for moving, so the office looked even bleaker than usual. She swallowed hard and tried to compose herself.

Mr. Buckley went around his desk and sat down, swiveling his chair to face her. He opened the book where he had it marked and carefully laid it face-down on his desktop. Kelly couldn't see the title of it. Then he took off his glasses and laid them beside the book.

His first questions were easy: How was she doing? How did she like her job here? Had the recent overtime hours been too much? He didn't look at her while she answered, and Kelly even wondered if he was really listening or just biding his time until he got around to telling her they wouldn't be needing her anymore.

It was odd, though. Mr. Buck wasn't known for softening a blow. If he had something to say, he usually said it very directly. Like a few days ago right outside the break room when he told Jillian, one of the floorwalkers, that she ought to try talking more like a grown woman instead of a little girl. And when he told Lester not to wear any more T-shirts to work with questionable words or pictures on them. When Lester asked him in a joking manner what he meant by questionable, Mr. Buck said without smiling, "I think you can figure it out, but I would err on the side of caution if I were you."

His next questions to Kelly got a little more specific: Could they count on her for at least ten extra hours a week until after the move? What did she think of the new building? Would she mind sharing an office with the floor supervisors? Had she come up with ideas yet for a theme for the grand opening? And for the two large front window displays? Was there anything in particular she needed for those? Had Dustin talked to her yet about setting up a new monthly budget for window displays? Was she getting the cooperation she needed from Les and Mo? Did she have any suggestions for how the day-to-day business at the Bazaar could run more smoothly?

Slowly Kelly was beginning to realize that he didn't seem to be working around to the subject of firing her; rather, he seemed to be assuming she would be around for a good while longer. She relaxed a little and rested her back against the back of the chair.

And then there was a pause. Mr. Buck leaned forward and put his elbows on his desk. Still no eye contact; instead, he stared at the book on his desk. "Thank you, Ms. Kovatch. All of that is very interesting information you've shared with me." Another pause, a longer one. Mr. Buck turned his chair a little and gazed at the wall. "However, that's not why I've asked to see you."

Kelly's heart started thudding again. Here it came.

"In your father's house are many children, are there not?" He spoke lightly, almost teasingly, still looking at the wall.

Kelly wasn't sure at first how Mr. Buckley could possibly know this—if he was speaking literally, that is. She had never talked to him about her brothers and sisters, not that she could remember. Nor was she sure if he intended the biblical allusion. Although she had heard him quote from the Bible before, it was always from the Old Testament, usually something spoken in a mocking tone.

"Well, yes, we do have a big family," Kelly said.

Mr. Buckley turned back to his desk and sat forward in his chair again. He ran a finger over the cover of the book. "And several besides yourself are daughters?"

"Yes." It was funny the way Mr. Buckley sometimes lapsed into a formal way of speaking while at other times he would put together a whole string of catchy slang expressions, often followed by an explanation of the history of a certain phrase. And sometimes he would combine the two, like the day he had described a phone conversation as "a humdinger of a hostile encounter." Her younger brothers were still laughing about that one at home. He was also known for correcting people's grammar.

He continued to trace the swirled design on the cover of the book. "Tell me, Ms. Kovatch, what do you think your father would do if one of his daughters hated him?"

Kelly didn't know what to say. First of all, she couldn't imagine such a thing. She and her sisters adored their father. He didn't talk or laugh a lot, especially since their mother had died, but he was like the big bolt in the middle of a machine that kept all the parts from flying off. If she ever got married, she would want somebody kind and steady just like her father. He was content to stay in the background, preferred it that way, in fact, but he would also step forward and do hard things if he had to.

Something about the way Mr. Buckley was asking this question, hunched over his desk, his words heavy and slow, told her it wasn't a hypothetical situation. There was a long silence as Kelly prayed for an answer, and then he lifted his head and looked straight at her. She had to say something.

"Well, I guess . . . he would probably start out by . . . trying to figure out why."

He nodded slowly, still looking at her. "Okay, let's say he knows why. And let's say she has a pretty good reason to hate him. Then what does he do?"

Another silence. Kelly was thinking hard, praying for the right words to come.

"Well, maybe she doesn't really hate him," she said cautiously. "She could just be . . . a little confused."

He raised his eyebrows as if not convinced but willing to hear more.

She paused and took a deep breath, then suddenly sat up taller and leaned forward. "In fact, I'm quite sure, Mr. Buckley, that she *couldn't* really hate him. She might act like it, but deep down in her heart I think she loves him. She acts like she hates him because she's mad—you see, she's mad at herself for not being able to hate him because that's what she *thinks* she wants and that's what she might think he deserves, and she's also mad at *him* because of . . . the problem, whatever it is. But she's really a very lonely, unhappy person inside, and she's waiting for . . . well, for . . ."

"For some vision or wonder?" Mr. Buckley said. "Some thunderbolt? Or for a quieter sign? For the latter rain maybe?"

"Well, yes . . . *yes*, that's a good way to put it, Mr. Buck." The words came to Kelly in a rush, though she didn't know if they were the right ones. "I think she desperately wants her father's love, even if it seems too late for it. But it's not too late. It's never too late for love. The fields need those latter rains just as much as the early ones."

Mr. Buckley gave a sad smile. "Yes, Ms. Kovatch, yes, they do." He sighed and dropped his eyes back to the book on his desk. "Unless the corn is already parched."

"But . . . you could still try," Kelly said. She didn't know what else to say.

He reached forward and turned the book over to the marked page. "I was just reading something before you came in." He put his glasses back on and scanned the page. "Here it is: 'Like a dry shell on the beach, waiting for the tide to come in.'

Daphne du Maurier said that. It's a good description, don't you think, Ms. Kovatch?"

"Well, yes," she said. "And it does imply, doesn't it, Mr. Buckley, that the tide is sure to come back in?"

He closed the book and stood up. "Thank you for your thoughts, Ms. Kovatch. I appreciate a young person with a head on her shoulders. I've kept you long enough."

Kelly stood up to leave. Her mind was suddenly flooded with things she could have said, but the opportunity was over.

Mr. Buckley walked her to the door and opened it. As she passed through, he called to Caroline, "Ms. Kovatch has agreed to keep working for us, Caroline, in case you're wondering what we were talking about. And if you'll come in here now, we can write up a memo to Dustin about getting her salary raised."

The two women's eyes met. Kelly wondered if she looked as surprised as Caroline did.

NINETEEN

Moment of Truth

Just over a week later, Caroline overheard the strangest thing. She was pinning the next week's work schedule and a new announcement to the employee bulletin board in the break room when

Kelly Kovatch arrived. It was fifteen minutes before nine o'clock. Caroline had come to work at eight-thirty today because she was planning to ask Mr. Buckley if she could leave before five.

Kelly couldn't see Caroline since the bulletin board was back in a little alcove by the two vending machines, but Caroline stepped around the corner to see who was here early. Kelly stood at the sink, her back to Caroline, rinsing out a mug. She was wearing a green plaid jumper and a short-sleeved white blouse, and her red purse was sitting on the counter beside her. Her father had given her the purse weeks ago for her birthday. She had told a couple of the girls at lunch that even though it wasn't the color she might have chosen, she wouldn't tell her father that for the world. She carried the purse every day regardless of what color clothing she was wearing. Caroline would never do that herself, but she had to admit that it must simplify life not to always be changing purses.

She stepped back to the bulletin board to remove last week's schedule and rearrange a few other things. This bulletin board was too small for all the unnecessary trivia Mr. Buck wanted on it. He had told her he was going to make sure there was a larger one in the new building, so she hated to think of what else he would want to start posting. The only thing people cared about was the work schedule, but he couldn't get that through his head.

She took down a notice about a safety video everyone was supposed to view and moved it over to make room for a new announcement about the employee appreciation picnic coming up the weekend before the move. While she was doing this, she heard someone else enter the break room.

"Well, hey, hey, look who's here," the voice said, and Caroline recognized it at once as Lester Lattimore's. It was an irritating voice—reedy, with a sarcastic edge. "Fancy that—us both getting here early on the same day," he said to Kelly. "People might think we was doing this on purpose—you know, meeting for a little . . . uh, close fellowship. Ain't that what you church people call it?" He laughed. His laugh was also irritating—a high-pitched cackle. "We better watch it or somebody might find out and start a rumor, saying me and you got us a thing going early in the a.m. here in the break room."

Kelly didn't say anything. Caroline peeked out and saw that she was still in front of the sink, drying the mug with a paper towel, her head down. Lester hopped up to sit on the counter beside her at the sink. He crossed his arms and tucked his fists underneath his biceps, then glanced down to admire them.

He leaned in closer to Kelly. "What? You not going to talk to me this morning?" he said. "Again? You know, I'm getting awful tired of you always giving me the cold shoulder. How come you don't say nothing? You think you're too good for me? Is that it?"

Kelly didn't say a word, didn't look at him, just kept her head down and continued wiping off her mug, going over and over it with the paper towel. It was clear to Caroline that this must not be the first such conversation between these two, though it really couldn't be called a conversation when only one person talked.

Lester was apparently enjoying himself. "You know, like I told you before, there's lots of girls who'd give anything if I was to take them out in my car somewhere, but you act like a block of wood ever' time I try to be friendly. And me just trying to help you out. Girl like you needs somebody to show her what a good time is, help her get over all her hang-ups." He raised his voice. "Hey! Don't you got nothing to say?"

Kelly suddenly set the mug down hard on the counter and wadded up the paper towel with both hands. "Yes, I do," she said. "I do have something to say." She lifted her head and looked right at Lester. Even with him sitting on the counter, she was so tall their eyes were almost level. They were only about three feet apart. She grabbed her purse from the counter and hooked it over one arm.

Lester's grin faded a little, and he unfolded his arms like he was getting ready to defend himself. Maybe he was afraid she was getting ready to hit him. Caroline half wished she would.

"Let me answer your questions first," Kelly said, "and then I have a couple for you." Her voice was a little shaky, and she kept squeezing the balled-up paper towel between her hands. But she didn't back down. "You asked me why I don't talk to you and if I think I'm too good for you. First, I don't talk to you because I don't trust you. I think you like to treat me the way you do just to get a reaction, and you make fun of people you consider weaker than you. That's not very nice and not very brave, either. But part of it is my fault because I've been too scared to say anything. But that's going to change—and it's only fair that I talk to you first instead of going to somebody else."

Caroline was full of wonder to be witnessing such a thing. Kelly seemed to be gaining confidence. Her voice was stronger and louder now. "And no, I don't think I'm too good for you. I'm not too good for anybody, Lester. We're all on the same level in God's sight. We're all sinners in need of his mercy." She held up the paper towel. "We're all disposable, in fact, just like this wad of paper, but the amazing thing is that God loves us anyway. And he can straighten us out and smooth out all the wrinkles and put us to use again."

Caroline wanted to give a little cheer for her, even though she also wanted to laugh at that business about the paper towel.

Lester opened his mouth but nothing came out. Caroline was glad to see how foolish he looked sitting on the counter with his mouth gaping and his little round owl eyes blinking in the middle of his round face while a girl gave him what-for. Lester was always strutting around, smarting off. It was a great satisfaction to see him at a loss for words. But even if he could have thought of something to say, Kelly didn't give him a chance. Now that she had gotten started, the words wouldn't stop.

With hardly a pause, she said, "And now here's my question for you, Lester. Have you ever given *any* thought to what you're doing with your life and where you're headed when it's all over? Don't you know that what you're doing right now has eternal consequences? If God called you before his judgment throne today to give an account of your behavior, how would you explain yourself? But here's another question: I wonder if you've ever heard that God has made it possible for you to go to heaven if you . . ."

Just then the telephone in the break room rang. Caroline pulled her head back into the alcove. She was almost as stunned as Lester appeared to be. This was certainly a side of Kelly she had never observed. She was fairly sure she could get them both in trouble with Mr. Buck—Les for being fresh with Kelly and Kelly for talking about religion at work. Those were both things she knew Mr. Buck wouldn't like.

The telephone kept ringing. Now, who would be calling the break room extension before nine o'clock in the morning? Caroline wondered. Well, she wasn't going to answer it. If it was somebody calling in sick, they could call Nora's number the way they were supposed to.

It rang five times before Kelly finally answered it, and when Caroline peeked back out, she saw that Lester was gone.

The next day Ben left the Bazaar around three o'clock. Usually he didn't stay this long on Saturdays, but everything was upside down with the impending move. Ever since he'd gotten home from Flat Rock, it had been this way. His whole life seemed unsettled and off schedule.

He had spent a good part of the afternoon today with Dustin and Roy, going through the new software program for inventory and accounting, trying to streamline it for the Bazaar. Actually, he had just sat there mostly, listening to the other two talk it through. It was going to be great once they got the bugs worked out, but Roy, the tech expert, said it needed a lot more tweaking. They had to have it up and running by the time they moved, so Roy, who was a little high-strung anyway, was even more so now.

Even on good days Ben found it hard to be around Roy, who could be a poster boy for Computer Geeks of America. LaTeesha liked to tease him, ask him questions like whether he ever just chilled out in front of a James Bond movie or hung out at pool halls or went to drag races.

Ben had a bad headache. He hated staring at a computer screen that long. And now his Saturday was all mixed up. It was too early for supper at the K&W Cafeteria even though he was getting hungry. He didn't feel like going to the library or bookstore when his head was hurting, but he didn't want to go home yet, either, because Athena might still be there cleaning. He needed a few groceries, but he didn't like going to the grocery store on Saturday.

Everything seemed to be pressing in on him. Part of it was all the accompanying hassle of the move, but he knew another big part was the baggage he'd brought home from Flat Rock, not the suitcase kind. That trip had not been a vacation in any sense of the word.

As he was pushing open the back exit to the employees' parking lot, he almost collided with Kelly Kovatch, who was just arriving. She gave a little startled jump and said, "Oh, hello, Mr. Buckley."

He knew she wasn't scheduled to work today since she had already put in over fifty hours this week. And even if she was, it was a funny time to be showing up, only a couple of hours before they closed for the day. "Hello, Kelly," he said. "What is this—a busman's holiday?"

She gave him a quizzical look. "I beg your pardon?"

"Never mind. It's just an expression. It means showing up on your day off to be sure things are . . . well, it doesn't matter. I'm surprised to see you here is all." He was on the outside now, holding the door open.

"Nora called and asked if I could run in to help out on the floor," Kelly said. "Gilda had to leave suddenly for some reason, and they couldn't find anybody else to sub her zone. It's only for a couple of hours, so I don't mind. Nora said things are really busy today."

Ben didn't know anything about Gilda's leaving early, but he didn't need to, either. That's why he hired competent people like Nora. He nodded. "Yes, the moving sale still seems to be going strong. People are coming out in droves." Actually, he was afraid some of the vendors were getting carried away with their markdowns. J.J. and Seth had been busy all day loading big items into trucks and vans and trying to schedule home deliveries.

Besides meeting with Dustin and Roy, Ben had spent a good bit of time circulating around the various exits, watching customers leave with armloads of purchases. He had a bad feeling that the vendors were going to clean themselves out of merchandise before the move and then not make timely plans for restocking before the grand opening. He imagined complaints from customers on Labor Day about the nearly empty showrooms.

He needed to have Caroline send out a cautionary e-mail to all the vendors right away.

"Well, I better go let Nora know I'm here. See you Monday, Mr. Buck." Kelly started away, then stopped. "Oh, I meant to tell you, I asked my father your question. I didn't tell him who it was or anything, just told him somebody at work was talking about a family situation last week. I asked Daddy what he'd do if one of us girls . . . you know, got really mad at him."

This was the last thing Ben wanted to talk about right now. Still, he couldn't help being curious.

"He said he'd have to think about it first," Kelly said. "I believe I already told you that a lot of times he tries to figure out what my mother would say or how she'd handle a problem, and that helps him decide."

Ben felt a prickle of annoyance. He didn't want to hear about this again. But he nodded politely. "Yes, you told me that."

"So then a little later," Kelly continued, "he said he'd been thinking about my friend's question, and he thought the best plan might be to try loving the girl back to his heart. He said he remembered lots of times when my mother would just drop a touchy subject with one of us and wait for the right time to bring it up again if it still wasn't resolved. And in the meantime, she would show that child some extra attention—do special things together and buy little treats and such." She smiled at him, an anxious-to-please kind of smile.

Oh, the irony of it all. Here he was listening to Kelly's report of her father's report of Kay Kovatch's child-rearing advice. Kay Kovatch, the very woman who had caused a breach in—well, the irony was too much. Evidently Kelly hadn't understood the circumstances. She seemed to think this was only a little difference of opinion. She didn't realize that when he said one of his daughters hated him, he was talking about the real thing, not just some temporary minor friction.

But he never should have asked her such a question in the first place. People from families like hers couldn't begin to comprehend the problems normal people faced. They couldn't imagine the kinds of looks Erin had given him last month—well, the few times she looked at him, that is. Most of the time she had simply stared at the floor or gotten up and walked out of the room whenever he showed up.

He tried not to look or sound as put out as he felt. "Thank you, Kelly, I'll keep that in mind." He lifted a hand. "Well, so long." All the way to his car he kept seeing her dark, sincere eyes and hearing her last words: "Do special things together and buy little treats and such." As if Erin were a sulky child instead of a grown woman. But what did he expect from an upright Girl Scout type like Kelly, whose view of life was so simple and innocent and narrow? He couldn't force himself to be too hard on her. She was only trying to be helpful.

He got in his car and started it but didn't put it in gear. What to do? Where to go? He heard Kelly's perky voice again: "A lot of times he tries to figure out what my mother would say or how she'd handle a problem, and that helps him decide." Ben wasn't sure he would admit that so openly if he were Kelly's father. It seemed like a wimpy way for a grown man to get through his days—to depend on his dead wife to help him make up his mind about everyday situations.

But suddenly, right there in the parking lot of the Upstate Home and Garden Bazaar, Ben had a swift, painful moment of truth. Maybe his defenses were down because of the heat or his general physical exhaustion or the lingering effects of the family vacation. Or maybe because yesterday had been one of the bleakest, blackest Fridays ever, seeing and hearing things all day that reminded him that he was a man without the love of wife or children. Without the love of anybody, really.

Or maybe it was just a combination of everything. Whatever it was, it hit him hard: Who was he, Ben Buckley, to talk about men being too wimpy and dependent to get through their days by themselves?

He thought of all his little rituals for filling up time—the way he puttered around in his yard and hung out in libraries and bookstores, his cautious obsession with the stock market, his careful and unvarying rotation of television programs and restaurants, all his trivia collecting and list making. Boiled down to its essence, his survival strategy was one of avoidance and escape. Day after day after day. None of it had made him happier. Richer yes, fatter definitely, older, too. But not happier. Not even smarter.

He raced the engine a little. Still he didn't move.

Compared to his own methods of coping, Kelly's father suddenly seemed like some kind of hero. Hercules or Rambo or Conan or Braveheart. Like Og, king of Bashan, the last survivor of the remnant of giants, whose bed was nine cubits long. And wasn't it a grand thing that he could pluck out such a minute detail from the Bible—from a book he didn't even believe in?

So what if Kay Kovatch's husband groped his way through every day asking himself what his wife would do? Was that any worse than what Chloe Buckley's husband did? So what if he knew that nine cubits came out to thirteen and a half feet? Or how much a pound of sand would weigh on Mercury or how long the attention span of a goldfish was? What did it matter if he knew a million answers to a million questions? Those quiz games he had won in Flat Rock were empty victories when his own children seemed like strangers.

He thought of Erin's words he had overheard that night: "All I'm saying is that there's something wrong at the very core of a man who can ignore his own children for years and years and years." And he agreed completely—there was something wrong with a man like that. He thought of the way Adelaide and Lavinia snuggled in Vera Bridgewater's lap and called her Gramma, yet stared at him with big eyes and called him nothing.

Ben put his car in drive and eased forward. He left the employee lot and drove slowly through the main lot toward one of the exits. He could go to the gym for an hour and try to sweat off another pound to add to the four he had somehow managed to take off. Maybe that would help clear his mind and lift his spirits. But he would need to go home first and get a change of clothes, and he didn't want to do that. Besides, his back ached from sitting so long in front of the computer. The thought of sweating on a treadmill held no appeal when his whole life seemed like one long treadmill.

He circled around and stopped in a far section of the parking lot. Rows of crape myrtle behind him were dropping white blossoms, which scooted across the hot pavement as light as snowflakes. He looked at the Bazaar. Maybe he should leave for a month and come back after the move. He wondered what it would be like to leave Greenville and start driving west, not stopping till he got to the Pacific coast.

He thought of Kelly's father again—he doubted that he ever had to think of what to do with himself on a Saturday afternoon. He thought of how full and noisy such a house would be compared to his own, which would be deathly quiet when he got there later tonight. But thanks to Athena it would be spotless, whatever that was worth. And his laundry would be done—all neatly folded and stacked on his bed.

Well, this was dumb and unproductive. Gas wasn't free. He couldn't sit here all day with his engine idling while he tried to make up his mind where to go. He flipped on the radio. A song was playing, an old song Ben hadn't heard for years: "I'll be seeing you in all the old familiar places." This wasn't the version he remembered; this one was being crooned by some younger Sinatra wannabe. The kid was full of himself, wringing every ounce of sap out of the lyrics by pausing dramatically, half-speaking certain words, even interjecting a rueful laugh at one point.

Normally Ben would have turned off such a song, but he sat there and listened to the whole sorry thing. It must have been the mention of the park and the carousel that gave him the idea of going to a park. He could go to one here in Greenville or—though he knew he shouldn't—he could drive over to Derby, to the park a few blocks from the old house on Amaryllis Street. It had a little paved walking trail around the perimeter, a standard quarter-mile in distance—or at least it used to. He could take a few laps around that. It would give him some exercise without all the

301

bright lights and loud music of the fitness center at the gym—and without all the sweaty well-toned specimens doing twice as much on the machines as he could do.

He knew that going to Derby was probably a mistake, but it felt like a step off the safe path, a small adventure, which was something he hadn't felt for years. Never would he claim he had heard Chloe say, "Go to the park"—he wasn't one for voices from the great beyond—but he couldn't help thinking she might approve.

TWENTY

Part of Another Life

Evidently this was the place to be on a Saturday afternoon, although it didn't even look like the same park Ben remembered. It had undergone a major facelift and expansion sometime during the ten years since Ben had moved from Derby to Greenville. A row of young oak trees with pale green leaves edged the sidewalk next to the street, and beds of pink and white begonias surrounded the large marker that bore the new name: Oaktree Recreation Complex. Ben parked his car in the parallel spaces along the curb closest to the monkey bars and got out.

It was easy to see why they were called monkey bars. Children swinging and hanging and climbing and chasing, all of it accompanied by shrill monkeylike chatter and squeals. The only stationary thing besides the bars themselves was one little boy sitting by himself sculpting a series of small ridges in the sand with the aid of a spoon and a stick.

The park was a mixture of old and new. There were pieces of brightly colored playground equipment that Ben couldn't even name, yet he thought it was interesting that all the kids were congregated around the old standards—seesaws, swings, and a long, wavy silver slide—all of which looked exactly like the ones from years ago only repainted. A boy was pushing the merry-go-round, his feet churning up dust until he hopped up to ride. The park planners must have squeaked in under the wire, before all the new safety codes had gone into effect.

Before they were married, Ben had brought Chloe to this park several times. They liked having the merry-go-round to themselves in the dark. They would get it going really fast, then swing themselves up and lie down on their backs on opposite sides, their hands locked above their heads as they watched the stars whirl in a big blurry wheel. After the merry-go-round stopped, they would lie there talking for a long time, their hands still touching.

One August night Ben spoke right during the fastest part of their dizzy spin. It was a misty, windy night, the stars partly hidden by patches of clouds. He called out to Chloe above the whoosh of the wind and asked if she wanted to marry him, and she called back, "Is New York City big?"

When he came in late that night, wet from rain, his mother was waiting up for him in the kitchen. She was sitting at the table dipping a tea bag up and down in a cup. Above the wisps of steam, he saw the worry on her face. He heard it in her voice, too, when she asked him where he had been all that time.

He still remembered the sound she made—half moan, half sputter—when he answered, "Chloe and I were lying down together in the dark." He had waited just a moment before explaining, which was mean of him. As usual his mother didn't appreciate the humor, had looked like she wanted to throw the contents of her cup at him. She said she and Mrs. Quantrille had been ready to call the police.

When he calmly proceeded to tell her he had asked Chloe to marry him, she was even more dismayed. "You proposed on a *merry-go-round*?" she said. His mother thought proposals should be big, elaborate affairs. Weddings, too. Later she had been appalled that Chloe was making her own wedding dress out of white dotted Swiss and that they planned to be married in a field. "Think of your *guests*!" she had protested. "People don't want to go tromping around in a field!" Then they don't have to, Ben told her. They were inviting only a few people anyway.

Ben stood for a moment scanning the park from left to right. In many ways it seemed like a scene from the fifties or sixties. Derby still had that small-town, family-oriented feel. A game of kick-ball was in progress at one end of the far field while a group of soccer players had claimed the other end. The old walking path still followed its same course but had been widened and resurfaced. The large grassy area in the center of it was devoted at the present time to Frisbee throwing, the main attraction being a little dog that dashed and leapt about, snagging Frisbees right and left. Ben headed for the path, glad to see that it wasn't overly crowded.

Over by the picnic shelter, several boys were playing basketball on a concrete court. Other people were just sitting and talking, mostly adults, mostly women. Ben was sorry to see that most of the benches around the track were thus occupied. He would prefer not being observed as he walked. He could imagine the things that might be said as he passed by, things like "That man looks like a good candidate for a heart attack. He ought to take off at least twenty pounds." They would have no way of knowing he was working on it, had in fact already lost a few.

He waited until there was a good-sized gap between walkers and stepped onto the asphalt track. A mile—that's what he would walk. He looked down at the asphalt. Even though it was only something people walked and spit on, composed of common bitumen, it could almost be called pretty—its smooth blackness shot through with sparkly glints.

Four laps around the track—that would be a decent workout for a Saturday afternoon. He was getting hungrier by the minute, but he would feel less guilty about eating an early supper if he could get in a good walk. He set out briskly.

Almost immediately a jogger passed him. From the back, the jogger looked like one of those Kenyan distance runners—lean and fit, with corded calves and thighs. He was wearing thin nylon shorts, the very short kind, and a tank top. Ben watched him weave in and out among the walkers and wondered why the man didn't go somewhere else to jog, somewhere with long open stretches instead of all these poky people in his way. Probably because he wanted to be noticed, wanted all these poky people to say, "Wow, look at that guy. He's a machine."

Once again Ben felt a wave of resentment toward young people. They couldn't conceive of the day when their legs wouldn't be so strong, when their feet and back would hurt, when they would pinch their waist and feel inches of flab. Somebody needed to inform that jogger that there comes a time in life when you have a lot in common with an old mattress. You sag and creak, your springs are sprung, you get dumped by the side of a road somewhere.

Halfway around the track, Ben passed an old woman sitting on a bench with a baby stroller beside her. No doubt she knew a thing or two about sagging and creaking. The child in the stroller was fast asleep. The woman, who was wearing an Atlanta Braves baseball cap and a huge orange T-shirt with a glittery yellow sunflower imprinted on it, smiled broadly at Ben. Actually she looked more like she had just felt the pang of a pinched nerve, but he figured it was a smile when she followed it up with "Hello there, young man. It's sure a fine day for getting some exercise!" She had a deep, clotted voice, her words seeming to come from the back of her throat as if she were gargling them.

Ben nodded and smiled but kept going. The South was full of these eccentric old women who struck up conversations at the drop of a hat. His own mother had been quite a talker herself, having inherited it from her mother, who had spent most of her waking hours on the telephone.

Before the first lap was done, Ben was sweating. But he had good reason, he reminded himself, since it was over ninety degrees today. The jogger passed him again, loping along as if hardly trying. Ben pushed himself to go faster on the second lap, even passed several other walkers, but then he slowed down again halfway around. He was breathing hard. He certainly didn't want to have to give up before he'd finished four laps, and for sure he didn't want to keel over on the track and have to be borne off in an ambulance. He tried to pull his stomach in and hold it, but it was too much to think about. He thought of the old joke about "furniture disease"—when your chest falls down to your drawers. It used to be funnier than it was now.

When he passed the old woman this time, she said, "Keep it up. You're doing just fine!" She had her cap off now and was using it to fan the child, who was still asleep. Her short gray hair was smashed down damply against her head. She had a magazine open in her lap, though Ben doubted that she had read a word of it. She called out to another walker behind him: "You sure are light on your feet, honey!" At least his grandmother hadn't gone around calling people *honey*. That was the ultimate old-woman Southernism.

As he approached her the next time around, she was bent down adjusting the strap on one of her sandals. Ben had never seen such big feet on a woman. She was wearing white ankle socks, and several inches of her mottled, lumpy legs showed between those and the voluminous blue pants she was wearing. The magazine was now spread out facedown on the bench beside her cap, and Ben saw the title: *The Banner of Christ*. He wasn't at all surprised. The South was full of religious people, too.

He was hoping she wouldn't see him this time, but she sat back up just before he passed her. "Good for you, you're on your third loop already!" she said. He wondered if she was keeping up with everybody else's progress the way she was his. All the other people sitting on benches were engaged in conversation, for which he was thankful. Nobody but the old woman was giving him a second glance.

Just then a Frisbee hit the ground near the track and skipped up again. The little dog, a Jack Russell terrier, came tearing toward it and took a flying leap, pirouetted in midair, and caught it neatly in his mouth. The old woman hooted. "My lands, I never did see such a plucky little dog in my whole life! He's nimble as a wet noodle!" Then she laughed so hard she emitted a little snort. Ben didn't know if she was addressing somebody in particular or everybody in general, or maybe just herself. "We used to have a dog," she added loudly, "but cookies was about the only thing he'd do tricks for."

Somewhere on his desk at work, Ben had a list of sentences that ended with prepositions. He might have to add this one: *Cookies was about the only thing he'd do tricks for.* Though it ended with only one preposition, it was still a colorful sentence with the subject-verb disagreement added in. Though the old rule against ending a sentence with a preposition had long since fallen by the wayside, he still had fun correcting Caroline, who had a great fondness for prepositions at the ends of her sentences. In fact, it was a jewel of hers that had inspired him to start the list in the first place. He had been standing in front of her desk one day reading something aloud from his *Say It Ain't So, Joe* book when she suddenly put her hands over her ears and declared, "What did you bring that book I didn't want to be read to out of in here for?"

After the jogger breezed past him again, Ben briefly considered jogging a little distance himself but quickly decided against it. No need to push it. In his khaki pants and polo shirt, he wasn't dressed for jogging anyway. His Docksiders were fine for walking but not for running.

As he neared the old woman on his fourth lap, she seemed to be looking for him. "There you are again!" she called. The stroller was now empty, and a little girl was sitting in her lap. The woman seized the child's hands and clapped them together. "Here, let's clap for the nice man taking his afternoon constitutional, Rosemary Jean. Just like your mama and daddy are doing!" Rosemary Jean smiled up at him, a sweet startled smile. She reminded Ben a little of his granddaughter Lavinia, Grant's younger, with her big eyes and loose blond curls.

He waved and nodded at the old woman, who offered him another painful-looking smile and called out, "Four loops makes a whole mile, you know!" He looked at the walkers up ahead of him, wondering if any of them might be Rosemary Jean's parents. Probably not. They all looked like fairly normal-sized people. Anybody related to the old woman would have to be the size of the Jolly Green Giant.

He finished up his last lap and walked over toward the picnic shelter, where there was a drinking fountain. He took a long drink, then sat down at a picnic table and watched the kids playing basketball a few minutes. A boy waiting to get into the game was standing alongside the court twirling a basketball on his finger—or trying to. He wasn't nearly as good at it as Chloe had been at his age.

Ben headed back to his car. As he passed the track, he saw the jogger on the grass now, walking around in little circles, stopping every few steps to shake his legs. To Ben's surprise, the man was much older than he had thought. From the back he had looked like he was in his twenties or thirties, but his face said more like fifty or sixty. Ben liked him even less now.

Ahead of him Ben saw the old woman again, walking along slowly now, holding Rosemary Jean's hand. The woman had put her baseball cap back on. She looked even bigger standing up than she had sitting down. A man and woman were with her, walking slightly behind her, and Ben was pleased to see that the man, who was carrying a cooler and lawn chairs, needed to take off far more weight than he himself did. The younger woman was pushing the empty stroller.

For some reason he thought of a line from a Barbra Streisand song. It was one of her signature songs, one that Chloe used to have fun wailing, fluttering her eyes and contorting her mouth in the same affected way Barbra Streisand did: "People who need people are the luckiest people in the world." Like everything else, it had lost its humor.

The old woman was leading Rosemary Jean in the same direction as Ben's car, so he slowed down. He surely didn't want her to see him again and launch off into another conversation. All he wanted to do right now was get in his car and go to the cafeteria to eat, then go home.

But unfortunately, the old woman turned around to say something to the other two, and when she did, she caught sight of Ben. She immediately started waving. "Yoo-hoo! Hello there again! I sure hope you had yourself as nice a time at the park as we did! Isn't this the prettiest little park since they've done refurbished it?"

Ben groaned inside. But he waved and smiled. "Yes, very nice, thank you." He was sorry to see them stop at a station wagon directly in front of his car. The man opened the back and started stashing things inside while the younger woman lifted the child and set her in the car seat inside. Ben walked forward slowly. The old woman was evidently waiting for him.

"This here's our car," she said, pointing.

Ben smiled again. As he walked around to the driver's door of his own car, the old woman said, "Is that one *yours*?" and then set about exclaiming over the coincidence of their being parked right next to each other.

"Do you live here in this neighborhood?" she called.

Ben shook his head. "No, I live over in Greenville." He opened the door and put one foot inside. He had only the smallest shred of hope that she would catch the hint that he was in a hurry.

"This here's my daughter and her husband," she said, then laughed. "I call him my son-in-love instead of my son-in-law. Don't I, Willard?" Willard acknowledged that she did. He lifted his head and gave Ben a friendly smile.

"You ready to go, Mama?" the younger woman said, closing the door. She also smiled at Ben.

Ben could have told her the answer to that. No, her mother wasn't ready to go. Old women like her were eaten up with curiosity about everybody they met. And they assumed that everybody else was just as interested in them and wanted to become their newest best friend.

"I never did catch your name," the old woman said. " 'Course, I might not of caught it 'cause I didn't *ask* it!" She laughed a honking sort of laugh. "Mine's Eldeen."

"I'm Ben." He eased himself inside and stuck his hand up to wave before closing the door.

By now the man had finished up in the trunk and had opened the back door on the driver's side, presumably for his mother-in-love. Ben backed up as far as he could without bumping the car behind him and waited as the younger woman helped her mother off the curb and then between the two cars and around to the door. Before getting in, the old woman looked back at Ben, cupped her hands around her mouth, and said something. He couldn't tell what it was, but he waved again.

Glancing in the rearview mirror as he pulled away, he tried to imagine what it would be like to be headed home with the four people in that station wagon. The thought of his own house, freshly cleaned and empty right now except for his cat, suddenly seemed like a very sad thing.

Though he hadn't planned to drive by the old house on Amaryllis, he found himself headed in that direction. It was only a few blocks away. He stopped in front of it and looked at it for a short while. A few things had changed. A new mailbox, new black shutters, potted petunias on the porch. It seemed like part of another life to Ben. What a long, winding road he had traveled since living there as a teenager—and then again with his mother and children. The Quantrilles' house next door hadn't been kept up. The grass was overgrown, and the screen door had a big rip in it. Two dirty children were sitting on the front steps eating Popsicles.

Even though he knew he shouldn't, he turned left instead of right out of the Montroyal subdivision, then drove the mile and a half east to Sherborne Street, then two more blocks and a right turn onto Fairfield. And then he was there, right in front of the only house he and Chloe had lived in together, the house where she had been vacuuming the floor that Friday afternoon over twenty-one years ago. Someone had put in a new sidewalk and flower beds in the front yard, and a woman was standing beside the driveway with a garden hose, watering some rose bushes. The two maple trees flanking the driveway had grown so much that their branches were touching. Ben stepped on the accelerator. He needed to get back to Greenville.

On his way out of Derby, though, he passed Charity Bible Church. He had a sudden thought: Maybe the old woman at the park attended this church. Maybe she knew Kelly Kovatch and her family. Maybe she had been attending for many years and had even met Chloe on one of those long-ago Sundays she came. The marquee in front of the church read, *O COME, LET US WORSHIP THE LORD TOGETHER. PLEASE VISIT US THIS SUNDAY!*

Not a chance in the world, he thought. He quickly turned on his radio, but it was a song without words this time, one he didn't know.

TWENTY-ONE

Heathen Land

Labor Day dawned gray, drizzly, and unseasonably cool for September. Kelly was up earlier than usual since today was the grand opening for the Bazaar's new location. By seven o'clock she was dressed and downstairs in the kitchen. All the employees had to be at work by eight this morning. Even though Mr. Buckley's memo in Friday's paycheck said there would be sweet rolls, juice, and coffee available for the staff before the doors opened, she decided to have a bowl of oatmeal before she left. That would be better for her than sweet rolls.

Ten minutes later she was sitting at the breakfast bar eating when her father walked into the kitchen wearing an old pair of jersey shorts he used for pajamas and a faded red T-shirt that used to be Kirk's. The shirt, which was snug on her father, had white bleach splotches all over it from when Kirk volunteered to clean the bathhouses at summer camp last year. Kelly never had understood why bleach had been slung around so freely, but sometimes with Kirk it was best not to ask questions. She knew from experience that anytime Kirk got involved in a cleaning project, unexpected things happened and cleaning was not always one of them.

"Morning, Kelly," her dad said. He headed for the coffeepot.

"Hi, Daddy, I didn't expect you up so early. I thought you'd try to sleep a little later on your day off. You want some oatmeal?"

"I might fix some later." He inserted a filter in the cone and spooned in two scoops of coffee, then ran water in the glass pot. After he got the coffee going, he took a loaf of bread out of the breadbox. "I woke up and decided to get on up. No use lying in bed when you can be up doing something." He got out a knife and plate and set them next to the loaf of bread. "Anyway, I didn't want you being the only one working on Labor Day. I'm going to crawl under the house this morning and try to figure out why the boys' room never seems to cool down. I think the duct must've pulled loose."

"Get them to help you," Kelly said. It was something her mother used to say whenever her father got started on some home repair job. Her mother wanted them all to learn how to do as many things as possible. She was big on versatility; she had liked to see the girls working outside sometimes and the boys in the kitchen. She had made sure all her sons knew how to sew on a button and follow a recipe, and Kelly herself had helped her dad with several woodworking projects. Not long ago he had shown her how to check the oil and change a flat tire.

Her father got butter and jelly out of the refrigerator and set them on the counter. "You think we made the right decision?" he said.

She didn't have to ask what he was talking about. She knew it had been heavy on his mind for weeks now, and tomorrow was the day it was going to start. "It's the only decision possible, Daddy," she said gently. It was the same thing she'd said numbers of times already. "They can't teach themselves here at home, and the private school would cost too much."

"Maybe I ought to get a loan." That was something he kept coming back to. He felt sure that Kay's mother would lend him whatever he needed for the children, even though he knew she wouldn't be very cheerful about it and would take it as another opportunity to deliver one of her lectures on being able to provide for whatever size family you chose to have.

Kelly shook her head. "We all prayed about it, remember? We talked about it and took a vote, and it was unanimous, remember?" She glanced at the clock on the stove. She was almost finished with her oatmeal. If she could leave by seven-twenty, she could get there early to see if there were any last-minute jobs to do. She hoped LaTeesha remembered the balloons—the final touch for the window display. They were going to tie them to the chair backs at varying heights.

It had been Kelly's idea to use the birthday party theme for the grand opening since the move happened to coincide, at least close enough, with the end of the Bazaar's fifth year in business. The window display had been fun to put together, and she had gotten no end of compliments on it. Mr. Begian had been effusive in his praise: "Ah, Miss Kelly, it is away from this world. You did yourself out with this one!" Mr. Begian was funny. It often took a little creativity to interpret his meaning.

Her father put a slice of bread in the toaster, then got a coffee mug out of the cupboard. At first they had all tried to do everything for him in the kitchen like their mother used to do, until he told them one night that he didn't want that, that he needed to learn his way around. He still let them pack his lunch and fix his supper and do his laundry, but he always got his own breakfast now, though he did everything slowly and methodically.

Kelly scraped out the last spoonful of oatmeal and took her bowl to the sink. "You could come by the Bazaar today. I told you about the live radio broadcast they're having, didn't I?" she said. "You can sign up for all kinds of prizes. Who knows, you might win a free year of car washes or a bird-bath or something."

He smiled. "Maybe we should all come. If we all signed up, we'd have a better chance of winning something."

"Well, if you do, be sure to look for me. I want to show you around and introduce you to people." Kelly grabbed her lunch sack and her red purse, then took the keys to the Taurus off the little row of hooks by the back door. "Bye, Daddy," she said, blowing him a kiss. "I'll be working late, so remind Kerri to save a plate of supper for me."

Caroline, Nora, and Byron were already at work when Kelly arrived. They were getting the sweet rolls and drinks set out on one of the tables in the new break room, or the staff lounge, as the sign on the door said. It was a bigger room than the old one, with fluorescent lighting and two new dinette sets against the wall on the kitchen side. The walls were painted a pale shade of green, and the carpet was a dark green with gold flecks—decisions Mr. Buckley had given over to Kelly and Caroline. The gold sofa from Mr. Buck's old office fit perfectly on another wall, along with an overstuffed chair in a green and gold plaid and a magazine table between them.

Kelly put her lunch in the refrigerator and was helping set out paper plates and napkins when LaTeesha walked in. LaTeesha was always a flashy dresser, and today she was wearing bright bubble-gum pink Capri pants with a stretchy pink-and-orange polka-dot top and tall platform sandals that tied several times around the ankles. She was carrying a pink beaded purse the size of a pillow-case—but no balloons. Kelly's heart sank.

LaTeesha held out her hand. "*Look* what she brought me!" In her hand were eight or ten balloons of various colors, none of them blown up. LaTeesha's sister was supposed to have furnished a dozen inflated helium balloons from the gift shop where she worked. "She said the dumb pump busted yesterday, so she couldn't blow them up. So she comes home late last night with *these* wonky things! I could've choked her. I would've called you, but I knew it was way past your bedtime." She dug in her purse and pulled out a little roll of yellow crinkle ribbon. "And she gave me *this* to tie them with."

"Well . . . it's better than nothing," Kelly said. "Hey, don't worry. We'll make it work." She smiled at LaTeesha and took the balloons and ribbon from her. At least the balloons weren't all the same color. They would do fine, maybe better than the helium ones now that she thought about it. These would give the display a slightly retro flavor.

LaTeesha cocked her head and made a face. "You know, it's really okay to go ahead and lose it once in a while, Double K. At least frown a little bit and poke your lip out. You always Miss-in-Control-of-Herself. Miss-No-Sweat-and-Hang-Loose and Easy-Does-It. I keep waiting for the day you gonna cut loose and stomp around and cuss somebody out. I want to be here to see that!" She threw her head back and laughed. LaTeesha had a hearty, resonating laugh that sounded like it was amplified, and she laughed a lot. You never had to ask if she was at work on a certain day; you could always hear her even if you couldn't see her.

Kelly shook her head and smiled. She wished she were as good as LaTeesha thought she was.

Melody and Jillian walked into the lounge together.

"What's so funny?" Jillian asked LaTeesha. In spite of the chilly weather, Jillian was wearing a very short white eyelet dress today, and her blond hair was piled on top of her head with several loose spirals strategically arranged around her face.

"Oh, nothing," LaTeesha said. "I'm just trying to tell Kelly she can't keep losing her cool and cussing up a blue streak every time something don't go her way."

Jillian's mouth dropped open.

"It's a joke, Jillion-Dollar Baby," LaTeesha said. "Like if I said she was *fat*, see? It's the opposite. Like if I said you was *ugly*, okay? Or your dress was *black*. Or your hair was *red*." And she laughed again. LaTeesha had a way of laughing at people without seeming to make fun of them. Of all the people at work, Kelly liked LaTeesha the most.

"Oh, *you*!" Jillian cried, flapping a hand at LaTeesha. "I can't ever tell when you're teasing!" Then she immediately spotted the full-length mirror next to the restroom door and headed straight for it, as if to make sure she was a pretty blonde wearing a white dress.

"I've got to get these balloons blown up," Kelly said to LaTeesha. "You want to help?"

"Oh, honey, I can't," LaTeesha said. "I got to keep my breath sucked in all day or else I'll pop right out of these." She looked down at her pants. "Not even sure I can sit down. I 'bout couldn't get them zipped up this morning. Ask some man to help you. They got plenty of hot air, 'specially the ones that work around here." She laughed again and then left to check out the sweet rolls.

More employees were arriving every minute. Mr. Buckley walked in with Dustin and Roy. Lester came in shortly after. The room was filling up, and people were already drinking coffee and helping themselves to the sweet rolls and doughnuts.

An idea suddenly came to Kelly, and she headed toward Les before she could change her mind. This could be a very bad idea, but something told her to try it. Les saw her coming and quickly looked away, then stepped behind Roy. He had carefully avoided her for the past couple of weeks, which suited her fine, but she walked right up to him now and held out her hand with the balloons in it.

"Hi, Les. I need somebody to blow these up. Would you do it for me?"

His eyes darted to hers, then to the balloons in her hand. Maybe he thought she was playing a trick on him.

"They're for the window display," she said. "They're a last-minute substitute for the helium kind, but I don't think I have the strength to blow them all up. I'd really appreciate your help. Let's move over there by the counter where there's more room."

She wasn't sure he was following her, but when she got to the counter and turned around, he was a few steps behind her, a puzzled look on his face. She set the balloons on the counter and handed them to him one at a time. He blew them up easily and was surprisingly adept at stretching the ends and tying them off. She was pleased that they were all different shapes as well as colors: long and thin, short and round, medium and oblong, even two squiggly-shaped ones. After each one, she said thank you and took it from him, though neither of them looked directly at the other. She set them gently on the counter.

After the last one was done, he brushed his hands together and said, "Is that all?"

Kelly held up the coil of yellow ribbon. "Well, I've got to go find scissors so I can tie them to some chairs."

Les pulled a little Swiss army knife out of his jeans pocket. "Show me how long and I'll cut."

Ben took a cup of orange juice but turned away from the sweet rolls. They were good ones, he saw, the kind that were swirled and sticky, with pecan pieces on the top. He took his cup of juice and went to stand by the bulletin board. He would wait until eight-thirty to get everybody's attention and then would give his little pep talk, which was folded up inside his shirt pocket. He had typed it out himself on his manual typewriter.

He had memorized the opening: "As a wagon driver might do to assist his horses in pulling a load out of the ditch, so I'm calling on each of you to put your shoulder to the wheel as we begin a new era here at the Upstate Home and Garden Bazaar. Not that our company is in the ditch." Then he would pause for laughter. He had incorporated a number of quotations by famous Americans about hard work and honesty—nothing all that great, really, but it seemed appropriate for the occasion.

He scanned the room. He was pleased to see that the new staff lounge was big enough to hold everybody comfortably. That was nice to know in case he ever wanted to call them all together like this again. It was a clean, cheerful-looking room.

Across the room he saw a couple of balloons bobbing among all the heads. Kelly seemed to be the one holding them, but it looked like Lester was helping her with something. Ben didn't know why he should be surprised, but he was. He had gotten the idea that Kelly didn't have much to do with Les.

He shifted his position to get a better look. A more mismatched pair than Kelly and Les would be hard to imagine. Surely Kelly wouldn't be interested in somebody like Les. Surely she would set her sights higher than that.

He worried suddenly that she might have so little experience with men that she would be easy prey for somebody like Les. He would have to keep an eye out. Maybe Caroline knew something. He would have to check with her as soon as he could. Certain things just couldn't be allowed. He thought of the laws of separation in Chloe's Bible, forbidding the mingling of different elements—the planting of corn and wheat in the same field, the weaving together of wool and linen in a single garment, the yoking of an ox with an ass.

But maybe he was totally misreading the situation. Kay Kovatch would have fostered an evangelistic mindset in her children, so maybe Kelly considered herself an undercover missionary here in the heathen land of the Bazaar. Maybe she had her sights set on Les as her first convert. Yes, Ben would definitely have to keep his eyes open.

TWENTY-TWO

Clear Leading

It was two weeks after the grand opening, and Caroline was eating a late lunch in the new staff lounge. Gilda and Roy were the only others in the break room at the time, neither of whom was anybody she wanted to have a conversation with.

Gilda was always finding ways to mention her bright and shining star of a son, and Roy, with his little ratlike face and wispy mustache, was just plain boring, not to mention peculiar. She had seen him in the hall one day carefully studying the evacuation diagram for the new building, talking to himself as he traced the route with his finger.

So while she ate her chicken salad pita and drank her Diet Coke, Caroline pretended to be engrossed in reading a magazine someone had left on the table. It was one of those news magazines, almost as boring as Roy, but she did finally come to a page that had pictures and reports of celebrities who had gotten married, divorced, or arrested in the past week. She also read some movie reviews, but none of them sounded like anything she'd be interested in.

She finished up her lunch quickly and discarded her trash. Noting a spill on the counter—something dark and sticky that some lazy person couldn't be bothered with—she opened the cupboard under the sink, where the household cleaners were kept. There she saw two cardboard boxes labeled "Break Room" and remembered that she had stashed them there when things got so crazy right before the grand opening.

She wiped up the spill, then pulled the boxes out and opened the tops. It was mostly odds and ends of dishes, which she had suggested throwing out instead of packing for the move. But Mr. Buck had said, "Waste not, want not," which she took to mean no. They obviously weren't very important if no one had even missed them in two weeks, but it was always a doomed endeavor to argue with Mr. Buck. Too bad they hadn't all gotten broken during the move, but someone had wrapped them individually in newspaper as carefully as if they were fine china, not mismatched castoffs. Probably Kelly. Caroline couldn't think of anybody else who would go to this kind of trouble.

She was tempted to stick the boxes back under the sink unpacked, but as sure as she did that, Mr. Buck would buzz her on the intercom one of these days and say something like "Caroline, quick, bring me that green plate with the chipped edge." No doubt if he knew they were still unpacked, he would have already done it.

She set the boxes on the counter, then slipped off her navy sandals and got up on a chair. Since nobody ever used the dishes anyway, she sure wasn't going to waste her time washing them before putting them away.

She quickly got into a rhythm, unwrapping each dish, dropping the newspaper on the floor, setting the dish on a shelf. As she worked, her thoughts went to the movie she had seen for the first time last night. She always liked to review the plots of good murder mysteries after watching them. She had run across this one on television—something titled *The Doll Murders*. It was about a serial murderer whose victims looked just like the antique dolls in his deceased grandmother's collection, which he kept enshrined in his basement, propped up on a long shelf inside little decorated casket-like boxes.

It was a smart, pretty woman detective who figured it all out, but only after she went to his house while he was away and snooped around. When she found the dolls, she knew she had the right man because all the dead women had been found propped up in various poses, dressed in fancy Victorian costumes just like the ones the dolls were wearing. She snapped pictures of the dolls and was headed back up the stairs when, of course, the camera shifted to the driveway, where the killer was just arriving home.

Right then Seth and J.J. burst into the break room laughing, and Caroline almost jumped out of her skin. She looked down at her hands and saw that she was clutching a plate still wrapped in newspaper, holding it in front of her like a shield. And furthermore, it happened to be the front page of the Greenville *News* she was looking at, with part of a headline visible: *DEAD IN CAR*. She unwrapped the plate and saw the rest of it: *MAN FOUND DEAD IN CAR*.

In the first sentence of the article she saw the name of the victim: Percy Hopkins. She felt sure she had heard it or seen it before, but she couldn't remember where. She put the plate away, then looked at the article more closely: *Percy S. Hopkins, 86, was found dead in his car of a single gunshot wound to the head late Tuesday night when firefighters responded to a report of a fire at his residence on State Park Road in North Greenville. The fire started in the kitchen and spread to the other rooms of the house before firefighters could control the blaze.* She skimmed to the end of the article: *A note was found with the body. The death has been ruled a possible suicide, but details are being withheld until further investigation.*

Seth and J.J. monkeyed around as usual as they got drinks from the vending machine, but they finally left. The last thing she heard one of them say was "And this guy is on his back kicking for all he's worth while the leopard is, like, foaming crazy at the mouth trying to eat him alive." Seth and J.J. were always trading farfetched stories that were supposedly true. From the way they talked, all they did when they weren't at work was play video games and watch YouTube.

She looked back at the newspaper she was holding. She wondered why she wouldn't have seen this article in the newspaper. Such a story would certainly have caught her attention. But checking the date, she realized that would have been the week she had been gone on her beach vacation in August. She looked at the name again: Percy Hopkins. It was irritating that she couldn't place it. She prided herself on her good memory for names.

Oh well, maybe it would come to her later. Maybe Percy Hopkins was the name of a character in a book she'd read. She finished with the dishes and set the empty boxes beside the trash can for Mo or Les to take.

As she started to leave the lounge, she noticed several things still hanging on the coat hooks just inside the door, things left there from the grand opening: a couple of sweaters, a raincoat, a jacket, and a hooded sweatshirt. It had been cool and rainy that day, so people had worn them to work and then evidently forgotten them. She had told Mr. Buckley they shouldn't put up with all kinds of personal items being left in the new staff lounge, that they should routinely clear them out and donate them to Goodwill. He had agreed and had already included a note on the last weekly memo to that effect. Apparently no one had read it.

Caroline walked over and swept the items off the hooks, then found a pen and printed a makeshift note on a paper towel: Anything Still Left on Fri Will Be Thrown Away! She was in the process of laying the things out on one of the tables when Mr. Buckley opened the lounge door and said, "Oh, there you are. I need you to do something." She felt like telling him she *was* doing something, but she held her tongue. Saying the first thing that came to mind usually wasn't a good idea with Mr.

Buck. He always managed to make a federal case out of the simplest remarks. Any little thing she said could lead to either a rebuke or a big hairy explanation about word origins or grammar or where Timbuktu was or the life expectancy of elephants. It was very tiresome.

He remained in the doorway while she finished. Over the years she had perfected the art of filling up time and space with extraneous motion just so people didn't get the idea that you were somebody to be bossed around. Pretending to be concentrating very hard, she picked up the red hooded sweatshirt to pull out one sleeve that was stuffed down inside it. It was faded and limp from wear. She held it by the shoulders in front of her and shook it, then folded it quickly and laid it on the table with the other things.

And right at that moment it hit her. Percy Hopkins was the name of the neighbor who said he saw a man sneaking through the Buckleys' backyard after Mr. Buck's wife was strangled in her kitchen with the cord of the vacuum cleaner twenty-one years ago. She had read his name in the newspaper article recapping the unsolved murder. And the killer was wearing a red hooded sweatshirt—at least that's what this Percy Hopkins person had claimed.

The triple coincidence of seeing his name in the newspaper just minutes before picking up a red hooded sweatshirt while Mr. Buck was standing at the door was spooky. A *red* sweatshirt, not any other color, and a hooded one at that. She made a mental note to go back and reread the article about the murder tonight at home to check the name, although she was already ninety-nine percent sure she had it right. Of course, she realized that it was entirely possible that two different men could be named Percy Hopkins.

"Is it an especially nice fabric, Caroline?" Mr. Buckley said from the doorway. "Are you going to stand there stroking it indefinitely?" She turned around to see him peering at her over the top of his big dumb-looking reading glasses. She didn't know why he didn't take them off when he wasn't reading. Maybe he had finally decided to just keep them on all the time to avoid misplacing them. She ought to buy him one of those long chains to go around his neck, the kind old women wore.

She restraightened the articles of clothing slightly, moved the sign over a few inches, and then walked to the door. "All right now, what can I do for you?"

He narrowed his eyes at her and then turned his head and looked up at the ceiling as if listening for something. He often did this before answering her, as if considering her tone. Or, more likely, just marking time, making her wait until he was good and ready to respond, especially if she had made *him* wait. Mr. Buck never wanted anybody to forget he was in charge. He looked back down at her. "That new vendor is here," he said. "He wants to see the available spaces so he can choose one."

"He's early," Caroline said. She hated it when people came a whole hour early and then expected everybody to drop everything and work them in.

"I've been talking with him while you were—" he glanced toward the table behind her—"while you were in here folding things. He came when you were at lunch, but I decided not to bother you. I took him to my office and answered all his questions, of which there were several dozen, and now I'm ready to pass the baton to the next runner. I told him I'd find someone to show him around. That would be you."

"Where's Kelly? I thought that was part of her job. She knows more about the new layout than I do."

"She's busy."

Caroline wondered what she was busy *doing*. In her opinion Mr. Buck was beginning to show favoritism toward Kelly, always holding her up as an example of the ideal worker, always looking out for her in a fatherly way. Like the day he called Caroline to his office and asked—this still made her laugh—if she knew of any "romantic interest between Kelly and Lester, either one-way or mutual." Caroline had told him that was completely out of the question, that she knew for a fact that the two of them could barely tolerate each other, to which Mr. Buck had replied, "Well, that's good to hear," and then told her to find him a new pair of nail clippers because his had disappeared from his desk drawer.

And Mr. Buck's partiality didn't just stop with Kelly herself. Caroline had strong suspicions, for instance, about one of the prize drawings on the day of the grand opening, when Mr. Buck had pulled an entry slip out of the bucket and, without even looking at it closely, announced "Charles Kovatch!"

That was Kelly's father, who had shown up just a few minutes earlier with four younger Kovatches who looked like clones of Kelly. The whole thing was fishy. Their name slips would have been right on top, but she had seen Mr. Buck reach down to the very bottom of the bucket and pull out a slip. And Charlie Kovatch, a big, tall whooping crane of a man, had looked so puzzled that Caroline wondered if he had even filled out an entry. But off he went carrying a brand-new weed eater just for being related to Mr. Buck's pet employee.

Caroline herself felt hot and cold toward the girl. Sometimes she wished she had a daughter like her, or a daughter-in-law, but other times she wanted to tell her to get a wardrobe update, put on some makeup, and join the twenty-first century. At least she had bought herself a couple of new outfits lately even if they did look like they came from Kmart.

"Well, I don't even know how much space this

vendor needs or anything," she said. "And I've got to type up next week's schedule for Nora, and . . ."

"Caroline." He said it like a weary parent dealing with a difficult child.

Before it could turn into a reprimand, she said, "Oh well, all right then, if you'll move out of the doorway, I'll go give him a tour. Even though a *lot* of other people could do it better than me."

He didn't move. "Better than I. You need the nominative case there. It's an elliptical clause, with the pronoun serving as the subject. You wouldn't say, 'Better than *me* could do it,' would you? Please tell me you wouldn't say that."

"Oh, Mr. Buck, I wish—" But she stopped. She knew how these conversations could drag on indefinitely. She wasn't going to give him the pleasure of having something else to correct.

He waited a moment, then said, "If wishes were horses, beggars could ride." Then he stepped out of the way and let her pass.

Whatever that was supposed to mean, Caroline thought as she marched down the hall. She didn't see any connection at all between horses and beggars.

At six o'clock that day Ben was getting ready to pull away from the back entrance of the Bazaar in his Lincoln Town Car when he saw Kelly exit the building and walk toward her Ford Taurus. She was wearing a black skirt with big yellow flowers on it and a yellow blouse. Her clothes usually hung on her as if they belonged to a larger older sister, but today she looked different, as if she had actually bought something just for herself, something that fit. He wondered if LaTeesha had anything to do with it. He knew the two of them had started taking their lunch break at the same time. He surely hoped Kelly wouldn't start dressing like LaTeesha.

He pulled out of his parking place slowly and rolled down his window. He stopped alongside Kelly and said, "I keep meaning to ask how that new weed eater is working."

Kelly smiled. "Oh, it's great, Mr. Buckley. My brothers do yards, so they especially appreciate it. Our old one was on its last leg, so the timing couldn't have been better."

Ben nodded. "I think your father said it was being held together with rubber bands and tape." He let his car creep forward a few inches. "Well, good night, Kelly."

"Good night, Mr. Buck."

He put on the brake. "I don't know that I ever thanked you for all the extra time you've put in since the move. And before, too. You're doing a good job."

"Everybody has worked hard," she said. "But thank you. I love my job, Mr. Buck. It's more than I ever hoped for. I feel like . . ." She hesitated, then lifted her chin just slightly. "Well, I don't know if

I ever told you that my whole family prayed about it together every day, and then when you said you'd hire me, well, we knew it was God's clear leading."

He waved to her as he slowly pulled away. It came as no surprise that she would connect her job with her religion, of course, but it gave him a funny feeling to know he'd had a hand in what somebody considered "God's clear leading."

After work several evenings later Caroline walked into the office of the Derby *Daily News*. She felt very proud of herself for coming up with the idea even though she was a little disappointed that it had taken her so long to think of it.

It had been as easy as pie to call the newspaper office from work to ask about looking at something in their files. She knew from experience that the requests of timid people were often turned down, so she had been very assertive with the woman on the phone, not really asking but telling her exactly what she *needed*, not just wanted, and when she would be able to stop by. The woman, who identified herself as Mavis, had fallen all over herself to answer Caroline's questions over the phone, had been so chatty, in fact, that Caroline had finally cut her off and told her she had a call on another line.

The woman coming forward to greet her now, or *waddling* forward, had to be Mavis because she had already launched into a greeting that went on and on. While she talked, Caroline took in every detail of her appearance.

Mavis was plump, to put it kindly, but seemed perfectly content with her size, along with every other aspect of her life—her age, which was probably close to Caroline's own, her thin frizzy orangish hair, her hearing aids, her polyester pants, her *DIXIE PRIDE* T-shirt, and especially her job of "morgue librarian," a title that gave Caroline the creeps. It was only one of the many hats she wore here at the newspaper office, she said cheerfully, and she was always glad to accommodate folks this way because it made her feel like all her long hours of cutting up newspapers and filing the clippings away were finally worth something.

She told Caroline to take her time. She wasn't going home for at least another two hours, and it might be longer if her husband called and said his truck still wasn't fixed, even though this was the *third* time this month he'd had it in the shop, and . . . Caroline finally interrupted and told her she was on a tight schedule, which wasn't exactly true, and asked her where she could sit to read.

"Oh, sure, sure," Mavis said and pointed to a table. She handed Caroline a file folder labeled "Murder/Buckley, Chloe," and before leaving, she grew serious and asked gently, "You related to the victim?"

Caroline lowered her eyes and said, "Well, in a roundabout way, yes."

Finally she was alone. She hung her purse over the back of the chair, took a deep breath, and opened the folder. For more than forty-five minutes she read, proceeding straight through the articles in the folder, which were all in chronological order with the date neatly printed at the top of each one.

When she finished, she closed the folder and sat back in the chair. She felt overloaded yet unsatisfied at the same time. It was all so very, very interesting. Again she wondered why it had taken her so long to think of checking all the newspaper articles from twenty-one years ago. There were so many fascinating things about the case.

She opened the folder again and reread the first article, then skimmed the second one, which repeated a lot of what was in the first one but added some new information, such as the names of the two neighbors—the woman named Leah Jorgensen, who had been the first on the scene, after the little boy had run to her house, crying, "My mommy! My mommy!" and the man, Percy Hopkins, who lived on the street behind the Buckleys' house and had been the only one to offer the smallest bit of evidence about the killer.

Caroline stopped reading after the second article and considered Percy Hopkins' testimony about the man in the hooded sweatshirt, a clue that had dried up to nothing. It was a heavily wooded neighborhood, according to the description, so it would have been easy to start in one place and emerge a couple of miles away. But it was odd—if a person was up to no good, prowling through people's backyards and walking into houses in broad daylight to kill somebody, he wouldn't wear something as conspicuous as a red sweatshirt that could be spotted by anyone glancing out a window. Not if he had any sense.

She started rereading the third article, which told about how the police searched high and low but came up with nothing. No evidence of forced entry, no fingerprints except those of the family, no footprints since the backyards were all covered with dead leaves and pine needles and then swirled around by the gusty March winds, and certainly no red sweatshirt with or without a killer inside. This article also confirmed that there was no evidence of sexual contact and no sign of robbery.

And here in the third article was also something very interesting. Caroline had never stopped to think about the possibility of Mr. Buck himself being considered a suspect. How awful for him. It was the unlocked back door, his unknown where-abouts for several hours, and—this was the most suspicious—a fairly recent insurance policy on Chloe Buckley's life that raised the biggest questions about his guilt. Caroline closed her eyes. To think she might be working for a murderer! She couldn't get a picture to form in her mind of Mr. Buck actually committing murder, wrapping the cord around his own wife's neck, but what if he had hired someone? But she couldn't imagine that, either.

In the end he had been cleared. In the next article she read about the waitress's testimony, the restaurant receipt, the father-in-law's public statement in his favor, and then the lie-detector test—he had passed that with flying colors. And the unlocked back door—well, it was concluded that anyone in the family could have done that by accident.

She was glad for him, of course she was. Even though he was a far cry from being a dream boss, she would hate to think of him in jail for the past twenty-one years. Or executed in the electric chair. A shudder went over her.

She finished the second read-through and closed the folder again. So that was that. But *who* had done it? Somebody had to be responsible, and maybe he was still running around loose. This case would make a bad movie, a horrible book. A vacuum cleaner killer striking in the middle of the day yet eluding capture for over twenty-one years. There could be no story unless there was an ending. A mystery couldn't leave you hanging.

Fifteen minutes later she was leaving the newspaper office, having finally gotten away from Mavis, who hovered around while Caroline photocopied the articles, recounting the whole history of the Derby *Daily News* and how she first started working there when she was "fresh home from college." Caroline hid a smile. She couldn't help wondering what kind of *college* somebody like Mavis had gone to. Probably some little backwater junior college.

She ordered a ham and cheese calzone at the drive-through window at Luigi's Little Italy, then drove home. She kept looking down at the photocopies on the passenger seat. She was going to change clothes and then read them all again while she ate her supper. Surely there was a clue somewhere in all of those articles. It could be something really obvious. She knew one thing—from what she had read, she wasn't very impressed with the police and detectives who had handled the case. If she had been part of the investigation, she never would have let go of the case. She imagined herself as a little bulldog, gnawing and shaking an old rag until it unraveled.

TWENTY-THREE

Something Legitimately Fragile

Finally the corn was boiling. Erin looked at the clock again. Where had the time gone? And what had ever possessed her to invite people for dinner on a Sunday afternoon? Just because the Galloways had invited them to their house two weeks ago, was that any reason to turn around and reciprocate so soon?

She tossed a bag of potato chips onto the kitchen counter. "There, put those in a bowl," she told Reuben.

"Yes, ma'am," he said. He was humming something she couldn't put a name to.

"Not that one," she said when he reached for a mixing bowl. "Get a nicer one from up there." She bobbed her head toward a cupboard as she dumped a can of pork and beans into a saucepan. "Hand me a spoon, will you?"

Reuben laughed. "Hey, I can't do everything at once. Which is it, chips or spoon?"

"Spoon right now," she said, holding out her hand. "Quick, don't just stand there. I'm trying to come up with some kind of imitation baked beans here." She snapped her finger. "Come on, they'll be here in fifteen minutes. We can't waste time talking." She heard the pup out on the back porch, whimpering. "Did you get new dog food like I told you to yesterday?" she said. "That other stuff is disgusting. Eskie just sniffed around at it this morning."

He handed her a small dessert spoon. Of course—with Reuben you had to be very specific.

"That's all we need around here," he said, ripping open the bag of chips. "A canine snob. Who does he think he is, turning up his nose at my dog food? Mewt eats anything we give her. But to answer your question, yes, I did get the new stuff. Paid an arm and a leg for it, too."

"Wait, don't do that yet. Can't you remember anything? Put in a napkin first."

"What?" He popped a chip into his mouth.

"A napkin. Unfold a paper napkin and put it in the bowl first. It absorbs the extra grease. You ought to know that by now—I've only done it every time we've had potato chips in the past ten years. Get out the box of brown sugar, will you? And the bottle of vinegar." She squeezed some mustard into the pan of beans, then some ketchup, and stirred it all together.

"Hey, will you slow down? What's the big deal, anyway? If they get here before we're ready, they can just wait. You're making this sound like the countdown for a space shuttle or something. They can come in here and watch us finish up." He was concentrating on trying to get the edges of a paper napkin apart.

"How's the chicken coming?"

"I don't know. I stepped inside a minute ago to get the basting brush, and you've been barking orders at me ever since. It might be burned to a crisp, for all I know."

She jerked her head around. "Get out there and check on it!" She put the spoon down and walked to the pantry for the brown sugar and vinegar. Reuben could be so efficient in every other room of the house, but in the kitchen he had only thumbs and two left feet. At least he could manage the grill in the backyard. He was quite adventurous with meat, in fact, and often pulled off successes, though he could never remember afterward exactly what he'd mixed together for the marinade or what temperature he'd cooked it on or for how long.

Reuben slapped the unfolded napkin back on the counter and pretended to be pulling his hair out. "I need counseling. I'm living with a mentally unstable female," he said as he strode toward the door. He was wearing his leather-fringed vest and moccasins today. For some reason he often took off his cowboy clothes on weekends and turned into an Indian.

"Hold on, didn't you want the basting brush?" Erin called after him. She grabbed it from the drawer and threw it to him.

He caught it neatly. That's one thing he could do—anything that had to do with catching or throwing or hitting or kicking.

"And now she's throwing things at me," he said. The screen door slammed hard behind him. She heard him say something to Eskie, and then he started humming again.

Erin turned off the burner under the corn. She sprinkled some brown sugar into the beans and poured in a little vinegar. She stirred it some more, then added salt and pepper. She tasted it. Not bad. She got out the barbecue sauce and stirred in a little of that and tasted it again. Better.

She suddenly remembered the bacon in the freezer. She could add some of that. It was the expensive already-prepared kind, something she would never have bought. Reuben teased her constantly about her inconsistent shopping habits. Only the very best pet food would do, for instance, yet she hated to spend a dollar for a name-brand grocery item if she could get an off brand for ninety-nine cents. She was always fussing at him when he came back from the grocery store with unauthorized purchases, such as the bacon.

She got it out now and read the directions. Okay, this would work. A couple of strips in the microwave, crumble it up, and stir it into the beans. That would make it more like the baked beans her grandmother used to fix.

A few minutes later she was spooning the beans into a CorningWare dish and setting them in the oven. She rinsed out the saucepan and stuck it in the dishwasher. Then she unfolded the napkin, arranged it in the bowl, and emptied the potato chips into it. Now to set the table.

As she zipped around laying out plates, silverware, and napkins, she ticked off the menu items. Chicken on the grill, baked beans, potato chips, bread, corn on the cob, raw veggies and dip, tea, peach cobbler. Not bad for somebody who didn't consider herself a cook.

She was halfway proud of the cobbler, which was sitting on the stovetop. It was Shelly's recipe, one she had gotten from a Savannah cookbook and e-mailed to both of her sisters, along with a glowing description of her own triumph with it at a big family dinner for Mark's grandparents' wedding anniversary. "It looks and tastes like you spent hours on it," she had written, "but it's a breeze to make! Easy as pie, ha ha!" Then she had added one of those stupid little sideways winky-smiley faces made out of a semicolon and a parenthesis.

Reuben had gone from humming to singing. Now she recognized what the song was. It was from the Cinderella musical they had attended in Flat Rock two months ago. She thought of all the excited little girls in the audience that day wearing their princess dresses and fake tiaras, her nieces included. Once upon a time she had had her own princess dress, along with a little silver crown and slippers. But that was over twenty-five years ago, when she foolishly believed wishes really did come true.

"In my own little corner in my own little chair"—those were some of the words of one of the songs Cinderella sang. Reuben was messing them up, though. "In my own little corner of my own little world," he sang, "I can fly wherever I want to fly." It was a funny song for a man to be singing, but Reuben wasn't the typical man. She wondered where he wanted to be flying right now. She knew if he had his way, they would spend half the year traveling and seeing the world. She was the one who liked to stay put in her own little corner of the world, not him. He was the idealist; she was the realist. He dreamed; she held back.

Eskie started howling, a curiously thin and eerie sound for a dog called a husky. Reuben broke off his singing. "Hey, you, don't ruin my concert!" He laughed and started singing again, even louder. "In my own little corner by my own little grill, I can sing whatever I want to sing." Reuben could be extremely silly.

Erin took the vase of roses off the table, poured out the old water and added fresh, then put it back. She got the little dish of lemon slices out of the refrigerator and put it on the table next to the butter. She looked around to see if there was anything else she had forgotten. Oh yes, the glasses for the tea. She took them out of the cupboard and set them on the counter.

She had always hated this part about having company. All the planning and cooking and then the jittery rush at the end. It was hard to believe this whole dinner was actually her idea—and with a couple they hardly knew at that.

They had met Holly and Clark Galloway only once, with the little girl they had adopted from China a year earlier. Susannah had just celebrated her third birthday. Erin knew that the real reason the Galloways were coming for Sunday dinner in a few minutes had nothing to do with Holly and Clark but everything to do with Susannah.

She couldn't explain it and hadn't tried to. Normally she came up with all kinds of excuses whenever Reuben suggested inviting people over, which he had pretty much quit doing. And never ever would she willingly subject herself to company that involved children. So when she told Reuben a few days ago that she had called Holly Galloway and invited them for dinner on Sunday afternoon, he had felt her forehead and asked if the September heat was getting to her.

There was no analyzing it. All she knew was that two weeks earlier she had seen Susannah Galloway for the first time and had thought about her every day since. It was at church, of all the unlikely places. Though church wasn't a normal part of their weekend routine, and though churches had disappointed Erin time and again, for some odd reason that Sunday she had shrugged and gone along when Reuben suggested it.

A small church without even a real denomination in its name, it was packed to the gills that day. They had been squashed in at the end of a pew near the back. Right in front of them had sat a couple near their own age with a little black-haired Asian girl. Erin, who avoided children whenever she could, couldn't take her eyes off this one. And, oddly, the interest appeared to be mutual. Off and on during the entire service, the little girl had peeked over her father's shoulder at Erin. Not at Reuben or any of the other dozens of people around her, but at Erin. Most children gave her wide berth; she didn't wear a sign that said, "I Don't Like Kids," but they all seemed to know.

The couple introduced themselves after church and invited Erin and Reuben over for an impromptu meal, which turned out to be a ham and cheese omelet with a Caesar salad and Klondike bars for dessert. And somehow before she and Reuben left the Galloways' house that day, Susannah had ended up sitting in Erin's lap, studying her face up close with her bright little eyes. "That's really funny," Holly had said. "She doesn't usually have much to do with other adults." Erin thought she was the most beautiful little girl she had ever seen.

She heard the porch door open and slam again, then Reuben's voice talking to Eskie: "Okay, hang on, you whiny mama's boy, you. I'll get you something to eat in a minute. We can't have you out here making all this racket while we—oh no, you don't! Hey, stop it! Get down. You can't have any of this!"

Erin yanked open the back door. "Here, give me the chicken," she said. Reuben was squatting down, laughing and holding the platter of chicken above his head as Eskie leapt around him. Leave it to Reuben to stop and pet the dog while he had their dinner in his hands.

And just then she heard the doorbell ring from inside. "Hurry up and feed him," she said. "Then wash your hands and help me get ice in the glasses. I'll go get the door." Eskie had scampered over to nose around her feet by now, but she gave him a gentle kick. "No, no, get away. I've got stuff to do." This was another upside-down thing. Usually she loved dogs, all kinds—everyone at work called her Dog Woman because she had such a touch with them—but she was having a hard time learning to like this one. It certainly wasn't his looks; he could be on a calendar of "World's Cutest Puppies." And it wasn't the breed. She had told Reuben for years that her dream was to someday have a husky.

Forty-five minutes later they were finishing the meal. Susannah's bib was spotless since she had eaten only raw carrots and celery, bread, and potato chips—all very charmingly, her little fingers as deft as a raccoon's. Pushed up close to the table, she sat primly on the stack of books they had arranged on one of the kitchen chairs. She didn't make a peep, at least nothing Erin could understand, but Clark said they had been told this was typical of children adopted at her age. Since she had already begun absorbing Chinese language patterns before they brought her to the States, it would take her a little longer to reprogram the verbal part of her brain to English.

"But anybody can look at her and tell she's very intelligent," Reuben said. "She'll probably open her mouth one of these days soon and say something like 'My soul is enraptured over the colorful foliage of deciduous trees in the autumn.' "

"Well, if she lived in your house, maybe," Clark said, laughing. "In ours she'd be more likely to talk about negative correlations and reducing volatility in one's portfolio." Erin hadn't really caught what kind of job Clark had except that it was something to do with finances.

They all laughed, and Susannah looked from face to face, smiling happily, her fine black hair swinging prettily from side to side, all silky and uniform like a tassel.

Eskie suddenly started scratching at the kitchen door, emitting excited little yips. Evidently he didn't like the idea of people having fun while he was stuck out on the porch.

"Oh, you have a dog?" Holly said. "May we let Susannah pet him?"

And before it was over, Reuben had gotten the camera and taken a picture of Erin sitting on the floor of the porch holding Eskie in her lap so that Susannah could pet him. And then for good measure, Reuben brought Mewt out of the back bedroom so Susannah could see her, too.

"Wow, a dog and a cat both," Clark said to Erin. "Did you bring them both home from the animal shelter?"

"The cat, but not the dog," Erin said. She watched as Susannah turned away from Mewt and back to Eskie now, clapping her hands and chortling with glee as he wiggled around in Erin's lap.

"Oh yeah?" Clark said. "Pet store?"

But Erin didn't feel like getting into all that. If she told them the dog was a gift from her father, she knew that would only lead to more questions, and she didn't want to ruin a perfectly good day by thinking about her father. She shook her head. "No, private breeder." Which wasn't a lie. After her father had found out from Reuben that Erin loved huskies, he had contacted a private breeder. No dog pound mutt for her father, of course, only something that cost a lot of money.

"How did you come up with the name Eskie?" Holly said.

Reuben spoke up. "It's short for Eskimo since they were, you know, bred up in the Arctic somewhere to pull sleds and such. Actually, people who know all about the history of words think the word *husky* is probably just a corruption of Eskie."

"How interesting," Holly said.

Erin gave Reuben a look. She knew exactly where he must have heard that. There could be only one person who would have offered this tidbit of information. Now she understood why Reuben had suggested the name as soon as he arrived home with the dog after meeting her father in North Carolina, halfway between their two houses. No doubt her father had given him the little etymology lesson over lunch that day. She refused to consider what else they might have talked about as they ate. She had never asked, and Reuben hadn't offered.

"Okay now, how about some dessert?" she said, rising to her feet suddenly and dumping Eskie on the floor. "Let's go back inside, and I'll get it dished up."

By the time they had finished the peach cobbler, Susannah was sitting in Clark's lap, her head against his chest, her eyelids fluttering.

"Looks like we need to get somebody home for a nap," Holly said.

"Oh no, not yet!" Erin didn't mean to sound so desperate. She felt her face flush as everyone's eyes turned on her. Even little Susannah opened her eyes to stare at her. Erin cleared her throat and tried to sound casual. "Well, I mean, I wonder if Susannah might like to take her nap on our bed? If she would, could you stay a little longer and tell us about . . . how you got started in the adoption process?" She didn't look at Reuben, but she knew his mouth must be hanging open.

Ben changed the channel quickly. The National Poker Championship was not something he wanted to watch. Slim pickings on Sunday night, even with cable. He came to a soccer game on another channel. One of the commentators was British. Ben liked the humorous expressions British sportscasters used. Somewhere he had started a list of them, things like "Look at him, tacking along the fairway as if he's a yachtsman" and "Oh no, the cat is among the pigeons now!"

He watched the soccer game for a minute. "We have some particularly robust action on the field today," the British commentator said. "There's more shirt-grabbing than at a department store sale." A few months ago Ben would have written that one down, but more and more he was losing interest in such things. A few days ago he had even thrown away several lists at work as he was weeding through the stacks of papers Caroline had boxed up from his old desk.

He looked at his last can of beer sitting on the table beside his recliner. Still unopened, it had sat out too long now and wasn't as cold as he liked it. Somebody scored in the soccer game, and the commentator started yelling, "GOOOOOOOOAL!" Ben began flipping channels again. He found one with some kind of obstacle course set up for contestants to get through. There were subtitles in English, with a Japanese-sounding announcer. A very hyper Japanese. He switched to the Off-Road channel and found a bowling tournament for wheelchair players.

He turned off the television and got up. He returned the can of beer to the refrigerator and closed up the bag of pretzels. Ink appeared at his feet, meowing. She'd already been fed, but Ben opened another can of tuna and scooped the whole thing into Ink's dish. The cat didn't hesitate but fell to eating. She wasn't stupid. If somebody was offering extra tuna, she wasn't going to stand around.

Ben looked at the clock on the stove. Time was all out of whack. The day had seemed interminable, yet it was too early for bed. He left the kitchen and wandered into the study. He hadn't turned on his computer today and saw no need to do so now. He never checked stock prices on weekends. He looked at his bookshelf a moment but turned away. He didn't see a thing he wanted to read. This was awful. He needed a ritual for times he couldn't settle down, which seemed to be happening far too often lately. But he knew that wasn't at all what he needed—more rituals. He thought of all the hours he had wasted in his lifetime. Not just hours, but months and years.

He wanted to fix things with his children, had been trying to, but there was a limit to what a person could do. You couldn't force yourself on other people, not even your own flesh and blood. Or maybe *especially* not your own flesh and blood. You could do only so much, and that was it. Then you had to wait, maybe forever.

As he walked back into the hallway and headed toward his bedroom, he heard a light scratching sound somewhere overhead and stopped to listen. Maybe it was just a branch scraping against the roof—or maybe it was something in the attic. He thought of the battle with mice his father had waged in the attic of their first house many years ago, a battle they had finally won only after financing a professional exterminator's summer vacation. The sound stopped, then resumed, but lighter than before.

He went to the kitchen for a flashlight, then came back to the hall and pulled down the attic door. He unfolded the ladder and started up. The ladder creaked under his weight, and he stopped to listen. Nothing. At the top he pulled a string to turn on the light—a single bare bulb. He looked around, then stepped up into the attic. It was hot and stuffy, and he had to stoop as he started searching, moving boxes and shining his flashlight around.

But he found nothing. No sign of anything. No mouse droppings, no nests, no chewed-up bits of paper. He climbed back down and stood in the hallway. Just as he started to fold the ladder back up, he heard it again—a little scrabbling sound. He quickly climbed the ladder again and aimed his flashlight all around. Still nothing.

Again he poked around among the boxes. Maybe whatever made the noise was *inside* one of them. But he couldn't start opening all of them and going through them. There must be at least three or four dozen, some of them quite large. He needed to get rid of all this stuff, whatever it was. Just load it all up and take it to Goodwill. He would never miss it. Some of it had been in his mother's attic when she died. She had always been reluctant to throw anything away. Obviously, he was more like her than he wanted to admit.

Well, he would have to give this up. His back was hurting from stooping over, and he was starting to sweat. As he moved toward the ladder, he noticed something written on the side of one of the boxes he had shoved around. It was the word *fragile* printed in tall, skinny letters, the *i* dotted with an asterisk. He recognized it instantly as Chloe's printing.

He lifted the top and found it full of photo albums and scrapbooks. Evidently Chloe had originally used the box for something else, something legitimately fragile. Even though he told himself not to, he reached for the album on top. *Inexorable* was the word that came to his mind. Unyielding to reason.

He moved over under the light bulb and opened it. His eyes fell on a picture. Of all the pages he could have opened to, it had to be this one. Erin was wearing a princess dress, and he was wearing an old pair of shorts and a ratty T-shirt. The two of them were dancing, Erin standing on his feet in ballerina slippers, her head thrown back, laughing up at him as if he were the love of her life instead of her ordinary father.

There was an empty slot next to the picture, and Ben knew exactly which photo had been there at one time—the one in his wallet, of him holding Lydia and Erin. A quick glance at the other pictures on the page told him it must have been the twins' birthday. There was one of the two girls blowing out candles on a cake, another of all four children wearing party hats. Grant was only a toddler. Shelly, not looking at the camera, was trying to straighten his hat.

He looked back at the picture of Erin and him. "Impossible"—that was the name of one of the songs in the Cinderella musical they had all attended in Flat Rock. And that was the only word to describe the photo. Impossible that there had ever been a time when Erin had looked at him that way and danced with him.

TWENTY-FOUR

Common Things Like Trees

The bride was a girl Kelly had known ever since they were in Mrs. Thompkins' Sunday school class together as kindergartners. Chelsea Loftis was marrying a boy she had met a little over a year ago at a camp in Virginia where they were both counselors for a summer.

Kelly had never before attended an autumn wedding, but she thought October was a beautiful month to be married. All the way across the top of the choir loft partition lay dark green magnolia leaves interspersed with yellow, red, and orange mums and daisies. Chelsea's three sisters were bridesmaids, and they wore dresses in a soft shimmery gold fabric.

Kelly liked the formal diction of wedding ceremonies—things such as Pastor Shamblin was asking right now: "Chelsea, do you take Andrew to be your lawful wedded husband?" And "To have and to hold from this day forward." She thought the way Pastor Shamblin performed weddings was perfect. He didn't rush anything, but he didn't drag it out, either. He managed to make it both solemn and joyful, which was exactly what a wedding should be. Kelly listened carefully to every word of the long question and then to Chelsea's bold answer: "I do." It seemed like a very big promise she was making.

Kelly and her sister Kimmie were sitting right behind the bride's family, so they had a good view of everything. Kerri was back in the fellowship hall, helping to get the reception set up, and the younger children were at home with Dad. "Let's see," Kirk had said when they discussed it at supper last night, "do I want to spend Friday night at home playing games and watching a movie, or do I want to go to a wedding and watch two normally sane people get mushy and drip all over each other?" He had scrunched up his face as if in deep thought and tapped a finger against his lips. "Wow, that's *really* a hard decision."

The groom's sister was singing a solo now, accompanied by trumpet and piano. The printed program said the title of it was "Your Heart Is My Treasure." Kelly had never heard it before. The melody had a haunting quality, echoed by the trumpet, but the piano accompaniment was light and rippling. Another blending of solemn and joyful.

Chelsea and Andrew were holding hands, facing each other. They made a nice-looking couple. Though Andrew wasn't tall, he was certainly tall enough for someone as petite as Chelsea. They looked into each other's eyes as if totally unaware of anyone else in the whole auditorium. " 'I will hold it gently,' " the sister sang, " 'for it is the treasure of my heart.' " It was a different kind of solo for a wedding at their church—not really what you would call a spiritual song. But Kelly immediately changed her mind. No, it was a song about love, and the Bible was full of love.

Andrew bent his head closer to Chelsea's, and she smiled up at him. Kelly knew she would never be able to do that—look at a man that way in front of a whole roomful of people. Her older sister, Krista, had done it in her wedding. She and Neil had recited their vows to each other and then had sung a duet together, all the while gazing into each other's eyes. But Kelly knew it would embarrass her to no end to do that publicly.

Her mother had talked to her often about the dreams she had for her. Whenever they had prayed together, just the two of them, her mother always thanked God for Kelly's "special gifts" and expressed her happy assurance that God was even now "preparing a godly husband" for her second daughter the way he had for Krista. Unfortunately, no eligible young man had seemed to notice her special gifts yet.

Though Kelly knew marriage could be a wonderful thing, she couldn't generate any confidence that it would happen to her. Kerri and Kimmie were always talking about weddings. Kerri, who had recently started apprenticing with a caterer, was taking detailed notes in a special notebook about all the weddings and receptions she was helping with, and Kimmie, who had an eye for fashion, drew sketches of wedding dresses all the time, even though at seventeen no prospects for a husband had yet materialized.

But at least Kerri had a boyfriend. She and Jared King had been keeping company for almost a year, though most of their dates were limited to sitting by each other in church. Jared was taking courses at Greenville Tech to be a paramedic and was saving his money to buy a ring.

Kelly had never had a boyfriend. Around boys she didn't have the friendly, easy manner of her sisters. She could never think of anything to say. It was irritating that she could talk freely and naturally with anybody else, but not boys her own age. No one would ever want a bump on a log for a girlfriend. And certainly not for a wife.

Lately she had been thinking a lot about the fact that God didn't ordain marriage for everybody. She had read a book from the church library titled *Single Sainthood*, hiding it between two other books after she checked it out so that no one would see it and ask questions or tease her. It was written by a woman in her fifties who claimed to be "single by choice." And it was a good book. The author told her story well, giving thanks from beginning to end that God was teaching her in her unmarried state to find him all-sufficient. Active in many ministries and involved with the lives of a dozen nieces and nephews, she seemed to be happy and fulfilled. And very funny—Kelly had laughed out loud many times as she read the book.

That was something she had always admired in others—a quick sense of humor. Several of her brothers and sisters had the gift—Kevin, Kirk, and Kimmie especially—but she had missed out. She could *appreciate* a good joke; she just couldn't tell one.

She was willing to accept singleness if that was what God wanted. At times she wished there were the equivalent of a convent for girls like her who weren't Catholics but were interested in a life of quiet seclusion—praying and meditating and doing simple work. But more often she dreamed of going to college, though she knew that was very expensive. She had been praying about it for almost a year now, but she hated to bring it up with her father when he still seemed so lost without her mother. Maybe she could save enough of her salary to take a night course at some point.

Before her mother died, Kelly had tried to relieve her mind one day by telling her that she wasn't worried about getting married, that she could be content to stay single. "Well, that's fine, sweetheart, but don't resign yourself to anything yet," her mother had replied, her eyes full of concern. She tried to raise her head from her pillow. "You're very young. God works in mysterious ways. People get married at all ages, so keep your mind and heart open." Kelly had felt bad about upsetting her.

She wished God would give her a clear signal. If she was meant to be single, she could focus on that and stop being stirred up by feelings of hope whenever she went to a wedding or noticed how nice certain boys were—for example, Gilda Bloodworth's son, Ryan, who always spoke to her politely whenever he came to the Bazaar to see his mother. She tried not to look for him every day, but she couldn't help it. She liked his deep voice, his blue eyes, his black hair—she liked everything about him. She knew Gilda played the piano at a Nazarene church, so she thought maybe Ryan went to church, too. She wouldn't consider marrying anybody who didn't, of course. She didn't know much about the Nazarene church, but from things Gilda said, she thought it might be a good church.

Looking at Chelsea and Andrew now, Kelly tried to imagine how different it was going to be for Chelsea to wake up *married* tomorrow morning. She tried to put herself in her friend's place—to be in love with someone for more than a year, then to have a wedding and suddenly be transformed into his wife. To have prayed for and practiced chastity for that long, and then after a thirty-minute ceremony to have the full privileges of marriage— well, that had to feel like you were participating in a miracle.

Kelly had a great deal of curiosity about the physical part of marriage even though she tried not to dwell on it. Her mother had told her the facts, very clearly and honestly when she was fourteen years old, had said it was "a beautiful and sacred part of marriage" and had asked if she had any questions. Kelly had shaken her head at once; she was sure she must have turned twenty shades of red. She did have questions, plenty of them, but she never would have dared to ask them.

The solo ended with the words " 'With my life for all my days I will guard my treasure—the treasure of your heart.' " Andrew's sister had a pretty voice. The ending slowed down, and the last note leapt up a full octave, then hung in the air like a row of silver bells.

Now came another part Kelly liked about wed- dings—the exchange of rings. "Andrew, what token of your love do you give to Chelsea?" Pastor

Shamblin asked. And then came the most serious words a little later, after the vows were exchanged: "What God hath joined together, let no man put asunder."

Kelly knew that marrying for life was considered an outdated concept by many people today. She had heard disparaging comments at work about marriage. Mostly it was women complaining about their husbands' faults or about men in general. Caroline often said things like "No sir, no more men for me. Marriage is for the birds, and I'm no bird!" It seemed to be something she very much wanted for her son, Donald, however, for she was forever advertising his bachelor status to Kelly and the other single girls, along with his high-paying job and personal charms.

Kelly wasn't convinced of the personal charms, though. Back in August she had overheard Nora ask Caroline how her vacation at the beach had gone. She was pretty sure Caroline was referring to Donald when she told Nora, "I should have had my head examined for inviting him to go along! We weren't even speaking by the end of the week. I would just throw him some money every day and tell him to go somewhere and entertain himself. Some vacation—I'll never make that mistake again!"

Chelsea and Andrew were facing the congregation now. "It gives me great pleasure to present to you Mr. and Mrs. Andrew Doyle," Pastor

Shamblin said. "Andrew, you may kiss your bride."

Kelly both wanted to look and didn't want to. But she did. Andrew lifted Chelsea's veil very gently and kissed her tenderly, though not too long. Kelly looked down at her hands in her lap and wondered if ten years from now her ring finger would still be as ringless as it was right now. She knew her father had taken her mother's engagement ring and wedding band off her hand after the visitation at the funeral home. She had seen them on his dresser for a while, and then they disappeared.

Maybe someday her father would feel sorry for Kelly, after all her younger brothers and sisters were married and she was still single. Maybe he would let her wear her mother's diamond ring out of pity. It was only a small diamond, but her mother had worn it proudly.

The organ and trumpet sounded the first notes of the recessional, and Chelsea and Andrew started back down the aisle, beaming at everyone and walking quite fast. Kelly tried to imagine how it must feel to know you had only a few photos and a reception to get through before you could throw your bouquet and then get in a car and drive away with your husband. On your honeymoon. A married woman for the rest of your life.

Kimmie touched her hand and gestured toward the aisle. Kelly saw that their row was being dismissed to go back to the reception. As she and Kimmie walked out, she felt everybody's eyes looking them up and down. People were probably wondering right now when Kelly was ever going to find a boyfriend and get married. They probably wondered how she felt about her younger sister Kerri dating Jared King while Kelly herself orbited through life like a lone moon.

"Whoa, why are you walking so fast?" Kimmie said to her once they were in the church lobby. "Are you in that big of a hurry to get to the food?"

Unable to think of a witty comeback, Kelly simply said, "Oh, sorry, I didn't realize I was."

They moved along with the crowd back to the fellowship hall. Now for the reception. She would hug Chelsea and tell her how happy she was for her. And she was. She wouldn't have missed her wedding for anything. It was funny how you could love something that made you feel bad.

Well, Kelly wasn't going to let her melancholy side get the best of her. She turned to Kimmie and smiled. "I can't wait to try that coffee punch Kerri keeps talking about. And did you hear her say they're having a whole table with nothing but chocolate? Truffles and fondue and something called mint twirls. And the groom's cake—that's chocolate, too."

"Oh, great," Kimmie said. "We'll be awake half the night with all that caffeine."

Kelly laughed, but she was ashamed of the

thought that sprang to her mind: All that caffeine wouldn't matter one bit to Chelsea and Andrew because they would probably be awake half the night anyway.

The Birthday of the Trees. Ben had never heard of that particular Jewish holiday. It was funny to him that it always fell in January or February, when the trees had no leaves. Tu B'Shevat—that's what they called it.

He was at Barnes and Noble with six books stacked on the floor by his chair and one in his lap. This book was the last of his evening's reading—or browsing. He had spent most of the last two hours just flipping pages, reading a sentence here and there. Except in *Heart Health*. He had read the first three chapters straight through before becoming discouraged over how much of the advice he had been ignoring for the past several years and how many men his age or younger had heart attacks every year. Even though he was trying to take steps to mend his ways, he knew it was an uphill battle. You didn't suddenly become Mr. Atlas at the age of fifty-eight.

Tu B'Shevat wasn't one of the high-profile holidays of the Jewish calendar. The book said that for modern Jews it mostly meant saying a prayer of thanks for trees, eating a piece of new fruit, and maybe planting a sapling somewhere.

He read through the words of a song often sung

on Tu B'Shevat. *Hashkedia porachat ve-shemesh paz zorachat.* A translation followed each line. This one meant "The almond tree is growing." He remembered something he had run across in Chloe's Bible recently. In the last chapter of a less-than-cheerful book called Ecclesiastes, the almond tree was used as a symbol for an old man, its white blossoms signifying his white hair. So the Jewish song celebrating the birthday of trees just happened to mention specifically the one associated with death. The implication was clear. No sentimental saplings for a Tu B'Shevat song. Only forthright reality: Born today, dead tomorrow. Ben closed the book.

As he rose to return his books to the shelves, it came to him that maybe it wasn't such a bad idea to have holidays for contemplating the gifts of simple, common things like trees. It certainly wasn't hard to think of reasons to be thankful for trees. Take books, for instance. There would be no books without trees. Take apples and oranges and all the other fruits that the *Heart Health* book said should be a regular part of your diet. Things he needed to stock up on and get busy eating. One Granny Smith apple a week wasn't nearly enough. Maybe he should stop at a grocery store on the way home and buy a bag of tangerines.

He left the Barnes and Noble parking lot and turned toward home. It was dark, so he couldn't see the trees clearly, but he knew many of them had already started changing colors. Maybe he should drive back up toward Flat Rock sometime soon just to contemplate the trees. He could do it on a Saturday or Sunday. Not quite yet, for the peak season for color was still a few weeks off. But he couldn't wait too long, or all the leaves would drop to the ground and die.

Sitting in the police station now, Caroline felt a tingle of excitement just watching the men and women in uniform moving around. Even the two officers standing over by the window talking and drinking coffee looked more important than regular people drinking coffee, even if one of them did have fat little chipmunk cheeks.

Once again Caroline was seeing proof that there was no end to what a person could find out if she only asked the right people. She was even more proud of herself right now at the county Bureau of Law Enforcement than she had been at the Derby *Daily* newspaper office two weeks ago and at the Greenville *News* office a few days after that. The average person probably had no idea that these kinds of police reports were available for the public to read. But Caroline smiled a small, self-pleased smile, for she knew she was no average person.

Two weeks ago she had been thinking how much she would enjoy being a crime reporter for a newspaper, but now she was fantasizing about being a criminal investigator on the police force. She knew she could make a name for herself. Or *could have* made a name for herself. If only she were thirty or forty years younger and had the luxury of starting over, she would never have darkened the door of that community college where she took secretarial courses. For sure she never would have married the smooth-talking car salesman who turned out to be a royal dud of a husband. And she never would have ended up with a dead-end second-rate job at the Upstate Home and Garden Bazaar, working for a boss with more than a few loose screws.

If she were younger, she would beg, borrow, or steal whatever it took to get into whatever kind of school it was that trained detectives. She would amaze all her instructors and eventually be offered a plum job with a big police department some-where. They would give her the hardest cases, and she would solve them.

After reading everything about Chloe Buckley's murder that she could get her hands on at the two newspaper offices, the idea of asking to read police reports came to her. It had been a simple matter to get the case number, pay the fee, request the copies, and come here to pick them up. She had gone over and over the pages at home. One night she had spoken directly to them, in fact, all spread out on her kitchen table along with her handwritten notes and photocopied newspaper articles. "*Somebody* did it!" she said. "Tell me who it was!"

Now she was on to something else. It was the report of Percy Hopkins' death she was preparing to collect and take home. And also his son's death. She had already read them both and was now waiting for copies to be made. Maybe there wasn't any connection, but she had discovered that Percy Hopkins' retarded son had died only eleven days after Chloe Buckley—in the house right behind the Buckleys' no less.

Leon Hopkins' death had been ruled an accidental overdose. According to the reports, the boy—or rather, the forty-year-old man—besides being mentally handicapped, had suffered from an obsessive-compulsive disorder concerning medications, in particular pills. His father had to keep them under lock and key so his son couldn't get into them. Apparently it wasn't a matter of attempting suicide; it was just a desire to swallow pills. There were more than five documented incidents of trips to the emergency room to have his stomach pumped.

But on the last trip Leon Hopkins was dead on arrival. Ironically, his father, wild with grief, had to be sedated.

Caroline considered for a long moment what Percy Hopkins' life had been like with a son like that. Evidently no wife to help him, just him and the boy at home all day and all night. It wasn't hard to imagine the feeling of despair such a father would feel. She wondered why he hadn't put him in an institution somewhere. But if Percy were going to commit suicide, it looked like he wouldn't have waited until after his son died, over twenty years later—that part didn't really make sense.

Suddenly Caroline's own life seemed very carefree in comparison to Percy Hopkins'. Donald drove her nuts, it was true, but at least he was smart and independent. At least she didn't have to watch him night and day to make sure he didn't overdose on pills and kill himself.

TWENTY-FIVE

Divine Means

The whole time he was talking, Ben knew Mo could hear every word he was saying to Lester, but he didn't care. Maybe it would do him good. Ben and Les were standing just inside the doorway of the storeroom while Mo was on the far side of the room by the sink, his head bent, pretending to be cleaning paintbrushes over and over. Ben could imagine what he must be thinking: "Whoa, never seen Old Man freak like this."

Ben was almost as mad at himself as he was at Les. How he could have let Les get by with so much for so long was incomprehensible. And inexcusable. Where were the standards he always claimed to uphold here at the Bazaar? Why had it taken Caroline's report this morning to spur him to do what he should have done long ago? Caroline and Les had had their run-ins before, but they had always blown over. Caroline was constantly looking for things to pick at Les about, and Les was always talking back, but this was over the top.

"So did you forget that, or did you simply choose to ignore it?" Ben said now. Arms folded, he was blocking the door, looking down at Les. "I'm very interested in your answer, not that I'll believe it since you've destroyed what little bit of trust I had in you. There was a time when I thought you were harmless, that all your loose talk was just for show. I even thought you were humorous at times, but not anymore. I can't imagine what was going through your head to say something like that to a woman. But back to my question. I'm curious— did you forget what I said about watching your language, or did you think it applied to everybody but you?"

Les, his thumbs hooked in his pockets, looked puzzled—no doubt a ploy to stall for time. "Hey, I can't even remember . . . but sometimes things slip out, you know?" He shrugged. "It's no big deal. You know *her*. You know how she always likes to—"

But Ben interrupted him. "That doesn't cut it, Lester, not at all. If things like that slip out, then I'd hate to hear what you say when you take the time to plan your little blowups. The things a person says off the top of his head reveal exactly what he is, and you have shown yourself today to have not only a filthy tongue but also a filthy mind. And it *is* a big deal. It was an awful thing to say, and I can't begin to imagine why you thought you could get away with it. But that's where you were wrong. This is the end of the line for you." He paused, then added. "You need to go check out and leave. For good."

Les looked like he didn't believe him, like he was expecting Ben to stop any minute and say, "Okay, I'm fooling with you, man. Just wanted to make a point. But let's watch it from now on, okay?" But Ben wasn't fooling, not one bit. They stood there glaring at each other.

"Let me get this straight," Les said. "You're going to believe—"

"No, hold it, you're not the one asking the questions here," Ben said. "You're the one listening. You're the one being told that it's all over." He stepped back and put a hand on the doorknob. "And furthermore, Caroline also told me this morning about some things you said to Kelly a while back. I wish I had known about that sooner. You would've been out on your ear before now." He pointed a finger at Les. "And Caroline had every right to tell me, so don't whine about it. It's all over now. I don't want to see you back here. We'll mail you your final paycheck."

For some reason Ben couldn't stop there. Words kept pouring out. He swung the door open, still talking. "We've put up with your hotshot ways long enough around here. I'm not paying anybody good money to act like a jerk on the job. That's the last time you're going to shoot off your dirty mouth like that inside my building."

But it wasn't. Les must have thought if he was going down anyway, he might as well shoot off his mouth a little more. Or a lot more. What came out now had to set some kind of record.

Ben wanted to pick him up and sling him down the hall, but his anger was spent now. He didn't say anything, just opened the door wider. The only thing left for Les to do was stomp out, yelling and cursing at the top of his lungs, calling Caroline every name in the book. And Ben, too—he had some choice names for him, too. All the way down the hall, through the warehouse, and out the back exit. He ran out of new things to say so he started repeating it all. When the back door clanged shut, all was quiet.

Ben stood in the doorway a minute and watched Mo lay the brushes out on a paper towel to dry. On his way down here, he had already thought about what it was going to mean to fire Les, but now that it was over, it hit him hard that the Facilities Management Team was now cut in half. He knew Mo must be thinking the same thing, wondering how he was going to keep up with all the work by himself.

Mo glanced back to see if Ben was still there, but

didn't say anything, and neither did Ben. He would wait and talk to him later, after he had cooled down.

Mo turned the water off, then grabbed some trash bags and headed out the door past him, avoiding his eyes. He was walking faster than he usually did, as if he wanted to get away from there before the Old Man thought of a reason to fire him, too. Ben knew there was no love lost between Caroline and Mo, either, but at least Mo knew how to keep his mouth shut.

Well, no use standing around all day. What was done was done. Ben knew it wouldn't be easy to replace Lester, but he needed to get the ball rolling. No time today to waste on piddling, as Caroline called it.

The following Monday morning Ben was in his office at the Bazaar, sitting at his desk. He had already made his presence known by a quick round past all the showrooms, had passed the time of day with a couple of employees, and had read all his e-mails.

It was Dustin who had finally talked him into getting his own computer here at work, telling him that it was highly inefficient for the CFO to have to walk the length of a basketball court every time he wanted to discuss money with the CEO.

Ben had jokingly suggested that Dustin and Caroline trade offices so he would have to walk only the distance of a Ping-Pong table, to which Caroline had responded heatedly: "That's easy for you to say! You wouldn't be the one running back and forth all day with your tongue hanging out! It's bad enough being right outside your door." Ben had clasped his hands and replied, "Caroline, your trials and tribulations have broken my heart. They are unique. I've never heard anything like them." Dustin had laughed, but Caroline had turned on her heel and left, flinging back, "Nobody knows what I have to put up with!"

Overall, Ben had to admit that the computer was a good idea, though he could already see how it was going to clutter up his time at work. Dustin seemed to think Ben loved spreadsheets as much as he did and that he needed and wanted to see documentation for every single penny coming in or going out. "I hire people I trust and trust the people I hire." This was what Ben had e-mailed him just minutes earlier, along with a brief note that Dustin could spare him things like the cost of three new first-aid kits or the inventory updates and price increases for all the cleaning supplies.

Though he should have qualified it by saying, "I *usually* hire people I trust." Lester Lattimore was a case in point. Lester had been a bad decision, one Ben had kept around far too long, overlooking his sorry behavior because he was a good worker and because, after all, he was only a grunt. But "only a grunt" was a lame excuse. As he had told the staff repeatedly, a team was only as good as its weakest member.

And Jillian Denton—she was another weak link. Giggly, pushy, superficial, Jillian liked to roam outside her zone and talk at great length with other employees. Nora had already reprimanded her once. Since then the girl seemed to have built-in radar to tell her where Nora was at all times, so even though they hadn't caught her wandering in a couple of weeks, he knew from Caroline that it was still going on. Her radar also resulted in her showing up directly in Ben's path far too often to call it accidental, always armed with some inane question or comment, always batting her eyes. Always a whole lot of shaking going on.

He wished he could address the matter of her slinky clothing, but he didn't want to give her the satisfaction of knowing he had noticed. Maybe they needed an official dress code for all the floor employees. Other places had such things. He had seen one posted in the dining room of a country club a couple of years ago, when he had been invited to a dinner for potential investors in a posh new development outside Greenville. There were even penalties listed for country club members, ranging from a written reminder to a hundred-dollar fine. Maybe he should write up a dress code and then include it as a memo in this week's pay-checks. The wording might be a little tricky. How could you quantify things like slinkiness?

Like Les, Jillian had been easy to ignore because she was only a floorwalker, but there was that *only* again. He couldn't believe how lax he had been. Good CEOs didn't hide out in their offices. They got involved and stayed that way.

Hiring a replacement for Lester had to be the first matter of business this week. Not that it would happen today unless he got lucky, but they needed to at least get some interviews scheduled. Roy had posted the job opening on their Web site on Thursday, the very day Ben had fired Les, and Caroline told him just minutes ago that they already had four applications submitted online.

He pulled them up now and read through all four, then e-mailed Caroline to contact three of them for interviews. He also told her to come to his office afterward to talk about this week's memo. He would run the dress code idea past her. Maybe the floorwalkers should have a uniform of some kind—dark pants and a white shirt or khakis and a colorful polo. He wrote "uniform?" on a pad of paper.

Just then a new e-mail popped up on his screen. It was from his investment broker. Emmett Anders was another example of hiring somebody you could trust. Emmett had done well for him over the years—very well—to the point that Ben now left it all in his hands with perfect confidence. Even during bad cycles, Emmett had somehow managed to make money for him, or at least to keep from losing money. "Good guessing comes from years of paying attention" was something Emmett liked to say.

Ben opened the e-mail and read it. *Thought I'd try again,* Emmett had written. *Sell or keep?* Ben could almost hear the sigh that must have accompanied the e-mail. It was a medical supplies stock Emmett kept asking to get rid of. Normally Ben didn't want Emmett to ask him anything. He hired him to manage his portfolio, and that's what he wanted him to do. This was the only stock he had told Emmett to leave alone. He had never offered an explanation, and Emmett hadn't pressed for one. He did keep bringing it up, though.

Ben had bought the stock twenty-one years ago after he'd gotten the check from Chloe's life insurance. At the time he couldn't bear the thought of using the fifty thousand to buy anything, not even something for the children. If the company failed and he lost it all, he reasoned, then good riddance. He certainly didn't deserve the money. Not after treating Chloe so badly those final weeks.

But the company had succeeded. Ben looked at the computer screen again. Pretty amazing, really. Today the stock was worth a little more than five times what he had paid for it twenty-one years ago. It had been up even higher but had slipped in the last quarter. Emmett kept telling him the stock had peaked, that it was facing some heavy competition from a couple of new companies. "Greedy leads to needy" was another one of Emmett's favorite things to say.

He knew Emmett was itching to reinvest the profit. It was something he loved to do, and he no doubt already had a plan. Two hundred fifty thousand dollars, two hundred grand of it in profit—oh yes, Emmett could have a lot of fun with that.

A thought suddenly occurred to Ben. It was something he had never considered before.

Just then Caroline showed up at his door, a yellow legal pad in hand. He glanced at her, then back to the computer screen. He was still thinking. It was a radical thought, one he was sure Emmett didn't have in mind. But it wasn't Emmett's money.

Caroline sat down in front of his desk and clicked her ballpoint pen several times to signal she was ready. Out of the corner of his eye he saw her reposition herself with a little flounce. He heard her sigh, then clear her throat.

He felt the idea filling up his mind, settling in. What if he had Emmett sell the stock and transfer fifty thousand, the original investment, into something else—and then what if Ben took the two hundred thousand profit and divided it among his four children? What if he sent Shelly, Lydia, Erin, and Grant a check for fifty thousand each?

He doubted that any of them would refuse the money or have trouble figuring out how to spend it. Not even Shelly and Mark, with Mark's recent big-bucks promotion. Ben remembered the days of early marriage with young children, trying to stick to a budget with some new expense always springing out of nowhere. If one of their parents had sent them fifty grand out of the blue, he would have felt like he had hit the jackpot. He would have had a dozen ideas for how to use it.

"I thought you wanted to talk about the staff memo!" Caroline said. "I'm sitting here ready."

He turned to look at her. "Yes, I do and you are. Thank you."

He turned back to the computer. He could tell his children the truth—that he had made a nice profit from the sale of a stock, so he thought he'd share it. Or he could just tell them nothing. Just send them the money. He felt sure it was something to which Chloe would give her nod of approval.

He glanced out the window at the car dealership next door, its red and white pennants flapping all around the perimeter of the lot, its electronic marquee flashing *HOT DEALS! DO IT TODAY!*—not nearly as nice a view as the mountains from his second-floor window at the old building. He wasn't much worried about Shelly, Lydia, or Grant, but he tried to imagine what Erin would think when she got the money. Maybe she would think he was trying to buy her affection. Maybe it would make her mad. But then, maybe it wouldn't. You couldn't always hold back because of maybes.

Maybe she and Reuben needed money right now for some worrisome expense.

The word *godsend* flashed into his mind. Something desired that comes as if by divine means. Similar to a windfall—an unexpected piece of good fortune. He remembered coming across it not long ago in his *Say It Ain't So, Joe* book. Medieval peasants were prohibited by law from cutting down trees for firewood, but if a strong wind blew one down, they could thank nature and chop it up without penalty.

He would do it. Now that he had decided, he was suddenly seized with worry that it might be too late. Things could turn south with the stock market in the blink of an eye. What if he had waited too long? He hit Reply and started typing: *Sell and transfer . . .*

Caroline stood up abruptly. "Mr. Buck, are we going to talk about the memo or not? I have a whole lot of other things I could be doing instead of sitting here."

He didn't look up. "Ms. Mason, you're not sitting, you're standing. Now please sit back down and wait. I'm in the middle of writing a very important message that might make a difference in someone's life."

"Well, of all things!" Caroline said, but she sat back down.

In a few keystrokes it was done and sent. Something he had read in Chloe's Bible years ago suddenly came back to him: *He shall divide the spoil.* Was it Moses who said that as he blessed the twelve tribes of Israel before he died? Or was it Jacob when he blessed each of his sons before he died? What if it was Jacob's blessing to his youngest son, *Benjamin*? Wouldn't that be ironic? He would have to look it up sometime.

TWENTY-SIX

Swirl of Stars

Even the gorgeous autumn colors of Virginia in late October weren't enough to lift Erin's spirits. It had been a horrible week so far, with very little hope for improvement. Usually her favorite month, October was totally uninspiring this time around. Not just uninspiring but sinister. Erin had never before thought of autumn as a time of dying, though she'd always known that's really what was going on in nature. But the crisp air and clear blue sky and all the reds and golds used to make her feel very much alive. If there was ever a month she could call a happy month, it would be October. But now she felt she was suddenly getting to know October in a new way, like a close friend who suddenly turned on you.

She was almost finished disinfecting and hosing out the eight empty concrete cubicles in the west kennel. Less than a month ago Dirk had been joking that they were going to have to start building high-rise cubicles to house all of the larger dogs. But these cycles happened regularly, so nobody was really worried. Animal Control deliveries would suddenly increase and adoptions would drop off, then it would go in reverse. August, September, and October were typically slow months for adoptions, but they always picked up in November and December, when parents came looking for cute pets for Christmas presents.

Two weeks ago Erin had been the first worker to hear two different dogs—a Lab mix and a bull terrier, housed side by side—coughing the dry hacky cough that was the telltale sign of kennel cough, along with the usual nasal discharge. The staff took immediate measures to isolate them, but by then it was too late. Within days the infection had spread through the kennels in both the receiving and adoption houses. It swept through with a fury, like the stiff winds that were stripping the autumn trees earlier than expected this year. The howling of the wind seemed to make the dogs more nervous—the ones that were still alive. Howling winds and howling dogs. Everybody's nerves were frazzled.

Weldon said it was the worst epidemic he had ever seen in his thirty-plus years of working in humane societies. With a single pet, kennel cough was usually nothing more than a week-long annoyance, but in an area where numbers of dogs were confined, some of them already in a weakened condition, it could be deadly. Seventeen dogs had died so far, and another fifteen or so sick puppies had been euthanized.

Some of the sweetest dogs were gone. But Erin wouldn't let herself cry, not even two mornings ago when she learned that the pure-bred miniature schnauzer had died the night before. He had been at the shelter less than two weeks but had already won the hearts of all the staff. Cynthia had been the one to find him peering out of a basket early one morning, bright-eyed, with a big red bow tied around his neck and a nametag that read, "My name is Julius Caesar." Someone had left him by the front door, his pedigree papers rolled up in a little scroll, secured with a gold cord and tucked into the basket with him.

Dirk had concocted a story about Caesar: The puppy was a gift to a widow from her children, who hoped it would ease her loneliness. But before her husband was cold in his grave, an old boyfriend of the widow's had breezed in to ease her loneliness in a different way. Jealous of the new pup, who liked to sleep in the widow's bed, the boyfriend had planted evidence against Caesar all around the house—little "accidents" in shocking places, ripped cushions, tipped-over houseplants, and such.

"The innocent namesake cruelly betrayed just like the emperor," Dirk had said. The boyfriend then graciously offered to find a new home for the pup, according to Dirk's story, and the widow tearfully agreed—thus, Cynthia's discovery of the basket by the front door early one morning. The sad part, and this was fact not fiction, was that Caesar had already been chosen by a family, his adoption papers drawn up ready to be signed, when he had been stricken with kennel cough.

Erin wrapped the hose and walked back inside the building. In the staff room she took off her rubber shoes and apron, then disposed of her latex gloves and lathered her hands again. Infectious tracheobronchitis, the technical name for kennel cough, was an airborne disease but could also be transmitted by hands or clothing. For this reason all of the personnel had to take extra precautions. Erin's hands felt raw from all the scrubbing lately, but she thought of Eskie at home and soaped her hands and arms once more, then rubbed them with hand sanitizer for good measure.

Her stomach felt hollow, and though she had never fainted in her life, she felt like such a thing might be possible right now. She leaned against the edge of the large sink and closed her eyes. She had skipped lunch two hours earlier, canceled on Reuben again, told him to stay away from the kennels. She didn't want to run the risk of his carrying the bacteria home. But she was hungry and knew she couldn't keep going without something to eat. She still had half a turkey sandwich in the refrigerator, left over from a few days ago, so she went to get it. If only she could sit down for a little while and get something in her stomach, she knew she would feel better.

"If anybody needs me, I'll be out back," she told Cynthia on her way out. "I won't be long."

"Okay, honey," Cynthia said. She was holding a freshly bathed large white cat, kneading the fur between his ears. "We got those two adoptions at three, so I need you to help with the Siamese." Though they had canceled all adoptions for dogs until the epidemic was under control, they were still trying to keep up with the cats.

"I'll be back by then," Erin said.

Cynthia looked down at the cat and made a smoochy kissy sound. "My buddy here's getting him a new home, aren't you, fella?" The cat twitched his ears and let out a plaintive meow. His fur was long and silky, the purest, most exotic white Erin had ever seen. She couldn't help wondering, though, if the new owners had noticed that he was slightly cross-eyed.

She stopped at the vending machine for a drink and then hurried out to the picnic tables by the old barn. She sat on the bench and put her head down on her arms. She hadn't slept well lately. Part of it was the crisis here at work, and another part was the uncertainty and frustration at home. Unfortunately, the cost of adopting a baby was a lot more than the sixty-nine-dollar fee for a pet adoption here at the Humane Society. As in at least twenty thousand dollars more expensive. That was how much the Galloways had told them to be prepared to pay if they applied for a child from China. And that didn't include travel expenses or the home study fee. Some adoptions were less than that, but some were more.

It was the kind of money she and Reuben didn't have sitting around. And since adoption agencies did a thorough investigation of a couple's finances in order to see if they could afford to raise a child, a loan was out of the question. She couldn't help thinking of all the ways they could have saved money over the ten years they had been married, but she and Reuben were a lot alike in that they didn't mind spending money. Investments, savings, careful budgeting—those kinds of things had never been high priorities.

So it looked like the adoption route was blocked for now—which could be just as well. Erin knew there couldn't be another little girl as beautiful as Susannah. She would hate to always be comparing a daughter of hers to the Galloways' perfect child.

Another discouraging factor was that the Galloways said adopting from China could be a two-year process. Right now two years sounded like an eternity. And there were so many possibilities for things to go wrong in an adoption. Holly and Clark had told them about a previous effort of theirs to adopt here in the States. They had gotten all the way to the day of the official exchange, and then the birth mother backed out and wouldn't sign the papers.

Erin wondered if maybe she and Reuben were destined to be one of those childless couples whose pets substituted for children. She remembered a former neighbor who had a separate photo album for each of her three toy poodles. She and Reuben could do that for Mewt and Eskie. They could schedule them for Olan Mills portraits, buy them Christmas gifts, take them for walks in a baby stroller.

Well, she was getting extreme, as usual. She sat up, sighed, and took a bite of her sandwich. The leftover turkey had a funny taste—or maybe it was just the lingering smell of disinfectant on her hands and clothes. She took another bite and then a long drink of her Pepsi.

She heard distant squeals and laughter and looked up to see four small children chasing one another around the house across the road from the Humane Society. Situated on a small rise, it was a tan house with brown shutters and a fenced yard with more dirt than grass. The children were too close in size to be siblings, and since the number differed from day to day, Erin had always figured it to be a low-budget day care. A short, round woman came out the front door holding a glass of something and settled herself in a lawn chair. The wind was blowing briskly again today, and golden leaves from a big sycamore flurried about as the children raced through the yard.

Erin finished her sandwich quickly and threw her trash away. But she wasn't ready to go back to work yet. She took her drink with her and walked down the path behind the barn. She hadn't been to the old pet cemetery in many months. When she first started working here, it was one of her favorite places. Reuben had teased about it often: "Nothing I enjoy more than eating lunch with my wife in the pet cemetery. It's so peaceful. There's a little bench we like, right by the pink marble head-stone that reads, 'Little Bit, My True Friend.'"

Erin couldn't explain her attraction to the ceme-tery, to cemeteries in general, really. Maybe it was something a lot of melancholics felt. Many nights she dreamed about her mother's grave, wondered if she could find the place, wondered if anybody kept it cleared, put new flowers on it. She had never visited it since the day of the funeral over twenty-one years ago.

For years she had suppressed the thought of going back, for she had vowed after college never again to set foot in the town where it happened, the town where her father still lived—or at least within a few miles of where he lived now. He had moved from Derby over to Greenville some years ago, into a new subdivision.

The pet cemetery wasn't a big area, no more than twelve feet square. Weldon said there was a time when people had regularly made arrangements to bury their pets here, but it had fallen into disuse over the last ten years or so. The path suddenly ended, and Erin stepped off to walk between the little headstones. The grass had grown up so high that some of them were hidden.

She felt better now, not quite so hollow inside, though she still had a mild headache. She walked slowly, reading the inscriptions on the markers: "Tuxedo, Good Ole Cat," "Sugar, Beloved Companion," "Buttons, Faithful Seeing Eye Friend," "Pixie, 1968–81, Miss Elsie's Precious," "Tiger, WHS Mascot." She remembered how Reuben used to stop midsentence while they were eating their lunch out here. He would cup a hand to his ear and say something like "Shh, did you hear that rustling through the trees? I think it was the ghost of little Tippy, Happy Playmate."

Poor Reuben. Always trying to make the best out of a situation. Erin sometimes felt twinges of guilt when she thought of the life he had always dreamed of living somewhere out West in the wide-open spaces. But those were the dreams of a little boy, and he was a man now. Grown men didn't race around on horseback yelling, "Giddyup!" and going from one adventure to another—shootouts and cattle drives and busting broncos. They got jobs and married women who kept their feet on the ground. They paid mortgages and bought life insurance and kept their cars running. "At least I still get to climb trees," Reuben had liked to joke when they were first married. But that was before he had fallen and hurt his back. Now he didn't even do that.

She stopped and drank the last of her Pepsi, then returned to the path and started back toward the main building. She was mad that she had let herself get off on Reuben's disappointments. She didn't like to think about all that.

Anyway, it wasn't as if she herself didn't know what it was like to have to give up dreams. There were plenty of things she wanted but hadn't gotten. Or hadn't wanted but had gotten. She hadn't asked to come home one day as a ten-year-old and see her mother lying dead on the kitchen floor. She hadn't asked to get stuck with a father who was never home even when he was there.

Sure, she'd had a grandmother who didn't let a speck of dust settle anywhere, who made a major production out of cooking full-course meals and keeping up with laundry, who even mowed the yard. But a grandmother was no replacement for a mother, especially one like hers. Erin still felt bad about the way she had resisted her grandmother's attempts to fill in at home. All those years, all the time and energy—things children never appreciated. Erin recalled all her sulkiness and protests, even a few temper meltdowns. Once she had made her grandmother cry by refusing to hug her. But she didn't want to think about any of that now. She had been a kid—the only thing she understood back then was that both of her parents had disappeared. One of them couldn't help it, but the other one could.

She knew she had stumbled into a certain measure of happiness when she met Reuben, but marriage wasn't a big rosy romantic bubble you floated around in. It wasn't the great fixer of problems or the fulfiller of dreams. It didn't guarantee motherhood, for example.

She passed the barn and crossed the parking lot. Time to clear her mind now and get back to work. She saw Weldon's boogeyman van just pulling in at the far end of the long, curved driveway, coming back from another delivery to the crematorium. Usually they took dead animals to the landfill, but the county required them to cremate when an infectious disease was involved. Julius Caesar's mischievous little face suddenly rose before her— his alert eyes and gray beard, his perky ears and blunt muzzle. She imagined his adoption papers catching fire, the edges shriveling slowly at first and then quickly burning down to a little heap of gray ash.

A few minutes before three she was headed toward one of the small adoption rooms with the Siamese cat and all the paper work when she felt her cell phone vibrate inside the pocket of her jeans. She knew it was Reuben; no one else ever called her. She felt a flush of irritation. He knew she didn't like him to call her at work, especially when things were so busy and tense around here right now. She decided to ignore it. He could leave a message if it was important.

She went into the little office cubicle and sat down. She put the Siamese in her lap, keeping a hand on his back, and set the adoption papers on the table beside the starter kit containing the food samples, the collar, a toy, and some coupons. Her phone started vibrating again. The cat must have felt it because he stiffened and tried to jump from her lap. "Hey, hey, it's okay," she said soothingly. She picked up the cat and cradled him with one hand, then stood up and fished out her phone. It was Reuben's number on the screen.

She flipped it open. "Quit calling. You're spooking the cat," she said. "I can't talk now. I'm getting ready to do an adoption."

"Okay, I'll tell you later what came in the mail today," Reuben said. "Call me when you have a minute. You won't believe it." And he hung up.

He could be so exasperating. She called him back. "Okay, make it snappy, before the people get here."

A couple of weeks later Ben left the library an hour earlier than usual. He stopped by the grocery store for yogurt, something new he was trying for a bedtime snack, and then drove home. He pulled into his driveway and went to the mailbox.

It seemed later than it was for some reason, not only by the clock but also by the calendar. By the clock it was only fifteen minutes past eight, but it seemed like it was at least ten-thirty or eleven. He would like to blame his confused sense of time on the fact that daylight savings time had ended, but he knew that a single hour's change couldn't begin to account for the way time was creeping. By the calendar it was only the fifth day of November, but it seemed like December, probably because there were already Christmas decorations everywhere you looked.

At the mailbox he stopped and looked up into the sky. No stars tonight. The moon was a faint globe of diffused light behind a cobweb of cloud. Weather-wise, October had been a very unpredictable month this year. Lots of rain and cooler than average temperatures. He opened the mailbox and found it full—a stack of regular mail on top of a large padded mailer.

Once inside the house, Ben set his grocery bag and the other mail down on the counter and opened the padded mailer. He knew what it was. He pulled the book out and studied the cover. The title—*The Windmills of Consciousness*—was centered near the top, in large sensible black letters, and the author's name—Vera A. Bridgewater—was printed in smaller letters across the bottom. In the background was a muted pattern of blue windmills overlaid with a graph and bright green lines, the kind you saw on heart monitors.

Ben had ordered the book through Amazon, had paid $59.95 plus tax and shipping for it. It was a hefty volume, almost six hundred pages. Inside the back flyleaf he read the author bio, only a brief paragraph: *Vera A. Bridgewater received her MA from Boston University and her PhD in psychology from the University of Chicago. She has taught psychology at the University of Virginia, the University of Toronto, and the University of Vermont. She has published numbers of articles in professional journals as well as a book of essays titled* The Other End of the Tunnel. *She currently lives in Burlington, Vermont, with her husband, Reginald, a photographer.*

A small black-and-white photo appeared below the bio. Ben wouldn't have recognized her as the same woman he saw in Flat Rock almost four months ago. The woman pictured here looked twenty years younger. Her hair was dark and long, piled on top of her head, and she wore a placid smile, as if sorrow had never touched her.

He turned to the front of the book and leafed through the opening pages. The copyright date was only three years earlier, and the dedication read, *Reggie—As always it's for you, darling.* He scanned the table of contents, noting chapter titles such as "The Riddle of Consciousness," "A Single Self?" "Seat of Awareness," "When the Brain

Rewires Itself," "The Shades of Memory," "Navigating the Waters of Death," "Inside a Baby's Mind."

He flipped through the book, skimming over phrases like *stress hormones, heightened activity in the amygdala,* and *old-fashioned Freudian psychotherapy.* He stopped at a sentence: *Emotion is often the master over reason when it comes to moral dilemmas: If you have only seconds before a burning building collapses, whom do you push to safety—your ninety-year-old mother in her wheelchair or the infant triplets in their perambulator?* Ben paused to ponder for a moment: first, what he might do in such a situation; second, why an American writer would have used the British term *perambulator*; and, third, did it matter that they were triplets as opposed to a single baby?

He scanned through the index. This part must have added countless hours to the actual writing. Maybe she'd had help cataloging all the terms. Maybe Reggie Darling had put down his camera and given her a hand with the alphabetizing.

He closed the book and studied the cover again. *The Windmills of Consciousness*—Ben wondered if Vera was in any way alluding to the 1960s song "Windmills of Your Mind." He remembered the song well, winner of an Oscar in 1969 for Best Film Song after it was featured in *The Thomas Crown Affair*, though Ben hadn't seen it until several years later. The windmill song was the background music in the scene where Steve McQueen was flying a glider.

He hadn't thought of the song for years, yet the words came to his mind now as he stood in his kitchen: *Like a circle in a spiral, like a wheel within a wheel, Never ending or beginning on an ever-spinning reel.* A pretty good description of his life, now that he thought about it—nothing but endless circles.

Sometimes circles did end, however, and sometimes there was a pattern. *Like a carousel that's turning, Running rings around the moon.* When he and Chloe lay in the dark on the merry-go-round all those years ago, watching the swirl of stars overhead, eventually the circles slowed and stopped, and the sky ended up looking exactly like the constellation diagrams in books. At least the lights of heaven knew their place.

Okay, enough philosophizing. Too late in the day for that. He set Vera Bridgewater's book down and picked up the rest of the mail. As he shuffled through it quickly, he almost missed the postcard, which was stuck between the phone bill and a piece of junk mail that said *DATED MATERIAL, OPEN IMMEDIATELY.*

He knew a postcard could be considered the lowest form of written communication, implying that the sender was not only stingy with his time and money but also didn't care who read the message. And the message itself was likely to be obligatory or perfunctory. All these things were probably true of this postcard since it was from Erin.

He had already heard from his other three children. Shelly had called the very day the check arrived. Her thanks had been effusive, with a self-righteous edge. "We'll be tithing part of it, considerably more than ten percent in fact, because our church is starting a building program for a new gym, and then we're going to give some to Mark's sister—you know, the one I told you about whose husband left her after he was fired from his job—and then we've been wanting to get our front yard landscaped because we think it's always a good testimony to do our part in keeping up the neighborhood." As if he wanted this kind of report. He was glad when she stopped to take a breath and suddenly said, "Oh, Dad, sorry, I need to go now! Mackenzie just got home and wants to show me her first report card of the year!" Without covering the phone, she broke away to say, "Is it straight A's as usual, honey?"

Both Lydia and Grant had called within days, too. Not long calls, but sincere, and somewhat shocked. Neither specified their plans for the money, but he didn't want them to. It was enough that they were pleased and thankful.

Days had gone by, two full weeks, without any word from Erin. But now, a postcard. It was a plain white card, the kind you bought at the post office, with the postage already imprinted on it. No "Dear

Dad." She launched right into the message. Four brief sentences in Erin's handwriting, a mixture of cursive and printing.

We got the check. We have plans to use the money down the road. It was a big surprise and will be a real help. Thank you. And then *ERIN* printed in small neat letters, all capitalized.

Reuben had added a note: *Impossible things are happening every day! Thanks for giving us hope.* He had signed off with only an *R*.

Ben wondered if Reuben had quoted from the *Cinderella* lyrics on purpose. And what did he mean by *giving us hope*? Did he and Erin have some kind of problem that nobody knew about, something money would help fix? He read the postcard again, then set it on the kitchen table.

"Who can know the interpretation of a thing?"— this was a question he had come across in Chloe's Bible recently. And he had read on, looking for the answer to the question, only to come at last to a verse that said a man can try all day long to figure things out—the good and the bad, all the work under the sun—but in the end even a wise man can't find the meaning.

He took the cartons of yogurt out of the grocery bag and arranged them in the refrigerator. Then he chose the Very Berry flavor, peeled it open, and took it to the table. He got a spoon and sat down. He propped the postcard up against the salt and pepper shakers and read it again, slowly.

TWENTY-SEVEN
An Ordinary Man's Heart

It was three-thirty in the afternoon when Kelly went to the staff lounge. She got one of her half-pint cartons of milk out of the refrigerator and the little bag of green grapes left over from her lunch, then sat down on the sofa. She didn't always take an afternoon break, but she had been so rushed at lunch today that she had eaten her sandwich standing up. This was the first time she had been off her feet all day.

The grapes were good, not too tart but sweet and very firm. She ate several and then opened her carton of milk. It was nice in here when she was by herself. Unless she was with LaTeesha or Gilda Bloodworth, she much preferred eating alone even though she rarely did so anymore.

She thought of the book she was reading now, a biography of the missionary Amy Carmichael, and of something she had read just last night: *Toward those who made no pretense of being Christians, Amy felt pitiful, purposeful love.* She had read the sentence over and over, putting her own name in. That's the kind of love she was praying for—not just to have it but to show it. She knew, though, that you couldn't show people love if you avoided them.

The door opened and Seth and J.J. entered the lounge, laughing and goofing around as usual. Here were two boys who certainly qualified as *those who made no pretense of being Christians.* Kelly never could understand much of what they said. They were always referring to movies and video games, and they loved to talk about cartoon characters she had never heard of: Strong Bad, Homestar Runner, Coach Z, The Cheat, and Bubs. Today J.J. was wearing a T-shirt that said *VOTE FOR PEDRO* on it. Kelly had no idea who Pedro was.

Seth and J.J. never gave her the time of day unless they were having fun at her expense. They were good at disguising it, much better than Les had ever been and not nearly as mean, but she knew whenever they talked to her, which wasn't very often, there was something else going on underneath. She caught the looks that passed between them and knew they probably repeated things she said and laughed about them later in private. But generally they ignored her.

She ate another handful of grapes and took another drink of her milk. She hoped they would get their snacks and leave. Sometimes they did that, but sometimes they stayed in the lounge to eat. She picked up somebody's discarded newspaper and pretended to be reading it.

Seth and J.J. were in front of the vending machines making their selections. One of them said something, and the other one laughed and said, "Oh yeah, like *whatever*!" Kelly heard more laughter and the kerplunks of things being dispensed from the machines, and then a sudden groan. "Idiot machine! I didn't want this! These make me want to puke!" She looked up to see J.J. holding a cellophane package of miniature cake doughnuts.

Seth was convulsed with laughter. "You punched the wrong number! I watched you!"

J.J. hurled the package at him. "So why didn't you say something, you retard?"

Seth put his drink down, and they threw the doughnuts back and forth several times, along with insults about each other's intelligence. They kept moving farther apart and throwing them harder, laughing the whole time. Finally J.J. stopped and squashed the package between his palms as he made a vulgar noise with his mouth.

"Hey, wait. Maybe *she* wants them," Seth said. He raised his voice. "You hungry for a snack?"

Kelly knew he was addressing her. Even though they hadn't yet acknowledged her, they couldn't have missed seeing her. One thing she had learned about men and boys was that they always liked an audience. The more immature they were, the more they liked it when somebody was watching.

She glanced up and shook her head.

"What's wrong? You don't like doughnut mush?" J.J. said. He walked toward her, holding the package by a corner. What was inside looked nothing like doughnuts now. The cellophane was split, and a few crumbs fell to the floor.

Kelly shook her head again and smiled. "No, thank you."

Seth came up behind J.J., a Mountain Dew in one hand and a Snickers bar in the other. The two of them stood there staring at her.

J.J. motioned to her milk. "Are you drinking one percent because you think you're fat? 'Cause you're not. You could be drinking whole if you wanted."

Behind him, Seth made a sputtering sound.

Kelly held up her carton. "No, this is whole milk."

"Oh, okay," J.J. said. Then, "I like your sleeves. They're real big. Did you make them yourself?"

Kelly glanced down at her pink blouse, then back at J.J. He looked totally serious. "No, I bought this," she said. She was puzzled. Her sleeves weren't big at all; at least she didn't think they were.

J.J. held up the package of pulverized doughnuts again and swung it back and forth. "You know what these remind me of?" He swung them a few more times, then said, "Smashed tater tots." He looked back at Kelly. "Do you like tater tots?"

Kelly stood up. "Sure, I like tater tots." She walked to the trash can and threw her trash away, then headed for the door. She didn't know what was going on here, but she was tired of these pointless questions. It was awfully hard to feel pitiful, purposeful love toward these two.

"Do you like them with fish?" J.J. asked. "'Cause I could catch you a delicious bass." She heard Seth give another snort of laughter.

At the door she turned around. She knew her face was as pink as her blouse. All she could think of to say was "Well, thank you, but I like them with sloppy joes better."

J.J. and Seth laughed as she opened the door. As it swung shut behind her, she heard Seth say, "Man, you got skills, J.J. You're really good at hooking up with chicks. Too bad she doesn't know about Uncle Rico's *enhancers*. She could sure use some." And they laughed again.

Kelly checked her watch and went to find LaTeesha, who was always a good source of information. She found her in the new Anything Glass showroom, taking some of the figurines out of a locked case for a customer to look at. "This one here is one of my favorites," she heard her say. "Way he's all squatted down on his hind legs like he's ready for action!" The customer told her it was a gift for her mother, and LaTeesha laughed. "Oh well, then we better scratch that. Your mama might not want to look at a tiger sitting on her dresser every day. How about this little dancing girl here? She's real pretty!"

Kelly busied herself across the aisle, straightening knickknacks on a shelf, until LaTeesha's customer thanked her and said she was going to keep looking.

"Hey there, Kayko, how's it going?" LaTeesha said, walking over to Kelly. Kayko was LaTeesha's latest nickname for her.

"It's going fine, but I just had the strangest conversation with J.J.," Kelly said. "I think I must've been missing something. Sometimes I feel so . . . well, like people are talking in circles."

"Honey, Jaybird's head is empty. Everybody knows that. If there's any gray matter up there, it's not brains; it's just dust bunnies. He talks in circles 'cause he can't think straight. So what was it he said?"

Kelly repeated the conversation, trying to remember every word. LaTeesha kept nodding and saying, "Yeah, uh-huh, go on, go on." At the end she laughed. "Napoleon Dynamite," she said. She told Kelly it was "this movie that's so dumb it's funny." It wasn't a new movie, she said, but people who liked it never seemed to get tired of watching it and talking about it, "like they in some kind of cult or something." By the time she explained the basic plot and main characters—Napoleon, Kip, Uncle Rico, Pedro, and Deb—Kelly had to agree with the dumb part. To start with, she couldn't believe any high school kid would have a name like Napoleon Dynamite. But maybe the movie was one of those things you had to see before you thought it was funny.

"So okay, you never saw it—I can believe that easy enough," LaTeesha said, "but you standing there telling me you never even *heard* of Napoleon Dynamite? Don't you know *nothing* about movies, Kayko?"

"Well . . . sure I do," Kelly said. "We sometimes watch movies on Friday nights at home."

"Yeah, like what? *Moses and the Ten Commandments*?"

Kelly laughed. "We have watched that one. But we watch a lot of different things. We saw *The Sound of Music* last week and *Ben Hur* a couple of weeks before. And *The Apple Dumpling Gang*—we're watching that tonight. Again."

LaTeesha whistled. "Woo-hoo. Watch out, honey, you be getting wild. How about *Mary Poppins*? You seen that one?"

Kelly nodded and smiled. "Several times. But I do have younger brothers and sisters, remember."

LaTeesha grinned and shook her head so that her big jiggly earrings made little clinking noises. "You make me laugh, you know that? But hey, listen to me, girl. This here's the U. S. of A. we live in. It's a free country. You can watch any kind of movie you want to. World's a big place, big enough for all kinds of folks." She threw her head back and let loose with her big hee-haw laugh. "I got to feel good knowing there's somebody like you in the world, Kayko. I mean, it's like you living in the Little House on the Prairie or something."

411

Kelly shook her head. "They didn't watch movies back in those days."

LaTeesha lifted her hands and stepped back in mock surprise. "Hey, jump back, everybody. Kayko almost told a joke!"

Kelly knew she was only teasing, but she did pause to wonder if a sense of humor might be something you could develop if you kept trying. Maybe LaTeesha would rub off on her a little in that way. She checked the time again and told LaTeesha she had to go. She was meeting with a new vendor in a few minutes, a man who dealt in Brazilian folk art. The Bazaar was getting more and more multicultural. This man was a native of São Paulo and spoke Portuguese, but he was bringing his American wife along to do most of the talking.

Kelly saw Seth and J.J. just leaving the staff lounge as she approached. Normally she would have slowed down to make sure they didn't see her, would certainly not have initiated a conversation with them, but for some reason she heard herself calling out, "Oh, J.J., by the way, your friend won, didn't he?" They both turned around and looked at her blankly. Kelly pointed toward J.J.'s T-shirt. "Pedro. He won the election, didn't he?"

She knew it was nothing to feel proud of, but she couldn't help it. There was just the tiniest bit of satisfaction in deflecting somebody's teasing, in involving herself with somebody totally different from herself, even if only for a moment. Maybe that was the first step to showing purposeful love—finding out a little about someone else's world. She turned down the hallway to her office. Behind her, she heard Seth and J.J. laughing again, but this time it didn't sound as mean.

Supper was almost ready when Kelly got home that evening. She washed her hands in the laundry room sink, then stood in the doorway a moment, watching the beehive of activity in the kitchen.

"Karla, you forgot the napkins," Kimmie said as she filled the glasses with ice. "Kirk, quit fiddling with that and put these on the table. Wait, Kitty, that needs a hot pad under it. Okay, everybody, get to the table! Kyle, grab the tea pitcher. Careful, it's full. Hey, stop eating all the chips, will you?" Kimmie saw Kelly in the doorway. "Hey, Kelly, would you grab a new jar of pickle relish from the pantry?"

Kerri called out, "Kimmie, are these the only chips we have? I thought we had a new bag of the wavy kind Daddy likes." Above all the chatter, Kirk was singing a song called "David and His Slingshot" in a little-boy voice.

Within minutes they were all finally seated. They were eating supper later than usual tonight, but that was typical for a Friday night. Either Charlie or Kelly often worked till seven on Fridays, and Kerri sometimes had catering events now to help set up for the weekend. It also seemed like one of the younger children was always needing to stay for something extra after school on Friday—some meeting or team practice or rehearsal.

Hot dogs, baked beans, coleslaw, and chips—it wasn't a fancy supper, but it was one they all liked. Kirk's first batch of hot dogs on the grill had been not just hot but burnt to a crisp, which had necessitated starting all over. And ironically, it was all because of a dog.

Kirk started recounting the whole story for Charlie and Kelly, how he had put the hot dogs on the grill, then turned them, then heard a horrible ruckus coming from the direction of Kyle's duck pen. He had run to check it out and found a big stray dog loping away through the back gate with one of the ducks in his mouth. The side of the pen was bashed in and the little door was wide open. One of the other ducks was also missing, and the remaining one was in the corner of the pen, quacking weakly and flapping its wings, one of which looked broken.

The story went on, but Kelly lost the thread of it. She glanced at her father. She knew what he must be thinking: that abandoning a duty to chase a dog was only further proof of Kirk's irresponsibility. Her father had a lot of patience, but somehow Kirk had a way of driving him to the end of it.

She turned her attention back to the story. Kyle was talking now, excitedly telling about how he and Kirk had followed the stray dog's trail for a while by means of blood spots and an occasional feather, but they finally lost it in the woods and came home to find their sisters hopping around the grill in a panic and spraying water from the garden hose onto what was left of the hot dogs, which by now looked like sticks of charcoal.

Kyle showed no signs of grief over the loss of his ducks. Evidently the excitement had made up for it. He protested loudly, however, when Kirk suggested serving up the wounded survivor as duck chop suey. "Well, okay," Kirk said, "but we need to fix his wing somehow. Hey, I got it! We'll use duck tape!" There was laughter at that and a few groans.

Kitty spoke up and said she might write a story about a feisty duck who outsmarted a dog. "I could name him Quackerjack," she said. Kitty had a quick wit. She often read her stories and poems to the family after supper. A few days ago she had written one about a clever pig named Cunningham. *Cunning ham*—Kelly wondered how she had ever thought of that.

The conversation finally moved away from the ducks, and Karla started telling about something funny that went wrong with an experiment in science class that day, after which Kelly shared something Mr. Begian had said to her that day at work.

"He got so excited when he found out the ebony cabinet had sold," Kelly said, "that he started talking in one of his other languages. And then he stopped all of a sudden and said, 'Oh, my words! I beg your pleasure, Miss Kelly. All I say is that it is a jubilation! It is . . . horry-dunky!' " Everybody at the table laughed. They all liked hearing about Mr. Begian and LaTeesha and Caroline and some of the other people Kelly knew at work, several of whom they prayed for by name during family devotions.

Kimmie asked Kelly how the new guy was working out—the one they had hired to take the place of Lester. "Well, not too bad," Kelly said, "but not too good, either. Definitely not horry-dunky yet. He's got a lot to learn."

Kerri began describing the upcoming Thanksgiving dinner she was helping the caterer plan for a big family reunion in a hotel ballroom. She was right in the middle of listing all the dishes on the menu when Kirk interrupted with "Hey, maybe they'd like a big platter of tender, home-fattened duck!" Kyle tried to kick him under the table.

Finally the meal was over and the table cleared. Kelly knew the younger children were eager to start the movie, but she glanced at Charlie and said, "Daddy and I have something we need to talk to everybody about before we leave the table." Everybody's eyes were on Charlie instantly. He pushed back his chair and crossed one leg over the other.

"Well, Kelly has been offered the chance to take some college classes, and we talked it over and think it's a good opportunity, but we wanted everybody's opinion, since it would mean pitching in to cover her jobs at home so she could have time to study." He stopped and looked at Kelly. "You want to tell them how it came about?"

So Kelly told her brothers and sisters about the day a couple of weeks earlier when Mr. Buckley had called her to his office to ask her if she'd be willing to work on a college degree, a few courses at a time, in something like art or interior design. He had looked into several good programs at colleges nearby, and she could start in January. The incredible part was that he was going to pay for it.

"He told me that employers often do this sort of thing, since it's for the company's benefit in the long run," she said. "And even though I wasn't sure he wanted to hear this, I told him I had been praying for a long time about someday being able to go to college, but I never ever expected God to answer my prayer by dropping it into my lap this way. In fact, I told him it seemed so easy and so sudden that I would need to pray some more and talk to my father about it."

"And what did he say then?" Kimmie said. "Did he quote something else strange from the Bible?" Many nights at supper Kelly told them about things Mr. Buckley said at work, some of which they recognized from the Old Testament, yet she also told them he seemed suspicious, even scornful, of religion in general. They had been praying for him for months.

"Well, he did quote from the Bible," Kelly said, "but it wasn't strange at all, really. In fact, he put me to shame. He said he wanted to understand— was I saying my God could work all kinds of miracles in lions' dens and fiery furnaces and such, yet couldn't lay it on an ordinary man's heart today to offer a free college education to one of his employees who had an excellent spirit within her?"

"Is that what he said—'an excellent spirit'?" Kerri said.

Kelly nodded. "And I don't know how I ever had the courage, but I said, 'Mr. Buck, you're starting to sound like a preacher now.' I told him I was glad to know he had read beyond the first five books of the Bible, all the way to Daniel. I said he was talking like a wise man now, not just a smart one."

"And what did he say then?" Karla asked.

Kelly, who had always enjoyed her roles in plays at church, acted it out for them now, imitating Mr. Buckley. "He leaned back in his chair this way and looked up at the ceiling for a few seconds. Then he said, 'Wise is as wise does, Kelly. Believe me, there's plenty I don't have figured out yet. No secrets revealed to me in night visions.'"

Then she looked around the table and became Kelly again. "I reminded him that Daniel prayed to

God for wisdom to reveal those secrets. And he said yes, he supposed there were people who were on praying terms with God, but he wasn't one of them."

There was a brief moment of silence, and then Kirk spoke up. "Well, I say she should go for it. Covering for her at home won't be hard since she doesn't do much of anything anymore anyway . . . anyday anytime . . . anywhere anyhow . . . anybody else?"

Charlie gave him a look that said *This is no time for joking around.*

The others started talking all at once, asking questions and finally agreeing that it was an offer too good to pass up. The only hesitation voiced was from Kitty, who said to Kelly, "Does this mean you can't read to me before bed every night?"

Kelly shook her head and said it didn't mean anything of the kind.

TWENTY-EIGHT

Appointed Cycles

It was while she was in the dentist's chair the next week that Caroline finally began to put two and two together. "And she was bawling her eyes out the whole time," Luanne said to her. "Here, you're drooling, sweetheart, use this." She put the little suction device in Caroline's hand.

Luanne had worked for Dr. O'Rourke for over thirty years, and for most of those thirty years she'd been talking. But at least she wasn't one of those dental hygienists who asked a lot of questions while probing around inside your mouth. Instead, she just delivered running monologues about things that interested her, expecting no commentary from the person in the chair, although Caroline did manage an occasional "uh-huh" or a sniffy little laugh if she thought something was intended to be humorous.

Right now Luanne was talking about something she had listened to on talk radio on her way home from work the day before. The topic of the day had been honesty, and the host, obviously hard up for something new to talk about, had posed the tedious old question "In what kinds of circumstances is it all right to tell a lie?"

Caroline wished Luanne was talking about something else because honesty was one of those subjects that had started making her uncomfortable lately. Part of it was a result of working around Kelly Kovatch, who took honesty to ridiculous lengths, always deliberating before giving an answer, often restating things she thought might be misunderstood. Another part of it was a little nagging sense of guilt over Lester Lattimore's getting fired.

If there were a way to rate everybody in the area of honesty, Caroline knew she wouldn't score very high marks, but she also knew there were times when you were *forced* to lie or else just did it accidentally, without thinking. She didn't like to use the word *lie*, however; she preferred to use *euphemisms*, which was a big word she had learned from Mr. Buck. She did admit that she sometimes fudged or colored the truth. If she used the word *lie* at all regarding something she said, she always modified it with the word *white*. She also comforted herself with the fact that there were plenty of times she was *very* honest, coming right out and saying exactly what she thought.

"So this poor woman can hardly talk, she's blubbering so hard," Luanne said, "but she plows right ahead, telling this story about raising these four children all by herself after her husband left her high and dry. And the host, he's just letting her go on and on. Who knows, maybe he got up to go take a bathroom break.

"But anyway, this woman gets to telling how she found out by accident that one of her sons was involved in robbing a bank and killing a teller, somewhere up in Ohio, I think it was, and how she confronted him about the evidence she'd found and how he smacked her around and told her she better not tell a soul, or else she'd be plenty sorry. Anyway, she tussled with her conscience for the longest time, crying in her bed all day and night and thinking about the family of that poor girl that got killed but also knowing she could send her own son to jail for the rest of his life if she went and tattled to the police."

Luanne broke off for a few seconds. She was working on the back side of Caroline's bottom front teeth now, frowning fiercely. "You must be drinking a lot of tea and coffee, honey," she said. "You got some serious staining going on back here."

She reached up and adjusted the light, then started in again. "Anyway, she finally she got up from her bed and put on her clothes and drove downtown to the police station and told them everything she knew and gave them her son's name and address. And you know what?" Luanne kept right on with her scraping, not waiting for an answer. "That boy's been in jail for over twelve years now. No chance for parole. He shot the girl point-blank, right in the face. I mean, part of me has to *admire* that woman for telling the truth since it seems like you can't trust anybody these days to really be honest, but another part of me wonders how she could do that to her own son. Of course, it doesn't sound like he was much of a son if he threatened her like that, but still . . ."

Caroline closed her eyes tight as Luanne kept talking. She'd heard about a new, completely modern dentist's office in Greenville that put headphones on the patients so they could listen to music or sound effects while they were in the chair. The dentist was only in his thirties, though, and charged outrageous prices, according to her hairdresser, whose sister went to him. If it was a long procedure, he even let his patients wear a special contraption like a big set of glasses that showed a whole movie.

Right now that sounded very attractive to her. She didn't like to think about some woman in Ohio whose sense of right and wrong was so strong that she turned her own son over to the police. It made Caroline think of all the times she'd kept quiet about the truth or else twisted it, even when it hurt somebody, and all the ways she had explained away lies she had told.

She thought again about Lester. Nora had said one day recently that she heard he had gotten a job at a nursing home, doing repairs and general maintenance. Caroline hoped they kept an eye on him there. With a mean streak like his, those old people weren't safe for a minute. He might disable the brakes on all their wheelchairs or unhook their oxygen tanks.

She still couldn't believe Mr. Buck had actually fired him. After that, how could she go back and confess that she may have exaggerated just a little bit? After all, she knew Lester must have said such things about her behind her back, so it wasn't an *outright* lie. She'd heard him use plenty of bad language in the past, so it hadn't been hard to come up with something he might have said, probably *did* say, about her. And then the business about his

423

harassing Kelly in the staff lounge—well, that part was pretty much the truth, maybe only slightly embellished.

". . . the way your kids can make you look so bad," Luanne was saying. She laughed and then paused to squirt water in Caroline's mouth. "There, use the suction again." Then she went back to scraping. "And she looked right at me with a straight face and said, 'No, Mom, I never said that.' I asked her what she thought I was, stupid? I told her I *knew* she did so say it because I heard her with my own two ears."

Caroline hadn't caught who it was she was talking about now, but it must be her daughter, who always wore black and had piercings all over her body. Luanne paused again and returned to a back molar to scrape some more, then stopped and used the little mirror to check every tooth.

This whole cleaning process embarrassed Caroline. You could be so conscientious about flossing and brushing, but then you came to the dentist and still had to endure all this scraping and had to hear the dental assistant make little grunting sounds as she worked to remove all the plaque that your special toothpaste and mouthwash were supposed to prevent. Evidently the advertisements for those products had some honesty issues, also.

"And I told her she better thank her lucky stars children aren't put to death these days for disobeying, the way they used to be back in Bible times, or she'd have been buried under a big pile of rocks a long time ago," Luanne said. She put the mirror down and started applying paste on the little electric whirligig. Finally, she was getting near the end. This was the only part of the cleaning Caroline could tolerate. Except for the whirring and the faint background music, all was quiet for a few minutes while Luanne concentrated. Caroline could feel little flecks of the paste flying out of her mouth.

"I always wondered," Luanne said, "if they ever made the parents throw a rock at the kid, too, or if it was some kind of committee that did the whole thing. Can you imagine using your hands to kill your own child?"

Caroline was glad she didn't expect an answer. She remembered countless times when she'd felt like choking Donald, and not just when he was a child. Just days ago, in fact, he'd stopped by her house and taken her stepladder and electric screwdriver so he could mount new speakers in his bedroom. He hadn't even asked, had just come by on his lunch break and taken them out of her garage, the same way he'd taken any number of other things—things she had no hope of seeing again unless she went to his house and got them back. Even then they were likely to be broken.

". . . though I did hear of a man once that killed his own son when he was threatening his mother with a butcher knife," Luanne said.

All at once a thought pushed itself up through the haze of missing ladders and screwdrivers and the combined drone of Luanne's words and the dental equipment. It was as if something suddenly jolted loose in Caroline's mind. She even jumped a little. The whirring stopped. "Sorry, did I hurt your gum or something?" Luanne said.

"Nuh-uh," Caroline said, and gave her head a little shake. Luanne started again.

Caroline's mind was now racing as fast as the little brush was rotating over and around her teeth. What if, just *what if*, it was Percy Hopkins' *son*— the retarded man—who had killed Chloe Buckley? Supposedly he was under lock and key and the ever-watchful eye of his father at the time, according to what she had pieced together. But what if he'd managed to slip out one day? One of the reports cited all the odd circumstances of the crime and quoted one of the investigators who called it the work of "either an incredibly lucky amateur or a brilliant career psychopath." So what if the lucky amateur was a mentally retarded neighbor?

Caroline knew it was a huge stretch. She back-tracked through her thoughts. No, they had searched the whole neighborhood; surely they wouldn't have overlooked any possibility that close. And anyway, why would somebody like that want to kill Chloe Buckley? But would somebody like that even have to have a motive? She pushed the theory forward. What if Percy Hopkins knew his son did it and couldn't decide what to do afterward? And what if he had wrestled with his conscience the way that woman in Ohio had, and what if . . . Her thoughts were tumbling over each other now. It was absolutely the remotest possibility, but it *could* fit together.

"Hey, sweetie, you all right?" Luanne said. She touched Caroline's shoulder and raised her voice. "I said you need to suction again."

Caroline nodded and moved the device around in her mouth. Luanne put more paste on the brush and resumed her polishing. "I told my husband one time that it was a good thing I didn't have a gun in the house or else he might come home one day and find me or Angie lying dead on the floor. Or maybe both of us. I tell you, that girl can make me madder than both her brothers put together. I told her I hope she ends up with a kid just like herself someday so she can get a taste of her own medicine."

Caroline went over it all again. She knew the idea was out in left field, but it really could account for all the strange details in the case. As far as she could tell, however, there would be no way in the world to prove any of it since the key people were all dead. Surely she wasn't to be defeated this way, with all that time and effort wasted on just a *possibility*.

She thought about all the weeks and weeks she

had spent collecting every conceivable related fact she could get her hands on and then all the hours and hours at night sitting at the dining room table with everything spread out in front of her, mulling over it all backwards and forwards. She thought about her dream of marching into the office of the chief of police one day and laying out the solution to the crime, then getting her name and picture in the newspaper. Maybe they would even give her a couple of other cold cases to work on.

She had felt out of sync in so many ways during these past weeks, living all those other people's lives at night while she tried to keep a handle on her own during the day. More than once Mr. Buck had commented on her distracted state of mind. Just yesterday he had said to her, "Caroline, did you swallow a bug? You look distraught, confused, and mildly ill." And more than once he had caught her staring at him. "Are you admiring me again, Caroline?" he had asked her recently. "Still, after all these years? What is it this time?"

"I said that does it!" Luanne was standing now, one hand on her hip, her brow furrowed, staring down at Caroline. "Are you overtired, honey? You act like you're in zombie land or something. Here, let's get you sitting up a little. Maybe it's all the blood rushing to your head. Although that's usually what's supposed to make you feel more clear-headed." She raised the chair, then pushed the bright light to the side. "Dr. O'Rourke will be in to check you in a couple of minutes. You going to be okay if I leave you by yourself? You're not going to pass out on me, are you? You want a drink of water or a magazine to read or something?"

"Oh no, you go right ahead," Caroline said, waving a hand. "I'll be fine. I've just got a lot on my mind is all."

Caroline sat in the chair and thought about the only bit of testimony from the only neighbor who saw anything—the account of a man in a hooded red sweatshirt. More than one mention was made of Percy Hopkins' emotional state of mind, of the words he repeated over and over: "She was such a beautiful woman! And she had those four little children." But surely that would have raised suspicions. Surely the police had questioned him at length and satisfied themselves that his tears weren't linked to any kind of guilty knowledge. Well, not necessarily. That would be assuming they were in the least bit competent, which Caroline wasn't so sure about.

She heard Luanne with another patient in the room across the hall. ". . . and the doctor said it wasn't just broken, it was *shattered*. They had to put all kinds of hardware inside her to fix it, and she's still not able to walk. She's no bigger than a button, so I'm wondering how she can even lift her leg if it's got all that metal inside it, and . . ."

Caroline wished Dr. O'Rourke would hurry up.

She was eager to get home and go over every piece of paper on her dining room table again. The thought of a newspaper headline flashed into her head: *LOCAL SLEUTH SOLVES OLD MURDER CASE.*

Normally Ben would have been home less than an hour by this time of night and would be in the den watching the ten o'clock news in his recliner. Tonight, however, he had once again dispensed with his trip to the library and had come home after eating supper at Ruby Tuesday, which was not his normal place to eat on a Wednesday. He had not dispensed with his reading, however. He had been at it since seven, three solid hours in the same book instead of skipping around as he often did. It was Vera Bridgewater's book, and he'd been reading it for the past week, several chapters a night.

Now, at a few minutes past ten o'clock, he was standing in the kitchen in his boxer shorts pouring a tall glass of cranberry juice. He knew it was not a good idea to be drinking anything at this time of night, certainly not a lot of it, but he kept forgetting about his juice earlier in the day, and besides that, he wasn't sleepy yet anyway. He disliked the taste of cranberry juice and the way it made the inside of his mouth feel so dry and shriveled up, but since it was one of the other things the doctor had recommended, he was trying to stick with it.

He took his glass of juice into the room he called

his office. He wondered if Vera Bridgewater had a Web site. Surely so—everybody else in the world did. He turned on his computer and sat down at his desk. A brown apple core and an open can of salted peanuts sat on the desktop from the night before. He scooped out a few peanuts, took another drink of his juice, and put the plastic lid back on the can. He tossed the apple core into the trash can and then typed the name of the book publisher into the browser on the screen. They probably had Web sites for all their authors.

From there it was a simple matter to find the complete list of the publisher's authors and titles. He clicked on *The Windmills of Consciousness* and soon found himself looking at the author's home page, which included a link that said "E-mail Vera." Never in his life had he contacted an author after reading a book, and he surely wasn't going to start now. That was the kind of thing kids did after reading one of J. K. Rowling's books.

He saw another link that said "Comment on Vera's Book" and clicked on it to see if other people's comments were accessible. They were. He was halfway through reading the second one when he stopped himself. Why should he care what other people thought of her book?

He returned to the "E-mail Vera" link and clicked, just out of curiosity. He sat there for a moment thinking about what he might say to Vera Bridgewater in an e-mail, if he ever decided to write her. He got up and went into the den to get the book.

He came back and set the book down on the desk next to the computer, then stared at the windmills on the cover for several long seconds. The word *quixotic* popped into his mind. He doubted that Vera would appreciate the connection if he pointed it out to her. Don Quixote, the helplessly impractical idealistic hero who went around sparring with windmills, and Vera Bridgewater, the writer of a book that pretended to have all the answers about the mysteries of human consciousness.

He could also point out the fact that the windmill made a fine symbol for the whole human race— spinning around and around but never going anywhere. Unlike Don Quixote and Vera Bridgewater, however, windmills were immensely useful. For eleven or twelve centuries now they had been grinding corn and pumping water and, more recently, generating electricity. Besides that, they made nice pictures for calendars and stationery.

Ben looked back at the computer screen. *Write your message to Vera in the box below,* it said, *and click on the windmill icon to submit.* He could think of plenty to say about a book full of high-sounding theories concerning something as unknowable as consciousness, but nothing he would dare send to her. There was a box to fill in his own name, so he did, though he knew he would never have the nerve to write anything or, if he did, certainly not to click on the windmill icon to submit it.

He took another swig of his cranberry juice and looked back at the book. In many ways it impressed him, but he wondered if it was mainly because of its size. He couldn't begin to estimate how many hours it would take to put together something like that. He thought of Vera Bridgewater and what a small woman she was. He imagined her laboring over it late into the night for years. He wondered if she had composed the whole manuscript on a computer or if she was one of those old-school writers who still preferred to write by hand. He had great respect for anybody who undertook to write a book and kept at it until it was finished. He remembered hearing Brittany say at Flat Rock that it had taken her mother over seven years to write the book and that her father had died just days before Vera received the first copy from the publisher. So the dedicatee never got to see it or hold it in his hands.

Ben tried out a few words: *Vera, I've read your book and want to* . . . He deleted it and tried again: *Vera, it has been almost four months since we were together at Flat Rock.* No, that sounded too cozy. He tried again but deleted that one, too, after only three words. Clearly he could never write a book; he couldn't even get a few sentences of an e-mail put together. He tried again—*Hi there, Vera, you might remember me and then again you might not*—but he backspaced until that one disappeared, too.

Well, so, which was more ridiculous—fighting windmills or sitting at his desk in his boxer shorts, trying for the right tone in an e-mail he was never going to send anyway? *Hello, Vera. Your book was very thought-provoking.* He got rid of that, too.

He picked up the book and leafed through it. Impressed or not, he was also highly skeptical of most of it. It was laughable that psychologists and neuroscientists and philosophers and all the rest of them could state these kinds of things about human consciousness with such confidence. This chapter about how the brain could rewire itself, for instance—how *cognitive approaches* could help someone *process grief* or how people could be counseled out of disorders like depression and compulsive behaviors—well, he would have to see stronger proof than a couple of isolated studies here and there before he could believe all that.

He remembered what he had overheard Vera herself say at Flat Rock, when she admitted to the great gulf between mind and heart when it came to dealing with her own loss. He didn't want to rub it in, but he did hope she felt something akin to shame when she thought about her book and all its easy answers to the hard things of life.

He turned to another page, on which Vera cited a study of a group of nuns in Germany whose hours of meditation supposedly altered the activity in the left prefrontal cortex of their brains to measurable degrees. On this same page, she asserted that the higher differential between the left and right sides of this part of the brain was somehow determined to be *an indicator of greater contentment and baseline happiness*, though in Ben's opinion, she didn't go nearly far enough in explaining just how such a thing was determined.

The clear suggestion, he read under a picture of a serene-looking nun inside some kind of imaging tube, *is that positive thinking is indeed powerful and, furthermore, that it can be trained.* On the very next page another caption read, *Writing Therapy: Sometimes the mere act of putting one's thoughts on paper can result in a new understanding of some aspect of the problem.* This picture showed a man, his brow furrowed, writing something at a desk. Unlike Ben, however, he was fully clothed.

Ben looked back at the computer screen. *Hello, Vera,* he typed. *I read your book and thought I would try the mere act of putting a few thoughts on paper in an attempt to understand some aspects of my problems.* He read it over. Sarcasm was not at all appropriate for a friendly, casual e-mail to his son's mother-in-law. But he didn't delete it. *Off and on for years now I've been trying to train myself to think more positively, but to no avail,* he added. *Nevertheless, I did enjoy certain parts of your book. The cover, for instance.*

He was loosening up now, especially since he knew Vera would never see it.

Those windmills have whirled around in my mind day and night, "like a clock whose hands are sweeping past the minutes on its face," as the old song goes, a song you surely must know as a child of the sixties and seventies—or at least I'm assuming you are, as I am, a child of that era, judging from circumstantial evidence. I surmise the two of us to be of approximately the same vintage, with "the mellow bouquet of an autumn orchard."

The words were coming swiftly now. It occurred to Ben that if a book didn't have to make sense, then maybe he could write one after all.

Speaking of vintage, Gertrude Stein once said that people don't necessarily get better as they age, "only different and older," an observation I consider wise, though much of what Ms. Stein wrote was full of fog, her most quotable line being, as you surely remember, "Rose is a rose is a rose is a rose."

Also speaking of age, T. S. Eliot once said that the years between fifty and seventy were hardest because "you are always being asked to do things and yet are not decrepit enough to turn them down." I wonder if a successful author like yourself finds this to be the case. For my part, I am rarely asked to do things. At my place of work, I am the figurehead on the prow of a sailing vessel.

But what of all that? At this point you must be saying to yourself, "This man utters nothing but balderdash"—an intriguing word, balderdash, *harking back to sixteenth-century England, originally referring to odd combinations of liquors, such as beer and wine, of which you must surely think I have had my fill to be writing these things to you at this time of night.*

He stopped and read what he had written. He remembered the term *stream of consciousness* in some college course he had taken years ago. He pressed on.

Speaking of time, I'm sure you will agree with me that it is a curious thing, time. Sometimes it seems to lag like a youthful transgressor on his way to the woodshed, and other times it seems to rush headlong like a mountain stream after the spring thaw, tumbling toward a lake or a river and eventually the sea, which, as you know, is never full—that is to say, never too full, for certainly the sea is full enough, as all things have their appointed cycles, the sun and the rain and the wind that goes to the south and then returns to the north, swirling in its ceaseless circuits, which brings me back to the cover of your book and the windmills of my mind.

He stopped again, surprised at the outflow of words. Maybe he had discovered his voice and, along with it, a new hobby to fill time. None of it mattered, of course. He wouldn't be sending this to Vera Bridgewater or anybody else. He took another drink of his cranberry juice and resumed.

You and I have something in common, Vera,

*besides our coming of age during the same years—
and besides our two granddaughters. I think you
know what I mean. It is likely that you have been
more successful than I in finding peace as the
remaining half of a married couple. Do you have
other tricks of healing besides those presented in
your book? Are you, for example, a privately religious woman? Can you sing of triumphant faith?
Even when the fruit on the vine withers, when the
fields yield no good thing, when there is no herd in
the stalls, do you yet rejoice and walk with hinds'
feet upon high places—to borrow from the prophet
Habakkuk?*

Ben paused. He felt the tension in his shoulders.
He knew in his heart that it was the chapter about
how to deal with death that had most annoyed him
about her book. And even though he also knew that
life had shot holes in many of her easy theories, he
still held it against her that she had ever been so
sure of herself in the first place.

Jaw clenched, he continued.

*In one of the anecdotal studies you included, you
mentioned the woman who wrote a list of her late
husband's most irritating habits and a few of his
notable misdemeanors and kept it in her purse.
Whenever she became overwhelmed by the sorrow
of his death, she would take out the list and read
through it. I wonder, Vera, if you have found this
strategy helpful yourself in dealing with . . .*

He stopped. Now he was turning spiteful. Time

to quit. No more stream of consciousness. No more venting. Time to shut down the computer.

He dropped his head and rubbed the back of his neck. How dumb to let himself get carried away like this. Now he would be up most of the night, and not just because of the cranberry juice. Foolish acts brought regrettable consequences. He closed his eyes and swung his chair around.

He would never understand how the half-full glass of juice had ended up so close to the edge of the desk that his elbow caught it, nor how, as he tried to grab it with one hand, he could have so forcefully knocked the keyboard and mouse across the desktop with the other, but one thing he did understand was that the windmill icon on the screen had suddenly come to life and was merrily twirling around. He stared at it in disbelief. Surely this was just a bad dream. Surely there wasn't cranberry juice all over the keyboard. Surely he wasn't sitting here reading a message that said *Thanks for contacting Vera!*

TWENTY-NINE

The Sound of Many Voices

It was too long a trip to make over two days, but there was no sense in continuing to complain about it now that they were finally within fifty miles of their arrival. The big accident on Interstate 77 had cost them over an hour already, a fact that didn't seem to faze Reuben at all. He kept pointing out sights along the very roundabout detour they were taking through little podunk towns in South Carolina.

"Look, that must be a peach orchard," he said.

Erin stuffed the road map back into the glove compartment of the truck and slammed it shut. "I can see for myself." She knew more than enough about the state of South Carolina. Reuben seemed to forget she had grown up here.

Four hundred forty long miles from Roanoke, Virginia, to Savannah, Georgia, on Thanksgiving Day, along with everybody else on the East Coast who had waited until today to travel—a crummy way, in Erin's opinion, to spend a holiday. And in a truck no less since her car had chosen this morning for the Check Engine light to come on. At least it was a decent-looking truck, though, and got fairly good gas mileage, not like the rust bucket he had traded in.

She looked again at the clock on the dashboard—1:43. They had left home a little past six that morning, after having to transfer everything from her car to Reuben's truck. If not for the accident, they would have been in Savannah by now.

"Want to call Lydia and tell her we'll be there by two-thirty?" Reuben said. "She might be wondering whether to make the gravy yet."

"You mean Shelly might be wondering," Erin

said. Erin would be surprised if Lydia did anything more than put brown-and-serve rolls in the oven. She made no move to get her cell phone out. "I told them two hours ago we'd be late. Joey said they'd see us when they see us." She nudged the brown paper bag on the seat between them. "We've still got cookies and cheese crackers if you're hungry. There's an apple, too."

"Nah, don't want to spoil my appetite," Reuben said. He turned on the radio and switched stations for a few seconds, then turned it off again. He pointed to a stand of trees. "Can't believe there's still so much color left down here." A flock of birds in formation passed over the highway, dipping low as if going in for a rest stop somewhere beyond the trees. "Seems a little late to be migrating," he said. "Maybe they ran into bad weather or somebody in the group got sick." He laughed. "Flight delay." A few minutes passed, and Reuben got his own cell phone out and handed it to Erin. "Here, call them. I'll talk. I hate to leave them guessing."

She found the number and pressed Send, then handed it back to him. "What you really hate is the thought of them eating without you."

"That, too," he said. "But I refuse to feel guilty for thinking about food on Thanksgiving Day." Someone answered on the other end. "Hey, Lydia," Reuben said cheerfully. "Say, you haven't started eating yet, have you? Erin is getting all worried about that. She made me call."

441

As a matter of fact, Erin was plenty hungry, though she didn't mind the late arrival. Late meant shaving a couple of hours off their total time. At least this visit wasn't going to go on and on like the Endless Week back in the summer. A big turkey dinner, a little time of sitting around after that, then bedtime. That took care of today. Then tomorrow they would stop back over for a little while before they had to leave again. She was glad she was scheduled to work on Saturday. The sooner they left, the better.

Another improvement over summer was that they were staying overnight in a motel this time. Lydia and Joey had offered to put everybody up in their new house, but they warned it would mean roughing it, sharing bathrooms and sleeping on the floor. They had plenty of space upstairs but didn't have beds yet. It wouldn't be so bad if it were just Lydia and Joey, but it wasn't. It was the whole messy tribe again. Still, two days at Thanksgiving was sure a lot better than five days at Christmas, which was the first idea Shelly had pitched. Thankfully, Grant and Brittany were going on a cruise at Christmas, so that suggestion got shot down.

Reuben was laughing when he got off the phone. "Joey was howling like a hound dog in the background. Lydia said he kept snitching food so they had to banish him from the kitchen. They're waiting for us. She said Grant and them just got there. They ran into traffic, too."

They drove in silence for a while. Erin wondered, but wasn't going to ask, if her father was there already. She was holding out hope that he had decided at the last minute not to come. She knew for sure Shelly and her family had gotten there yesterday. She could imagine Shelly bustling around in Lydia's kitchen right now, taking over as usual, sizing up the assigned dishes everyone was bringing to see how they compared to the ones she had brought. She had bossily sent recipes, which Erin had refused to use.

Erin felt a spark of self-satisfaction at the thought of the sweet-potato casserole and apple pie sitting on the floor right behind her seat. She and Reuben had made them together last night after supper from recipes she'd never tried before, from a cookbook she had hardly opened during the whole ten-plus years they'd been married, a fact Reuben had teased her about when he took the book off the shelf and pretended to be blowing dust off the cover. She had told him she didn't want him clowning around, that she had to have his help, even if he was a klutz in the kitchen.

Amazingly, he had done much better than she'd expected. He had peeled apples, chopped pecans, even mixed a few things together. Never mind that the kitchen was a total wreck when they finished; at least they got a good-looking casserole and pie out of it. Afterward Reuben was so proud of his kitchen performance that he had shooed her out to take her bath while he cleaned up. After he went to bed, she sneaked back in and took care of everything he'd overlooked.

They passed a cyclist along the side of the road. All decked out in royal blue spandex and a yellow helmet, he was hunkered down, moving forward with the efficiency of an arrow. Reuben swung out to give him plenty of room.

"Did you know a lot of the Canadians that landed on Juno Beach after D-day carried bicycles with them?" Reuben said. "Brits used them, too, but not the Americans." For weeks now he had been asking Erin if she knew this or that about D-day, the subject of a thick book he was reading. "I wonder if your dad knows that," he added.

"He probably knows what brand of bicycles they were and how much each one cost," Erin said. Several times since the trip to Flat Rock, Reuben had talked admiringly about how easily her father had answered all the questions in that dumb Schooldays Trivia game they had played. In the past months she had noticed him reading a lot more than he ever did before—books, newspapers, magazines, whatever he could get his hands on. Though he hadn't mentioned it specifically, she strongly suspected that he was hoping they would play the game again at Lydia's house.

A little farther on, just before getting back onto the interstate, they passed a farmhouse set back off the road where several children were playing football. A little black-haired girl was flying across the front yard, the football clutched in both arms. At the end she stopped, raised the ball, and did a little victory dance.

"Did you tell Lydia yet?" Reuben said.

"No," Erin said quickly. "And I don't want you telling anybody, either. It's too soon. The whole thing might fall through before it's over, and then we'd have to put up with everybody asking questions and feeling sorry for us."

"Don't you think we could tell Dad? I mean, since it's his money we're using."

"No," Erin said. "It's not his money. It's ours. He gave it to us. We don't have to submit a report. And I wish you'd stop calling him *Dad.*"

Reuben didn't say anything for a few minutes. Then, "I hope Mewt and Eskie behave themselves while we're gone. Clark said they'd be by to feed them tomorrow after they eat lunch with Holly's brother."

"I know. I'm the one who told you that." Erin tilted her seat back a little and closed her eyes. She knew she couldn't sleep, but she needed some quiet time to prepare herself for the next twenty-four hours.

It was twenty minutes past two o'clock when Ben pulled up to the curb in front of Lydia's house. He'd planned to get here an hour earlier, but he had done something that morning that he hadn't done for years; he had overslept. The alarm didn't go off. At least that's what he was telling himself. He distinctly remembered winding the clock last night before bed, then pulling out the little peg on top to activate the alarm. He had even reached over after turning out the light to make sure it was sticking up. But this morning when he woke up an hour late and stared at the clock, it was lying on its face against the lamp and the little peg was pushed down. So much for trusting only a wind-up alarm clock for important wake-ups.

He turned off the ignition and looked at Lydia's house. Sitting close to the street, it was a boxy-looking two-story, neatly but sparsely landscaped. A large banner featuring a turkey wearing a Pilgrim hat with his tail feathers fanned out behind him was hanging from a mounted pole by the front door. Nobody was watching out the window or bursting from the front door to greet him, thank goodness.

He studied the cars that filled up the double driveway. Two minivans and an SUV—his children were so unimaginative. He wondered if the new silver Suzuki was Shelly and Mark's. Maybe they had scratched their original plans for the money he'd given them and decided to put it toward an SUV instead. But what did he care? He'd told them all to use it however they wanted to.

He knew he ought to get out of his car and let them all know he was here, but he couldn't make himself move. He needed a little more time. When he had called Lydia this morning to tell her he was getting away late, she had told him to drive safely, had said they wouldn't start dinner without him. Very likely they were all inside right now watching the clock and listening to their stomachs growl as he sat out here stalling for time. Suddenly he had a thought: He could turn the engine back on and quietly pull away from the curb, then go somewhere and call Lydia to say something had come up and he wasn't going to make it after all.

But another thought immediately crowded in on that one. It was something Vera Bridgewater had said in the last e-mail she had sent him. *Frankly, it wouldn't surprise me*, she had written, *if you didn't come up with some excuse to miss spending Thanksgiving with your children, especially since you know that I'll be there and it would be hard to look me in the eye. I know all about people like you. We call them Avoiders.* Ben hated being thought of as belonging to a certain type. There was no way he was going to give her the satisfaction of being right. He was going to march in there and look her right in the eye—in a few minutes.

He reached into the back seat for the gift Kelly had wrapped for him at work the day before. Kelly was the one who had suggested he take a hostess gift for Lydia. She had even recommended a few things at the Bazaar that she thought would be appropriate for the occasion.

He held the gift up and looked at it from different angles. Lydia would probably think it was a coffee table book, but it wasn't; it was a picture. He wasted a little more time plucking at the mass of curlicue ribbon on top of it. Kelly had wrapped it in gold paper and used fall colors for the little twirly cascade of ribbon. Finally he opened the door and got out.

He heard a vehicle behind him and turned around to see a black Ford Ranger truck pulling up to the curb behind his Lincoln Town Car. Erin's husband, Reuben, waved to him. Erin appeared to be looking straight ahead. Ben stopped on the sidewalk. He wasn't sure which was better—continuing on his way to the door to face Vera Bridgewater inside or stopping and waiting for the daughter who treated him like he had scurvy.

Wait for her. This was what he heard in his head. Reuben got out of the truck and trotted up the sidewalk toward him, extending his hand and saying something about traffic and detours. He was wearing lime green Crocs instead of the cowboy boots he'd worn at Flat Rock last summer, but he still moved like a cowboy, loose and lanky. He had on jeans and a flannel shirt with the sleeves rolled up to the elbow.

Ben held out his hand and allowed it to be shaken. He didn't remember who had told him about Reuben's background, but it came to him now that it couldn't be true. Reuben had none of the signs of being passed around from one foster home to another. Whoever told him that must have been mistaken.

Behind Reuben, Ben could see Erin getting out of the truck on the passenger side. She pushed the seat forward and leaned in to get something, then slammed the door shut with a foot.

Reuben spun around. "Hey, don't try to carry those," he called. "I'll get them." He glanced back at Ben and threw his hands up. "She doesn't know what the word *wait* means," he said, and then he took off for the truck, calling out, "Hey you, put those down. I'll carry them. You might drop them—you're just a *girl*!"

Erin relinquished one dish to Reuben but insisted on carrying the other one. She trailed behind him as he started back up the sidewalk toward Ben.

No, stay where you are, the voice told Ben. *Wait for her*. Easy for the voice to say; it had no idea what it was like to wait for someone who couldn't stand the sight of you, someone whose low opinion was entirely justified. Ben stepped to the side and let Reuben pass him. He would have preferred by far to lead the way and ring the doorbell, but he made himself do the hard thing. He lifted his eyes and looked right at Erin, but her eyes were averted. *Give her the present*, the voice said. No time to argue with the voice and explain that it was a hostess gift for Lydia. It wouldn't have listened anyway.

"Here, let me trade you," Ben said. He reached

449

out and put a hand on the dish she was carrying, all but forcing it from her. It was a glass pie plate covered with foil. Once he had it, he held out the gift with the other. "This is for you," he said. No time now to worry that she might not like it.

She frowned and looked at it for a long moment without moving to take it.

Someone had already opened the front door. Behind him Ben heard several people talking at the same time. He heard Joey's laughter, and Shelly's voice saying, "Well, it's about time!"

"Here, it's for you. Take it quick before I drop it," he said to Erin, holding it out farther. "Careful, it's breakable."

"Come on. Hurry up, you two!" Shelly called.

Erin reluctantly lifted a hand and took the gift from Ben. Not a word, no eye contact, not even the smallest smile. But she accepted it. Ben quickly turned and walked toward the door. Shelly stood waiting, smiling tightly, one hand on her hip and the other motioning them forward, an impatient little crease between her eyes.

At the door Joey took the apple pie from him and peeked under the foil. "Well, hello there! You look good enough to eat!"

Reuben punched Joey in the arm and said, "Okay, how about we dispense with the small talk and get on to something more important—like *where's the rest of the food?*" The two of them laughed like boys.

"Come on," Joey said. "We'll storm the kitchen together. They can't keep us out if we've got food!"

Shelly, wearing a red-checked chef's apron over her slacks, held up a hand. "Wait, everybody has to take off their shoes by the door." She pointed to the cream-colored carpet and shook her head. "Lydia just had this put down a week ago, but it's sure not a very practical color for an entrance. Especially in a house with little kids." She reached up and gave Ben a quick peck on the cheek, then took the casserole dish from Reuben and headed off down the hall, calling out, "Wait, Joey, bring the pie this way. I've got the desserts set out on the buffet. The rest of you hurry up so we can get started! It's all ready. Wash your hands, and come on to the table—this way. You can use the hall bath right there on the left. Somebody be sure to close the front door!"

Ben stepped aside and motioned Erin in ahead of him, then shut the door. While he bent to untie his shoes, Reuben slipped off his Crocs and placed them next to a small Ficus tree in a brass pot by the door.

"Sure smells good in here," Reuben said. Erin took her time removing her clogs, then straightening them and setting the gift next to them. Maybe she was hoping someone would step on it.

She heaved a sigh. "Okay, lead the way," she said to Reuben.

Left alone by the front door, Ben took off his sneakers slowly and placed them next to Reuben's green Crocs. He picked up the present from the floor and stood it up against the wall. He could hear the sound of many voices down the hallway. Someone shouted, "Hey, Michigan scored again! When did that happen?" A child wailed and then stopped abruptly. He heard Shelly's voice: "No, not there! It goes down here on this end. Turn the TV off!"

It came to him again that he could leave. He could pick up his shoes right now, open the door, and make a dash for his car before anybody missed him.

"So you did come after all." He looked up to see Vera at the end of the hall. Framed in the open doorway, she looked even smaller than he remembered. Her hair was shorter and curlier than it had been last summer, and she was wearing a pastel blue sweater, gray slacks, and what looked like fluffy white bedroom slippers on her feet. If he didn't know her voice, he might mistake her for one of the grandchildren.

He forced himself to look right at her. "Of course I came."

"So let me guess," she said. She started down the hall toward him in her fuzzy slippers. "You were standing out here by yourself, thinking about leaving, weren't you?" She stopped and folded her arms.

Ben tried to look incredulous. "Leaving? After driving all this way? No way am I going anywhere before I eat." She might have written a big, thick book about psychology, but that didn't give her any right to act like she was a mind reader.

Lydia appeared at the doorway behind her. "Hi, Dad, glad you made it!" she called out, waving what looked like a gravy ladle. She came down the hall toward him, passing Vera. She gave him a brief, awkward hug. "So how do you like our new house?" she said, looking up at him, her eyes shining. She couldn't possibly know how much she looked like her mother.

"Very much," Ben said, smiling. "I like it very much. I especially like what I smell coming from that direction." He nodded back toward the doorway to the kitchen.

He had never seen Lydia's old house, of course, the starter home she and Joey had moved out of a month ago, the home they had originally planned to live in only a couple of years instead of nine.

"We've got a lot to do before we're really settled in," Lydia said, looking around, "but we never could have done any of this without your money."

"It wasn't mine, really," Ben said. "But I'm glad you could use it. Now, can we eat?"

"Well, sure. Come on," she said, laughing and waving the gravy ladle over her head. "The food is this way. We've had the awfulest time keeping Joey away from it."

Vera had disappeared from the hallway, which suited Ben fine. She was probably off in another room, analyzing someone else's shortcomings.

Ben followed Lydia down the hall in his stocking feet. He heard Shelly's voice somewhere up ahead. "Okay, everybody, find your place! If we wait any longer, we might as well call it Christmas dinner."

THIRTY

Rising Moon

Caroline stacked the plates and carried them to the sink. Donald had already gotten up from the table and was from all appearances preparing to leave. He had agreed to eat Thanksgiving dinner with her, but she knew that coming over for a meal didn't mean he was going to hang around and visit afterward. And of course it would never enter his mind to pick up some of the other dishes on the table and bring them over. He was standing by the table, scratching his belly and making the kinds of prenap sounds men make after a big meal. Emitting a loud yawn, he raised his arms to stretch. His rumpled gold velour pullover rode up above the waist of his large sweat pants, showing a bare roll of flesh around his middle, covered with dark curly hair.

Donald had inherited three things from his father: his tendency for food to run to fat, his basic laziness, and his hairiness everywhere except on the top of his head. Caroline never had been the kind of woman who valued hairiness in a man. She clearly recalled the first time she had seen her former husband, who was her boyfriend at the time, with his shirt off. She had turned away in mild horror at the sight. A hairy chest was one thing, but a hairy *back* was another. She should have taken that as a warning that he was more like a gorilla than a human being.

Ever since the day Donald was born, Caroline had received the same surprised looks from people whenever she introduced him as her son. Sometimes they looked back and forth between the two of them as if saying, "You're kidding, aren't you? So is he *adopted*?"

If mothers got gold stars for trying, Caroline knew she would have earned a truckload of them. All his life she had tried her best to get Donald to care about his looks and his clothes, to watch what he ate, to show some initiative so some nice girl would be interested in him.

And there's the product of all your trying, she told herself now as she watched him hike up his sweat pants with one hand and dig inside his ear with the other. "You can turn on a game in the den if you want," Caroline said, coming back to the table for more dishes. She wasn't ready to be alone again today. She had spent all morning in the kitchen and wasn't looking forward to another hour or so of cleanup, followed by a long afternoon and evening by herself. Even watching a football game would be better than that. Donald could have the whole couch to himself; she would sit in one of the chairs. She might do some reading, try another crossword puzzle, maybe even curl up on the loveseat for a nap herself. "There'll be plenty of turkey for sandwiches if you want one later," she added, though she had little hope that he was going to stick around that long.

"Nah . . . I think I'll . . ." Donald took his finger out of his ear and examined it. But he appeared to be thinking about her offer. At least he didn't move toward the door. Caroline headed back to the sink carrying two serving bowls. It usually worked better, if anything worked at all with Donald, not to act like she cared much about what he decided to do.

She plunked the bowls down on the counter and opened a cupboard. Her Thanksgiving Day cheer had evaporated. She hated this part of serving a meal almost as much as the cooking itself—transferring all the leftovers to smaller containers. She scraped the green beans into a small dish and clamped a plastic lid on top. Now she had to go to all the trouble of labeling things or else she'd forget what they were. It was all such a bother. She should have just offered to take Donald out to eat somewhere today instead of spending all this time in the kitchen. He obviously didn't care whether

. . . She glanced over to find him gone. She knew he hadn't left the house or she would have heard the door open and close.

A loud honking sound came from the hall bathroom. Another similarity she'd almost forgotten about. It was odd how something like a certain way of blowing your nose could be passed on from father to son, even when the father had been around so little during the son's growing-up years. This sound was soon followed by a rolling belch, then the flush of the toilet, followed seconds later by another flush and then the running of water at the sink. The water went on and on, much longer than he could be using it to wash his hands. This was typical of Donald—he always seemed to think water and electricity were free. Caroline knew his landlord must have regretted a thousand times that utilities were included with his rent.

Caroline went back and forth to the table several times for the rest of the dishes and then back once more to gather up the tablecloth, which now bore a large red splotch and a smear of butter where Donald had been sitting. By the time she had shaken it out by the front door and come back to the kitchen, she could hear the sound of the television from the den. She took the tablecloth over to the washing machine and sprayed spot remover on it.

She went back to the kitchen counter and turned her attention to the turkey now. She would slice off enough for a couple of sandwiches just in case Donald wanted one before he left. Now that he had the ball game on, there was at least a small chance that he would stay for a couple of hours.

On second thought, she put the knife down, covered the whole turkey with foil, and stuck it in the refrigerator right on the platter. She would tend to it later. As she began scraping dishes in order to load the dishwasher, she suddenly remembered something she'd heard that annoying Gilda Bloodworth say at work yesterday when someone asked her if she was having a lot of company for a big Thanksgiving dinner.

"Not a lot if you mean quantity," she had said in her chirping voice. "It'll be just Ryan and my sister Zootie. But if you mean *quality*, why, yes, I'm having a *lot* of company!" She had laughed and wrinkled up her nose in that childish way she had of showing pleasure, then added, "The three of us always have a big Scrabble tournament after dinner on Thanksgiving! Both Zootie and Ryan are cutthroat when it comes to Scrabble. Me? I do well to think of three-letter words. I just play for the fellowship."

Caroline glanced at the clock. It was going on four already. She tried to imagine what it would be like to be Gilda Bloodworth right now, playing Scrabble with her son and sister. It was a strange thing for a boy Ryan's age to like to do—play Scrabble with his mother and aunt. And Zootie—

458

what a ridiculous name for a grown woman. But at least Zootie was spending Thanksgiving with her sister. Caroline's own sister had said she was too tired right now to drive to Caroline's house or to cook dinner if Caroline drove to hers. Linda could be so antisocial at times. Caroline suspected that she might be entertaining a man at her house over Thanksgiving—that was probably the real reason behind her so-called tiredness.

From the direction of the den, all was quiet except for the sound of the football announcer. Donald was probably sprawled out on the couch with his mouth gaping open. For a moment Caroline thought of all the other people she knew at work, and she wished she could peek in on their houses right now. She wondered about Mr. Buck— he had driven to a daughter's house today, somewhere on the coast. She had overheard him telling Kelly about it one day. She had hung around trying to listen in without being obvious, but the two of them had walked out of the lounge together and down the hall toward the showroom floor.

And the Kovatch house—she wondered how they did things on Thanksgiving Day. Especially now that Kelly's mother wasn't there. Did all the children crowd into the kitchen together to fix dinner? Did their father help out? Maybe they just had something practical and easy like spaghetti or hamburgers. She wondered how many people there were around their table today.

Caroline slammed an empty pot into the sink and ran some water into it, then gathered up a handful of dirty silverware and started rinsing it. More than once she had wished she had more children, at least one more, maybe a daughter. Daughters could usually be counted on for a little more help and company than a son, especially a son like Donald. A daughter might offer to make part of a holiday dinner, might even want to have it at her house. For sure she would pitch in with the cleanup afterward.

Caroline thought of LaTeesha and Nora and Melody and Dustin and Byron and little mousy Roy and Mo and all the rest of them at work—how were they spending Thanksgiving Day? With a little twinge of guilt, Lester Lattimore came to her mind. She wondered if he was having to work today at the nursing home.

She tried to imagine what kind of son Lester was to his mother. Surely no better than Donald, probably worse. She wondered what the mother of Lester Lattimore would be like, whether she would have cooked a big turkey dinner today with all the trimmings or whether she was lying drunk in a trailer park somewhere. As much as Caroline had disliked Les, there was no denying that things hadn't run as smoothly at the Bazaar since he was fired. Manny White, the new man Mr. Buck had hired, tried hard but was several cards short of a full deck.

All of a sudden she realized she was just

standing there at the sink, rinsing the same serving spoon over and over under running water. She turned off the water and quickly deposited the spoon into the dishwasher, then started adding other things as fast as she could, without rinsing. This was a good day to test something: LaTeesha had announced the other day at work that nobody in her whole family except herself knew the right way to use a dishwasher. "They all act like they insulting the dishwasher or something by loading it up with dirty dishes. All that scraping and scrubbing and rinsing—like we bowin' down to Queen Kenmore, hoping she won't get mad at us for asking her to do what she was *made* to do!"

LaTeesha had gone on to compare it to her aunt in Chicago, who was a lawyer and paid somebody to come clean her house every week, "except she always got to go running around straightening everything up before the gal show up to do her job! I told her, 'Aunt Jaz, for being so smart, you sure missing the whole point here.'"

Caroline had her doubts, not only about the dishwasher theory but also about somebody like LaTeesha having a lawyer for an aunt. But as fast as she could, she cleared the stove and countertop, throwing everything into the dishwasher before she could change her mind. She added the detergent, then closed the door quickly and started the machine. If this didn't work, she would sure let LaTeesha know about it tomorrow.

As she wiped off the counter, moving down its length with slow, circular motions, her thoughts went back to Mr. Buck. She wondered what he was doing right now at his daughter's house. She wondered if he bored his children to death with all his little useless, stored-up facts. She wondered if they got as annoyed with him as she did, the way he turned everything into a school lesson. The last thing he'd said to her out in the parking lot of the Bazaar yesterday was "You know, don't you, Caroline, that we owe a great debt to Squanto? Without his help, the Pilgrims probably wouldn't have survived their first winter, and we might not be celebrating Thanksgiving tomorrow."

"Oh yes, Mr. Buck, I've been thinking about Squanto constantly, all week long," she had said right before slamming her car door. He appeared not to have heard her. As she drove away, he was standing by his car gazing up into the sky, which, as far as she could tell, looked just like it did every other day at that time. She had felt like rolling down her window and yelling, "Would it ever occur to you just to say something simple like 'Happy Thanksgiving. Have a nice day off'?"

Caroline had reached the end of the counter now. She stopped wiping and glanced over to the desk, where she had stacked all her notes and file folders of copied pages about the murder. She had wrestled for days over how to lay it all out to someone—and exactly who that someone should be. She didn't expect to be taken seriously, at least not at first, so she had to be sure the whole thing was meticulously planned out, that she hadn't overlooked anything, that every single detail fit into place.

At least once a day she went through the long version, but at random intervals, like now, she ran through the short one: Knowing his son had killed a woman, it drove Percy Hopkins a little crazier and a little crazier to the point that one day he knew he had to execute justice with his own hands by taking a life for a life, even if it was his own flesh and blood. So it was Percy Hopkins himself who actually gave his son all those pills, or rather left them out where he could get to them—many bottles of them, all kinds.

Making them accessible was all it took, since taking pills was one of the boy's compulsions. Caroline had read that in one of the reports. She imagined him popping them into his mouth, any kind he could get his hands on, one right after the other until somebody stopped him or he passed out. He must have liked all the different colors and shapes of pills. Bottle caps were obviously no deterrent; *childproof* meant nothing because he wasn't a child, not in that way.

So on the day Percy went over the edge, he had brought the boy into the room—Percy's own bedroom, where he kept all the medicine and his gun in a small locked tool chest under the bed—and he got the tool chest out and put it on top of the bed and helped him fit the key into the lock and open the lid. Then he left the room. He must have listened fearfully from the other side of the door, wondering if the boy would get curious about the gun while he was ingesting pills. He must have been torn about which kind of death he preferred for the guilty one—overdose or gunshot.

As time stretched out, he must have known which it would be. He must have heard water running in the bathroom as the boy got drinks to help him swallow the pills. After he finally tiptoed in to check, he probably waited just a little longer to call 9-1-1, to make sure the damage was done this time. And then, of course, everybody concluded the boy had done it to himself, as he'd tried to do all those other times, and Percy Hopkins acted so overcome and agitated that the only thing held against him was neglect, and even that was mitigated by his great show of grief and his long years of caring for his son. And then at some point after that he moved away from the neighborhood out to a little house near Paris Mountain, where he finished losing his mind one day at a time until he eventually set a fire and then killed himself.

Caroline rinsed the dishcloth and hung it over the faucet head to dry. She knew she might have some of the details not quite right. Such as tiptoeing into the bedroom to check on his son. She wasn't sure why she kept imagining that he tiptoed. Or actually helping his son unlock the chest instead of unlocking it himself and then pressing the key into the boy's hand to transfer fingerprints.

She still couldn't quite decide how to go about telling what she knew, but it had to happen soon. The weight inside her was growing too heavy. Mr. Buck needed to know the truth. She never thought of it in terms of *possible* truth or what she *thought* she knew. In her mind it was now fact. So what if it wasn't provable? Many of the big things in life weren't provable in a tangible way, but that didn't make them any less true. Like love or pain. Or like life after death.

Which was the subject of another one of Mr. Buckley's startling questions recently. He often brought up the most unpredictable things, right out of the blue. She had been in his office watering the plants on his windowsill. He had a book open on his desk and was typing something into his computer. Without a word of warning, he had suddenly stopped typing and said, "Caroline, as you stand there today watering plants that you know will eventually die, I can't help wondering if you believe in life after death. Not for plants, for people. What are your thoughts about heaven and hell?"

Though she was tempted to say, "Well, I'm not sure about heaven, but working for you has taught me a lot about the other place," she didn't. She couldn't say anything for several seconds, but she could tell he was waiting for her. Though she faced the window, she knew he had swung his chair around in her direction. She watched the last of the water trickle out of the long, curved spout of the watering can and soak down into the soil of the philodendron. She took a deep breath to slow her heart. There was no way he could know that these were questions that sometimes troubled her lately, especially at night when she was trying to get to sleep.

But she had no intention of telling Mr. Buck the truth—that more and more whenever she told a lie, she imagined that she heard the crackling of a big bonfire and a low, resonant voice calling as over a great empty chamber, "That's one more log to make the blaze higher." She took another deep breath and finally turned to face him. She made a conscious effort to pitch her voice higher. Brisk and upbeat—that's the tone she wanted. "Really, Mr. Buck, those are very personal questions," she said. She held the watering can against her with both hands, cradling it like a small pet.

He looked at her over the top of his glasses, which sat a little cockeyed on his nose, and nodded. "Well, yes, I guess they are," he said. "You don't have to answer."

As if she needed him to tell her that. "Dustin is coming in to see you at two," she said. "I have the file on my desk. I'll go get it."

He swung back around and leaned over the open

book on his desk. As she walked to the door of his office, he said, "Well, now, here's something interesting. Did you know there are white-blooded fish in Antarctica that can live in below-freezing salt water because they secrete a kind of organic antifreeze?" Like so much of what Mr. Buck said, it deserved no response.

Caroline turned out the light in the kitchen now and walked down the hallway toward the den. As she drew closer, she could hear Donald's snores rising above the sounds of the football game. She was starting to feel a little sleepy herself. It wasn't a bad prospect for Thanksgiving afternoon, really—taking a nap in front of the television, with her son nearby. It might not be the best Thanksgiving she'd ever had, but it certainly wasn't the worst.

In the dining room Kelly blew out the pumpkin candle—now burned down to only three-fourths of a pumpkin—and watched the plume of smoke rise toward the ceiling. It made her think of a poem she had written when she was fourteen, a poem about the brief but useful life of a candle. Her mother had thought she was going to be the next Robert Frost.

She leaned over and straightened the centerpiece. Surrounding the candle was an arrangement of colorful leaves, acorns, squash, and miniature corn cobs she had put together early this morning after getting the turkey in the oven. She took one last look around the dining room, making sure everything was back in place. She couldn't remember a Thanksgiving Day that had stretched out as long as this one. It had been so different without her mother this year. Through the window she saw her brothers out in the driveway looking under the hood of Keith's newest restoration project—a two-tone yellow and green 1953 Ford. Dusk was already coming on, but the car was pulled up under the light mounted on the corner of the garage. Kirk and Kyle were darting around the yard, throwing acorns at each other.

Kelly turned out the dining room light and went back to the kitchen. Kimmie, Karla, and Kerri were finishing up with the dishes, and her father was standing at the counter by the stove, slowly, methodically cutting the rest of the turkey off the carcass and placing it in a large cake pan.

Seeing a bag of garbage by the back door, Kelly picked it up and took it outside, past the duck pen over to the garbage cans lined up behind the garage. She deposited it, then walked out into the middle of the backyard and looked up into the sky. The wind had picked up again. She didn't remember such a windy fall. It was a gray sky, with scarflike wisps of purple and pink streaked through it. The rising moon looked like a silver dollar behind the dark filigree of tree branches along the back fence. She felt a sudden ache at the sight of such ordinary beauty right here in her own backyard. She rubbed her hands up and down her arms against the November chill. A song or poem—that's what such a sky begged for. Or a painting.

She thought of how happy her mother would be to know she was starting college in January and that as an art and design major she would get to take classes in drawing and watercolor. She could even take a creative writing course as one of her electives. It scared Kelly a little to think of being in a class like that, but it excited her, too. It seemed too good to believe that she was going to have an opportunity like this. Some mornings she woke up and wondered if she was imagining things. But Mr. Buck had already sent in the money for her registration and the first semester of tuition, and she already had a letter of acceptance on her dresser upstairs.

A sudden gust of wind stirred the trees and a flurry of fallen leaves swept around her feet. Someone opened the back door, and the sound of a baby's cry came from inside the house. Both Keith and Kenny were staying overnight tonight, along with their wives and children, so there was a long evening ahead. She knew she ought to go inside and see if one of her sisters-in-law could use her help with a baby, but she needed just another minute out here by herself under the sky. Sometimes she couldn't put a name to what it was she felt with so many people around, even her own family. She adored her nieces and nephews, but having them around always reminded her that what had seemed to come so easily for her older sister and brothers might pass her by.

She couldn't help wondering if Mr. Buckley had had a nice Thanksgiving Day with his children. She hoped his daughter liked the cross-stitched poem. Kelly herself had shown it to him one day in a new showroom at work and suggested he get it for a hostess gift. This daughter, the one in Savannah, had a baby.

She heard the slam of the car hood in the driveway. Her brothers tromped through the back porch and into the house, all of them talking and laughing. Kirk was bringing up the rear, making noises like a speeding car being chased by the police. They all disappeared inside, leaving the back door open. Kelly was glad they hadn't seen her in the backyard.

She looked up at the moon again. Pray for Mr. Buck, that's what you should do right now, she told herself. And so she did. With the wind whipping around her, she looked up into the gray and purple sky and prayed that Mr. Buck would keep reading his Bible. Last week he had told her he had gotten all the way to the book of Zechariah. "So far," he had told her, "the Israelites are still hanging in there. Those prophets are funny, you know. I mean, every one of them, it's the same thing over and over. One minute they're pronouncing doom and destruction on all the people for their whoremongering ways, and then the next thing you know, they'll turn around and say something like 'God's going to blow his trumpet against the chariots of your enemies and gather you up like his little children and bring you again to Jerusalem.'" He had paused to laugh, then added, "Seems like God has a hard time making up his mind."

Kelly hadn't known what to say. How did you explain to somebody like Mr. Buck that the story of the Israelites wasn't funny at all and that you didn't tease about something like God Almighty not being able to make up his mind? She knew one thing—she needed to study her Bible a lot more to be able to keep up with Mr. Buck. And she had to be willing to speak up when the opportunities came.

She looked back at the house and saw a light go on upstairs. She saw her father at the kitchen sink now, his head bent. Through the back door floated the sounds of home. "Hey, watch what you're doing!" someone said, followed by a loud thump. Her father's head came up. Before starting inside, Kelly took one last look at the sky, its colors already fading. The moon, still rising, was just above the treetops now.

THIRTY-ONE

Between Two Testaments

Well, you made it through another one. These were the words that went through Ben's mind on Friday as he got into his Lincoln Town Car in front of Lydia's house. It was just after two o'clock in the afternoon, close to the same time he had arrived yesterday. Only twenty-four hours, but it had seemed much longer than that.

Not wanting to appear too eager to leave, he stuck a hand out the window and waved as he slowly pulled away from the curb. Shelly and Mark, still loading up their SUV, paused to wave back, along with Lydia and Joey, who were standing in the driveway seeing everyone off. Lydia was holding the baby, bouncing her up and down, while the other children chased each other around the front lawn. The dog, a little blond terrier mix named Buster, was leaping about with them.

Shelly whirled and spoke to her three, who immediately stopped running and dutifully waved to their grandfather. *Marionettes* was the word Ben thought of as they stood side by side waving in unison. Lydia's Isaac hurled himself at Quentin from behind, grabbing him around the knees, and the two of them tumbled to the ground, Isaac

472

squealing with laughter. Shelly frowned at them and said something to Quentin, who stood up immediately and brushed off the knees of his jeans.

The others had already gone. Grant and his gang had left right after breakfast this morning, and Erin and Reuben not long after. It was a funny look Erin had shot Ben's direction as she and Reuben said good-bye to everyone—a mixture of puzzlement and disgust. At least that's the way he read it. Not a word had she said about the gift. Ben wasn't even sure she had opened it, but he thought she probably had. He thought the gift might be the reason for the funny look. And understandably—not a good idea to give your daughter a gift intended for a baby if she was childless and in her thirties. Any fool should know that.

Ben rolled up his window and gave a sigh, part regret and part relief, as he accelerated. Now to get back home, far away from Savannah, which was a nice enough city if you didn't feel like an outsider among your own children and grandchildren. And far away from Vera Bridgewater, too, who might be a nice enough woman if you didn't feel like she was always collecting evidence against you, applying uncomplimentary labels to everything you did and said. Not that the two of them had even exchanged more than a few dozen words during this visit, but he could just see the little gears in her mind turning around and around every time he glanced her way. Little windmills trying to analyze his consciousness.

He thought about the look she had given him over her shoulder, through the window of Grant's van as they backed out of the driveway. Not puzzled and disgusted like Erin's, but half-amused and half-pitying, as he read it. She was wearing a little black-and-purple knit cap with a purple tassel on top, pulled down snug over her hair, and she had turned her small oval face to look at him, her eyes the color of smoke. Not that he could see the color of her eyes from that distance, but he had seen them enough to know exactly what color they were. *Inscrutable*—that was the word. Inscrutable eyes the color of smoke.

She had lifted a hand to tuck a strand of hair under her cap, a gesture he had misinterpreted as the beginning of a wave. He started to wave back but caught himself and scratched his ear instead. Vera turned back around in her seat to say something to Lavinia and Adelaide. He wondered what she was saying in her low, scratchy voice.

Well, it was over, and he was glad. He had done it again—had shown his children he wasn't afraid to take his place among them. And he hadn't forced himself on them; they had invited him to come. Maybe they were hoping he would decline. They had no way of knowing how much he wanted to. But the voice wouldn't let him. *You need to go,* it had said. *This is good and right, and it will get easier*. And he had shown Vera Bridgewater that she didn't intimidate him one bit. He could hold his head up and look at her without flinching.

He turned on the radio and found a station playing classical music. It irritated him just slightly that the only question he had missed in the Schooldays Trivia game last night had been in the category of Art and Culture, at the "Graduate School" level, which meant it was harder and worth more points than one at the "Grade School," "High School," or "College" level. It was a question about a twentieth-century French composer named Francis Poulenc, whoever he was. Ben intended to find out the first chance he got.

The most irritating part was that Vera Bridgewater had answered the question correctly on rebound and earned ten extra points for her team. And she had gone on to answer another question about another composer named Sergei Rachmaninoff, but at least Ben had heard of that one, had read an article about him in a magazine years ago. Russian guy, a pianist with such long fingers that people with normal-sized hands had trouble playing the music he wrote. Many critics were hard on him during his lifetime. Someone had likened one of Rachmaninoff's symphonies to a musical version of the ten plagues of Egypt.

Ben turned onto a busy street that would take him to the interstate. Traffic was heavy in the city, to be expected on Black Friday, but he was hoping it wouldn't be horrible on the freeway. As he sat at a traffic light, he glanced overhead and saw a blur of dark birds sailing by. It reminded him of something else he needed to look up. Two things, really.

"One way of looking at thirteen blackbirds"—it was something Vera had said at the table yesterday at Thanksgiving dinner, when a flock of noisy starlings had lighted in a holly tree just outside the dining room window. She had immediately laughed and said, "Oh, never mind, that wasn't funny at all. I didn't even mean to say it." Ben doubted her. He thought she enjoyed being cryptic, making people think her mind was packed so full of esoteric things that it couldn't contain them all. He wondered if he should tell her that blackbirds and starlings were from two different families of birds.

Brittany, who was wiping a spot of sweet-potato casserole off Lavinia's pink shirt at the time, had cried, "Oh, please, Mother, *please* don't start reciting your weird poems," and to the rest of them, she added, "And please don't ask her to explain. She's been on this poetry kick lately, but it's all stuff that makes absolutely no sense. Like that stupid 'Thirteen Ways of Looking at a Blackbird.' That's her current favorite." She dipped her napkin into a water glass and resumed rubbing.

Ben wondered which it was—one way of looking at thirteen blackbirds or thirteen ways of looking at one. He assumed Brittany had it wrong. He couldn't imagine two different ways of looking at a blackbird, much less thirteen.

At the other end of the table, Isaac had set up a fuss about something, and Mackenzie said, "He already had one roll, but he dropped it and Buster's eating it."

Shelly had gasped. "You mean that dog is still in the house?"

"He's under the table," Mackenzie reported, her eyes bright with the thought of someone getting in trouble.

Vera wasn't a woman to take offense easily. Ben remembered all the little lines radiating from around her puckered mouth as she calmly observed Brittany's continued assault on the stain. He remembered her slow, wry smile and the words she spoke at last, almost as if to herself: "Well, I light a small fire in the rain." She was seated right across the table from him, but never once did she actually look at him during the meal. *So who's afraid of making eye contact?* he had felt like asking her.

So "thirteen ways of looking at a blackbird," or vice versa, and "a small fire in the rain." And Francis Poulenc. He didn't have to take a trip to the library; he would Google them as soon as he got home tonight. Maybe he would dash off an e-mail to Vera if he found out some interesting and offbeat tidbit she might not know, something breezy and casual to show her he was just a normal guy, not all hung up trying to hide, avoid, deny, or cover up.

Or maybe he wouldn't; maybe he wouldn't write her ever again. He surely didn't want her to think he was trying to impress her or that it bothered him in any way that she might know more than he did about music and poetry. Big deal. He knew a lot more than she did about other things.

He recalled one of the questions he had answered in the trivia game, about the United States buying the Virgin Islands from Denmark for twenty-five million dollars. It was one of the easier ones, actually, but he remembered Reuben's exclamation of "*Wowser*! Is there *anything* you don't know?" He also remembered how Erin had rolled her eyes and turned her head quickly toward the wall. She obviously thought Ben was showing off. If he had really wanted to show off, he could have told Reuben that he was misusing the word *wowser*, that it wasn't a synonym for *wow* but that it actually referred to a puritanical kind of person who got stirred up by minor vices. According to his *Say It Ain't So, Joe* book, the word was thought to be an acronym for We Only Want Social Evils Righted. He hadn't said any of that, though.

He got to the interstate and merged into the flow of traffic headed west. He turned on the cruise control and settled into the right lane. There was something light and cheerful playing on the classical station, a waltz maybe. He wondered if Vera would be able to identify it by name and composer. He thought he might start listening to more classical music and reading up on composers.

Listening to the waltz now, he wondered if people his age ever took up music lessons and succeeded at them. As a kid, his mother had made him take piano lessons. He was halfway good at it, too, but gave it up in junior high when it wasn't cool to like music, not the kind his teacher made him play. Vera played the violin. He wondered how good she was. Vera the Violinist. Vera the Violinist from Vermont. He ought to ask her sometime if she drove a Volvo.

It surprised him how often he still thought about what she had written to him in an earlier e-mail, one of the first ones after his accident with the cranberry juice: *It's hard to believe it was really a mistake,* she wrote. *I can easily believe that you told yourself you would never send it, but was there perhaps a suppressed desire, or a subconscious need, to establish contact, not necessarily with me specifically but with another human being, to let down your guard for a change and open up a line of communication? Could it be that you're tired of the wall between yourself and everybody else? You do understand, don't you, Ben, that you have erected a wall, that you live in a gated community of your own making? If you insist it was an accident, I suppose I can play along, but I'd rather we interact as adults instead of children.*

There had been more, a lot more, but those were the words he thought about most often. He had written her back hotly and at some length, trying to explain again how the accident had happened, but he had found himself at a loss to make it sound convincing. He had deleted much of it but kept the sentence that read *Do you perhaps have a suppressed desire, or a subconscious need, Vera, to tell other people what their problems are when you have more than a few yourself?* It obviously wasn't a suppressed desire, though, if she did it so freely.

"I light a small fire in the rain"—the words Vera spoke at the table came back to him. He suddenly remembered a camping trip when his children were young, possibly the last camping trip they had taken as a family. He had tried to talk Chloe out of the trip, had told her the weather in the mountains looked iffy, but she had insisted, had even laughed at him and called him a wet blanket and a worry-wart. She had the van all packed up and ready to go when he got home from work. It had started drizzling as they set up the tents, and by nightfall it was pouring. There was no lighting a small fire in that rain. He remembered saying to Chloe the words he knew he shouldn't say: "I told you so."

It made him mad that he couldn't forget that silly part of Vera's book where she talked about the woman who kept a list of her late husband's faults. Ever since he had read that, he had found things

480

about Chloe coming to his mind at odd times, things he didn't want to think about—like her stubborn streak when she got an idea in her head and the way she brushed off some of his ideas. And her habit of letting things run over in the oven and then never cleaning it up. And her refusal to wear a coat in the wintertime. And the way she left dresser drawers open for him to bang his shins on.

He turned up the volume on the radio. Now they were playing a march of some kind. He wished he'd never heard of Vera Bridgewater's book. For sure he wished he had never slipped up and sent her that first e-mail. And he wished she hadn't felt compelled to write him back. *You understand, don't you, Ben, that you have erected a wall?* What business was it of hers if he erected a wall or lived in a gated community? Not that he put any stock in her pet theories. It was all a bunch of psychobabble.

Ben glanced at the sky, which was a pale dingy gray, with dirty white clouds scudding low. He thought of the framed cross-stitched poem he had given Erin yesterday, the one originally intended for Lydia.

Do you know how many clouds
Every day go floating by?
Do you know how many stars
There are shining in the sky?
God in heaven has counted all;
He would miss one should it fall.

481

Do you know how many children
Go to little beds at night,
And without a care or sorrow,
Wake up in the morning light?
God in heaven each name can tell,
Loves you, too, and loves you well.

Next to the poem was a cross-stitched picture of an angel in a blue robe hovering over the bed of a small child, with yellow stars and a friendly, smiling crescent moon at the window. He had bought it from a new showroom at the Bazaar called The Eye of the Needle, which sold all kinds of needlework—everything from handmade quilts to crocheted bookmarks.

It was the cross-stitched pictures that Kelly had thought of for a hostess gift when he told her he was going to visit his daughter for Thanksgiving, the daughter who had a baby. And though there were many from which to choose, it was that particular picture and poem she had liked best, which didn't surprise him. Somebody like Kelly would naturally like one that mentioned "God in heaven" more than the ones about kittens and mittens and gingerbread men. He wondered if Erin would be angry when she opened the gift. He wished he had stopped to think about it before offering it to her. Chalk up one more strike against him in her book.

The music on the radio stopped, and the news came on. Same old stuff. Troubled economy.

Suicide bombings in the Middle East. Earthquakes. Tax increases. Political mudslinging. Holiday fatalities. But then, remarkably, this: "Early this morning a local woman had an unusual Thanksgiving blessing. When Annie Becker of Crossville, Tennessee, went out to get her paper, she found a cardboard box with her name on it beside her front door, along with a note that said, 'You were kind to me many years ago. I never forgot it. Thank you.' The note was unsigned. Inside the box were bills of all denominations, from ones to hundreds, totaling twenty-seven thousand dollars."

This was followed by an audio clip of the woman herself saying, "I got no earthly idea who done this. My whole life I always tried my best to treat people right, but I sure never expected nothing like this to turn up at my doorstep. This is like the windows of heaven pouring out so much goodness and blessing I just can't take it all in!" She sounded like an old woman, a very excited old woman with a high, warbly voice. Ben imagined her living in a run-down house, scraping by every month on a little social security check, writing letters, and looking in on her neighbors. And, of course, reading her Bible. He recognized the "windows of heaven" from the book of Malachi.

The news ended, and the music resumed, a Debussy prelude, the announcer said.

The book of Malachi was the last book Ben had

read in Chloe's Bible. He had finished it on Wednesday, the night before Thanksgiving. So right now, on the table beside his bed, the red ribbon marker in Chloe's Bible was resting squarely between the Old and New Testaments. Tonight he would be ready to start Matthew. Between two testaments—that's where he stood. That could make a good title for something—*Between Two Testaments*.

Ben drove along for many miles, thinking. The Debussy prelude ended and a Tchaikovsky symphony took over. He remembered realizing as he read the book of Malachi, slowly and seriously, how tired he was of picking out amusing phrases from the Bible to make fun of. And then he had come to the last verse. It struck him as a hidden thing he was meant to find.

He thought about the verse again now, on the day after Thanksgiving, driving from Georgia back to South Carolina: *And he shall turn the heart of the fathers to the children, and the heart of the children to their fathers.* He thought of his children, the only part of Chloe still left. He thought of them one at a time and spoke their names aloud.

"I do hope you're not thinking about hanging that up in here," Erin said.

Reuben kept on humming. He gave the nail one more tap, then set the hammer on top of the bureau. He picked up the cross-stitched picture and hung it on the nail. He stepped back to look at it, then straightened it and checked again. "There, that's got it," he said, and gathered up his hammer, pencil, and tape measure. He gave Erin a broad, goofy smile as he passed her in the doorway and pretended to bop her on the head with the hammer.

She followed him through the hallway into the kitchen. "How could you do that?" He didn't answer. "How could you just put it up without asking? I don't want it in there."

Reuben went out the back door onto the porch. She heard him bumping around, putting things away. "Hey, where's that white paint?" he called. "I think I'll get started on the rocking chair."

"You can't do that," Erin said. "Clark and Holly will be here in less than an hour."

"So? I've got extra paintbrushes," Reuben said. "Clark can help me."

"Stop it!" Erin said. "Stop pushing things!" She heard the shrillness of her voice and the sudden silence out on the porch. Reuben appeared in the doorway, a dry paintbrush in one hand. They stood apart, staring at each other for a long moment.

Erin felt her hands shaking. She clenched them together and pressed them to her mouth. She turned away from him and leaned against the counter. Why couldn't he take things slowly? Why did he have to be so childishly eager and hopeful? It was so risky to rush out and meet things the way he did. He should know that better than anyone.

"You're going to mess everything up," she whispered. "I just know you are."

He came to her and put his arms around her from behind, pulling her close to him. He was still holding the paintbrush. She took it from his hand and set it down on the counter harder than she needed to.

"Hey, hey, little girl, it's okay." He rocked her back and forth, his head resting on top of hers. "I won't paint the rocker white if you don't want me to. You want some other color?"

"That's not what I mean, and you know it." She allowed him to turn her around, but she wouldn't look up at him. "I just want you to *wait*. I don't want you getting things ready. And I don't want that picture hanging in there. I don't want to look at it."

He took her in his arms and held her a long while without speaking. She didn't wiggle away as she usually did but stood there listening to his heart beating. She rarely thought about the possibility of losing Reuben, but it struck her now that he was the one sure thing in her life, that without him her world, confined and cautious as it was, would come apart.

She also knew another truth: She loved the cross-stitched picture. Something in her did want to look at it and to hope with the same kind of abandon Reuben showed. But she was too afraid. About the child, of course—disappointment could come in so many ways. But also about her father. She was afraid to let him into her life. Doing that meant giving up her anger, something as familiar to her as her own name.

She thought of the picture and stiffened. She needed to keep it up. She needed to go into the room and read the poem every day to keep her anger alive, especially the second stanza about children going to bed at night without a care or sorrow and waking up in the morning light. Her father had no idea how far those words were from the way she had gone to bed and woken up every day of her life after her mother died.

"Come on, relax," Reuben said softly. "It's okay to let yourself hope, Erin. I can help you learn how." He swayed back and forth, humming something she didn't recognize at first. Then it came to her—it was one of the dumb songs again from the dumb Cinderella musical. "Do I Love You Because You're Beautiful?" Well, she knew the answer to that. She wasn't bad-looking, but she wasn't beautiful, not the way her twin sister Lydia was. Not the way her mother had been. No, it was the other way around. Reuben thought she was beautiful because he loved her. For some strange reason he loved her.

THIRTY-TWO

In Spite of the Cold

Ben slowly got up from the couch and walked stiffly to his recliner. He had been moving back and forth between the two all day. This was his third straight day off work. He couldn't remember the last time he had missed going in because of illness. From the top of the sofa, Ink raised her head and watched him ease himself into the recliner. She flicked her ears, then turned indifferently, leapt to the floor, and padded toward the doorway into the kitchen.

Ben yanked the afghan out from under him and threw it over his feet. What a lousy time to be sick, only two days before Christmas. Or depending on how you looked at it, maybe it was a perfect time to be sick, with his children planning to come for New Year's, all four of them. He had been thinking all day that he could use this as an excuse to renege on his invitation. He could make it sound like he was only concerned about his children's health, and the grandchildren's, too, of course. Didn't want to expose them to germs and all that. The voice kept saying *Don't you dare*, but he couldn't let the voice take over his life. Besides, the voice had been wrong before.

Unfortunately, he had to admit that he didn't feel

quite as bad today as he had yesterday and the day before, which probably meant he was recovering and would be completely well by December 30, the day they were all arriving. Maybe he shouldn't have been so diligent about taking the medicine Caroline insisted on bringing by and leaving in a paper bag in his mailbox two days ago. Four different kinds, with a handwritten note taped to each one, telling him how much to take and how often. As if he couldn't read directions on a box. Maybe he should stop taking it and try to drag this out a little longer.

His head still felt like it was the size of a pumpkin. Only a moderate-sized pumpkin now, but still quite heavy and full of mush. His cough was getting better, but he had a nasty coppery aftertaste in his mouth. Sinus headache, sore throat, drippy nose—he'd had the whole works. He thought he might have had a fever, too, at one point, but he never could find a thermometer to check it.

Ben looked around his den at the greenery, candles, and ribbon arranged on the mantel, then at the half-decorated tree in front of the window. Everything looked too new, too stiff and shiny, but it couldn't be helped. At least he hadn't gotten a fake tree. Chloe had always insisted on a real tree. Maybe when his head cleared, he would be able to enjoy the scent of evergreen. It was something he hadn't smelled inside his house in a long, long time. Or maybe he wouldn't enjoy it at all. Maybe it was one of those sensory impressions better left in the past. Maybe this whole Christmas business was better left in the past.

Athena was supposed to come again today to finish the tree and get the bedrooms upstairs ready for company, but he had called her and told her not to bother. She couldn't do anything else on the tree anyway since there were no more ornaments to work with. He'd been buying them and bringing them home from the Bazaar a few at a time. When you didn't usually celebrate Christmas, you didn't have boxes of decorations stored in the attic like everybody else.

He turned off the lamp beside his recliner and sat in the dark. The sun had already set, and through the den window the sky was deepening to black. Lights shone at a neighbor's house across the way—a single electric candle in each window. Athena had suggested the same kind of candles for his windows, but Ben had told her the mantel, the tree, and the wreath on the front door were more than enough for someone just getting back into Christmas.

He lay back in his recliner and closed his eyes. Everything seemed like so much trouble right now, especially the thought of company. At least he still had a week before everybody descended. He suddenly thought of something else—the church program he was supposed to attend. He groaned now to think about it. There was no way he could go to church tomorrow, most definitely not that church.

He ought to get up and call Kelly right now, or call Caroline and tell her to call Kelly, and say he wouldn't be able to make it. He still couldn't figure out what he had said that gave Kelly the idea he was planning to come. All he knew was that she had looked at him four days ago, her eyes as bright as stars, and said, "Mr. Buck, I can't tell you how much it means that you're coming to our Christmas Eve program at church next week!"

And apparently he wasn't the only one. He knew Caroline and Nora were planning to go, also Dustin and LaTeesha. He'd heard LaTeesha say to Kelly, "So what kinda play is this, K-K honey? You gonna be the Virgin Mary or what?" Kelly said no, one of her sisters was playing that part.

Well, he had a good excuse now. Nobody would expect him to go to church after being out of work for three days. At least his sickness was good for something—for now. He knew he would probably feel compelled to go to a service later to make it up to Kelly.

He drifted off to sleep and was dreaming about running through a maze of hallways while a fire alarm sounded, when he suddenly woke to the realization that the phone was ringing. He sat up and slowly swiveled the recliner around to face the desk. Probably a wrong number or somebody trying to sell something since every normal person would be out doing something fun tonight, two days before Christmas.

The phone stopped ringing and the answering machine took over. Whoever it was would surely hang up now. He couldn't think of anybody who would want to call him, and even if someone did, he knew he didn't want to be on the other end. He had already spent an exhausting twenty minutes on the phone with Shelly earlier today while she told him all about her plans for assigning meal preparation during their upcoming visit.

He tried to tell her he didn't want her doing that, that he had already talked to Athena and they could manage, but he had finally given up and let her talk. He couldn't remember a word she had said except at the very end: "So, see? You don't have to worry about a thing!" She hadn't even noticed his croaky voice or hacky cough, or, if she had, she hadn't commented on it. Maybe she thought he was faking in hopes that she would suggest canceling the visit.

Suddenly a woman's voice came on over the answering machine. "Ben." A pause, and then, "I thought you might be home, but I guess you're not, unless you're not picking up on purpose, which wouldn't really surprise me. I was thinking maybe you were in the kitchen trying out a recipe or wrapping gifts or trimming the tree in anticipation of this very *uncharacteristic* but nice thing you're planning to do for your children next week."

Another pause, a longer one. He had recognized her voice from the first word, of course.

He turned the lamp back on and sat there scowling at the phone as she continued. "You said something in a recent e-mail that I took to be unflattering, as you probably intended it—something about my lack of spontaneity, which, of course, is something you would know absolutely nothing about since you don't know me at all *and* since you're hardly one to be offering such a criticism. If you were home right now, we could talk about this, but you're not—or you're pretending not to be. Anyway, I was sitting here in my apartment just now, reading a novel, a rather sorry one set in the frozen wilderness of the Yukon Territory, of all places, when I suddenly felt a chill go over me, and the thought came to me, 'I will rise and warm myself by . . .' and I heard the answer almost immediately, suggested by your recent e-mail: 'by doing something spontaneous.' And then I thought, 'What better spontaneous thing to do than to call Ben, who accused me of not having a spontaneous bone in my body?' I believe that's the way you put it in your e-mail."

She paused again, made a gravelly contemptuous sound, then resumed. "You know, I ran across the word *glastnost* recently, g-l-a-s-t-n-o-s-t. It's Russian, but I'm sure you must already know that, being the word whiz you are. You must also know that it's a commodity *as scarce as hen's teeth* in your way of approaching life. So anyway, that's all for now. Take it or leave it."

And she hung up. Ben was pretty sure she had spelled the word wrong. He was almost certain it was *glasnost*, not *glastnost*. What an utterly strange phone call. That woman had more than a few loose cows in her pasture. He wondered briefly if he might still be dreaming. But he saw the red light on the telephone blinking on and off. For sure somebody had called. He got up from the recliner and walked over to the desk, stood there watching the blinking light for a few seconds, and then pressed Play.

It was definitely her voice. He listened to her message again, wishing he didn't feel so groggy and befuddled so he could make sure he wasn't missing anything.

Glasnost? Well, of course, he knew what that was. Mikhail Gorbachev's word back in the 1980s for the new Soviet era of free expression, open discussions, the lifting of bans, and such. Okay, so this must be only more of her tiresome commentary about Ben's *fear of engaging life*, as she had put it in another e-mail. *A commodity as scarce as hen's teeth in your way of approaching life*—where had she come up with that? And why had she stressed the phrase *as scarce as hen's teeth*? Obviously, she was mocking him. She had told him once that his obsession with the origins of words and phrases was a sad thing. Those were the very words she had used—*obsession* and *sad*.

He played her message back and listened to it a third time, all the way through, from the first word to the final *That's all. Take it or leave it.* How nice of her to give him a choice. He felt like calling her back and saying, "Well, I've thought it over, Vera, and I think I'll leave it," and then he could hang up as abruptly as she had.

Ink reappeared in the doorway. She stopped, front paws primly together, back slightly arched, and fixed him with one of her reproving looks. When he didn't move, she emitted a firm meow. Ink wasn't coy. When she wanted something, she let you know. No dropping subtle hints. No beating around the bush. No pussyfooting.

Ben smiled at his little joke. "Okay, okay. I know that look," he said. As he started for the kitchen, he pointed at the cat and added sternly, "You know, Ink, your obsession with tuna is a sad thing."

Kelly shook the paper bag that held all the pieces of glass and ceramic. They made a dry, clinking sound. She twisted the top of the bag tighter and wrote "Tile Pieces" on the side with a magic marker. Then she cleared off a space on the work-table and propped the finished mosaic against the wall. She hadn't realized it would be so heavy by the time it was done. She hoped it wouldn't pull the nails out of the wall when Mr. Buck tried to hang it. *If* he tried to hang it. She still wasn't sure she could get up the nerve to give it to him. It wasn't like it was a great work of art or anything.

She moved to the other side of her father's workshop and turned around to study the mosaic from a distance. She thought it was beautiful, though she would never say such a thing out loud. She had worked from a photograph she had seen in a magazine. *Two Blue Moons*—that was the name she had given it.

She backed up and sat down on an old stool against the far wall. She looked all around the workroom, then slowly let her eyes move back to the mosaic. She tried to imagine that she was just seeing it for the first time. What would she think of it if she had just now walked in and seen it propped up on the table?

It was hard to separate yourself from your art—she'd learned that a long time ago. That was one reason she didn't think she could ever be a real artist or musician or writer. She knew she would be too sensitive to the criticism of other people. She could do things secretly, just for her own enjoyment, but putting them on display for public scrutiny would scare her to death. But then wasn't courage one of the things an artist had to have? If you didn't have that, how could you ever get better? How could you ever dare to try in the first place?

She was worried about college. The closer it got

to January, the more nervous she was getting. What if her teachers didn't like her work? She had always sung and played the piano and flute and drawn her pictures and written her stories and plays for people who loved her—people whose tastes, if the truth were known, were probably not very highly developed. But now she would be thrown in with others and be expected to compete. Her teachers would compare her work with that of all the other students in the class and all the ones they'd ever known. What if they told her she should consider another course of study since she would never make it through the required art classes?

She was getting some good experience at the Bazaar, but she knew she had miles to go before she would be anywhere close to a professional designer. Whenever she recalled her job interview back in April, she was amazed that she'd sat in Mr. Buck's office and told him she could do anything he asked her to do. She could see now, from a distance of eight or nine months, how much her mother's high opinion of her had carried her through her whole life and right up through that interview. You hear your mother tell you for twenty-plus years how smart and talented you are, and you were naturally going to develop some confidence—some untested confidence. It was embarrassing to think about it now.

How in the world had Mr. Buck kept from

laughing at her during the interview? And what in the world had made him decide to give her a chance? Not that she wasn't working hard and helping out at the Bazaar. So far Mr. Buck and all the rest of them seemed to like her show windows okay and her ideas for advertising brochures and all that, but sometimes when she heard herself giving her opinions at work, she stopped and reminded herself of how little she really knew. She was waiting for the day when somebody would step forward and say, "And what gives *you* any kind of authority to say these things?"

She stood up and walked slowly toward the mosaic. What if she gave *Two Blue Moons* to Mr. Buck and he acted kind and said nice things about it but she could tell that deep down he thought it was amateurish? That would be horrible. What if he lugged it home out of obligation but then stuck it in a closet? Well, at least she wouldn't ever know about that. Kelly hadn't kept track of how many hours she had spent working on it, but she knew it was a lot. But she also knew that time alone didn't determine the worth of something. She wished she could tell if this was really any good or if she just thought it was because it was hers.

She stopped and stood directly in front of it. It was mostly shades of blue, with black and gray mixed in. And the moon itself was made out of pieces of a pale blue saucer and a cracked white perfume atomizer she had found in her mother's dresser drawer.

Even after she had removed the spray device, washed the bottle in hot soapy water, and pounded on it with a hammer inside a paper bag, the white shards had still given off a strong musky scent of the perfume. She knew she could put her face close to the mosaic moon even now and smell it.

The moon wasn't a full moon, which had been tempting to change. But she had stayed true to the photograph and made it a three-quarters moon. The sea was mostly dark blue and gray, with small pieces of the white perfume bottle for the moon's reflection, and shards of a broken mirror to give the effect of moonlight playing on the waves. The broad sky above the water was lighter —medium tones of blue and gray. Black fronds of a silhouetted palm tree, made from slivers of black ceramic tile, bent into the picture on one side, though Kelly had simplified them somewhat from the magazine photo. The caption of the picture had read "Moon Over the Sea in Casablanca," but it looked like it could have been taken in a thousand other places, even in Florida or along the coast of South Carolina.

She felt sure Mr. Buck would at least like the title she had given the mosaic even if he didn't like anything else about it. She had heard him explaining the expression *once in a blue moon* to Mr. Begian at the Bazaar several weeks ago, telling him that sometimes, but not very often, dust particles or volcanic ash or ice crystals in the atmosphere could make the moon look blue, so that *once in a blue moon* meant very, very rarely. Mr. Begian had listened with admiration and replied, both hands waving excitedly, "Mr. Buckley, I have sixty-one years of life, but only one time do I know a man with such a grand mind like you. Merchant in Morocco name of Jair who sold me exquisite fine wood. So once in *two blue moons* I meet a smart man like you!"

It was funny how something like that could lodge in your mind and then jump out at you while you were leafing through a magazine. The instant she had seen the "Moon over the Sea in Casablanca" picture, she remembered the overheard conversation and knew at once what she wanted to do for Mr. Buck's Christmas present to thank him for giving her a chance, first to work at the Bazaar and now to go to college.

Settling on the medium of mosaic had been easy; she had been wanting to try such a project ever since she had seen the new line of mosaic decorations in the Pomp and Pizzazz showroom at work. She had talked with Macon Mahoney about it, and he had explained the process and encouraged her to give it a try.

The door of the workshop opened, and Kelly spun around to see her father standing there.

"Oh, sorry, I didn't know you were out here," he said. "I thought you had already gone up to bed. I was coming out to cut the light off."

Kelly smiled. "You don't have to apologize, Daddy. It's your workshop. I'm the one trespassing. Come on in. I was just getting ready to leave."

Charlie stooped under the low doorway and walked in. "You're not trespassing, sweetheart," he said. "You know you can be out here anytime you want to be." His eyes came to rest on the mosaic, and Kelly heard his soft intake of breath. "So . . . is this what you've been working on?" He came over and stood beside her for a moment looking at it, then moved to the table and bent down to study it. "I don't know how you did this," he said at length. It almost sounded like his voice cracked, but Kelly knew that couldn't be. Her father wasn't one to show emotion on an everyday basis. Especially not over something like a picture.

She pulled the folded page from the magazine out of her pocket and unfolded it. "See, this is the picture I copied, so it's not really original. It wasn't all that hard; it just took a lot of time." She set the picture down and reached for the brown paper bag. She shook it again, then opened the top. "And here's all the leftover pieces from all the things I smashed. I thought I might save them for another project sometime."

Her father frowned at the magazine picture a long moment, then looked into the paper bag. He turned back to the mosaic.

"So do you like it?" Kelly asked.

He shook his head, looking back and forth between the picture and the mosaic. "But how did you do it?" he said. "When you told me you were going to make a mosaic, I didn't expect . . . anything like this. How did you do it?" He looked up and down the workshop table, as if searching for clues, then back at the mosaic.

Kelly laughed. "Somebody at work gave me a few tips, but mainly I just followed the instructions I got off the Internet," she said. "It had diagrams, too. I made some mistakes, but I learned as I went along. You don't like it, do you?" Of course, she knew he did.

He turned and put his arms around her but didn't say anything at first, then, "Yes, I do like it, Kelly. I just can't understand how you did it. I sure couldn't."

"Oh, Daddy, anybody could smash up some dishes and things and glue the pieces on a board." She pulled away. "Do you think Mr. Buck will like it?"

"If he doesn't, then he's not the smart man you say he is."

Kelly smiled. "I'm afraid you're not very objective, but I hope you're right." She reclosed the top of the paper bag and set it back onto the table. "Well, I'm off to bed," she said. She folded up the magazine page and stuck it in her pocket, then took the mosaic away from the wall and laid it flat on the table. At the door she turned back. "Night, Daddy."

"When are you going to give it to him?"

"I don't know. I was hoping to today, but he's been sick this week." It was okay, though—this way it gave her a little more time to decide whether to actually give it to him and what to say if she did.

With a sinking feeling, Caroline turned the last page of the book she was reading in bed, a thick book titled *So Many Clues*, and saw only three paragraphs remaining. She knew there was no way the story was going to be wrapped up in a satisfying way in only three short paragraphs. She flipped through the pages at the end, full of all kinds of footnotes and excerpts of newspaper articles and court transcripts, which had fooled her into thinking the story was much longer than it was.

With a sigh she turned back to the last page and started reading. She came to the final paragraph, read it slowly, and then said aloud, very deliberately, "What a cop-out." She slapped the book shut and dropped it onto the floor beside the bed. Honestly, to invest all that time reading about a real-life triple murder only to be hit in the face with the fact that it had never been solved!

The book jacket had given no clue whatsoever that the whole crime was left up in the air. All the little blurbs on the back cover made it sound like one of the greatest pieces of detective work in the past hundred years. She should have known better—a crime she'd never heard of, only ten years ago, in a southern state no less. She should have known the investigation had hit a brick wall, or she would have remembered it.

She threw back the covers and swung her feet out of bed. She sat on the edge of the bed studying her pedicure for a moment, wondering if she should switch back to red polish next time. This orangey-pink was getting on her nerves. A lot of things were getting on her nerves lately.

Reading before bed used to make her sleepy, but she had been reading for almost an hour and still felt wide awake. She looked over at the bathroom door. She didn't want to take another sleeping pill, but she knew if she didn't, she would lie awake for hours.

She shifted her eyes to the book on the floor and stared at it a long time. *So Many Clues*—what a joke. She reached down, picked it up, and put it back on the nightstand, but still she kept one hand on it, thinking. Slowly she picked it back up, laid it in her lap, and turned to the last page.

Slowly she moved a finger along under each word as she read the final paragraph out loud:

" *'Finally I had to accept the fact that some of the deepest, darkest secrets are meant to remain as such. We had followed this one for over four years and countless miles, climbing mountains, diving to the bottom of a lake, picking our way through the charred ruins of an apartment building, searching through reams of reports, hounding strangers while neglecting those dearest to us, only to come to the end of the trail, cold and empty-handed. So many clues but no answer. At last I knew what I had to do. I had to let go before my heart, too, was empty. I had to leave death behind and return to life.' "*

Caroline set the book aside and stood up. She had the most peculiar sensation, as if suddenly a giant loose peg inside her had quit rattling around and found its way into the right-sized hole. Slowly she walked out of her bedroom, through the hallway, and into the kitchen. At the table she laid a hand on the thick expandable folder of notes and photocopies labeled "Chloe Buckley." Any book about this case would have to be called *So Few Clues*.

For weeks on end she had been searching for the right time and the right way to tell Mr. Buckley her theory about his wife's death. She had watched him closely, trying to gauge his mood, trying to figure out how to start the first sentence. She had tried to put herself in his place: After almost twenty-two years, surely he would want to know who had killed Chloe—or who had probably killed her. It was the *probably* that kept nagging at Caroline.

And now she was hit with another thought, and from such an unlikely source, too—at the very end of a disappointing book: *Some of the deepest, darkest secrets are meant to remain as such.* She wasn't a religious person, but what if some mystical force had led her to pick up *So Many Clues* just so she would eventually come to the last paragraph and read those words? What if it was a message intended for her right now? She remembered something that naïve and goody-goody Kelly Kovatch had said to LaTeesha at work one day, something Caroline had shaken her head over: "I believe God brings the right people and events and things into our lives at just the right time."

Well, God hadn't dropped the book into her lap; she had seen it on the library shelf and chosen it herself. Caroline picked up the folder from the kitchen table but didn't open it. She knew every page inside backwards and forwards. *I had to let go. . . . I had to leave death behind and return to life.* Was that supposed to be some kind of warning? An astonishing thought came to her, astonishing in that she'd never considered it before: What good would come out of telling her theory to Mr. Buck or anyone else? The three people involved in the crime were all dead and buried. If her idea was right, then justice was not at stake. And though she hated to admit it, there was simply no way any of it could be proven.

Slowly she walked across the kitchen. She opened the sliding trash bin under the sink and gently laid the folder on top of an empty egg carton and pressed it down. She remembered that tomorrow was garbage day. She had meant to roll the garbage can out to the curb right after supper but had gotten distracted by a movie on television about two women hikers in a remote area out in Wyoming. While they were cooking their supper over a fire, they were suddenly taken at gunpoint by a man who shot and killed their dog, then threw their cell phones in a lake and forced the women to march in front of him to a deserted cabin.

It wasn't a great movie—*Dead of Night*, it was called—but she had spent two whole hours watching it in spite of several obvious implausibilities. The ending was a predictably happy one, with the two women working out a system to foil the man's evil intentions, even though one of them had a broken leg and a gash in her forehead before it was over. They had ended up killing the man with his own gun and sending up smoke signals— a particularly corny touch at the end—to catch the attention of a search helicopter. Looking back on it, she was struck with how she had wasted two perfectly good hours.

Caroline walked quickly back to the bathroom and got her robe. She might as well check the trash cans in all the rooms before taking care of the garbage. It was times like this that she was reminded of how handy it would be to have a man around the house. A man who wasn't afraid of work, that is. A man unlike either Donald or his shiftless father.

Back in the kitchen, she emptied the rest of the trash into the garbage. Only one corner of the folder was still visible. She still wasn't sure she could do this, but something led her on. She lifted the bag out and shook it a little to settle the contents, then tied the top securely. She slipped on her shoes, unlocked the door into the garage, and stepped outside. She felt something growing lighter inside her.

As she rolled the garbage can down the driveway, she breathed in the cold night air. The streetlight cast long shadows across her front yard. At the curb she stopped and looked around. All was still except for the softest sound of wind high in the trees. Though she was usually afraid of being outside by herself at night, for some reason the dark seemed friendly tonight in spite of the cold.

She positioned the garbage can just right, took one last look at it, then turned and quickly started back toward her house. She had the funniest feeling, as if she had just taken off an ugly outfit that was too big and put on something new and pretty, just her size. But she felt a little afraid. Would she wake up during the night and regret this? Would she run out here in the early morning and retrieve the folder? Or chase after the garbage truck, crying, "Wait! Wait! I need it back"?

She stopped and looked up at the yellow moon suspended among the stars. "That it might be fulfilled"—it was something Mr. Buck had said recently. Or maybe it was Kelly who said it. Whoever said it, Caroline didn't know why it should come to her now, but it sounded like something good and big to think about under a starry sky at Christmastime.

THIRTY-THREE

A Very Certain Plan

It was late on Christmas morning, and Kelly was getting ready to open her last gift in the den. Her father still hadn't opened any of his own gifts, which were stacked neatly at his feet, though everyone kept urging him to get started.

The whole family was noisily packed into the den, spilling over into the kitchen. All the children were here but Keith, whose wife had just had another baby. That made nine nieces and nephews now. She looked across the den at her father, who was holding his youngest granddaughter, the one named Kay. She was starting to get fussy.

"No squawking allowed," Kenny said. "Time to go to Mama." He took Kay from Charlie and handed her to her mother on the couch.

Kelly read the gift tag and smiled at her father, who was watching her now. She held the gift up, shook it, then started taking the paper off.

Krista's youngest, just learning to walk, lurched

toward Charlie with a big, wet grin on his face. "Here he comes, Daddy, be ready to catch him!" Krista called.

Charlie leaned forward and held out his arms. "Hey, there, Abe, steady does it. Can you come see Grandpop?" Abe stopped, his plump, stubby legs set wide apart. He swayed briefly before plopping down next to a small wad of wrapping paper, which he snatched up and stuck in his mouth. Charlie swept him up quickly and extracted the damp wad, which he tossed into the big cardboard box someone had brought in to collect the paper.

Kirk was galloping back and forth between the den and kitchen singing "Frosty the Snowman" in a shrill voice, with Jude, Kenny's three-year-old, perched on top of his shoulders, shrieking with delight. "Beep! Beep!" Kirk said. "Coming through! Clear the traffic jam!" He stepped over a little dollhouse, barely missing a toy truck. "Thumpetty thump thump, thumpetty thump thump, look at Frosty go!" he sang. His voice cut through all the other noise.

Kelly had the paper off now, but her father was watching Kirk with a worried look on his face—probably wondering if the day would ever come when he would sit still and be quiet, or maybe wondering how he would ever survive driving lessons, which Kirk had been begging for lately.

Finally he looked back at Kelly, and she opened the box. Inside was a red neck scarf. She took it out and looped it around her neck, then flung one fringed end behind her dramatically and put one hand on her hip. "It's perfect, Daddy!" she called out. "Thank you!" She knew it hadn't been easy for him to go shopping, but he had done it a little at a time—one gift for each child to add to the things Kay had stashed in her bottom bureau drawer.

Kevin stood up and let out a loud whistle. "Hey, who's ready to sing?" he said.

Kirk stopped his "Frosty" song and looked insulted. "Ready to sing?" he said. "What do you think I've been doing all this time?"

Kenny laughed. "I can think of several words for what you've been doing, squirt, but singing isn't one of them." He whisked Jude down from Kirk's shoulders and set him on the floor beside the couch.

Kirk burst out in fake sobs. "Maligned and mis-understood! That's the story of my life around here!"

"We can't sing yet," Karla said. "Daddy hasn't opened his presents."

"Oh, that's all right," Charlie said, "there's no hurry. I can do it after we sing."

But no one would have it. They all set up a clamor for him to open them now, so he took a deep breath and reached for the one on top, a small slender box wrapped in red and white paper, with a tiny green bow on top.

"That one's mine," Karla said proudly.

Everybody was watching him. Kelly knew he didn't like being the center of attention. Before, her mother had always helped him out. "That will go with your navy blue pants," she would say after he opened a gift, or, to one of the kids, "Perfect— how did you know he needed new socks?" All he had to do was smile and nod and say thank you. Of course, they all knew Kay was the one who told everybody what to buy him even though she acted surprised. But they were all on their own now, and so was he.

He pulled off the green bow, then peeled off the tape on one end.

It was a shiny black pen and pencil set. Not something he really needed. They had so many pens and pencils around the house they could equip a whole school. But he took them out of the box one at a time and held them up admiringly. He smiled at Karla. "These are sure nice, honey. I've never had a pen and pencil that matched." He twisted the pen to make the point come out. "Look at that. I'm glad it works that way instead of clicking." Karla glowed with pleasure.

Charlie finally made it through the whole stack and managed to think of something to say about each gift. Even Kirk's gift—a funny-looking wooden umbrella stand he had made in shop class at school. "This will be handy by the back door," he said even though it didn't strike Kelly as a very practical design. It didn't look like it would hold more than three or four umbrellas, and with such a small base it would probably always be tipping over.

"It started out as a lamp," Kirk said, "but I ran out of time for the electrical part." Kelly wondered if his shop teacher had suggested the change. Maybe he had stopped to think about all the things that could happen if Kirk started working with electrical wires.

Suddenly Kerri was at the piano, and they were all singing "Silent Night."

"All is calm, all is bright"—well, Kelly knew that didn't exactly describe how she always felt, but she joined in. As she sang, she looked around the den at all her brothers and sisters, her father, and all the little ones. She knew most of them were wondering the same thing: how the absence of one person could make such a full house seem so empty.

Later that night, after all the pumpkin and pecan pies were eaten and three loads of dishes were washed and put away, Kelly left the others watching *A Christmas Carol* in the den and headed upstairs to bed. Even though she had seen the movie a dozen times, she still wished she could stay up and watch the end. She liked the part when Ebenezer Scrooge woke up on Christmas morning and had changed into a different kind of man. But weeks ago when Nora was making up the holiday schedule, Kelly had volunteered to work the day after Christmas. Now she was wishing she hadn't, but there was no way out of it. She knew tomorrow was going to be a long day.

As she mounted the stairs, she couldn't help being glad that Christmas Day was over. She hadn't known she would miss her mother so much, that reruns of Christmases past would play through her mind all day long, that every time she turned around she would expect her mother to be there, giving directions and making everything feel warm and Christmassy.

She heard a cough behind her and looked back to see her father at the bottom of the stairs. She knew it had been a long day for him, too, but he had held up. This morning he had taken Kenny's two oldest for a walk down by the creek behind the woods to show them the new footbridge and a hollow tree trunk where a family of raccoons was holed up for the winter. Then before dinner he had worked on a jigsaw puzzle with the kids in the den and played a game of Uno that Kyle had gotten started. He had also carved the turkey and pork roast and helped stir the gravy.

Kelly stopped at the top of the staircase and waited for him. "You turning in, too, Daddy? You're not going to play Monopoly with them after the movie?"

He shook his head. "No, it's been a mighty full

day already." He was taking the steps slowly, like an old man.

When he reached the top, Kelly took his arm and walked with him toward the room at the far end of the hall. The nursery was what they still called it even though it was really a catchall room now. A small room no bigger than a good-sized closet, it used to have a crib in it for whichever baby happened to be the newest. Now, however, it held only old things: an old sewing machine, boxes of worn-out toys, a battered trunk, a rickety twin bed. This was where her father had insisted on sleeping this week so that Kenny's family could have his bedroom with the adjoining bath.

"I wish you could stay up with the others," her father said. "You've been working too much lately."

"Look who's talking," she said. "I'm not the one who worked fourteen hours yesterday."

Her father shrugged. "Oh well. That's what happens on Christmas Eve when you work for UPS." He paused outside the hall bath to check the thermostat on the wall.

Faint tinkly music was coming from the bedroom where Krista had put Abe to bed. Krista had a set of CDs she used for different purposes with her children. For nighttime it was a CD of hymns played by a handbell choir; for naps she preferred Strauss waltzes. Kelly wondered if she could ever be as easygoing and creative at motherhood as her big sister was—if she ever got to be a mother, that is.

She hadn't let on to anybody how low her spirits had been for the past week, after she had overheard Gilda Bloodworth at work tell Nora that her son Ryan had popped the question to a girl he had known since elementary school and they were getting married next summer. The last couple of days it had been harder than usual to be around her married siblings and all their children. And Kerri, who was only nineteen, was floating on air these days, ever since Jared King had talked to their father last week and gotten his permission to give Kerri a ring.

When they got to the doorway of the nursery, Kelly stopped. Her father went in and sat down on the bed to unlace his shoes. An old lawn chair sat beside the bed, and on it were his Bible and a stack of his clean underwear. He had brought in a couple of extra shirts and laid them on top of the trunk. His pajamas lay across the bed, an old pair of red flannel ones her mother had given him for Christmas years ago.

Kelly suddenly thought of something. "Say, Daddy, did you ever know a woman named Chloe Buckley?"

Her father frowned. "Chloe Buckley . . . no, I can't remember anybody named that." He pulled off one shoe and rubbed the bottom of his foot. "But I'm not good with names, so that doesn't mean anything. Your mother was the one who never forgot a name." He pulled off the other shoe and set them both under the lawn chair. "Why? Is she somebody I'm supposed to know?"

"Not especially," she said. "Mr. Buck told me last week that his wife knew my mother, but I wasn't sure if you ever met her. That's who Chloe Buckley is. Or was. Caroline told me she died a long time ago." Kelly didn't think she needed to tell her father all the gruesome details Caroline had shared with her.

"That's too bad," her father said. He picked up his pajamas from the end of the bed. "Your mother sure had a lot of friends, didn't she?"

Kelly nodded. "She sure did. And if she was a friend of Mr. Buck's wife, it finally makes a little bit of sense to me why he hired me in the first place—and why he's been so nice all along. I don't know why he waited so long to tell me, though."

Her father stood up and walked toward the door. "Well, he must have thought a lot of your mother." He put one arm around her and pulled her close. "Wouldn't she be happy to know he was paying for you to go to college just because his wife was her friend? I wonder if they ever visited our church."

"No, I don't think so," Kelly said. "Mr. Buck told me he hasn't been to church since he was a teenager. I was sorry he couldn't come to the Christmas program last night. But he promised to come to church one Sunday soon."

"Well, maybe he will. Is he still reading the Bible—do you know?" Her father's voice sounded tired and sad.

"Yes, I think so." She reached up and kissed his cheek. "Night, Daddy. Do you need anything?"

He shook his head. "No, sweetheart, I'm fine. Good night."

As she walked back down the hall, Kelly thought of another odd thing Mr. Buckley had said a week or so ago when he had suddenly appeared in the aisle outside the Kangaroo Kids showroom, where Kelly was busy wiping down the striped wallpaper some child had used as a drawing surface. She had given a little startled jump when she looked up and saw him standing there studying her, his hands behind his back.

"Oh, hi, Mr. Buck, I didn't know you were there."

"I didn't mean for you to," he had said. "It's like the parable. I'm the man taking a far journey. You know not at what hour I may appear." And with that, he had turned and sauntered away. She couldn't help wondering if that meant he was reading in the New Testament now.

Kelly stopped at the doorway of her dark bedroom. Through the window she saw the full moon shining like a big white button, perfectly centered within a triangular opening in the lacework of tree branches. She stood there for a long moment, marveling at such precise accidental alignment when so many other things in life seemed crooked.

Suddenly the fact that she was looking at the moon placed so exactly in the branches of the tree, like something drawn with a ruler and compass, was a very comforting thought. And the fact that it was in the sky every night, waxing and waning in its regular cycle, that it had hung in place since the creation of the world and would be there until the heavens passed away—suddenly it struck her as a clear reminder that God had a very certain plan for her.

Almost a week later Shelly was in the middle of a long story about a family at their church whose house had been destroyed by fire. It was New Year's Eve and they were all gathered in Ben's dining room, finishing up their dinner. Only a few slices of turkey and ham were still left on the two platters, and most of the other dishes were scraped clean. Shelly had been a little peeved that they had cut it so close on the food, but Ben was glad since it meant no leftovers to drag out of the refrigerator later.

Shelly was right in the middle of listing all the things she and Mark had bought and taken over to the apartment where the fire victims were living temporarily when she suddenly stopped midsentence, pointed to the wall behind Ben, and said, "Where did you get *that*?" They all turned to look.

It was Kelly Kovatch's *Two Blue Moons* mosaic, which Ben had decided to hang in the dining room, next to the big window facing the street, since it was the brightest room in his house, and since he could not only see the mosaic as soon as he stepped in the front door, but he could also see it from the den. Ideally, it shouldn't be hung on a wall but in a window so that the sunlight could shine through it, but this was the best he could do for now.

"Somebody at work gave it to me a couple of days ago," Ben told Shelly. "It's a mosaic."

"Well, I can *see* that," Shelly said. She turned to Mark. "Doesn't it remind you of that piece at the Coastal Art Expo last year?" Mark nodded. "It was this gorgeous mosaic of a waterfall," she told the rest of them, "and we both fell in love with it. But while we were standing there talking about buying it—the thing cost over seven hundred dollars!—somebody came right up and put a little sticker on it that meant it was sold! I was just *sick*, wasn't I, Mark?" Mark nodded again. "Did you say somebody *gave* this to you?" she asked Ben.

"Yes," he said, "she actually made it herself. She almost didn't give it to me because she didn't think it was very good."

Shelly got up and walked over to stand in front of it. Ben wished he hadn't said that last part. Shelly didn't need any encouragement to find fault. She surveyed it for a long moment, during which Lydia's Isaac set up a squall because all the mashed potatoes were gone. But after studying the mosaic for a while Shelly said, "Well, whoever she is, she needs to get glasses. I don't know why in the world she didn't think it was very good. Does this person make these to sell? Does she have a booth at your store? I might be interested in buying one."

Ben shook his head. "She's our designer," he said, "but she's cutting back to part-time next month so she can start taking some college classes. She just tried making this as an experiment."

Shelly sighed. "Well, anyhoo," she said, returning to the table, "since the Hortons weren't insured, they're going to need *every*-thing. But like I was telling the kids, this is what being a Christian is all about—helping those who are less fortunate. God blesses us so we can bless others. Right, kids?" Shelly's three nodded on cue, and she continued without missing a beat. "But I told Mark I can't understand anybody these days not having *some* kind of insurance, even if they're only renting, but that poor Barney Horton just can't seem to—"

But before they could hear what poor Barney Horton couldn't seem to do, Adelaide, who was leaning across the table trying to use the candle snuffer, knocked one of the candles over. Hot green wax spattered across the white tablecloth, and in her haste to pick up the candle, Brittany upset her cup of coffee. "Oh, Addy, look what we've done!" she cried.

"Ice cubes!" Vera said, leaping to her feet. "We need ice cubes! That's how to treat candle wax on a tablecloth!" She headed for the kitchen.

"Here, we need to clear the table," Shelly said, and everyone started stacking dishes.

As Brittany and Grant were blotting the coffee with napkins, Ben got up and followed Vera, feeling like he ought to do something since it was his house. But he was too slow. By the time he got to the kitchen, she was already coming back out, her head down, several ice cubes cupped in her hand. He didn't have time to get out of her way, and there outside the kitchen door they collided. For such a little person, she was solid. She plowed into him, her head against his sternum. Ben thought of those ramming pillars against the doors of a medieval castle. To his embarrassment, he actually heard himself say, "Oof." He also heard the clatter of ice cubes against the hardwood floor.

She looked up at him, clearly exasperated. "Did you want something?"

He stooped to pick up two cubes that had ricocheted off the baseboard, not trusting himself to speak. Amazing that a run-in with someone Vera Bridgewater's size could knock the wind right out of a person.

He stood and deposited the ice into her hand. As she looked up at him impatiently, Ben suddenly wanted to tell her about all the women over the years, several of them readily available right now and many of them quite young, who had made it obvious that they would give their eyeteeth to keep company with him, very close company. He thought of all the different ways he could answer Vera's question. "Did I want something?" he could say. "Well, let's see, how about some respect from you for starters?"

Instead, he looked her in the eye and said, "I thought you might need me to reach something for you on a high shelf . . . since you're so . . . short."

Vera heaved a big sigh and pushed past him. But at the end of the hall, she turned and gave him a long, not altogether disapproving, look.

THIRTY-FOUR

After Rain

On an unseasonably warm Tuesday in the third week of January, Ben came to work an hour late. Over the years he had missed a few days of work here and there for one reason or another, but never in the history of the Upstate Home and Garden Bazaar could he remember showing up late.

Though she didn't speak actual words, the look on Caroline's face said, "What is this world coming to?" Ben could see that she was plagued with curiosity, and for this reason he looked quickly away and pretended to be preoccupied with pleasant thoughts. He even started humming as he walked past her desk.

"Mo said Manny spilled a whole gallon of bleach on the floor of the men's restroom a while ago," she said.

Ben quit humming. "Well, I hope they got it cleaned up," he said cheerfully. He stopped at the door of his office and added, "Now that I think about it, maybe that's exactly what that floor needed. I was noticing recently how discolored the grout was getting."

Vexation was written all over Caroline's face. She was wearing an iridescent blue blouse with a frilly collar and earrings with clusters of tiny blue metallic rods dangling a full three inches below her earlobes, like miniature wind chimes. Her strawberry blond hair was swirled around in a style that wasn't entirely becoming, though Ben couldn't say exactly why. Sometimes he couldn't help wondering if she ever got tired of trying so hard not to look like she was sixty years old. Right now, sitting there in her tight-lipped pique with her eyes crimped up at the corners, she wasn't hiding her age very well.

Doubly thwarted was what came to Ben's mind—thwarted first because she didn't know why he was late and thwarted again because she didn't get the response she wanted about Manny's spill.

Ben knew everyone at the Bazaar must be wondering what had come over him, to hire Manny in the first place and then to keep him on. There was a time when he would have had no patience with such an employee. It seemed that someone was always having to sweep up after Manny, literally. Last week he had knocked over one of Mr. Begian's ceramic urns with the mop handle. Pieces had flown everywhere. He had also put a long scratch across the front of a cherry buffet—resulting in an impassioned speech by Mr. Begian: "Look at what he does! He makes of my show-room a sore-eye!"

Why Ben had hired him was simple—because he was the only one who showed up for an interview after Lester was fired—but a big part of the reason he had kept him went deeper. He had seen Manny's wife drop him off at work one morning in a beat-up truck with a missing bumper. And he had also seen the wide eyes of two small children peering over the dashboard. A softie—that's what he was turning into, though he surely didn't want it to show. Employees tended to get sloppy when they knew their boss was a softie.

But at least Mo had some help keeping up with Manny's accidents now, for just two weeks ago Ben had rehired Lester Lattimore, increasing the Facilities Management Team to three. Well, three if you were counting just bodies, but only about two and a fourth if you were counting *able* bodies.

So far Lester was keeping a low profile, and Ben

hoped it stayed that way. As far as he knew, Les and Caroline had avoided each other, and he hoped that stayed the same, too. Les didn't know the whole story behind his being rehired, didn't have a clue about the note Caroline had put on Ben's desk one morning after Christmas: *I've been thinking about something*, she wrote, *and it's been bothering me. I may have overstated what Lester said to me a couple of months ago. It's hard to remember exactly because we were both upset that day, but maybe I shouldn't have accused him like that.*

Upon further questioning, it was clear to Ben that she remembered that day quite well and was suffering from a guilty conscience. Which in itself was remarkable. He didn't recall Caroline ever acting sorry for anything she said. Though it was tempting to scold her soundly, he took it easy on her. He could tell she felt bad enough. After a few quieter-than-usual days at work, during which Ben had found himself missing her bluster, she had returned to her old self, at least in observable ways. Caroline wasn't one to carry remorse to extremes.

She sighed now. "Nora was here wanting to talk to you. I'll tell her you're in. She's having fits with the schedule for next week. Melody up and told her she's got to go to her sister's wedding in Missouri, and Byron had already said he was taking three vacation days, which he told her were *nonnegotiable*. He said his wife needs a change of scenery so he's taking her to the beach. In January!" She picked up the phone and punched a button. She cast her eyes to the ceiling. "That boy's wife leads him around like a trained pony."

"And bleach is a good disinfectant, you know," Ben said. "So at least the floor should be nice and clean now."

"Hi, Nora," Caroline said. "He's here, finally."

"And compared to other things he could have spilled, it's relatively cheap, too," he added.

Caroline set the receiver back down very firmly. "Then maybe we should just tell him to spill a gallon of bleach on the floor every day from now on, since there are so many advantages!"

"Well, maybe not every day," Ben said. "Maybe just once a week." He turned and went into his office, closing the door behind him. He knew he probably shouldn't tease her that way, but he had gotten so used to it, it was hard to stop.

Caroline stared at the closed door. He had started doing that more and more—closing the door—and she was certain it was because of the telephone conversations, which she had been hearing a whole lot more of than she used to. She couldn't ever catch his exact words, but she could tell by the rise and fall of his voice that they weren't business calls. Sometimes she heard him break off and chuckle.

Only once had she tried listening in and only long enough to see who was on the other end, of course, but Mr. Buck had been too quick. He had been right in the middle of a sentence when he had stopped suddenly and said, "Caroline, I'm on this line. That's what the light means. Have you forgotten how the phone works? Or is there some kind of emergency?" One thing she did find out, though, for she had heard someone laughing in the background right before Mr. Buck stopped, and it wasn't a man's laughter. Phone calls to a woman behind closed doors, coming to work an hour late—something was definitely going on.

Caroline knew from past experience, however, that the more inquisitive she acted, the more secretive Mr. Buck would get. He was infuriating that way. It was very hard, though, to act disinterested when you wanted to know things so badly, especially if there was some kind of romantic relationship developing, for instance, in which case Caroline wondered just how well this woman knew Mr. Buck. She could see how someone could fall for a man like him, who looked okay on the outside—well, more than okay for somebody his age, especially since he had taken off a little weight—but any woman should be forewarned about his many odd, irritating habits.

Caroline took a few moments to collect herself before she continued with the letter she was typing to a new vendor who was opening a showroom called Paper Stuff. The man, who had no computer at home, had sent Mr. Buck an old-fashioned letter by snail mail with a list of questions a mile long, and Mr. Buck had written out a response that went into excruciating detail. Had written it by hand, of all things, instead of typing it and e-mailing it as an attachment so she could just print it out. Half of these things were in the orientation material she had already mailed the man, but Mr. Buck had addressed each question, never once starting a sentence with "As specified in the information packet you received . . ."

Personally, Caroline thought Paper Stuff was a weak concept, too general to catch on. Why, paper stuff could include anything from magazines to kites to sticky notes. But she had learned by now to wait and see. Sometimes the silliest ideas were the biggest hits. She picked up Mr. Buck's handwritten letter to try to make out a word that looked like *perspicuous*, though she didn't know of any such word. She didn't know why he couldn't just use ordinary words like normal people.

Just then Mr. Buck threw open the door of his office and rushed out. "I just heard gunshots down in the parking lot," he said. He hurried out into the hall, calling for Dustin to come with him. Caroline immediately went into his office because she didn't have a window in hers, but nobody outside looked in the least bit concerned about anything. She waited until she saw Mr. Buck and Dustin, both in their shirtsleeves, exit the building and walk out into the parking lot looking around.

Then she heard the sound again, a single explosive *pow!* and at the far side of the parking lot she saw an old jalopy of a car creeping toward the exit, backfiring as it jerked along. Well, so much for gunshots. Caroline had to admit that part of her was disappointed it wasn't gunshots. That would have sure put the Bazaar in the news—a shooting in the parking lot! She looked back at Mr. Buck. Dustin was pointing, and they were both laughing.

As she turned from the window to leave, she suddenly remembered the photograph on Mr. Buck's bookshelf, something she hadn't had a chance to examine closely yet, since it had just appeared yesterday. From the couple of passing glances she had sneaked, she could tell it was a family picture, though something about it gave the vague impression that no one in it was especially happy. Just as she started toward the bookshelf, however, she caught sight of something on Mr. Buck's computer screen. Something very interesting.

Usually the most exciting things she ever saw on his computer were the sales figures for the previous day at the Bazaar or a panicky note from Nora or stock quotes or the online weather and news, but this wasn't any of those. It was an e-mail he was in the process of answering, a personal e-mail from the looks of it, though he hadn't even finished the first sentence yet.

Although I have the same advantage over the peerless Reginald that you have over Chloe—

*namely that you and I are alive and they are not—
I am nevertheless struck by the fact that*—That was
as far as he had gotten. Caroline stepped back and
looked out the window again. Mr. Buck and Dustin
were walking back toward the store entrance, still
laughing. If it couldn't be gunshots, at least
Caroline was grateful that the old backfiring rattle-
trap of a car had *sounded* like gunshots since it had
given her this chance to see Mr. Buck's e-mail.

She looked back at his computer screen. She
didn't have long, so she couldn't read the entire e-
mail he was replying to, but she did have time to
see a name—Vera Bridgewater—and to scan the
first part, in which the woman apparently kept
quoting Ben's own words back to him:

*Yes, indeed, mysteries abound. And change is
possible. I was happy after reading and rereading
your e-mail last night that you are beginning to
"envision tomorrow with faith and hope."
Remember, the ability to look backward and forward in time is a distinctively human trait. That
should be of comfort the next time you "don't feel
quite human." I agree that faith and hope are "two
very big words not to be used lightly," but . . .*
Caroline heard a noise and looked up to see Nora
standing in the doorway.

She immediately picked up the first thing her
hand touched on Mr. Buck's desk, which happened to be a small index card with writing on it,
and held it up. "Oh, hi, Nora, I just came in to get

this. He just stepped out a minute. He'll be right back." She walked quickly toward the door, talking the whole time and waving the card around. "We heard something out in the parking lot that sounded like a gun, so he ran out to check on it, but it wasn't a gun at all, it was just a silly old car—just a false alarm, thank goodness, so I'm sure he's on his way back in, unless he decides to stay out there and have a picnic since it's so warm today—isn't it nice after that cold spell last week? You can come on in and sit down if you want to." At the door she stepped aside and motioned Nora in.

Nora looked at her over the top of her little skinny glasses but didn't say anything as she walked over to one of the wing chairs and sank into it. Though she was a sturdy, large-boned woman, she moved with an easy grace and had a catlike way of scrutinizing people with her slanty, unblinking eyes. Today she looked tired, though, like it was late afternoon instead of only a few minutes after ten. Caroline didn't envy Nora her job for a minute—trying to make everybody happy with the schedule, keeping track of tons of government regulations, supervising all the floorwalkers, handling employee and customer complaints. There were worse things than being Mr. Buck's secretary, and Caroline knew it.

She sat back down at her desk and looked at the index card in her hand. It was Mr. Buck's handwriting, and, strangely, it was unfinished just like his e-mail reply. And like so much of what he wrote down on his slips of paper, this made no sense to her, although it sounded like something out of the Bible. Caroline's knowledge of the Bible was spotty, her experience with churches having been limited to her wedding day forty years ago—not a day she remembered fondly.

She laid the card on her desktop and traced the words with her finger as she read them again slowly. *Him that overcometh will I make a pillar in the temple of my God, and he shall go no more out: and I will write upon him the name of*—That was all he had written so far. Him that overcometh *what*? Caroline wondered. And who would want to be made into a pillar in a temple and not ever be allowed to go out again? That sounded like some kind of punishment to her. She gave her head a little shake and clucked her tongue. Mr. Buck had to be the most—

All of a sudden she felt someone standing in front of her desk, and she knew without looking up who it was. How had he gotten inside and upstairs so fast? She could kick herself for being so careless. She only hoped that he wouldn't notice the card or, if he did, wouldn't recognize it as his. Very calmly she turned it facedown and turned back to the keyboard to resume typing, pretending not to notice him.

"Where did you get that?" Mr. Buckley said.

She jumped a little and adopted a look of surprise. "What?"

He reached forward and picked up the card, then held it right in front of her nose and said, "That."

Caroline pushed her chair back to gain some distance and then stood up. She was no match for Mr. Buck in height, but she wasn't going to let him think he was intimidating her. She lifted her chin. "You must have dropped it when you went tearing out of your office," she said. "It looked like a piece of scrap paper, but I thought I better ask you before I threw it in the trash."

They stared at each other for a long moment, during which Caroline remembered the lie she had told about Lester and how it had haunted her. She also suddenly remembered her mother slapping her face many years ago and saying, "You don't even have the sense to look guilty when you lie." She had laughed about it when she told her friends later, though it didn't seem funny anymore. Lying easily wasn't anything to be proud of when you were going on sixty-one. For the briefest second she considered telling Mr. Buck the truth: "I accidentally picked it up from your desk when Nora came to your door and thought I was reading your e-mail." But even that wasn't the truth, really. It wasn't an accident that she had picked it up, and she was indeed reading his e-mail.

She opened her mouth to say something else, then closed it, then opened it again. "Well, I should have left it where it was. I'm sorry." There, that was true.

He didn't reply but kept staring at her, one side of his mouth twitching the way it did sometimes when he was trying not to lose his temper.

"So what about the gunshots?" she said. "What was that all about?"

"They weren't gunshots."

"Well, that's good," she said. She waved a hand toward his office. "Nora's in there waiting for you." She sat back down and sighed. "I've got to get back to typing this letter. We could have saved time and postage, you know, if you had just called this man instead of writing all of this out for me to type." She knew that would divert him, but she didn't want to press her luck, so she added, "But heaven knows, I'm used to all the busywork by now, so you can save your breath because I know exactly what you're going to say next—*you*'re the boss, and you get to tell *me* what to do. And I agree, so let's don't get started on all that."

He gave one of his short, sarcastic grunts of a laugh. "I ought to buy you a yo-yo with your name on it, Caroline," he said. He stood there a moment longer, then added, "Anything you see in my office from now on should stay there. Don't bring anything out here to yours. It might be personal."

She felt like saying, "And just what's so personal about a *Bible verse* written on an index card?" But she didn't dare. She typed two more words, then leaned forward and pretended to be engrossed in reading what she had typed on the screen. She wondered why he should want to buy her a yo-yo, but she wasn't about to ask. If she ignored the comment, maybe it would show him how unimportant she considered it.

To her relief he walked away, and within seconds she heard Nora's low voice in his office. She wasn't worried about Nora telling things she shouldn't. She and Nora might have their occasional differences of opinion, but they understood each other. When it came to Mr. Buck, the two of them had an unstated agreement.

Late that afternoon Ben was reading an interesting online article about adopting children from China. Reuben had sent him the link to a Web site called Hope Abroad. He had just read, *Your child may have* love marks *on the stomach or chest, which are scars resulting from a Chinese tradition involving acupuncture needles or medicinal plants* when Caroline's voice came over the intercom. "You never did go to lunch, did you? Kelly Kovatch just got here and said she's supposed to see you."

"Tell her to come in." Ben ignored the question about lunch.

Kelly appeared in the doorway, a file folder in one hand. She was wearing a brown corduroy skirt and a pink sweater with brown wooden buttons.

Once again Ben noticed that she looked more stylish than she used to. One day she had even worn a pair of black slacks and a red turtleneck sweater to work, and LaTeesha couldn't quit exclaiming over it all day. "Can't get used to seeing our straight-up six o'clock girl in *britches*!" she had kept saying. It must have embarrassed Kelly because she hadn't worn them again.

Ben took off his reading glasses and stood up. "Come on in and have a seat," he said to her. After she sat down, he said, "Okay, I'm ready, go ahead." As she talked, he leaned back in his chair and stared up at the ceiling. From time to time he glanced at her and nodded.

It had been Ben's idea for her to give him a weekly review of her classes, and this was her second one. She finished reporting on her Art Appreciation class, then proceeded to Principles of Design, and finally to Introduction to Written Communication, or Intro to Writ Com, as she said everyone referred to it. It was clear that she didn't consider her three classes merely as a duty.

After she finished, he gestured toward the folder she had set on the edge of his desk. "So is this the paper you wrote for your art class?"

She nodded and handed it across the desk to him. Ben opened it and read the title: "A Lopsided Moon." He thanked her and then stood up to see her out. He intended to keep these reports very businesslike from start to finish. Otherwise he was afraid she would feel compelled every time to tell him again how grateful she was for the chance to go to college, and he didn't want that. She had told him a hundred times already.

After she left, he put his glasses back on and took the paper out of the folder. He wouldn't take time to read it now, but he flipped through it, picking up a phrase here and there, until his eyes came to rest on a sentence near the end: *Art that treats only the pretty things of life, casting everything in the rosy glow of perfection, is narrow and dishonest.* He stopped and read it over. It wasn't something he expected Kelly Kovatch to write, and he wondered for a moment if somebody like her, whose whole life had been so sheltered, could really believe such a thing. But he did remember seeing her up in the Blue Pomegranate one day not long ago, intently studying one of Macon Mahoney's linocuts titled *Where Things Get Chopped*—a picture of a very cluttered kitchen counter.

He turned back to the first page of her paper and looked at the title. He wondered if she had been thinking of the moon in the mosaic she had given him. He had always known she had an artistic bent, but he could still hardly believe she had made something so beautiful with her own hands—and had given it to him.

He put the paper back in the folder and swiveled his chair around to face the photograph on his bookshelf. It was one Vera had taken at his house on New Year's Day, of him and all of his children and grandchildren. No rosy glow of perfection there. Maybe it was a distortion of the lens or maybe all of them really were leaning away from each other slightly.

Except Shelly. Her mouth set in a determined smile, she had an arm around each of her sisters and appeared to be trying her best to pull them toward her. The three of them were sitting on the couch, and both of the twins wore strained smiles. Erin wasn't looking directly at the camera. Ben himself stood behind his daughters, between Joey and Mark. If he didn't know them all, it would be hard to put the couples together since everyone was mixed up.

Reuben, standing between Grant and Brittany, was holding Lydia's baby, and the other six children were sitting cross-legged on the floor in random order in front of the couch. Mackenzie was sitting by Isaac, holding both of his hands as if to keep him from touching anything he shouldn't, such as the Christmas ornament he had yanked off the tree and broken right before the picture was taken.

He thought of what Vera had said on the phone one night before they all came to visit: "You know, Ben, you have four great kids, and they all have part of you in them. They all survived what they went through and turned into smart, strong, good adults." Ben had to agree with that. But Vera had continued: "So once you apologize for something, if you really mean it, you shouldn't keep beating yourself up about it."

And suddenly he had realized a simple truth. That was something he had never really done. He had acted sorry, or tried to, but he had never spoken it. And so, on the first night of their visit, he had told them all he had a few words to say— words he wouldn't have to say if he had been the father he should have been after they lost their mother, words that couldn't make up for his long absence from their lives, words he should have said long before now. And he looked at each of his children, one at a time, and said, "I'm sorry."

He walked to the bookshelf, picked the photo up, and studied their faces. Vera was right. They were smart and strong and good. That was a lot to be thankful for.

All in all the visit had gone well. They had played some games and shared some laughs around the table, and one night Reuben had read aloud a children's picture book titled *My New Family* and told them about the baby he and Erin hoped to get. And before they left, Erin had looked at Ben and said, "Thank you."

His eyes came back to Shelly in the center of the picture. Funny how someone could sometimes grate on your nerves yet could nevertheless make good things happen that no one else seemed to think about. If it weren't for Shelly, he knew the whole family never would have gotten together three times over the past six months. They still had a long way to go, but it was a start. He would have to tell Shelly what a good daughter she was the next time he talked to her.

Caroline tapped at his door and stuck her head in. "It's after five-thirty. I'm finally leaving. Bye." She shut the door, and a few seconds later he heard the rapid click of her heels as she left the office and headed down the hallway. Ben had no doubt that she would use the extra half hour she had stayed today when it came time to negotiate her departure on Friday.

He put the photo back on the shelf and returned to his desk. Through the window he saw that the sun was setting, the sky streaked with ribbons of color. But it would rise again after the night was over. He turned his chair toward the linocut above his sofa, the one Kelly had talked him into buying. He opened a drawer and took out a piece of paper Macon Mahoney had given him. It was a copy of William Cowper's poem, the words to the hymn that had inspired the linocut.

> Sometimes a light surprises the Christian while he sings;
> It is the Lord who rises with healing in his wings.
> When comforts are declining, he grants the soul again
> A season of clear shining, to cheer it after rain.

He turned the paper over and read the note Macon had written to him. *A light may surprise in different ways, Ben. Sometimes it's a blinding road-to-Damascus light, but more often it's a faint glimmer far away but growing steadily brighter, the distance shrinking. Be ready, friend.*

Ben looked back at the poem. He knew he didn't qualify as a Christian. Not yet. Though he had no right to relate any of this to himself, he couldn't help it. He didn't know how long a season of clear shining might last before the rain came again. No one did. But for now there was hope abroad. Not of his own doing, none of it. It had come quietly, like a small candle moving toward him in the dark.

JAMIE LANGSTON TURNER has been teaching for thirty-seven years at both the elementary and college levels and has written extensively for a variety of periodicals, including *Faith for the Family, Moody,* and *Christian Reader.* Her first novel, *Suncatchers,* was published in 1995. Born in Mississippi, Jamie has lived in the South all her life and currently resides with her husband in South Carolina, where she teaches creative writing at Bob Jones University.

Center Point Publishing
600 Brooks Road ● PO Box 1
Thorndike ME 04986-0001 USA

(207) 568-3717

**US & Canada:
1 800 929-9108**
www.centerpointlargeprint.com

Ben
wife
Chloe - murder